He cautiously pulled her closer. She initially tensed, but then relaxed in his arms.

He kissed her once more, savoring her warmth. Denise felt as if she were on fire, starting with her lips and blazing down into her center. She knew that she had to break his hold on her before she changed her mind. She took a tiny step backwards.

He gently pulled her to him again, so close that she could feel the beating of his heart.

He slipped his tongue inside her mouth, tentatively exploring and urging her to do the same. She responded eagerly, surprising them both with her bold and playful maneuvers.

Indigo Sensuous Love Stories

are published by

Genesis Press, Inc.
315 Third Avenue North
Columbus, MS 39701

Once in a Blue Moon

ISBN: 1-58571-070-9
Manufactured in the United States of America

First Edition

Once in a Blue Moon

by
Dorianne Cole

Genesis Press, Inc.

Acknowledgements

Many thanks to Paula Dawson, Bridgette Greer, and Kathleen Tucker for their encouragement, and to the editors at Genesis Press, Inc., who made a way out of "no way."

Dedication

To my husband, Steve; to my father, Talmadge; and in loving memory of my mother, Betty.

Chapter 1

"Like this, Aunt Neecy! Like this!" Jocelyn Thurman vigorously pumped her seven-year-old bottom to the beat, mirroring the pop idol on the television screen. Her little face was a study in lip-biting concentration, the same expression she wore when adding fractions or reciting poems from memory. Teaching her aunt the latest dance was proving to be an equal challenge.

Denise Adams had tried in good faith to follow her niece's precise instructions. Tried until tears of laughter ran down her cheeks and her lungs ached from the sight of Jocelyn wriggling like a tiny concubine in pink pajamas. She collapsed in front of the TV in her mother's living room, grabbing the child by her knees and pulling her onto the floor as well.

"Better be glad your grandma's not here," she advised, torturing Jocelyn with a flurry of tickles. "She'd beat both our butts if she caught you wringing and twisting like that."

Jocelyn now lay on her back, her short legs cutting the air with playful kicks. Her cardboard party crown rode sideways on the rows of her thin cornrow braids.

"I know what twisting is, but do you mean like ringing a bell?"

Denise turned to her twelve–year-old nephew, Malcolm Vaughn, who had taken advantage of the dance lesson to claim most of the couch. He was hunched over his gaming unit, fending off an attack by buggy-looking aliens.

"Malcolm, tell your cousin what 'wringing and twisting' means." Her request was met with silence, broken only by the announcer's description of crowds filling Times Square.

"Earth to Malcolm!" Denise shouted. He reluctantly peeled his attention from the galactic battlefield.

"Huh?" He blinked at her as if he'd been roused from sleep.

Denise shook her head with a knowing

smile. She'd responded the same way when she was his age, every time her sisters tried to lure her away from her books. And now here she was, spending another New Year's Eve in front of the TV in her mother's home, watching their children. Her sisters and their husbands had departed early that evening to attend a series of parties that would keep them out well past dawn. Malcolm's brother Marcus, now a college freshman, had bowed out of the children's party years before and was taking a date to a college party. Malcolm and Jocelyn would follow him before long, going out to embrace their grown-up lives. Even her mother, her most reliable companion, had gone to an overnight celebration sponsored by her social club at one of the downtown hotels.

"Never mind," she sighed. "Return to your battle station, lieutenant," she ordered, raising two fingers in a victory sign. "Ask your mommy to explain it to you," she suggested, turning back to her niece. "She's the family expert on wringing and twisting." Denise gave Jocelyn a quick hug, then readjusted their spangled party hats.

Denise turned off the lights just before midnight and huddled on the couch with the children, counting down the final seconds. When the ball dropped, she turned the lights back on and jumped and danced with them, blowing cardboard horns and cheering. After Malcolm and Jocelyn began to run out of steam, Denise filled glasses with sparkling cider for the three of them to toast the New Year.

"Any resolutions you'd like to share?" she asked as they sipped the tart, bubbly drink.

"Increase my average from the line," Malcolm responded quickly. "Run for class president in the fall. Keep my room clean. Help my dad more around the house—"

"But will you ever let him win when you two play "Tower of Doom" on the computer?" Denise inquired, already suspecting the answer.

"Never," he asserted calmly. "You gotta maintain respect, and he wouldn't respect me letting him win."

"I'll have to remember that next time your daddy and I get to arguing at the dinner table. And what about you, sweetie?" She let Jocelyn climb onto her lap.

"I'm going to read harder books and learn not to look at the keyboard when I use the computer." Her mouth stretched wide with a yawn as she set her glass down on the coffee table.

"Sounds like a really ambitious group here," Denise murmured approvingly.

"What about you, Aunt Neecy?" Jocelyn asked, leaning heavily against her shoulder. "Will you get married this year like you were supposed to last year?"

Denise was stunned for a moment. How on earth did the child remember? But yes, she had promised Jocelyn the coveted position of flower girl when she and Uncle Kenny got married. It must have been around this time last year, when she had been so sure...

"I don't know, sweetheart," she answered as honestly as she could. "But if I do, you'll be right up front with me, and we'll both be wearing the prettiest dresses your mommy has ever created." This seemed to satisfy the child; she planted a sleepy kiss on her youngest aunt's cheek.

"And on that note," Denise concluded, gently nudging Jocelyn to her feet, "it's time for your first good night's sleep of the new year."

After putting the children to bed, Denise heated a small serving of the collard greens and black-eyed peas she had prepared for the next day and filled a single crystal flute with champagne. She had recently read an article about creating one's own holiday rituals, so she brought her plate out into the dining room and sat at the head of the table. She lit a single candle and bowed her head. When Denise opened her eyes and picked up her fork, she was surprised to discover she had little appetite for her traditional meal. Shoving the plate aside, she took a sip of champagne and used a finger to trace the delicate patterns on her mother's ivory lace tablecloth. Her earnest ritual had served only to stir up ghosts of all she was missing on this night. Memories of her dead father. Thoughts of Kenny and Valerie, who were enjoying a romantic holiday in the Caribbean, the romantic holiday that should have been Denise's honeymoon. It would have been easier not to think at all.

Kenneth Hilton, Ph.D., was a professor of electrical engineering at the historically black Morris University in Washington, D.C. His keen intelligence had propelled him to the top of his undergraduate class each year, and Dean Adams had taken every opportunity to advance the young man's fortunes in the School of Engineering. Denise could remember the times her father had brought Kenny home for dinner when she was a little girl. There was no reason for him to have noticed her then; she was chubby, and rarely spoke unless spoken to. When they were reintroduced nearly sixteen years later, Kenny could scarcely believe that the attractive young woman with the shy smile was Dean Adams' youngest daughter. He asked her out immediately, and the three years that followed had been like a dream come true for Denise.

Kenny treated her well in all respects, and her family liked him. Her family, in fact, had begun to wonder aloud when the couple would do the right thing: start with a lavish wedding in the Morris chapel, settle down in an appropriate neighborhood and contribute two or three souls to the next generation of Morris graduates. Denise wondered, too, until Kenny asked her to prepare for a private wedding ceremony on Antigua at New Year's.

But she should have known something was up last fall when he asked for his key back. Break-ins in the neighborhood, he'd complained; he needed to change the locks. But the extra key she kept in her desk at the agency had worked perfectly on that fateful afternoon last October.

She had taken a taxi back to his townhouse, located about a mile southwest of the U.S. Capitol, to retrieve a book she'd left behind. Seeing his sleek Jaguar still in its assigned space, she told the driver not to wait. Kenny hadn't mentioned a change in his schedule, but she was sure he would take her back to work. Denise let herself in and ran upstairs, only to find him and Valerie, the dean's new secretary, in the bed she had vacated only a few hours earlier. She'd wandered back to her office in a daze, wounded and stunned into silence.

Sorry you had to find out that way. It was later that same day; she was sitting on the side of her bed, fresh tears springing to her eyes with each breath. He'd been meaning to tell her, but it would have been too hard to look into her sweet face and hurt her. Yes, he loved her but he was no longer in love with her. Didn't she know what it was like, needing to be with a certain person?

The rekindling of that painful memory had narrowed her throat and stifled what little appetite she had. She went to the kitchen and scraped her meal down the sink, pouring the champagne behind it. After checking the front and back doors to her mother's house, she went upstairs.

She tipped into her old bedroom to check on her youngest niece, two-year-old Joy Thurman. She slept peacefully, undisturbed by their mild carousing. Denise smoothed the edge of the blanket and set the favorite, balding teddy bear just outside the baby's reach. After checking on Malcolm, she stretched out next to Jocelyn on the narrow bed in her mother's sewing room. She calmed herself by matching her breathing to the slow, even rhythm of the child's. Before long, she drifted into a thick and troubled sleep.

Chapter 2

The cloud of steam dissipated, allowing Denise to see her reflection in the mirror on the back of the bathroom door. Her face still held a touch of roundness, a reminder of the baby fat she'd carried into her adolescence and beyond. She looked at her mocha-brown skin, at the braids that streamed past her shoulders, and the generous swell of bosom and hips separated by a small waist. What had Kenny called her? His little fertility goddess. His little miracle of engineering. His. His no longer, it seemed.

Denise contemplated last night's dream while she finished getting dressed for work. She had been riding in a car with the windows rolled down; she had felt warmth on her skin and the sky was a brilliant blue. She recalled the salty smell of the beach and the cheerful seaside houses, all sporting pastel flags that fluttered in the stiff breeze. She was in the passenger seat, but who was the driver? She tried hard to remember a face but she couldn't.

What difference does it make? she thought. I'm still in my little one-bedroom walk-up, it's January, it's cold and I've got to get to work. Her only driver on this day would be the too young and flirtatious operator of the bus route between her multicultural Adams Morgan neighborhood and the marble office buildings on Capitol Hill.

She would be starting a new work detail today, courtesy of Frank Wagner, her office director. Frank had hired an independent contractor last fall to upgrade the agency's computer network boundary systems, but he was beginning to lag behind schedule. The freelancer had corrected bugs in the programs that controlled traffic between the agency's protected network and the Internet, but he was still having problems with system memory requirements. To make matters worse, he had neglected to document his procedures for

the agency's records, which was where Denise
had entered the picture.

Frank had called her into his office a few
days before Thanksgiving and had immediately begun to apologize for what he had to ask
her. He said that she did not have to help pull
this contract together. That as second-in-
command of the firewall team and his best
technical writer, she had better things to do
than baby-sit a contractor. That he would
understand if she preferred not to work with
this admittedly difficult individual. But if she
would take on this out-of-office detail for, oh,
three short months, he would be eternally
grateful. Thanks to her father, she knew an
order when she heard one. She had managed
to keep a straight face when she told Frank
the detail would not be a problem.

He told her that the contractor's name was
Ian Phillips, a hot commodity on the network
security market. Frank must have dragged
this Phillips person around earlier to meet the
staff, but she couldn't put a face with the
name. When she'd made discreet inquiries
about him, her colleagues responded with
remarkably similar terms: arrogant, over-
bearing, impossible. But they'd all agreed
about one thing: Ian Phillips was as brilliant

as hell.

Besides, she mused as she pulled on her black tights, it might be good to get out of the office for a while. She'd decided on an easy, plum-colored knit dress and a pair of chunky black heels instead of one of the tailored suits she usually wore when working with contractors. The typical computer geek wouldn't know a Jil Sander suit from a straitjacket, so why bother?

This job has my name written all over it. Denise grimaced as she fastened her gold hoop earrings. *Caretaker of other people's children. Companion of men until they marry the women they love. Custodian of Frank's mad programming genius.*

"Stop that!" she scolded herself out loud. *It's only the third of January; two pity parties in three days are not acceptable.* What did that old song say, the one her sister Joanne used to play over and over? *Everything must change...*She thought about the previous night's dream again as she draped a series of ID-laden necklaces around her shoulders and shrugged on a heavy wool coat. *I'll have a hell of a time finding that beach in the middle of winter!* She grabbed her purse and backpack as she swept through the living room, pausing

only to give the front door an extra tug before
she hurried down the steps.

Ian Phillips started from sleep, flinging
the pile of blankets to the floor. He'd been
dreaming about Mexico again. He peered at
the chunky diver's watch on his wrist, the one
that had belonged to his friend Josh Morgan.
It was January third. The mere passage of
time now provided some small comforts: no
more forced gaiety, no more excuses for what
he did or did not do on New Year's Eve. No
more listening to the sound of his own footsteps echoing in the old agency building, most
of its inhabitants having departed for the holidays.

He rose and shuffled across the chilly
hardwood floor into the bathroom. Turning
on the light, he paused to look at his reflection
in the mirror hanging over the sink. The
straight, light brown hair that hung halfway
down his back was the same as always. But
the shadowy hollows beneath his hazel eyes
were new, carved out by months of mourning
and self-loathing. He padded over to the
shower stall and spun the faucet to the "on"

position.

He'd have to hurry. As Ian stepped gingerly into the stall, the showerhead dumped cold, then steaming water on his skull. He carried a few blurred impressions of that day last October: curtains of chilly, gray rain veiling the windows, Frank's face etched with exasperation and concern. You're one of the best...don't know what has happened...see if I can pull off a detail...if this doesn't work...

It was a new year, Ian mused, but he still hadn't managed to settle his old business. Josh was the one who'd convinced him to delay work on this contract last September. One last road trip before Yvonne and I tie the knot, he'd begged. Come on man, you've always been the smart one; this trip will clear out your head. You'll get back and knock that sucker out in no time. But Josh was wrong. The image of Josh's limp body, floating in the shallows off the coast of Cozumel, had thoroughly loosened Ian from his moorings and set him adrift on waves of despair.

The Smart One. That's who Josh had always told him he was from the time they were boys sneaking smokes behind the old apartment building in the upper east 80s of Manhattan. Or, the Good Looking One. Sure,

women always looked at Ian, and Ian certainly looked back, but he measured relationships
in terms of days and nights, and occasionally,
weeks. He'd always thought of Josh as a
shorter, sturdier version of himself, with long,
dark blond hair and blue eyes that could
seduce a woman on the other side of a room.
But of the two of them, Josh alone had the
capacity to love without reservation. He lost
his heart easily and often, giving himself over
to the majesty of the landscapes they'd
trekked or to the welcoming arms of a woman.

Who had Josh been? The Good One, Ian
would have answered without hesitation,
despite the pharmaceutical demons Josh had
battled since their teens. And who would Ian
be now that Josh was gone? He'd virtually
retreated from work, from life, for the past
three months, searching for an answer to that
question.

He soaped himself over quickly, taking a
little pride in the changes his body displayed
since he had become a regular at the gym
down near the Marine Barracks. Working out
had been another one of Frank's suggestions.
He had stopped eating regularly after Mexico,
and had become as skinny as his adolescent
self. Now he had to admit he was feeling bet-

ter, and the increasingly muscular physique under a snug sweater certainly wouldn't hurt his chances out in D.C.'s club scene.

Ian took a quick glance out the window to check the weather before he got dressed. A warmer-than-usual autumn had lowered the city's guard and made winter's tardy grip more cruel than usual. Hard-core nonbelievers shivered under their thin coats with raw, reddened ears and numb, icy toes. At least he wouldn't have to impress anyone today. He pulled on a turtleneck and fastened a flannel shirt over it. Black jeans, work boots, and an elastic band to restrain his hair completed his preparations for the day. He yanked an old ski cap down low on his head and grabbed an even tattier pair of mittens from the antique armoire in his bedroom, a gift from his parents. Making sure his security badges were tucked inside his jacket, he loped out the door of the townhouse and into the frigid morning.

He broke his trot down Pennsylvania Avenue to grab his usual 20-ounce cappuccino from the Italian bakery on the corner at 6th Street. The proprietor, a slight Ethiopian immigrant, knew his habits. Habib now steamed up a foamy cap of milk as soon as Ian's rangy form loomed up in the outside service window. Welcoming any opportunity to avoid small talk, Ian was grateful for their perfect, silent transaction

About ten minutes later his boots scraped up the well-sanded steps to the library. He flipped the necklace of identification badges in the direction of the security desk. The guards sat as stolid as cattle, eyeing the crowd of returning employees with indifference.

Ian took the stairs to the fourth floor two at a time, then sprinted down the hallway. No one seemed to be loitering, waiting for him outside his broom closet of an office. Relieved, he danced a little victory step as he unlocked the door. He didn't bother to turn on the lights but simply fell into the walnut professor's chair and rolled himself over to the desk that held his primary computer unit. He bumped it out of sleep mode and saluted as the monitor slowly revealed a desktop photo of snow-capped Himalayan peaks.

Nine-thirty, not bad—

"Mr. Phillips?"

The voice was low-pitched, but definitely feminine, with a hint of magnolia. He whirled around, tossing the worn backpack to the floor. A young African-American woman stood in the doorway.

"Okay, I'm here," he bellowed, raising his arms in surrender. "Is Frank putting on a special ceremony for the commencement of the detail? Should I have rented a tux?" The young woman probably thought he was out of his mind.

Her lips parted in a half smile instead.

"I hope not. My evening gown's at the cleaners." She stepped into the room and around his backpack, extending a delicate, cocoa-colored hand. "Hi. I'm Denise Adams. I'm here for the network security detail."

He stared up at her helplessly from his seat. Long braids framed her pretty face. Something in her expression, in the directness of her brown-eyed gaze, tied his tongue.

"Frank did tell you about this?" She enunciated her words slowly, as if he didn't understand English.

Alt, control, delete. Restart, Phillips.

"Uh, yes. I'm Ian Phillips."

He stumbled to his feet and extended the bedraggled right mitten. Realizing his mistake, he hurriedly tore it off with his teeth and pumped her warm, slender fingers.

"Ugh." She flinched and pulled her hand away. "I'm sorry." She smiled again, in apology this time. "Your hand is still cold."

"Oh, sorry. I always carry my coffee in my left. Hand, that is. Left hand."

Unable to think of anything more to say, he jammed his hands into his pockets and stared at the toes of his boots. His eyes traveled involuntarily to her shoes, up the curves of her legs in black stockings and snagged on the generous contours of her bosom. He drifted for a few seconds but bounced back to reality with a start.

"I said, is there a desk here for me?" The magnolia tones had withered and died, replaced by cold steel. She glared at him, her polite smile only a memory.

Not trusting his voice enough to risk an answer, he pointed in the direction of the project table that held the hardware he had failed to connect for the last two weeks. He also noticed the coat draped over her arm and the sleek black leather backpack that looped over one small shoulder.

"You can use that old coat rack behind the door. It has only one hook, but I don't need it." The terse click of her heels as she walked toward the rack was his only reply.

"Nice backpack," he mumbled.

She didn't look up as she arranged her coat on the lone hanger.

"Thanks," she offered curtly. "A present from my sisters."

"Oh? How many sisters do you have?"

"Two."

"I have a brother. Older." He watched as she strolled over near the door and flipped on the lights.

"Hmm." Denise walked back to the project table and began removing the plastic sheeting from the computer's components.

"I can give you a hand with that. It'll just take a few minutes."

"That's all right, I don't mind doing it." Denise Adams reverently touched each component with both hands as if she were conveying a blessing. Then she stopped and looked around until she remembered where she had put her backpack–on the floor next to the coat rack. She went to retrieve it, ignoring Ian. After fishing through the sack for a few seconds, she pulled out a battered plastic box that had been wrapped and re-wrapped with duct tape. She tugged at an edge of the dull silver adhesive that hung loose, pulled the container apart and extracted a screwdriver.

Ian couldn't believe his eyes. Needle nose pliers, bits, plugs, a wrench, and a soldering iron were neatly strapped into the kit's compartments. She carries her own tools!

"Do you have all the programs I'll need on zip?"

"I'll copy them for you right now."

Ian heard a low tsk sound as he shed his coat and sat down in front of his monitor. He pretended not to watch her reflection in the curved glass as he downloaded the necessary applications. Ms. Adams was smoothly connecting the monitor, the scanner and the zip drive to the central processing unit. She hummed softly to herself, executing a little gospel-inflected trill each time she was successful in fitting a set of the components together. It was about that time he noticed an unusual sensation, almost an ache, somewhere between his chest and his gut. The feeling was not totally unpleasant; perhaps he just needed to cut back on coffee.

After about half an hour she was ready to power up. The reflected image of Ms. Adams leaned forward against the desk, obviously searching for an electrical outlet. Her short dress hiked up a couple of inches before she jumped back to her feet and yanked it down. The sight of the knit material pulled taut against her high, round buttocks nearly drove his teeth through his lower lip. The ache wandered lower, into his groin.

She whirled around to face him, ready to challenge any evidence of an inappropriate thought on his part. He pretended to stare at the zip copy reports on his screen with scholarly concern. Satisfied, she returned to her task. Making one more furtive glance in Ian's direction, she dropped to her knees and crawled under the tabletop. No luck. She slipped back into her chair to consider what to try next.

Ian, having managed to get himself in check, risked an offer of assistance.

"The surge protector is a little tricky to reach," he suggested as blandly as he could. "Can I help you with that?"

She studied his face for a few seconds before she answered.

"Okay. I haven't been here long enough to know where everything is." Denise stood up and backed away from the table, not taking her eyes off him.

Ian rose and crossed the room to take her chair, blushing as he felt her lingering warmth. He nodded in the direction of his seat as he began to undo the tangle of cords that hung from the side of the table.

"Please, take mine." He nodded in the direction of his desk.

"That's all right."

"This might take a few minutes," he warned.

"I'm fine."

"I know, but you're making me nervous," he insisted, struggling with a particularly tricky knot in one of the cords.

"They say that performance anxiety is a common problem," she observed in a flat tone.

Ian dropped all the connectors on the floor and stared up at her. Denise, realizing what she had said, felt a flush of heat start at the roots of her hair and creep back toward her neck. She hid her face in her hands.

"Of course I didn't mean that," she said, shaking her head at her gaffe. "I guess we both need to start over, huh?" She gave him a hopeful look, needing his pardon.

"Are you kidding? A woman who talks dirty and carries her own tools?" He reached down to pick up the pile of cords. "I think I'm in love."

Denise laughed heartily, relieved that she

had not committed a fatal blunder. He looked up and offered one of his rare smiles, a gift in return for the lush melody of her laughter. Where had he heard those notes before? Ellington's "Black and Tan Fantasy"? Or perhaps a Coltrane ballad? And when might that sweet song erupt again? The ache in his chest persisted as he picked his way through the tangled wires.

Denise, still wary, took the chair he had offered, perching on its edge and gripping her knees together against potentially prying eyes. Here was an opportunity to do a little checking-out of her own. Ian Phillips was tall, she had noticed when he stood beside her. At least by a head and then some. His straight, light brown hair was pulled back with elastic, revealing two thin gold hoops that pierced his left earlobe. A couple days' stubble sprouted from his cheeks and chin, but the tawny mustache and goatee looked somewhat cultivated. He wore oval-shaped glasses with thin, tortoise shell rims; elegant and definitely not from Eyes 'r' Us. Speaking of eyes, he had those pretty hazel ones just like her best girlfriend Karyn Mitchell did. Did he use them to mesmerize women the same way Karyn could perpetrate a whammy on any male over the age of three? Nothing for you to worry about. Those smoldering looks were probably reserved for white women in general, and tall, slender blondes in particular.

As he crawled under the project table on his hands and knees, Denise could not resist a quick peek. Long, slim legs extending up into...hmm, not bad for a white boy. As he backed out again she redirected an innocent look toward the room's one window.

"All done," he announced. "Ready to power up?" He stood in a single, flowing motion, rubbing his hands together.

"Why not?" she agreed.

Denise finished loading the programs she needed around noon. Ian had been hunched over his keyboard all morning, working at something he didn't feel the need to talk about. They went their separate ways for lunch, and later returned to discuss the best way to complete the documentation process in the least amount of time. She was surprised and relieved to discover that he did not dismiss her ideas out of hand; they simply kept talking until they worked out their differences. They actually managed to hammer out a reasonable plan by four-thirty, which they e-mailed to Frank. Congratulating themselves for clearing a major hurdle on their first day of work, they began to relax with each other, gradually drifting into a discussion of their mutual pleasure in seeing the holiday season come to a merciful end.

"You too?" Denise was surprised to hear that the attractive man who sat across from her found the Christmas season as oppressive as she did.

"I didn't bother to go home," he responded, shaking his head. "Thanksgiving was scary enough."

"Do they bug you about not being married and when you're going to settle down?"

"Hell, that would be easy. At least yours are still talking to you. Wendy doesn't say anything to me anymore. She just makes a kind of tsk sound, the same way you did this morning. And she never takes her eyes off me; she just stares like a Jack Russell terrier."

"Wendy?"

"My mother."

"Your father doesn't talk to you either?"

"Ed? Oh, we just avoid each other. Fortunately their flat is large enough to allow that."

"You said flat instead of apartment. Were you born here?"

"Yes, in New York. We lived there 'til I was three, then it was the U.K. for the next ten years. Ed had teaching gigs in Edinburgh and London. We came back to New York when I was 13. This trace of an accent is Wendy's legacy to me. She's English and she'll die that way."

"You're lucky you got to live in a different country," Denise said wistfully.

"And what about you?"

"What about me? There's not much to say. I was born and raised and schooled here in D.C. I work for the government. End of story, nothing fabulous or unusual."

"You expect me to believe that? I don't meet a lot of women running around town toting a set of wrenches." Especially if they're as fine as you are, he added silently.

"You just haven't been paying attention." Denise checked her watch. It was nearly six o'clock.

"If there isn't anything else you can think that needs to be done tonight, I think I'm going to head out."

"You work for the government," Ian pronounced in a flat tone, a distant look clouding his eyes. He propelled his chair back toward his desk. "You should have gone an hour ago."

"I work," she replied testily, "until the job is finished."

"Suit yourself." He shrugged and turned to his computer. She had been dismissed.

She felt a prick of annoyance but decided to ignore it. He was right; it was time to leave. Glancing at the back of his head, she collected her things and headed for the door. Once again she stopped.

"Good night," she called out distinctly. He lifted his right hand in a slight wave, not bothering to look in her direction.

"No manners," she mumbled to herself as she turned away and walked out the door.

As the bus slowly climbed up 16th street, Denise stared out into the gloom at the buildings that lined the broad avenue. She wanted desperately to be somewhere else; somewhere as warm and colorful as last night's dream. But she'd missed her chance to decline Frank's request, so she would be spending the next three months in a box with Ian Phillips, Ian the Terrible.

As Denise alighted at her stop she felt the sting of ice pellets against her face, the crowning insult for a harsh winter evening. Sighing, she braced herself for the short walk home.

Denise was washing up the few dishes from her solitary meal when the image of Ian's beefy hands and long legs crept unbidden into her thoughts. Why on earth was she still thinking about that silly white boy? Your family's right, you know. Maybe you do need a man. And the sooner the better because you're getting sillier by the day! Next thing you know you'll be sneaking into those strip clubs for women out in the suburbs so you won't forget what the parts look like.

Dismissing her brief fantasy, she decided to heat a pan of milk for hot chocolate. She sat down to wait at her small kitchen table and peered out of the window that faced onto 17th Street. The sleet had thickened into clumps of wet snow, promising a miserable rush hour for the next morning. Below, a man and a woman hurried by, hand in hand, briefly illuminated by the amber glow of a street lamp. An echo of laughter floated toward her window, mocking her lonely watch.

Had she laughed that way when she and Kenny had traveled avenues emptied by snow and cold last year? He had been raised in Detroit and could not understand the typical Washingtonian's fear of an inch or two of snow. They'd often had whole restaurants, clubs, and movie theatres to themselves on those nights. Had her voice been borne skyward on some chilly blast of wind, taunting a woman who was as alone then as she was now? If it had, she reflected, the payback was hell.

She carried her mug of cocoa into the bedroom around eight o'clock. Turning on the TV for company, she crawled into bed with the mail and newspapers that had piled up during the holidays.

She was turning the pages of one of the tech tabloids when her eyes flickered over his name—Ian Phillips—followed by a glowing review of his new anti-virus software. She read through the article, feeling a tickle of pride for having some connection with his minor celebrity. But by the time she reached the last sentence, that pride had turned into discomfort. She felt as if he had followed her somehow, and invaded the usually safe harbor of her home, her bedroom. She imagined his picture was ogling her from the page, waiting for her robe to gap open and display a glimpse of cleavage. On an impulse she tossed the paper across the room and pulled out a fashion magazine from the bottom of the stack instead.

A few miles across town, Ian had worked steadily at one of his three computers until midnight. After undressing and stretching out across his big, empty bed, he lay awake for a while, thinking about his new assistant. She was smart, tough, and would not take any nonsense from him, all qualities he admired. Yet he sensed a vulnerability that softened her, made her seem delicate and tentative. She had other traits he found interesting: warm brown eyes, full, sensuous lips and a well-rounded figure. He rarely found this combination of characteristics in one woman, and so tastefully wrapped in smooth, dark chocolate. That wasn't an issue for him either.

The image of Stephanie, the corporate lawyer he'd met on a trip to the Caribbean a couple of years back flashed before him. He'd jumped on an air charter to Aruba at the last minute–the result of a nasty breakup, as usual. They were the only two souls on the plane who weren't gay or on a honeymoon; he'd asked if he could sit with her at dinner the first night. Stephanie was tall and slender, with caramel-colored skin and close-cropped hair. Bloody gorgeous, he remembered. She'd been a couple of years older than he, and on the run from the same kind of trouble. Freed by their anonymity, they'd spent hours entwined on pale sand or between linen sheets, rocking away the taste of their separate, bitter losses. They'd barely looked at each other as they boarded the plane for home a week later, mutually drained of emotion and self-regard.

But what the hell had made him think of Stephanie? Denise Adams and Stephanie Ross shared gender and a racial classification and that was the sum of it. A classification, Ed and Wendy had taught him, that was usually irrelevant, often harmful, and occasionally absurd. Denise could not be more different from Stephanie; beneath her serious demeanor lay sweetness, the kind that attracted kids and stray dogs and men looking for a place to hide. Stephanie had the highly polished looks of a model, but Ian suspected the blue veins that snaked beneath her skin conducted pure ice water. Denise had a soft, sheltering feel about her. Comfortable. What sane man would not want to rest his head against her sumptuous bosom, or lie between her smooth, cocoa-brown thighs?

Pleasant warmth stirred his groin again. He'd have to exert some discipline over that. Ms. Adams would not invite him to assume either of those positions; Good Girl was practically engraved on her forehead. There had to be a steady boyfriend and a line of hopefuls wrapped around the block, waiting for her to tire of him. No—more likely there was one well-educated, high-earning, racquetball-playing, African-American alpha male. A man as cool and good-looking as Michael Jordan, who fully appreciated the pleasures of her curvaceous body and razor-sharp mind. A virtual rocket scientist who could invent a thousand devices to prevent her from drifting into the arms of another, particularly a silly white boy such as himself. Although he hadn't seen a ring on her finger, Ian figured he'd better be careful–an alarm might go off if he happened to brush up against her in that tiny office. "Step away from the lady," a chip-driven voice would warn. He'd be better off accepting the truth, that she was probably in love with a man who was everything he wasn't. Lucky bastard, he whispered to himself as he closed his eyes.

Chapter 3

"I feel like Chinese."

Denise frowned and looked over her shoulder. Ian had turned his chair so he was facing her, his arms extended in a luxurious, late-morning yawn.

He'd lied about having parents, she thought. He had really been raised by apes. Computer code-writing apes. She turned back to her work, ignoring him.

He jumped to his feet and crossed the room in three long steps. Grabbing his jacket from the rack, he hesitated at the door.

"Aren't you coming?" he asked impatiently.

"Are you talking to me?"

"Do you see anyone else?"

"What if I don't want to go?"

"Nobody in her right mind wouldn't want to go to Mr. Kee's.

"Oh? And why is that?"

"It's the best Chinese food in town."

"No, but thank you for asking."

"Come on then, we need to get going before the lunch rush." His tone was urgent, ignoring her refusal. "It's not a big place and they sometimes bus people in from the Chinese Embassy."

"Excuse me, but did you hear what I said?"

"Yes, but I'm waiting for the right answer."

She sighed and rolled her eyes toward the ceiling. "Look, if you must know, I'm running a little low on cash right now and—"

"Not an acceptable excuse on your part. Lunch is part of the contract." He pulled back the sleeve of his sweater to check his watch. His eyes strayed back to her face, pleading without saying a word.

Denise thought for a second, her teeth nibbling her lower lip. Is he going to stand and stare at me like that all afternoon? Do I care if he does? She glanced back into his hazel eyes; his head was tilted like an inquisitive puppy's. It's just lunch, Denise, she thought.

What's the big deal? And when have you ever refused decent Chinese food? Surely he wouldn't try anything... Try what? What makes you think he even sees you that way? Except for those three short years with Kenny, nobody sees you that way, remember? You spent the morning deciding which video to take to your mother's tomorrow night, that is if she doesn't have other plans.

"Okay," she finally agreed, rising to her feet.

"That wasn't so hard, was it?" he remarked as he lifted her coat off its hanger.

She slung her small purse over her shoulder and approached him, reaching for her coat. To her surprise he refused to surrender it, holding the garment like a matador's cloak.

"Never let it be said that I have no knowledge of civilized behavior," he intoned, giving her coat a little shake. "Mademoiselle?"

She backed into her coat, eyeing him warily as she slid her arm into one sleeve, then the other. He was grinning as if she'd told him a good joke.

"Mademoiselle, encore." A broad sweep of his arm indicated that she should move through the door before him.

"Ma mère m'est apprendu ces choses," he

uttered with a flourish.

"I was beginning to wonder if anyone had bothered," Denise muttered under her breath as she stepped through the doorway.

Ian chuckled to himself as he switched off the light. She'd understood that his mother taught him manners. Just as he'd suspected, there was more to Denise Adams than met the eye. As if that weren't enough.

Denise swore she could feel her teeth rattle as the ancient cab tested every bump and pothole between Capitol Hill and downtown. She felt odd riding in a taxi with Ian, sharing its rear seat. He didn't talk much, but simply stared out the window as they passed the Senate office buildings, the Department of Labor, and the Tax Court. Within minutes they passed under the brilliant red arch over H Street, the entrance to Washington's Chinatown.

Mr. Kee's was located a few blocks away from the main drag of restaurants. It stood in a drab row of storefronts, many of which had been abandoned. Denise shivered and looked around anxiously as Ian paid the driver.

Leave it to him to choose a dingy dive like this, she groused silently, a perfect setting for either robbery or food poisoning. She was still staring up at the sign, beaten by rain and wind until it read "M Ke s," when Ian beckoned her to come inside.

She was surprised to step into a warm, rose-colored room illuminated with abstract neon lighting. The maitre d' nodded at Ian as if he knew him and led them to one of the booths that lined the left wall. A pot of steaming jasmine tea arrived as they removed their coats. Denise righted the small flowered cups and poured for both of them. Ian examined the sheet of green paper that came with the menus.

"The dim sum here is fabulous, you know."

"Really? It's been years since I've had any."

"Do you remember what you liked?"

"Maybe. There was shrimp wrapped in what, a clear wonton? And shark, I remember having shark."

"You're in luck–they've got both. How about starting with some pork rolls?" He turned the chart around so she could see the choices.

Once he placed their order Ian slid back

into the corner of the booth. He was quiet, almost a little awkward.

"So. How long have you worked for Uncle Sam?"

"I started right after college."

"Where'd you go to school?"

"Right here, at Morris University. A.B.S. in math and an M.S. in computer science. Where'd you go?"

"Everywhere, nowhere. I started at Harvard, screwed up notoriously, came back home to City University, courtesy of Ed. Tried a year in London. Then out to the West Coast with a friend to major in diving, climbing, and women. And got a computer science degree on the side."

"Climbing? Really? I've only seen that on TV. Do you think you'll do Everest?"

He laughed ruefully.

"We thought we would. Or at least K2." He turned serious again. "But no, all of that's over now." He could almost see Josh in his red jacket, waving to him from atop a sheer wall of ice. To speak about this now was to court disaster, to risk breaking down in front of this young woman. He quickly changed the subject. "Ooh, pork rolls," he said, glancing up at the approaching waiter.

Something in the way he said the words made Denise giggle.

"What?" Ian eyed the plate of dumplings that had been set between them.

"Ooh, pork rolls," she mocked. "You sound like my brother-in-law. If he were here you two would be wrestling for those by now. The problem is," she observed as she slid one of the fragrant delicacies onto her plate, "his appetite is starting to show. I remember when I was younger, when he was still with an engine company. We could barely keep weight on him back then. Mama and Lynn and I couldn't keep food coming fast enough on his off days; he ate like a horse!"

"He's a fireman?"

"Yeah. He's a white shirt now, a battalion commander."

"That's some righteous work, there. You know," he said, shifting plates to make room for the shrimp and shark dishes, "that's one of the few jobs left that you can draw a picture of and everyone knows what it is. In this city everyone wears a blue suit and does things that are totally theoretical. I'm a management analyst; I'm a programmer. What does that mean? Can a kid draw a picture of it and say that's my dad, that's my mom?"

"Oh, I don't know," Denise mused. "I'm still waiting for the day when we'll all be walking around in spandex suits like something out of science fiction. Getting ready for work would be a whole lot easier."

"Ugh," he groaned. "No more ladies in summer dresses? I hope I'll be long dead and gone when that happens."

"Don't worry; there'll be plenty of virtual reality arcades for you romantic types. Pay your money, push a button and you'll be able to float down a canal in Venice with your girlfriend while a gondolier in a striped shirt sings "Visse d'Arte...""

Ian's eyes widened at the reference.

"You're not one of those opera nuts, are you?"

"No, but you are talking about my mother."

"So now you'll have to come over here and kick my ass," he proposed with a sly grin.

"I'll settle for another order of shrimp dumplings," she responded, grasping the last one between her chopsticks. "I'm not crazy about it, but my mother was a singer in Europe when she was young. She still teaches classical voice at Morris. I go with her to a recital every now and then, but she knows she has to get with her music-teaching girls for full-blown opera. I've fallen asleep with my head hanging out in the aisle too many times. Some of their students have made it to the chorus at the Met and a couple are soloists, so they go up a few times during the season."

"Do you sing too? Wait," he interrupted himself, raising a hand. "Of course you do. You sing to yourself sometimes when you forget I'm around."

"Oh no," Denise sighed. "Just roll up a newspaper and smack me next time so I'll stop, okay?"

"Absolutely not," he exclaimed, pulling himself up straight on the banquette cushion. "You have a beautiful voice," he effused. "Even your laugh sounds like music!" Ian blushed, his confession having made him feel awkward once more.

"Wow! I don't think anyone's ever told me that." Denise offered him a shy smile, feeling her own face go warm at the compliment. "Aside from my mother, I'm the only one in the family who does anything with music. But I'm just an okay alto, that's all. I always thought it was a little strange that none of us ever took a serious interest."

"Your sisters?"

"Uh huh. Joanne's really artistic, creative in other ways. She can turn a brick and a plastic bag into a centerpiece or whip up a gorgeous dress out of the air, no pattern or anything. Lynn followed our father into education. You might have seen her on TV–she's the principal at the Niagara Charter School. Everything was fine for the first couple of years; her school out-performed every other one in the city on the national standardized tests. But now she's being investigated for falsifying scores–"

"What rubbish!"

"You've heard about it?"

"Absolute rubbish! Why would anyone think anything other than the fact that she's committed to teaching and has surrounded herself with people who feel the same?"

"Exactly!" Denise hadn't expected Ian to be aware of the story or agree with her point of view. "I know I would have gone off, punched somebody out and been carried off to jail. But no matter what's happening, she manages to radiate this tremendous aura of grace under pressure. We're all so proud of her."

"And what about you?" Ian asked.

"What about me?"

"What is it that makes Denise special?" He was leaning forward now, chin resting on the broad heel of his hand, looking at her intently. Something about Ian's penetrating look made her uncomfortable; she couldn't say what or why. She poured more tea into both of the tiny cups, trying to think of an answer to his question.

"Nothing I can think of," she concluded, setting the pot down on the table between them.

"You don't expect me to believe that, do you?"

"I'm not expecting anything, that's just how it is."

"Nah. I suspect there are at least a half-dozen amazing things about you."

Denise laughed out loud.

"Would you let me know if you find any? Lately I've been trying to figure out what I'm going to do with the rest of my life and that info could be helpful."

"That's easy. Before Tuesday I'd never met a woman who carries a soldering iron along with her lipstick and hankies."

"You're still bugging over that?" She rolled her eyes. "It's not a big deal; it's just convenient to have all the things I might need in one place. That's not special. A little neurotic, Lynn would say, but not special. What else?"

"Simplicity itself. You're awfully quick at math and, I suspect, anything that requires the ability to analyze systems."

"Okay. That's from my father; he was an engineer. What else?" she asked, beginning to warm to the subject.

"Hmm." Ian rubbed his chin thoughtfully. "I'll have to reserve judgment for now. After all, we've only known each other four days. But I'll find them, I'm sure."

"We'll just see about that." The combination of superb food and Ian's gentle teasing had made her sufficiently comfortable to toss back a snappy reply or two, the way she could around her family. Ian also convinced her to sample a couple more dishes and finish with a dessert of lemon tarts. A little over an hour had passed when she dabbed at her lips with her napkin and relaxed against the back of her seat.

"Would you like anything else?" Ian asked.

"Thank you, but I think my work here is done."

"Sure?"

"Absolutely," she protested with a wave of her hand.

Ian motioned for the waiter to bring the check. Denise reached for her purse.

"Please put that away," he advised, leaning to the right to extract his wallet. "Your money's no good here."

"But it's just—"

Ian deftly flipped a couple of bills onto the waiter's tray and waved him off.

"It's all part of the contract, mademoiselle."

"But—"

Ian slid off the banquette, pulling his coat behind him.

"I'll call for a taxi."

Denise noted his loose, athletic stride as he strolled across the floor. Definitely the outdoor type; she would have figured it out sooner or later even if he hadn't told her about his past. Ian picked up the handset of the phone that had a direct line to one of the city's cab companies. Once he'd put in his request, he returned to the booth where Denise was waiting.

"It'll be about ten minutes. Any more in there?" he asked, pointing to the stainless steel pot.

Denise poured the dregs into his tiny cup. "I think that's all of it."

Ian took a sip, then set the cup down with a start.

"Sorry!" he exclaimed. "I should have asked whether you wanted it. I've been on my own so much lately that my manners have suffered for it. You'll need to speak up for yourself more when you're with me."

Denise flashed him a suspicious look and reminded him of what he'd told her.

"Je pensais que votre mére vous est apprendé l'étiquette, c'est vrai?"

Ian shook his head, smiling at her fluency with the language.

"She tried to teach me table manners. I didn't give her much to work with." He shifted his weight on the cushion. "You're awfully good. Where did you learn?"

"From fourth grade on. Through Morris," she added.

"All this," he said quietly, leaning forward on his elbows, "and French, too."

He was looking at her again, nearly staring. He probably didn't mean any harm but she still didn't like it. Denise swung her legs out from under the table and fumbled with her coat. Ian quickly stood.

"Let me help you with that," he said, taking a step in her direction.

Denise visibly pulled back from the hand he extended toward her.

"No, that's all right. I can do it," she murmured.

"Please, I insist," he begged. "I owe you for taking the last of the tea."

"You don't owe me a thing. I'm fine, really," she asserted, dropping her gloves in the process. Ian quickly bent over to retrieve them. Their heads collided with a hollow thunk.

"Ow!" she wailed, the sharp pain trumping her usual reserve. Ian rocked a little on his heels, then fell backwards. He tried to sit up, rubbing his forehead and laughing. She began to giggle as well.

"Cab here," the maitre d' announced calmly from behind his newspaper, as if patrons screeched with pain and lay sprawling on the floor of his establishment every day.

"Let's scram!" Denise ordered, pulling on her coat.

"After you." Ian grabbed her gloves and pushed himself back up on his feet.

Ian linked his arm through hers, steering her toward the door. "Slowly I walk–" he began.

"Step by step," she responded, grinning broadly.

Chapter 4

Denise bounded up the steps to her childhood home two at a time despite the mid-winter darkness. On Friday nights the Adams women and their families usually gathered at their parents' house in the northern section of the city. The area, locally known as the Gold Coast, was home to many affluent and well-known African Americans. The Adams' elegant colonial was tucked away on a winding lane just off 16th Street, a few blocks to the south of the Rock Creek Park tennis courts.

When Denise arrived on the first Friday evening in January, Julia Adams, Lynn, Joanne and their husbands and children were already seated around the dining room table, poised to attack the red and white cartons from Hunan Paradise. Tossing her coat on the sofa, she rushed into the dining room to claim a seat and a plate.

"They were going to start without you, Aunt Neecy," Jocelyn declared. "I wanted to wait."

"Good evening, everybody. And thank you, sweetheart," she added, winking at her niece.

"Malcolm, why don't you say the blessing this evening?" Julia suggested. "Denise, if you can wait for a second, there's a seat on the other side. Just put Joy on Jo's lap."

Malcolm, the youngest son of Preston Vaughn and Denise's sister, Lynn, repeated the familiar grace in a swift, nearly inaudible murmur. When he was done, everyone shouted "amen" to make sure the prayer was heard. Then they all got down to the business of inspecting the various containers, spooning out the contents and enjoying the meal, all under a constant buzz about the events of the week. Julia noticed Denise was too quiet, as usual, and attempted to draw her last-born into the conversation.

"So how was your first week of the new year, baby girl?" she inquired.

"Oh, Mama!" Denise sighed heavily. "Ask

somebody else, please. You don't want to know." Denise unbuckled Joy from her car seat and lifted the toddler onto her lap.

"Of course I want to know! I asked you, didn't I?" Julia Adams was an instructor of classical vocal technique at Morris. The still-girlish pitch of her speaking voice hinted at her career as a young operatic soprano.

"Hmm." Denise paused to think for a moment. "I think I told you a little about it before the holidays, the detail I had to take? Well, this was the first week. He's supposed to be some kind of genius. One of the programs he's designed is probably going to be the next big thing in security applications according to some of the tech publications. But he's a real piece of work. Not as bad as the folks in the office led me to believe, but bad enough."

"Like what? What did he do?" queried Joanne, her hennaed dreadlocks quivering.

Joanne Adams Thurman's personality was as light and bubbly as champagne with tastes to match: she loved shopping, parties and gossip. On her most recent birthday Denise had given her Alice Roosevelt's famous quote framed in needlepoint: "If you don't have anything good to say, come sit next to me." Joanne's frothy exterior belied the drive and marketing savvy that had made her boutique, The Mango Leaf, successful for more than a decade.

"I don't think I had been in the office five minutes before he started staring at me," Denise complained.

"I'll have a warrant issued first thing Monday morning for a check-out in the first degree, Neecy," remarked Joanne's husband Maurice as he expertly twirled noodles around his chopsticks. "If we had capital punishment in D.C., he would definitely get the chair."

Maurice Thurman was developing a reputation as a formidable prosecutor in the Washington U.S. Attorney's Office. He'd started as a beat officer and had met Joanne when he responded to a burglary at the boutique. Maurice soon worked his way up to detective and passed the sergeant's exam. Graduating near the top of his class from Morris University's Law School, he passed the bar and landed a coveted invitation to join the U.S. Attorney's staff.

"The next big thing in computers, you said?" asked Preston Vaughn, Lynn's husband. "That means real money, doesn't it?"

Preston Vaughn was one of the four bat-

talion commanders in the city's fire department, overseeing a number of fire stations in
the city's northeast quadrant. Preston had
met Dean Adams during a training session
when he was an ambitious young lieutenant,
nearly twenty years before. They became
fishing buddies, then in-laws, after the Dean
invited the handsome fire fighter home for
dinner.

Denise nodded affirmatively, spooning
white rice onto her plate. Preston thought for
a moment.

"Then I'll get him some glasses and a see-
ing-eye dog, if he needs it. Girl, you need to
let him stare as much as he wants to! You're
a good-looking woman, why shouldn't he
stare? That's part of your problem, Neecy.
Nobody's even supposed to look at you."

"Hey Preston, it's a new year." Denise set
the spoon down, ready for battle. "Why don't
you get some new material? Something about
you this time. Maybe, oh, I don't know, something about that extra padding around your
middle? I know you play Santa Claus every
year for the poor kids in your district, but
don't you think it's about time to remove that
stuffing? Oh you can't? Excuse me, I had no
idea..."

"Ooh!" Jocelyn hooted, always apprecia-
tive of bad behavior by the adults.

"Damn, girl," Maurice chuckled. "You can
be so cold."

"I wouldn't laugh so quick if I were you,"
warned Joanne.

"And I would watch my language at this
table in front of my grands if I were you, too,"
Julia admonished.

Maurice bowed his head sheepishly.

"Yes ma'am. I'm sorry." But he covertly
reached around his daughter's chair to poke
his fellow Adams in-law in the ribs and whisper "damn" again.

"See, that's another one of your prob-
lems," Preston continued, undaunted.
"You're always so ready to jump on somebody.
You know I've been trying to deal with this–"

"You've been trying to deal?" Denise
leaned forward to better get Preston in her
sights. "Who are your partners, Ben and
Jerry?" Even Julia joined in the whoops and
giggles that followed Denise's observation.

"Come on, you two," Lynn chided. "One of
these days we're going to have a meal without
the two of you getting into it."

Lynnette Adams-Vaughn was tall, angular
and intense, much as George Adams had

been. Possessing advanced degrees in psychology and education, she was the principal of the Niagara Charter School in the City. Her close-cropped hair, West African wardrobe and elegant carriage lent her an air of austere sophistication.

"You know we love you, thick or thin, or at least I do." Lynn patted Preston's stomach. "But you're always picking at the girl! What do you expect her to do? Just take your trash all the time and not defend herself?"

"What I expect is for her to go out and find herself a man, get married and start having some kids."

"Preston, can we let that rest this evening?" Julia pleaded. Lynn whispered quickly in her husband's ear, reminding him that Denise was still hurting from her breakup with Kenny.

"But that's my point," Preston blustered, determined to have the last word. "You fall off the horse, you get back on again."

"What is the status of the investigation, Lynnette?" Julia posed the question both out of sincere interest and the hope that Preston would settle down.

Lynn had run afoul of the school system and the press many times because of her outspoken allegiance to an Afrocentric curriculum. The students' consistently high performance on standardized tests had often been the only factor preventing her removal. But her detractors had come up with a new approach; at the beginning of the current school year they had brought formal charges accusing Lynn of having falsified the scores.

"Nothing's changed, Mother. I have that continuation hearing before the Board next month, more of the usual racist dog-and-pony show. I don't know what else those Uncle Toms can ask me to do–pull up my dress so they can examine the elastic in my drawers?"

"They think that's where you wrote the answers and instructed the kids to do the same. Ain't that some sh—oh—sorry again, Mama Adams," Maurice apologized.

"You don't need to be sorry when you're right," Julia responded bitterly. "Every few years white people need to question black folks' intellectual capacity in the so-called 'interest of science.' Lord knows they do it all the time in private! When I was a young woman it was Jensen and Shockley. Then there was all that 'Bell Curve' nonsense a few years ago. I can't believe that in this day and age my daughter is on trial for running a school in which black children exceed national standards."

"Especially when the house Negroes are the ones conducting the investigation. And reporting on it," Preston added, eyeing Denise. "You better tell Karyn to let her man know we're watching him."

"Give Terence a break, Pres," Denise muttered. "He just got promoted to the city desk; they probably won't even give him that assignment. When's the next testing period, Lynnie?"

"March. I intend to let the chips fall where they may. And if they land in the 80th percentile again, so be it."

"Good! I'll get started on your ensemble for when the results are released and you have to talk to the press." Jo's creative sense was already at work. "Something fierce and elegant–"

"All kente cloth and dripping with cowrie shells?" Denise suggested.

"Wait!" Joanne's slim fingers were measuring the folds of imaginary fabric. "I can see it now: a gold damask buba, with a matching gélé."

"Maybe not, Jo," Lynn responded, giving her head a sorrowful shake. "If those Toms and their white overseers dare to accuse me of fixing the scores again this year, I'm gonna come down off those steps and whip some-body's... No, what you're talking about sounds like something I wouldn't want to get torn up, so don't even bother."

"Now baby, you know you can't win," said Preston. "If you come out swinging, they'll say it's typical. If you stand up there in your nice outfit as dignified as a queen, they'll start calling you "that arrogant black woman"! Before you know it, that'll be your name all over town. Might as well put it on all the checks and credit cards right now."

"You let me know," Julia advised, "when and where the next hearing will be. I'll round up the usual suspects." The ranks of Dean Adams' activist network had been thinned by age and illness, but its remaining members could still be counted on to fill a council cham-ber or courtroom with their moral authority whenever the cause of racial justice demand-ed their presence.

"They must be tired of this family, Mother Adams," observed Preston. "I thought my trial and the appeal wore them out."

"Maybe some of us can't march the way we used to, and we don't have to speak up because you younger folks have access to fancy lawyers now, but we sure can sit shoulder to shoulder and look ugly."

Lynn reached over and took her mother's hand, giving it an affectionate squeeze.

"Ugly? Never! Your and Daddy's friends are the most beautiful elder warriors on the planet."

"Here, here," Preston concurred, raising his glass with a nod in Julia's direction.

Denise examined the containers on the table and set them back down in disappointment.

"What's wrong, Aunt Neecy?" asked Malcolm.

"I've already had Chinese food today. And it was a lot better than this."

"Where was that?" inquired Maurice.

"Mr. Network Security was in the mood for Chinese, so he literally forced me into a cab and down to some place in Chinatown where I've never been. It's on G Street–Mr. Kee's. The food was good, though." She poked around in a few more cartons with no luck. "I think I'll just fix something after I get home." She popped a few sticky grains of white rice into Joy's mouth.

"Who paid?" asked Preston.

"You never give up, do you? He did," she admitted reluctantly.

"Good," he asserted, with a triumphant glance in Lynn's direction. "Now that's what I like to hear."

"Pres, forget it! He's white, plus, I suspect his parents are rich. And even if they aren't, he will be, no doubt about it. Two degrees of separation are two too much. End of story."

Preston shook his head, defeated at last.

"Too bad. Can't go there, not after what I've been through with the department. Still going through, to tell the truth." He was quiet for a moment, thinking about the eight years he'd spent in litigation against the fire department and the city for promotions he'd deserved and been denied. The hard-won decision in Preston's case had been instrumental in destroying the remains of the fire department's old-boy network.

"Amen," Lynn agreed. "The last thing you need is a white man! Life is hard enough without being in a relationship that just makes everybody mad."

"Oh, I don't know..." Joanne set her fork down, a suggestive smirk forming on her lips. "A little jungle fever might not be such a bad thing. It might give our Neecy a little cachet, a little mystery. She could stand to change that intellectual, upright church girl image."

"Why are you all always talking about me as if I were no older than Joy or as if I weren't here?" Denise snapped abruptly. "Doesn't anybody here ever read a newspaper or watch TV? What the hell would you talk about if I didn't exist?" Denise pushed her chair back and placed Joy on her mother's lap. "Please excuse me. I don't see anything worth eating or hear anything worth talking about!" She stood, tossed her napkin onto her empty plate, and fled to the powder room in the hallway.

"Why it's another Friday night at the Adams love feast," Joanne intoned sarcastically.

"Drama queen," Preston sniffed, emptying most of the carton of orange beef onto his plate.

Lynn reached over to give her husband a light smack on the forearm.

"What is wrong with you tonight? And not five minutes after I told you about her and Kenny! What did you hope to accomplish with that?"

"I didn't do anything!" Preston yelped. "Joanne's the one who made her leave."

"Me?" Joanne was indignant. "After all

your crap the girl had had enough! I was just making a helpful suggestion."

"Jungle fever? Oh well now, that's real helpful," Preston responded with a groan. "You think she sits around here all depressed now? Just let her get all messed up with some white boy. Then she'd really have something to be sad about."

"Just when I'd given up hope," Lynn interrupted, "the first intelligent word you've said since you sat down at this table."

"And what was that?" Joanne asked skeptically.

"Depressed, depression. She's having a hard time bouncing back from the Kenny thing. We'd actually started looking at wedding gowns. I know," she added quickly, noting Joanne's sudden frown, "that's your area. I meant casually looking, if we happened to be near a place."

"As much as I hate to see her get hurt, I can't say I'm sorry he's out of the picture." Julia's tone was emphatic.

"Really, Mother? I didn't know." Lynn leaned forward to look at Julia. "You never said anything."

"Denise seemed happy so I kept my mouth shut. But I never cared for the way he just appeared out of nowhere and started taking up all her time. Why wasn't he interested in her when she was heavy? She's the same person she was before. And I always thought he was too old for her."

"Things have always been so hard for Neecy," Joanne reflected. "First losing Daddy so young, then getting so sick the way she did."

"Yeah, but she lost all that weight, though. Now she's fine," Preston drawled, stretching the word into two syllables. "But you wouldn't know it for those clothes! I don't understand why a young woman would want to go around looking so old and tired. Joanne, can't you take her in hand, fix her up a little?"

"It's not that simple, baby," Lynn began. "Before Denise can change her outward appearance she has to accept–"

"Uh-oh," Maurice interrupted. "Pardon me, Oprah. Please tell us what feelings she should be feeling 'bout now. And what feelings will she be feeling if she don't fight the feeling? You feeling me, girl?"

"Maurice Thurman, if our children weren't sitting at this table I'd tell you to feel–" She made a sucking sound between her teeth. "Oh, never mind."

"Malcolm and Jocelyn, are you finished eating?" Julia raised her voice, implying what the correct answer would be.

"Yes, Grandma," Jocelyn answered promptly, sensing an opportunity to catch a forbidden cartoon or rerun. "May we be excused?"

"I'm not through, girl," growled Malcolm. "I'm not even finished."

"You are now, young man! Both of you go upstairs and watch TV now. And stay off those clean clothes in my sewing room!" The two cousins eagerly scraped back their chairs, raced out of the dining room and up the center hall stairway.

"They don't need to hear this." Julia poured herself another cup of green tea before passing the pot to Lynn.

"Thank you, Mother. As I was saying to the intelligent people here, otherwise known as women," she emphasized, rolling her eyes at Maurice, "Denise needs to see and accept herself as she is now. I would disagree with you to the extent that I believe that Kenny's attention was a wonderful new adventure for her and contributed to building up her self-esteem. And naturally she experienced some loss of that self-esteem after they broke up last fall. But I, for one, am not convinced that this rift in their relationship cannot be healed and–"

"What do you need, doc? A video of him doing the silly bitch?" Joanne laughed bitterly. "I might not have a Ph.D. in psychology, but I'm convinced! And they didn't break up–that fool drop-kicked Neecy, hard! Besides, doesn't anybody remember who Kenny was originally intended for?"

"Do you have to bring that up again?" Maurice shook his head vigorously.

"Well, it's true!" Joanne insisted. "Daddy assumed that Lynn and Preston had given him a track record."

"You know your father never would have forced you–" Julia began.

"You're damn skippy, Mama, or else I would have had my own personal civil rights march!" She paused to take a sip of tea. "And poor little Neecy! She came running into my room that first night he came to dinner, her eyes as big as saucers, asking if Kenny and I were going out on a date. She was so disappointed when I told her I wouldn't break wind for his sorry ass if he was suffocating. If she had been old enough, she would've gone in my place in a heartbeat."

"Yeah. Be careful what you ask for. She got her wish and then some," Maurice observed.

"She sure held onto that dream for a long time." Lynn pushed her back her chair. "All right folks, we need to apologize. I'm going to go get her. Try to look sincere, would you?"

Once inside the powder room, Denise had quietly pushed the door closed and locked it. She turned on the light and looked in the mirror, feeling shamed by the tears in her eyes.

What is happening to me? she wondered. *I used to be so strong. Now I feel as if I'm on the brink of going to pieces all the time. Men have left me before; I've gotten to the point that I know when they're going to leave before they do. But something is different this time. It feels so...final. As if I've shut a door on part of my life without knowing what's on the other side.*

Denise lowered the top of the commode and sat down, resting her forehead against the vanity's cool marble. She retraced the day's events in her mind, trying to understand how she'd been brought so low. Her thoughts wandered to Ian Phillips, recalling his genuine delight as he introduced her to unfamiliar delicacies and how he'd listened, really listened to her, his hazel eyes intense and full of light. At least a half-dozen things that are special about me, he'd said. Kenny had obviously missed those things by a mile. A couple must have flown right by her family, too. And to think, we've only known each other four days. Known each other. What did she know about Ian Phillips? Not much, really. He's smart, he likes talking to me, and his legs are so long... And he's white. He could never be part of her world, and she had no reason to assume he would ever want to be. She was sure...

She raised her head at the sound of fingers thrumming against the door.

"Honey, we're sorry." It was Lynn's husky whisper. "Please come back; we want to apologize."

"More likely Mama wants you all to apologize." Denise sighed and unlocked the door. Lynn stepped into the tiny room, looking down at her youngest sister with tender concern.

"I tried to explain to everybody how hard the breakup with Kenny has been for you.

We're really sorry." She paused to stroke Denise's tear-stained face. "And I'm worried about you, too. You seem more, I don't know, fragile than usual. Is something else going on? I mean, beyond what happened with Kenny? If there is," Lynn continued, not waiting for Denise to answer, "you might consider talking to someone about it. Not me, but somebody outside the family. I know the folks at the African-American Psychotherapy Center. It's in one of the office buildings near my Metro stop. There are a couple of outstanding female counselors on staff; I could hook you up if you like."

Denise wet one of the guest towels with cold water and dabbed at her eyes and cheeks.

"Thanks, but I don't think I've got much to talk about. There's some new stuff I have to deal with at the agency. I wish I could take some time off instead but this detail was scheduled back in October." She looked in the mirror one more time, pushing her braids away from her face. "And for once the work is really important. I guess I'm just a little overwhelmed. I'm the one who probably needs to apologize."

Lynn urged Denise through the door and out into the hall.

"Don't worry about that. We just want to be sure you're all right. We get a little wild sometimes but it's only because we care about you."

The dining room was unnaturally quiet when they returned. Joanne, Preston and Maurice all looked solemn. Preston stood and cleared his throat.

"Look, Neecy. Denise. We're sorry. We didn't know about–" Julia shot him another warning look. "We shouldn't have said those things. You're right, even your mother knows you're grown but we don't act like you are. And that's pretty bad. So..." He pulled out Lynn's chair and waited for her to sit.

"That's okay. I'm the one who should be sorry. I just need to get a grip." Denise's voice wavered a little. "And Mama, the language. I'm sorry." She slipped into her seat noiselessly and slumped forward.

Julia nodded. The room became so quiet they could hear the mantel clock ticking on the other side of the hall. Joanne finally broke the silence.

"If everybody's through being sorry, can we do dessert, please? You all were so busy minding Neecy's business that I almost forgot I brought cake."

No one spoke.

"I'm talking about a ten-inch chocolate mint torte, people!" Joanne bellowed the words like a comic playing a tough room. The cloud that had descended on the room finally vanished with smiles of anticipation and laughter.

As she helped clear the dinner dishes, Denise had already begun to dread the weekend looming before her. She would have preferred to get up and go to the agency the next morning. To go and work with Ian the Terrible.

Chapter 5

The first working day after Dr. King's holiday began badly. Denise had been reading journal articles into the wee hours and overslept. Discovered the new sweater she'd treated herself to over the weekend was marked a size too small and wouldn't keep the chill off hot coals. Got stuck in a traffic jam miles from Capitol Hill. Let herself into an office that was cold enough to hang meat in; the heat had yet to come up on their side of the building. Checked her backpack twice but couldn't find a scrunchy or headband to hold her braids off her face. Left her package of tea bags and cocoa on the kitchen table in her rush.

One of those days, Denise thought as she stood in the middle of the room with her hands on her hips. She was considering whether to go downstairs for a comforting hot chocolate or a work-fueling espresso when Ian burst through the door.

He rarely bothered with little courtesies such as "good morning" and usually simply glanced at her and kept walking. But this morning he stopped suddenly and stared at her, long and hard. How could he have known she'd be standing in the middle of the office, nipples erect from the cold, hard enough, he imagined, to pierce her thin sweater? That her braids would be hanging loose around her shoulders? That she would be wearing lipstick that made her mouth look as if she'd been eating summer berries? He was hard before he even got to his desk. He was so attracted to Denise at that moment he didn't trust himself to stay in the same room with her. She couldn't have known she looked like everything that made him crazy. He turned bright red, abruptly threw his backpack on the floor and stomped out of the room.

Denise didn't know whether to laugh or

worry about this new wrinkle in Ian's unpredictable behavior. She reflected for a few more seconds and, deciding in favor of laughter and cocoa, set off for the cafeteria.

When she returned Ian was in his professor's chair, scowling over a steaming cup of coffee. He was still wearing his gray wool topcoat.

"You should put my sweater on until the heat comes up. I left it in your chair."

"I'm all right. And with this cocoa I should be better."

"No, really. You need to put it on," he insisted.

"I appreciate your concern, but–" she began.

"I don't need your appreciation," he snapped. "I need you to stay well enough to finish this work. Just put on the damned sweater so we can start the next !" He didn't even bother to look at her.

She felt a shot of anger, followed, surprisingly, by tears. It must be because this is the last straw on a bad morning, she thought. Otherwise, I would tell him and Frank both what I think about this stupid detail.

Not trusting her voice to argue, she walked slowly to her chair and picked up the

Shetland wool sweater. It still held some of his warmth. As she pulled the garment over her head, Denise flushed with embarrassment, nearly overwhelmed by the aroma of apples, plain soap, beer and an undeniable maleness. Her head still reeling, she returned to her seat and opened her file.

After a while her mind cleared enough for her to lose herself in the work. When she called him over to look at her latest edits he didn't bother to get up, but just propelled himself over in his chair. He read through her document, frequently nodding in agreement and whispering "yes."

When he finished, he looked at her with a grateful smile.

"This is first-rate! I've been trying to find a way to say this but I can never manage to make it flow this way."

"Is it good enough for me to take this off now?" she queried sharply, pushing up the sleeves that ended well beyond her fingertips.

"What? Oh. I'm sorry." He had turned slightly in her direction. There wasn't a trace of his earlier surliness. "I shouldn't have barked at you like that. I guess I was going ballistic over this contract again. And I really don't want you to get sick, period."

"Don't be sorry." Denise's tone was sarcastic. "I'm relieved to see that everything I heard about you was true. I was beginning to be disappointed."

"How so?"

"Everyone I asked said you were difficult to deal with. Until a few minutes ago I almost didn't believe it."

"Takes one to know one."

"Are you saying that I'm difficult?"

"I think you're as difficult as hell, he observed. You just have better manners than I do. Your man must have his hands full with you."

"Don't have one," she murmured, her eyes fixed on the monitor.

"Leave it out!"

"What?" Her fingers stopped over the keyboard as she turned to look at him. "Leave it out?"

"You must be joking," he answered incredulously, "about not having a boyfriend."

"What did I just say?"

"Do you expect me to believe that?"

"You can believe whatever you want. I just told you." Denise began typing again, hoping Ian would be discouraged from pursuing the subject further.

He rolled his chair back and looked at her.

"But you're attractive and you're smart and-"

She shrugged and continued her edits, but he couldn't leave it alone.

"No way! Since when?"

She stopped and folded her arms.

"Why do you want to know?"

"Well, I just can't believe, I mean, if I..."

"Okay. Since last fall. And more so since he spent the holidays with his true love in Antigua." She was surprised the name of the island came to her so quickly, considering the effort she'd made to repress it. "Are you happy now?"

"But why did he break up with you?"

"Are you trying to say it was my fault?"

"No. What I'll probably say is that he's a flaming idiot. But right now I'm asking for information."

She laughed despite her reluctance to probe this still-tender subject.

"If I could answer that..." She dropped her hands into her lap and sighed, not having found a satisfactory response to that question for herself, let alone for someone she barely knew. "I honestly don't know."

"So who was he, anyway?"

"Dr. Kenneth Hilton, Kenny. He's a senior professor in the electrical engineering department at Morris."

Ian snorted. "He probably did you a favor."

"How could that be?"

"Engineers. Too many of them have their heads up their asses."

"How can you generalize about a whole group of people like that? My father was an electrical engineer and his head was on quite straight, thank you!"

"Trust me. And I didn't say all, just too many. But back to you. What about the others before him?"

"The others? You sound as if you're talking about a cast of thousands. There haven't been enough to make up a decent doubles match."

"It must be true what they say, then."

"What's that?"

"That everyone inside the Beltway is insane. Imagine: a whole city full of smart, gorgeous women working killer hours, then falling asleep with their cats in front of the TV every night."

"You know what else they say," she teased. "If you're not part of the solution you're part of the problem. Are you doing your part?"

He thought for a moment.

"Over the years I've probably done my share. The truth is, lately I've been thinking about what my life would be like with one woman I'm crazy about and a house full of kids."

"Really!"

"Is that so hard to believe?"

"You bet it is."

"Why?" He stretched his legs out to their full length and folded his arms behind his head.

"Well, you have this really defiant attitude. It's in everything you do: the way you wear your hair, the way you dress, and the way you relate to people. Well, most people. I don't know why but you've been almost civil to me, with the exception of this morning, of course. And as far as marriage is concerned, 'ever after' is a really hard thing, from what I've seen. It takes discipline, compromise and patience. No offense, but do you think you're ready for that?"

"That's a pretty grim view. What about 'happily ever after'? Tell me about that."

" 'Happily ever after'? It's only in fairy tales, where it belongs."

"Jeez, woman! Who told you that? I believe it's our duty as humans to at least attempt it! Haven't you ever had a grand passion, a little obsession, and a tiny fixation? Or in your case," he paused to give her a significant look, "been the object of same?"

Who the hell was he to probe her personal history this way, especially after the burst of anger he'd displayed toward her earlier? She decided it would be best to keep him at arm's length.

"I'd rather not say," she murmured, with what she hoped was a mysterious smile.

"Chicken." He pointed at her with light-hearted disdain. "I'll tell you the truth: I'm still waiting for mine. I'll know her when I see her. Was that Kenny guy your grand passion?"

She nearly laughed out loud trying to imagine Kenny in that light.

"Hardly. He was nice, and he treated me well. My family liked him."

"Zzzzz…" Ian mimicked a snore. "Nice. Nothing I can see that's either grand or passionate. How long were you with him?"

"A little over three years."

"Was it a sex thing for you or for him?"

"Excuse me?" Denise's eyes grew wide.

"What?" he asked with a careless shrug of his shoulders.

"I don't know you!" she replied incredulously. "I can't talk to you about those things."

"How will we get to know each other if we don't? We're going to be stuck in this broom closet for the next two months; we're going to know a hell of a lot about each other by the time we're done. I'm only trying to figure out why you stayed so long with this Kenny guy and the best thing you can say about him is that he was nice! Frankly, I'd understand better if hearing his name made you curse and throw things. At least that would show there was some feeling there once. You weren't thinking of marrying him, were you?"

"Why wouldn't I? I'm just an ordinary, everyday person. I'm not the kind who has grand passions, fatal attractions, whatever." She fluttered her fingers carelessly, hoping to convince them both that she wasn't taking the conversation seriously.

"You're not that kind of person? What, are there height limits on it now, like the ones for roller coasters? Or is it because you like to run around with your own little set of wrenches? You're not going to say that

African Americans don't have grand passions, are you? You can't listen to Ellington or Mingus or Coltrane and believe that, can you?"

The artists he had named were revered in her home, but it stunned her to hear their names roll so easily from his lips.

"How do you know about them?" she asked, her eyes growing wide with surprise.

"My father. Ed loves jazz. I grew up with all of it."

"That's deep," she exclaimed. "My father loved jazz, too."

They looked at each other and beamed, pleasantly surprised by this mutual discovery. Knowledge of this common ground gave her confidence to ask him a question.

"Okay. So what about children, though? How'd you decide about that?"

"I hadn't worked for a while." His smile faded as he suddenly stood and walked toward the window. "I was living with my parents, driving them crazy and vice versa. My brother Andy—he's a surgeon—belongs to Medicine Without Boundaries. He was going to a refugee camp in Rwanda; I asked if I could tag along. So he pulled some strings and off we went.

"I can't tell you..." His voice trailed off, his eyes focussed on some point in the distance. "The kids... It's still hard to talk about it. I watched Andy do some incredible things. I saw him fail, too.

"I was assigned to do construction, any kind of manual labor, actually. Our group would sometimes blow off to play with the kids who weren't sick or in shock from seeing their families murdered; I really got attached to some of them. I probably would have brought a dozen of them home if their government hadn't prevented it. Now I can't imagine going through life without having children. I hadn't thought much about it before, but I'm sure that I want as many babies as my lady will give me, and adopt or become a foster parent for a few more besides. That doesn't make much sense, I know, but it's still very real for me."

"I think I understand," Denise agreed solemnly. She remembered how the pictures of maimed and orphaned children had torn at her heart as well. "I love my sisters' kids but I want my own, too. Maybe it's selfish, but I want my own babies so much."

"You?" He turned to look at her, his eyes wide with amazement. "And I took you for the ambitious career woman type."

"I have to work, just like everyone else. That doesn't mean it's the only thing I want." It's probably the only thing I'll get, she thought to herself.

Ian returned to his seat.

"I don't think you have anything to worry about, Denise." He said it as if he had been reading her mind. "If there is such a thing as having it all, the way I think women mean it, you'll have it. You're smart, attractive–I'm repeating myself but it's true. You'll find the right guy, or he'll find you. I promise."

"I don't know about all that. I'll probably dance at your wedding first."

He deliberately wheeled his chair into hers, trapping her where she sat.

"Is that a promise?"

"What?" His sudden proximity made her uncomfortable.

"That you'll dance at my wedding?"

"Why don't you just roll out of the way so one of us can get some work done?" she grumbled, trying to position herself squarely in front of her monitor.

Flashing a mischievous grin, Ian wheeled back to his desk.

Ian was sipping a beer at Filmore's, facing the TV screen but taking in little of the basketball game that beamed down from it. He was still thinking about his near miss today. Perhaps this detail was not such a good idea, after all. One unguarded word or lingering, inappropriate glance could ruin his reputation and empty his pockets. A lapse of self-control could blow this foundation for a real adult life to hell. And more importantly, terminate all opportunities for spontaneous chats with Ms. Adams. Denise.

There weren't many people in the bar that night so he absorbed a blast of cold air each time someone opened the front door. He shivered, remembering that she had forgotten to return his sweater before she left for the evening. That didn't bother him; he liked the idea that she might still be wearing it. Besides, it looked better on her.

He finished his beer, signaled the bartender for another and considered taking a look at the menu. He wasn't in a hurry to rush back to an empty house but he didn't feel up to putting on the attitude that going to a club required, either. He decided to order a salad, steak sandwich and fries to eat at the bar.

He watched the hoop action on the TV for a while, but his thoughts soon strayed back to Denise. As she shyly revealed her intelligence, her hopes, and her natural sweetness to him, his response had been to open himself to her as well. He'd found himself revisiting old regrets and sharing his new dreams. Even sitting here at the bar he could visualize her sitting across from him, listening intently. A smile might play across her lips or else her soft, brown eyes would well up with tears as he described some hurtful thing. Thank God she didn't waste herself on that guy she was still pining over. He wondered how she would be with a man she had come to truly love and trust, whether she would lose some of her nervous, self-conscious edginess. A woman like that deserves to know she's loved, he thought, deserves a man who will lose himself for her.

At least, that's what I'd do if she were mine, he thought. If she were... That was the one thing he couldn't read in her face, what she thought of him. If she thought of him at all. No, not much chance of that, really. She was a few years younger than he was, and she'd admitted that she hadn't dated much.

Which probably meant she hadn't dated any white men, either. And she clearly had some religious scruples, always pausing to bow her head before she picked at a sandwich and read a book around one o'clock most days. He couldn't remember the last time he'd been inside a house of worship, other than to say goodbye to Josh.

He could understand why that engineer jerk appealed to her: He was a respected black academic and her family approved of him. He was safe, in other words. Safe enough to dump her like yesterday's garbage.

I'd never be a safe choice for her, Ian mused, but if I ever have the chance... What was he thinking? The last thing he wanted right now was to get hung up on a woman. Even if he felt blood rush to his face and elsewhere when she brushed by him in their tiny office. Even if he whispered her name as he dozed off some nights. No, he needed to finish this project and, for the first time in his thirty-two years, make some serious plans for the future.

Ian's dinner arrived; he attacked it ravenously. After settling his bill he decided to walk home, picking his way carefully through patches of ice and slush. When he arrived at home he undressed and fell asleep immediately, continuing to ponder the mystery of his quiet, comely work mate in his dreams.

Denise was still a little off balance when she let herself into her apartment that evening. Her conversation with Ian had been a revelation in many ways: They'd discovered common interests, shared desires and emotions. And he had even flirted with her a little. All of this was unsettling when she thought about the fact that they had two more months to spend together in that tiny office. At least you won't be bored, she thought as she tossed the day's mail on the coffee table and slipped off her coat.

Her discomfort turned to dismay when she realized she was still wearing Ian's sweater. She pulled it off over her head and carefully spread it out across the top of the couch. She would leave it there so she wouldn't forget to take it to work tomorrow.

The prospect of having to deal with Ian because of her own stupidity cast a pall over the remainder of the evening. Too distracted to read, she curled up on the couch and tried to watch TV.

Blasts of arctic wind rattled the windows and made her shiver. She didn't feel like getting up and walking all the way to the bedroom to get her robe out of the closet. She glanced up and saw Ian's sweater draped across the upright sofa cushions. She pulled it down into her lap to examine it, considered its owner, then cautiously slipped the sweater over her head and pulled the body down over her pajama top. The fresh reminder of his scent caused an odd sensation in the pit of her stomach, but she forced herself to ignore it.

Stretching out into a comfortable position once more, she tried to keep her attention on the dull parade of situation comedies in front of her, but her mind repeatedly strayed back to flashes of their earlier conversation. She could have kicked herself for speaking so openly to a white man she hardly knew. That was part of her problem, she knew it. Lynn had tactfully suggested that Denise consider seeing a therapist a couple of weeks ago. Maybe it was time to check her health insurance policy and start collecting a few names. But didn't she need to make up an excuse for running off with the sweater? And why was it so important that he not be angry with her?

It was only a temporary assignment, and Frank and the rest of the world knew Ian was at least a little crazy. She tried to balance competing explanations and excuses until she dozed off under their weight.

Denise was still conducting her internal dialog on how to handle the sweater as she strode down the hall toward their tiny office. Should she just leave it in his chair and say nothing? Or present it to him with a little self-deprecating humor?

She unlocked the door and turned on the light. Everything looked the same as it had yesterday evening. He hadn't left a nasty note on her desk or wired her chair to explode.

You're tripping, Denise, she decided as she hung up her coat. She pulled the nubby old sweater out of her backpack and placed it on his chair. Then she made herself a cup of tea and settled down to work.

Ian arrived a little before ten, as usual. She had trained herself not to utter a reflexive "good morning," knowing he wouldn't respond. He marched over to his desk without a word and bumped his computer out its sleep mode. Struggling out of his heavy top-coat, he briefly looked up in her direction.

"Look, I'm sorry about your sweater," she volunteered uneasily. "I didn't realize I was still wearing it until I got home."

"Not a problem." He showed no interest in her apology, looking away as her eyes met his.

Of course he wasn't interested, she told her herself, her cheeks flushing with embarrassment. It wasn't a problem because she was nobody and meant nothing to him. His legendary temper was reserved for people who mattered. What happened yesterday was an anomaly, a mere blip on the screen. As long as she did her work and occasionally entertained him with scenes from her lonely life he would be as gallant as a knight. Needing to walk off her disappointment, she pushed back her chair and headed for the door.

"I've got to go pick up some mail from Frank's office," she announced from the doorway. "I'll be back in a little while." He simply shrugged, as usual, flipping through the pile of papers on his desk.

Once the click of her high heels faded into the distance he picked up the sweater and held it against his cheek. He detected the faint aroma of tropical flowers, just as he did whenever he found an excuse to be near her. He inhaled deeply, eyes closed, until the sound of approaching voices intruded from the hallway. Ian hastily jammed the sweater into his backpack and sat down to work.

Chapter 6

Denise and Ian ended their first month together over a lunch of empanadas in a small Spanish restaurant on Capitol Hill. She had gradually adjusted to his practice of taking her to lunch on Fridays. Even on this day, when he would leave the restaurant and fly home to New York for the weekend, he stuck to his habit.

"Spinach, right?" he asked, poring over the menu.

"Yes, and the omelet?" she asked tentatively.

"That's good. Now the eggplant–" He hesitated, seeing her lips twist in a pained grimace.

"I take it you don't like eggplant?"

"Only when it's sautéed with peppers and onions. And then only a spoonful."

"I've never heard of that."

"The things you've never heard of would fill a dump truck," she shot back, giggling. "I'm sorry. That's something my father used to say."

"You're a mean little person, you know that?" Ian tried to appear hurt, but he secretly enjoyed it whenever she took a jab at him. He could tell that Denise was relaxed enough to let down her guard today. He would be free to enjoy her dry wit and look into her eyes without fear of reprisal. That was why he had initiated these Friday sessions, to memorize her sensuous features and rich laughter for the solitary days that would follow.

"Just for that, I'm getting the anchovies."

"Ick!" She shivered with distaste. "You're not hurting me, but please buy drinks for your seatmates this afternoon. They're the ones who'll be punished."

They both laughed, nixing the anchovies and choosing a shrimp dish instead. Once their order had been placed, Ian sat back in his chair sipping a glass of white wine as he watched Denise stir her tea in an absent-minded fashion.

"So, what's on tap for Ms. Adams this weekend?"

"Pretty much the usual, except Joanne has a fashion show on at the Omni on Sunday afternoon."

"And you're modeling?" He sat forward a little, obviously interested.

"I don't think so!" Denise laughed abruptly. "No, I help the models dress and make sure they go out on the runway at the right time, things like that. And write up sales after the show, pack up the inventory. It's tiring but it's usually a lot of fun, too."

"You should ask your sister to let you model. I think you'd be good at it."

"You don't know me very well, do you? I'd probably get my heel caught in a curtain, fall on my face, and bring down the entire walkway with me.

"I'm serious, Denise," he pressed. "I've never seen you come anywhere near the kinds of pratfalls you're talking about. You're quite graceful, actually. Next time, tell your sister you want to try it, okay?"

Denise was surprised by his compliment. What did he have to gain by flattering her?

Had he left his wallet back at the office?

"Only if you're around to absorb some of the flak that would fly if I did," she responded. "Girl," she began, imitating Joanne, "if you ruin one sale for me I will kill you. I can see it now—you don't know how to walk in heels. Tear one of my dresses, you will pay for it. You should have been learning how to walk like a woman instead of having your head in some damn book all the time..." She looked up into Ian's eyes as she finished, surprised that he didn't find any humor in her recital.

"Don't you believe any of that for a second. I'll tell her myself, if you like." His expression was still as serious as before.

Denise began to feel uncomfortable. Ian was getting far too caught up in her innocent attempt to make conversation. She took a quick sip of tea and changed the subject.

"So you'll see your parents this weekend?"

"I'll be staying with them. I'm really going up to talk with my agent." He sighed and rubbed his eyes with both hands. "It should be easier now that the holidays are over. I couldn't face going home then. Not without..." Ian fell silent, his attention turned inward. Denise waited quietly for him to return.

"I'm sorry," he said, shaking his head as if roused from sleep. He pulled his chair closer to the table. "I keep this up, you'll never have lunch with me again. Such fascinating conversation!"

"I didn't mean to bring up anything bad," she found herself apologizing.

"You didn't," he responded, seeing the genuine concern in her eyes. He reached across the table, rubbing the back of her hand to reassure her.

Her first urge was to pull away, but she found herself drawn to the study in contrasts. His big, ruddy hand easily covered her small, dark one. His fingers were rough and crisscrossed with scars of various ages; hers were smooth and unblemished. Risking a covert glance, she could tell he was contemplating the same image and felt the same sensations. When she dared look up again their eyes met. Denise expected him to look away after a few seconds but Ian continued to stare at her, as if he had asked her a question and was waiting patiently for her answer. She felt confused: there was an odd buzzing in her ears and her stomach dropped somewhere below street level. Worst of all was the twinge from deep within the place she thought she had willed back into numbness after Kenny left. The pressure and movement of his skin against hers had startled one nerve, then another.

No, she told herself firmly. This can't happen. I can't let it. She slipped her hand out from under his and took another sip of tea. When she looked up again Ian had relaxed against the back of his chair once more, but continued to study her with the faint trace of a smile. Before she could succumb to the urge to ask why he was staring at her, the waiter brought their selections.

They finished their meal in near-silence and, on leaving the restaurant, went their separate ways.

Bumped from his flight, Ian sauntered down the concourse with a drink voucher in hand, in search of the nearest barstool. The post-rehab Josh would have said he was self-medicating.

You bet your ass I am, mate, he whispered to himself. The prospect of two and a half fun-filled days with Ed and Wendy would set the most devoted monk off on a bender.

And what the hell was that about back

there at the restaurant?

Another kind of self-medication, Josh.

Did you see the look in that poor girl's eyes? Like a deer caught in the headlights! You should be ashamed.

Ashamed? Perhaps. But I'm not sorry.

Drawn by the aroma of stale popcorn and hops, Ian ducked into a dimly lit alcove. The station's bartender occasionally wiped at a glass, his attention consumed by the soap opera playing on the elevated TV. Ian slid onto the red vinyl cushion of one of the barstools, not really caring whether he was served or not.

What was that look in Denise's eyes? It seemed an awful lot like fear. Further proof of her intelligence. Any sensible woman would run screaming from him these days. But there was something about her that drew him, kept her on his mind. He couldn't say what it was.

That very morning he'd nearly bitten through his tongue trying not to laugh. She'd been standing toe-to-toe with him, her little legs sweet in black stockings, scolding him for the number of incomplete loops she'd found in his code writing. She was such an attractive woman: long, skinny braids, deep brown eyes and the exaggerated curves of a naughty doll. She would have been perfect for a role in one of his science fiction fantasies: a 21st century priestess exacting punishment from men who dared corrupt the Temple of Binary Logic. And the nature of the penalty? To be forced to attend her, to be her student and her servant, to look into her dark eyes and inhale the trailing notes of her fragrance, but never to touch, to embrace, to possess. All that bit about not having a lover was a device, her ladylike way of ordering him to mind his own damned business.

"Look, but don't touch, Phillips," he mumbled under his breath. His mantra roused the somnolent barkeep, who looked up as if seeing him for the first time.

"Sorry, how's that again?" he asked, taking a few steps toward Ian.

"Foster's," Ian said plainly, shoving the voucher forward. The bartender collected it with a sigh, then filled a glass mug with the lager. He placed the drink in front of Ian, who obligingly fished a crumpled dollar from his pockets and pushed it toward the server.

Ignoring the beer, Ian rested his head in his hands. For months he'd grappled with Josh's death, and eventually had found some peace in the passage of time and in work. But this preoccupation with Denise was sticking pins into his serenity, worrying the tender scar of his composure. His attraction to her and the constant struggle to deny it had turned into a daily battle waged in his brain and in his groin. He was used to being in control; now he was feeling his way in uncharted territory. Better that he be dropped naked into the depths of the Amazon jungle; at least he'd actually been there once and knew enough to take a good, hard look before each step.

Ian sat up, rubbed his eyes, and took a long draught of beer. His head was buzzing with expectation as it always had before he'd departed on a journey, but this feeling had nothing to do with the short trek to New York. The time he'd spent with Denise Adams was leading him down a path he'd long avoided, to a place he'd rarely seen sober or in daylight. For not only had she engaged his mind and body, but she was well on her way to winning his heart.

Chapter 7

"Now that," Denise concluded triumphantly, "is one good-looking algorithm, as my daddy would have said." She underlined the mathematical rule with three blunt strokes of the marker. Ian continued to stare at the whiteboard, but his mind had lurched away from the equation and toward an image of his lips against hers.

"So? What do you think?" She replaced the cap on the marker and set it down in the whiteboard's channel.

"Hmm," Ian murmured, reluctantly abandoning his fantasy. "Awfully impressive. I'll have to sleep w– sleep on it for a while. Where the hell did you find it?"

"Some online journal link to the University of Helsinki. I can't remember who wrote it." The confidence she'd shown while acquainting Ian with the formula suddenly left her. She returned to her seat, avoiding his eyes.

"I shudder to consider your 'serious' reading list," Ian observed with a soft chuckle. "Yours and your daddy's." He emphasized the last word in a gentle imitation of her southern accent. She turned and looked up at him, breaking into a smile that set his blood humming. He needed that smile, needed to keep her talking.

"You only have sisters, right?"

"Uh huh."

"I'll bet your father has a shotgun with each of your names on it."

"I don't think anyone is packing where he is."

"And where is that?"

"Up there." She pointed toward the ceiling.

"The secretary's office?"

"No," she responded with a wry smile. "He's in heaven."

"I'm sorry," Ian quickly apologized. "I'm

really sorry."

"That's all right." Denise shook her head. "You're really funny sometimes."

He looked at her closely.

"When you did that," he said, pointing upward as she had, "you looked so sure, like a little kid. Like you really believe that's where he is."

"I do believe it. He's up there, and sometimes he's here." She spread her arms wide, indicating the room around them. "But mostly," she whispered, "he's here." She was pointing to her heart.

There was that trusting, innocent expression of hers again. He turned away, believing it might break him in two if he looked at it too long. How could she be so composed speaking about her father? He could barely think about Josh without...That weird sensation in his chest reappeared out of nowhere.

"Ian, it's all right," she said, taking a step toward him, her voice full of concern. "I like talking about him. That's how he stays real for me."

"So tell me," he asked, taking his usual seat on top of the table by the window. "Tell me about your dad. What was his name?"

Denise walked over and sat down beside

him. "George Washington Adams. He was born and grew up in South Carolina, and his family moved up here when he was twelve. Even when he was little he loved numbers and building things and finding out how things work. A natural engineer, right? Anyway, he went to Morris for electrical engineering and practically stayed there most of his life, teaching and doing research. He was Dean of the School of Engineering when he had to retire."

"Had to retire?"

"Daddy had his first stroke when I was eleven. He was lucky the first time–there wasn't much physical damage. But two years after that he had several more. He was completely disabled and my mother stopped teaching to take care of him full time."

"You were pretty young then. It must have been hard for you."

"Yes, it was." The faraway look in her eyes betrayed her travel back to that place and time. "I was kind of a last minute surprise, and I think he always got a kick out of that. I can remember that when I was in elementary school, very young, he put a little desk and chair in his study at home. I used to go in there and do my homework while he wrote or read in the evenings. You always talk about how engineers are boring," she said, brightening. "My father wasn't! Sometimes, when he'd had a hard day or just wasn't in the mood to work, he'd put on his old jazz records and dance. We'd both dance sometimes. I knew all the words to his favorite blues songs, although I didn't have the slightest idea what they meant. And now that I know—talk about corrupting a minor!

"He encouraged me to be interested in math and science, which I was. He put up with stinky messes from my chemistry sets, helped me with junior science fair projects and didn't get mad when my white mice 'accidentally' ran free in the house. When I came to him with questions about my homework— now I can't believe how simple they must have been to him—he would patiently talk me through them, making sure I understood why things work the way they do.

"But it wasn't just about academics, though. Daddy knew a lot of folks around town and not just the rich, important ones, either. He used to take me with him when he did his 'visiting' on the weekends. He'd check in on some of the little old ladies from church, making sure their lights and heat and all were working."

"Your dad sounds like a real mensch," Ian mused. "No wonder you loved him."

"Mensch?"

"A word Jewish people use. It means a good person who's good to other people."

Denise nodded in agreement and gave him a shy smile. They both forgot about the time as she recounted more stories about herself and her father. They ended up sitting beside each other on the floor as the afternoon shadows lengthened.

"You haven't told me what he looked like," said Ian.

"Oh, he was slim, tall, dark and handsome. Like you," she teased, her tongue loosened from storytelling, "except for the dark part." She was relieved when Ian laughed at her tentative flirtation. "It's funny, you know. Kenny actually resembles him a lot."

Ian groaned.

"And I thought we could have one conversation without mentioning him."

"Why does he bother you so much?"

"Because he treated you like dirt and that makes me very angry," he growled. "You didn't, you don't deserve that."

Denise tried not to stare at Ian, unsettled

as she was by his unexpected display of emotion. Why did he react so strongly, so negatively whenever she mentioned Kenny? Her own family had not responded that way when she announced their breakup on that Friday night in December. They were sorry, of course, and murmured the appropriate condolences, but the conversation soon returned to holiday festivities. But here was a man she barely knew, and a white man at that, who turned red and clenched his teeth every time she called Kenny's name.

"I was only going to say—well, I guess that's one of the reasons why I was attracted to him. You see, Kenny was one of Daddy's undergrad students. He's very talented and Daddy was very impressed with him."

"Wait—I thought your dad died about fifteen years ago."

"That's right. When Daddy started bringing Kenny home for dinner sometimes I was still a little girl."

"So he's a child molester too?" Ian's jaw was tight again.

"Oh, stop! He barely knew I was there; I was just a fat little thing. He was always my dream back then. I used to imagine that we'd get married, with a fabulous wedding in the

Morris chapel. I'd wear a gown with a lace train that stretched from the altar all the way out onto the sidewalk. Kenny would fall in love with me all over again when I came down the aisle on Daddy's arm. We would start our family right away: A boy for him and a girl for me. Then we'd invent all kinds of indispensable things, just like Pierre and Marie Curie. But black, of course. And the Nobel prize? We'd have at least one apiece!

"Stop laughing, I was just a little kid!" she admonished Ian, who had stretched out on the floor next to her. His face had contorted into a reddened mask before he finally let loose a howl.

"I was trying not to, honestly," he pleaded.

"Yeah, right! As I was saying, I used to run into him occasionally when I was an undergraduate but he didn't have anything much to say to me, of course. Then a few years ago, after I'd been real sick and lost a lot of weight, the engineering school had a big banquet. Mama was invited because a chair had been funded in Daddy's honor. I was her 'date,' of course. Kenny came right up because he recognized her, but he couldn't believe who I was. I was wearing a dress Joanne had made for me; it was like the one Marilyn Monroe wore standing over the grate. It was made from deep blue satin and had a little jacket. He couldn't stop looking at me and practically begged me to go out with him the following night. It was so incredible, after years and years of thinking of him as an unattainable dream. We were together for nearly three years. Sometimes being with Kenny was like living out my silly fantasies. I had begun to hope..." she paused, reluctant to taste the pain again. "Until last fall."

"I wish your mother had found herself a real date," Ian grumbled as he pulled himself up to sit next to her. "And that you'd worn a potato sack or a barrel. Then you wouldn't be miserable and I wouldn't be pissed because you're miserable."

"Why should you care?"

"Because a woman like you deserves to have a man who loves you above all else. You shouldn't have to sit alone every night, grieving about what might have been. Maybe I'm selfish," he shrugged, "but I hate to see you hurting this way."

Denise fell silent, her heart turning over. Why had he said that, and what did it mean? Was he saying he had feelings for her? Or was he simply trying to be a good friend? A

Dorianne Cole

woman like you. What would a man like Ian
see but another short, dark woman in a city
filled with thousands more just like her? She
didn't have money or position, and her future
was probably tied to this government job.
There was nothing she could ever do or be for
him...if he were ever to ask.

She eyed Ian warily as he rested his elbows
on his kneecaps, his big hands dangling
between his legs. She was deeply ashamed of
her physical attraction to him; that alone
would earn a stream of curses from Lynn if
she were ever careless enough to mention it.
With his hazel eyes, straight chestnut hair
and angular jaw, he projected a European
ideal of male beauty. European male beauty,
she thought, a phrase Lynn would use. It's
still beauty, nonetheless.

Denise recalled the time around her
twelfth birthday when she was decorating her
room with posters of her favorite entertain-
ers. Lynn had looked on with faint amuse-
ment as she mounted blown-up photos of
Michael Jackson and Prince in places of honor
over her bed. But when she unrolled the
poster of British singer George Michael, Lynn
had broken into odd, unpleasant laughter. We
don't admire white men, sweetheart, she'd

said with a pitying smile. Denise could still remember how her cheeks had burned clear back to her ears, sensing she'd done something shameful. Crushed by yet another violation of the unwritten social rules that eluded her, she had promptly rolled George into a tight cylinder and tossed him into the trash.

She'd never forgotten what Lynn said to her that day. But the stubborn fact remained: she was attracted to Ian Phillips. And here she sat not an arm's length from him, sharing some of the most intimate details from her life. What more would it take for her to contemplate going to dinner with him, sitting next to him in a darkened movie theater, and perhaps even sharing a kiss? Not much, she concluded.

Denise hastily scrambled to her feet, brushing dust from her slacks.

"I've been talking too long–look at the time!" she exclaimed.

Ian, not in a hurry to end their conversation, glanced at his watch.

"It's just a little after five. We stopped work at a good place. Why don't you just relax," he invited, patting the spot she had just vacated. "I was enjoying listening to you."

"No! I mean, I'm sorry. I've really said too much." She picked up her things and backed away toward the door, grabbing her coat and scarf from the rack.

"I'll see you tomorrow, okay?" She hurried out, her footsteps echoing down the hall.

Ian leaned back and rubbed his forehead. He could have listened to her for the rest of the evening, watched her eyes light up or travel to a place in her past where he couldn't follow. He would have liked to take her for a leisurely dinner and then to her place, where perhaps he would have told her a few stories of his own.

Chapter 8

On the second Sunday in February, the Mount Zion Baptist Church Gospel Choir set the old gray foundation stones to rocking by eleven forty-five. Denise was clapping, swaying, and stomping, one of more than forty voices in close harmony. Karyn Baker Mitchell, her best friend since forever, was at her elbow, modulating the lush chords in a resonant alto. They'd known these songs longer than they'd known each other, had packed them between layers of muscle and bone while waiting to be born. Singing like this made Denise feel as if she'd been set free. Free from the daily round of work and family obligations. Free from the loneliness that lately had threatened to crush her spirit.

The organist had set the normally slow, solemn melody to a stuttering bass line, which she pounded out from the depths of the Hammond B-3. The baritone soloist took liberties with the verses, looping, stretching, almost caressing the words. The choir anchored the congregation to earth as they punched the refrain.

Denise couldn't say exactly when her voice failed, when her mouth would only shape the words as tears streamed down her cheeks. But before the congregation's last amens faded and Reverend Shelton stepped into the pulpit to take his text, Karyn had begun rooting around in her purse for tissues. Her raised eyebrows formed a question as she passed her friend the pink, peppermint-scented wad.

Denise could only shake her head, angry with herself, as she wiped her eyes. She cried at the drop of a hat these days, and the soul-stirring music had set her off again.

"Coffee after," Karyn leaned over to whisper in her ear. "I'll drive." Denise responded with a nod and a muffled sniff.

They'd met in elementary school on the first day of kindergarten, an accident of the

alphabet. Denise Adams, the placid child with
the round, dark face and Karyn Baker, the
lanky redbone terror, had quickly overlooked
their apparent differences to become bound at
the heart. The two had tackled everything
together, from multiplication tables and science fairs in elementary school to advanced
calculus and information technology at
Morris.

Karyn was a certified public accountant in
the Washington office of Alfred & Stokes.
Assertive and plainspoken, she'd taken on the
task of successfully shepherding one of the
firm's major clients through a harrowing
audit. She was now on the partnership track.

Her good fortune had carried over into her
love life as well. She'd married Terence
Mitchell, her grad school sweetheart, the previous September. Neither the bleak winter
weather nor the impending tax season could
dampen her joy.

After the service the young women hurried
out the back door of the church, bending their
heads into a chilly wind as they walked the
two blocks to Karyn's parking space. A few
flurries swirled around Denise's broad-
brimmed felt hat or caught and melted among
Karyn's honey-colored goddess braids. Karyn

stopped next to a new Mercedes sedan and activated the keyless entry.

"Girl, this is sharp!" Denise exclaimed as she peered in and tossed her hat onto the rear seat. "When did you get it?"

"At the end of December, thanks to that little something extra in the company Christmas envelope."

"I'll miss old Betsy," mourned Denise. "We had some good times in that car. But this is beautiful–and I don't even have a car yet."

"You don't need one! Nobody makes you stay at the agency 'til two o'clock in the morning. I wouldn't have this thing if A&S ever heard of the forty-hour workweek. Besides, this is one of the reasons I've been trying to get you to come out and play in the private sector with me. I don't want to be the only one stuck with these golden handcuffs!"

"Can't say I'm not tempted, seeing this beautiful thing," Denise murmured, removing a glove to stroke the leather seats. "You mean Terence doesn't wait up for you or come down to pick you up?"

"Are you for real? Now that he's on the city desk at the *Herald* his hours are even crazier than mine. At least I know I've got the annual descent into tax hell in front of me.

Speaking of which," she said, pausing to look at her friend, "I can't make the trip without knowing you're okay. What was all that about during the anthem? And don't tell me you were channeling Sojourner Truth."

"Don't worry. I'm sure she wouldn't even think about speaking through a wimp like me."

"You, a wimp? I don't think so! You might have gone into that hospital with a couple of fibroids but that infection almost took you over Jordan." The memory of nearly losing her best friend made her shiver. She switched the heater on full blast. "Ugh. I don't want to think about it."

"Me neither." Denise settled back against the headrest, making herself comfortable for the crawl downtown through 16th Street's post-church traffic.

"Any prospects yet?" Having polished off a generous slice of Oreo cheesecake, Karyn was ready to chat.

"If there are, they haven't let me know." Denise idly stirred her tea as she glanced down at the colorful mix of pedestrians on Connecticut Avenue. "Are you sure Terence doesn't have any brothers?"

"Four sisters, sorry." Karyn took a sip from her machiatto. "Is there anything new on the work front? Don't they ever bring any new blood into that joint?"

"I am the new blood except for a stray contractor or two. They're usually in and out, like this guy I'm working with now."

"This guy? Who's 'this guy'?"

"Oh, nobody. Wait," Denise stopped, raising a hand, "that's not true. He's definitely on his way to being somebody. Remember the network security detail I told you I had to take? That's the guy, and he has mass-market software product going into the stores, too. He'll probably need your services soon; shall I give him your card?"

"The question is whether you need his services. What's the deal? Is he married, gay, or what?"

"Or what," Denise replied with a frown. "He's white."

"And your point is...?"

"You need more of a point than that?"

"These days you can't afford to rule anything out."

"What do you mean, I can't? Just because you've exhaled, I'm supposed to make do with whatever comes along?"

"Girl, please! What is up with all the paranoia? I'm just trying to say that maybe it doesn't hurt to increase your pool of choices, at least just to consider–"

"Consider what? The look on Lynn's face if I brought a white man home? Or how long it would take her to throw him out on the sidewalk with her bare hands?"

"He's still just a man. At least you'd be dating within our species."

"In his case I'm not too sure about that either."

"Okay, okay! Sorry I brought it up." Karyn finally surrendered to Denise's obvious lack of humor with a wave of her hand.

Denise shrugged, looked out the window, then back at her friend. "He tried...he touched...no—he held my hand."

"What!"

"It was kind of an accident," Denise whispered.

"I doubt it!" Karyn pulled her chair closer to the small table they shared. "All right, what's the deal? I knew there was more to this."

"There's really not much to tell. He takes me to lunch on Fridays and this was a couple of weeks ago–"

"Takes you to lunch?"

"He's just a person who doesn't like to eat by himself. If I try to say no he always insists that it's part of the contract."

"You've spent too much time in tech world, girlfriend. On our planet it's called a date, remember?"

"Look, I can tell a date from a lunch and this was just lunch."

"A hand-holding lunch that you're still misty over two weeks later. Go on."

"I am not misty!" Denise insisted. "He had just asked me what I was doing that weekend—"

"Uh-huh. Trying to check out the competition."

"Are you going to hush up or what? I told him about Jo's show at the Omni. When I asked what he was doing he said he had an appointment with his agent in New York, and that he was going to see his parents, too. He was flying up that afternoon. When he mentioned his parents he, well, went into himself. He got quiet and started looking kind of sad. When he came out of it I told him I hadn't meant to say anything to upset him. He kind of touched my hand as if to say it was all right, but then he didn't let go. He just looked at me, as if he were trying to figure out whether I liked it."

"And did you?"

"Please. I snatched my hand back."

"What did he do?"

"He sat back and stared at me with this funny smile."

"Uh oh." Karyn's mischievous grin faded.

"What is it?" Denise whispered anxiously.

Karyn shook her head with an air of good-natured pity, her lips parting in a scarlet-edged smile. She began to laugh out loud as she drummed her fingers on the table. Denise still didn't get it.

"Hear that?" She pounded out a few more beats. "Sounds like jungle fever!"

Denise slumped back into her seat and stared at her best friend helplessly. She had hoped her more experienced friend would give her a better handle on the incident, but instead she was laughing as if it were the funniest thing she'd heard in weeks. She decided not to let her know how much the experience had both disturbed and excited her.

"Girl, I'd watch it if I were you. No telling what he might want to hold onto next. But I can guess."

"Then he'll be the famous one-handed

software developer."

"He'll need both hands for the parts I'm thinking about."

"You're nasty, you know that? And your seat in the choir isn't even cold yet."

"Haven't you heard, Neecy? I read somewhere that we church girls are hot stuff!" Karyn leaned forward, her voice dropping to an uncharacteristic whisper. "We love sex! We're into burning in the flames of the Spirit and transcending the body! Speaking of which, what kind of body are we burning and transcending here? What does he look like? Name an actor or something."

"No one I can think of. He's tall, got long, light brown hair. Kind of on the slim side." She fought the urge to smile. "Pretty eyes like yours. Really long legs."

"Sounds like he could be fine."

Denise shrugged. "Some people might say so."

"What do you say?" Karyn leaned forward again, her hazel eyes gleaming with anticipation.

"That it doesn't matter."

"What's his name?"

"Ian. Ian Phillips."

"Ian Phillips," Karyn repeated, trying the

name on her tongue. "Sounds very 'Masterpiece Theater.'"

"I guess. His mother's English."

"See! That's what I've always liked about you. Always so quiet and innocent, then you go and jump the fence and the Atlantic Ocean in a single bound! Denise and Ian. Ian and Denise, dahling." She extended a lacquered pinkie as she lifted her coffee cup.

"Mr. Ian Phillips and Ms. Denise Caroline Adams," Karyn intoned with an exaggerated English accent, "were joined in holy matrimony in a formal, yet charming ceremony at the British Embassy yesterday at exactly five o'clock, post meridian. A reception followed in the rose garden, during which the bride and groom were attempting to engage in the quaint Negro custom known as jumping the broom when the oldest sister of the bride grabbed the ceremonial broom and chased the groom across the grounds and whupped him smartly right in the middle of Massachusetts Avenue–"

"Yeah, the last part's about right, except Lynn would have locked me up in her basement long before the wedding."

"Uh-uh! Your maid of honor," Karyn asserted, jabbing a finger at her thin chest, "would have come and busted your timid behind out of there! I don't give a damn what Lynn would think about you hooking up with this Ian."

Denise tipped Karyn's cup and carefully examined its contents.

"What did they put in there? Caffeine's supposed to focus the mind, but you're seriously spinning out of control and trying to pull me along with you!" She set the cup down and looked into her friend's eyes. "I haven't hooked or jumped or crossed anything, and I don't intend to."

"I'm just trying to have a little fun," Karyn insisted, "which is what you should be doing with the situation. He's not going to be around forever so it won't hurt to use him to keep up your skills."

"And just what skills are those? I'm almost afraid to ask."

"Just keep a little flirtation going, if you want. Chances are, that's all he was doing with you."

"You didn't see his face, Karyn. You're not with him every day. I just have this feeling–I have to be careful."

"Careful?" Karyn repeated the word with a wry smile. "Why? Afraid you might give him a taste? Afraid you might find out you actually like a little cream in your coffee?"

"I don't intend to give him anything except a hard way to go." Denise's tone was emphatic. "Sometimes I don't know why I still try to talk to you."

"Because you know I'm always right." Karyn blotted her lips with a napkin and picked up the check from the server's tray. "Been right about everything for the last twenty-two years, ever since I told you to add some red to your picture on the first day of kindergarten."

"No you don't!" Denise tried to snatch the check from her friend's hand. "I'm not some poor orphan; it's my turn."

Karyn wrestled the bill from Denise's fingers.

"Save your capital, lil' orphan Neecy. Go buy yourself a new red dress for your next date—excuse me—lunch with Daddy E-bucks."

Denise tossed her another withering look, then stood to put on her coat.

"By the way," Karyn added as she snapped her purse shut, "what's on Mama Adams' menu this afternoon?"

"Are you going to start dragging your husband to my mother's table, too? The man might actually have a sense of shame, unlike some people I know." Denise paused to adjust her hat in the window's reflection. "Don't you know by now whether he can tell a frying pan from a flying saucer? I already know you can't."

"To tell the truth, we haven't quite gotten around to exploring each other's culinary skills. But if he has any, more power to him." Karyn gracefully arranged her cashmere ruana around her shoulders. "You know I'm my mother's daughter when it comes to the kitchen."

"Yeah," Denise agreed, recalling charred roasts that spurted blood and countless desserts with a mysterious, sour aftertaste. "Vernelle Baker might have brought you into this world—"

"But her cooking almost took me out," Karyn finished.

Their warm, womanly laughter preceded them down the stairwell to the first floor. Several male patrons peered over the tops of their *Heralds* or broke off conversation to look in the direction of the two young women. Giggles turned to gasps when Denise and Karyn stepped outside; the temperature had plummeted several degrees.

"So," Denise muttered through teeth clenched against the cold, "ten years from now you'll still be mooching Sunday dinners, bringing your husband and a half-dozen babies?"

"Sitting right across the table from you and Daddy E-bucks and your rainbow brats. He's gonna keep you pregnant 'til you're sixty, you know that."

"Shut up." Denise slipped her arm through Karyn's as they hurried toward the parking lot.

Karyn huddled closer to Denise for warmth.

"You still haven't said what's for dinner."

Chapter 9

"You never answered my question."

Denise had nearly been lulled into a doze by the patter of late winter sleet against the windows. Had there been thunder? She pulled herself up straight in her chair and considered going downstairs for some coffee to wake herself up.

"I said, you never answered my question." It was Ian, louder and more insistent this time. Probably signaling he was in a mood to talk rather than work. But her conversations with Ian always held the potential for danger; she preferred to keep him from the winding roads that always seemed to end at her heart.

"What question was that?" she asked,

almost wearily.

"Was it a sex thing between you and Kenny?" he inquired brightly, knowing he had hooked her attention.

Denise groaned.

"Why do you keep going back there?"

"I have to know. Well, I want to know. I'd like to know, if you'd be so kind…"

She reached under the table for her backpack and pulled out her wallet.

"I'll make a deal with you," she said, counting out four quarters. "Get me a small coffee and I might be able to speak in complete sentences."

"Done!" He sprang to his feet and swiftly crossed the room.

"Hey! You forgot the money," she called out behind him.

"Don't you get it?" he asked, pausing at the door. "It's all part of the contract." She could hear his now-familiar whistle fade as he drifted down the hall.

"Will you explain something for me? Every time I mention Kenny you start cussing. Then every time I turn around, you're asking me something about him. It's like you're having this love-hate relationship with somebody you don't even know."

Ian set her cup down on the windowsill, her usual seat during their talks. He shrugged while emptying sugar packets and small tumblers of half-and-half out of his pockets. He remembered how I like it, she noted with surprise.

"I don't know. Maybe if I can figure out what it was you saw in him, I can help you find a kinder, gentler version so you won't be so mopey all the time."

"I'm not mopey!" she retorted as she rose to fix her coffee. "And Kenny was very nice to me."

"You have an intriguing definition of 'nice,' Ms. Adams." He leaned back against the fake mahogany desk and kicked off his oxfords. "Does it also include a poke in the eye with a sharp stick, or a continuous loop of Barry Manilow singing?"

Denise rolled her eyes in Ian's direction as she eased herself onto the windowsill.

"And what makes you think I need you to find a man for me? And you better not say some of your best friends are black, either."

"Are you saying that being your man isn't

an equal opportunity gig?" Ian looked genuinely surprised. "What's up with that?"

"I never really thought about it. I mean,
why would it be?"

"Ha!" He folded his legs yoga-style.
"You're kidding, right?"

"No, not really. I don't know why any
white guy would be interested in me."

Ian shook his head.

"I could rattle a couple of reasons right off
the top of my head but..."

"Okay, beyond anything like that."

"What is there not to like about you?" Ian
inquired, as if the answer were obvious. "Are
you telling me that if I found a guy who's like
Kenny in every way, the walk, the talk, the
job, in the sack, everything–just like him,
except that he's blond with blue eyes–you
wouldn't go out with him?"

"I don't know. It's not something I ever
thought about."

"Okay, let's try it this way: what if he's
better than Kenny? What if he has everything
Dr. Kenny has, only better, right across the
board? What if he promises to love you like
nobody else, forever? Would you give him a
chance, just one chance to prove himself?"

Denise shifted impatiently on the windowsill.

"Do you have someone in mind or are you just having fun?"

"Denise, I'm serious." He was having a hell of a time keeping this exercise light and non-emotional, at least on his end. Denise chewed her lower lip and looked out the window, a good indication that she was finally ready to tackle his questions. She took another long sip of coffee before she spoke.

"It would be real hard. My family wouldn't like it in general and Lynn would kill me, in particular."

"Even if you were happy with the guy?"

"Let's just say that most of us are unable to imagine being 'happy' with any white person, and leave it at that."

"I'm not talking about an 'us.' Right now I'm only interested in whether Denise Adams can imagine being in love with somebody like m– I mean, a white man. And happy. Married, with a house full of kids. And a career. The whole deal, if that's what you want."

"I don't know, Ian. As a matter of fact this came up at dinner a while ago—don't ask me how—and as Lynn said, interracial relationships just make everybody mad. I think that white people assume that we think it's some great honor for us to become involved with them. Well, it's not," she declared, looking at him pointedly. "Most of the time our families don't like it one bit either. One of my uncles married out years ago, and my father practically treated him as if he didn't exist. I never even met the man until after Daddy's funeral.

"Besides that, black people you don't even know feel free to give you grief. There are times when we're walking to lunch that black men give me angry looks or make comments. And there's nothing between us, we're just coworkers."

"I never heard anything! When did this happen?" Ian demanded. "And why didn't you say something?"

"You don't hear it because it's not directed at you. It's for me."

"Things like what?"

" 'Jungle fever' or 'you need to come home, sister.' Even that you've contaminated me. Stuff like that and sometimes worse."

"You let me know next time, okay? I'll be happy to contaminate anyone who interferes with you while I'm around."

"Caveman, please!" She waggled her fingers at him dismissively. "Spare me. I can take care of myself."

"I don't doubt it. But you still haven't answered my question," he insisted.

"Can't distract you, can I?" She paused to look out the window before she spoke again. "Okay. I don't think a white man could ever understand what it's still like for us," she replied, purposefully emphasizing the last word. "What it's like to have to maintain a healthy paranoia, even if you're lucky enough not to have it justified every minute of every day. Because just as soon as you let your guard down, it never fails to come out of nowhere. No, let me step back: the paranoia's always justified. If the injustice isn't inflicted on you, personally today, it's being inflicted on someone just like you for the same damn stupid reasons. And that's what makes the us important. We're connected by that struggle across history, across all the colors we are, all the cultural differences and all the politics. I want whomever I'm with to understand that. I don't know if a white man ever could."

Ian pondered her words, his brow furrowed in concentration. "Isn't there a difference between experience and understanding, though? I'll be the first to admit that what you're talking about hasn't happened to me.

But I recognize bigotry and prejudice, and despise it."

"But that's exactly my point!" Denise blazed. "When does someone like you see it? Or do you assume simple, decent treatment is what you're due?" Her voice rose, tinged with bitterness. "I'll bet you don't realize that it's taken over twenty years of litigation for black people to be fairly hired and promoted here at the agency. If it weren't for people always pushing, fighting, and forcing change where it isn't wanted, I would never have been hired, and I probably wouldn't make a decent salary, either."

"You're right, of course," Ian quickly agreed. "Perhaps a white man would need to be with you over time to learn how to see what you already know." He regarded her anxiously, hoping this concession would calm her. Denise shrugged, then nodded in agreement. He breathed out a sigh of relief, grateful for the reprieve.

"So let's say," he continued, "there's this white guy–call him Kenny Squared–a brave, brilliant, handsome fellow, who does his best to understand and fully support the struggles of your people. He loves you and all the beautiful babies you'll make with him more than his own life. And every night you'd lie in his arms, safe and happy, wondering how you could ever question his feelings for you..." He paused, pleased with this version of his story. "Would you be willing to give him a chance?"

Denise stared into the bottom of her empty cup. He couldn't read her averted eyes but the familiar slump of her shoulders implied that his romantic scenario hadn't worked as well as he'd hoped.

Ian watched as she slid off the windowsill and returned to her desk. Denise stood, thinking for a moment, then started toward the door. She turned around, her expression suddenly sad and a little weary.

"Thanks for the fairy tale," she said with a weak smile. "Too bad it's not even close to my bedtime." The door quietly clicked into place behind her.

"Maybe one day," he whispered to himself, "it will be."

"Denise?"

"Um." Denise wasn't in the mood to be dragged into one of their conversations that afternoon. She knew she wasn't up to defending her point of view, let alone her heart, should he carry their talk beyond the boundaries of work.

"I'll be away tomorrow, Friday. There's a big trade show beginning in San Francisco and my agent wants me to be there. I should be back on Monday, but it could be as late as Tuesday. I'm taking a flight out tonight."

"That's great!" she exclaimed. For reasons that escaped her, she was genuinely happy for his success. Then she noticed his bland expression.

"Aren't you excited?"

Ian shrugged.

"Not really. I've gotten so far into this documentation I'd prefer to keep at it. You think you can hold down the fort, Ms. Adams?"

"I'll manage, Mr. Phillips. I'll probably get some real work done for a change because you won't be around to bug me all the time. Bring me back something good from Fishermen's Wharf, okay?"

"Come with me and pick it out yourself," he proposed. "I can get another ticket for you, you know." Warming to the idea, he came over and perched on the edge of her desk. "I could say you've been assisting me with the next release, which you have, in a way. Come on, it would be fun!"

He dared to hope she might take him up on his offer. At least he'd have someone to run around with in the evenings. They could check out the clubs and perhaps share a late dinner or two. And maybe, if the mood was right, he could tease out her feelings, see if there was any chance they could return to D.C. as more than work mates.

"Right!" she snapped sarcastically. "As if I could just jump up and fly to the West Coast at a moment's notice. No, you just get out of here so I can experience one of those three-hour lunches I keep hearing about. Let's see: shop, get a facial; shop some more, get a massage; and maybe a cute little fruit salad..."

"Come on! What would you have to do to get ready that can't be done by five o'clock?"

"For a young man you don't hear very well!" she pretended to shout. "Besides, it's not just a matter of what I can or can't do in a couple of hours. I have responsibilities, you know."

"No, I don't know! For the last two months all I've heard is quite the opposite. No husband, no kids, no lovers, and you've got two sisters around if your Mom needs anything. Sounds pretty easy, if you ask me. So why not throw a couple of your little dresses in a bag and–"

"Ian! I don't owe you any kind of explanation, but there's a big Democratic Party function at the Garfield Hotel Saturday night–"

"Oh, well," he sighed. It was a political town, after all. "My condolences, then. A few baked chickens and boring speeches never killed anyone. Quickly, "he added.

"That's not it. I'll have all my sisters' kids. They're staying with me because Preston and Maurice have to be there and–"

"You're not even attending the damned thing? What rubbish!" he snorted. "Better they pay someone and let you get away for a few days. Honestly, Denise, I think you let your family take advantage of you! It's awfully convenient, isn't it, for them to unload their brats on you whenever they want? What about you? What about your needs? I suppose they didn't have much to say when Dr. Kenny broke your heart, did they? Better for them to have their moment's notice nanny back, free of cost."

"You need to be quiet because you don't know what you're talking about," she shot back, frowning. Another lie, a big one. That was exactly how she'd felt when her announcement had barely evoked a comment at dinner that night. They all seemed to take it in as naturally as the air they breathed. No more frantic calls to teenagers they barely knew, no more frustration when the young women didn't bother to show up. Denise was back on her babysitting gig, more dependable than grandma. What was with this guy, anyhow? Were her thoughts playing out in front of him in 70mm, sound enhanced THX technology?

"Look, why don't you just go, okay?" She turned away from the distraction of his thigh resting against her desk, less than six inches away. "You said yourself you weren't really interested in going, so why should I want to?"

Ian sighed deeply.

"Why indeed?" He remained by her side for a few moments, then went back to his desk.

Ian decided to leave the office around mid-afternoon. He had not spoken a word to her since their heated exchange that morning. Denise looked around, hearing his computers power down, and was surprised to see him pulling on his jacket.

"You're leaving so soon?"

"No reason not to," he replied briskly. He looked at her directly as he hoisted the backpack and a large duffel bag onto his shoulders.

Denise looked back, fighting thoughts of jumping into a cab to zip home, then to the airport. Imagined the two of them flying together into the wan, late-winter sunset to San Francisco. She knew there was only one reason for her to go with him: to create an opportunity for the one thing she could never allow to happen, yet wanted more than anything she could think of.

"You'll have a good time," she predicted evenly.

"Perhaps." The tight set of his features relaxed a little; the hint of a smile played around his mouth. "Shall I bring you anything, then?"

She nodded.

"Yourself, back safe." The words didn't come out the way she wanted and were far more revealing than she'd planned.

Ian's eyes on her softened. His lips parted in a wide smile, full of unexpected light and warmth.

"Of course." His voice dropped to a husky

whisper. "That's part of the contract, too."

They fly business class, of course. Two wide, comfortable seats cruising over mountains, farms, and more mountains, all night long. Flight attendants serve a decent dinner, with a little champagne. As the night comes on everything but the jet's engines go quiet. They sleep, their reclining bodies as close as lovers'. Her head falls lazily onto his shoulder; he wakes for a moment and smiles, then drifts off again. The next day they sit behind skirted tables and answer endless questions about Ian's product. Private jokes, furtive touches, and long glances arc between them when no potential customers are present. The end of the day finds them sharing drinks and later, a fine dinner. They talk business, but there are also pauses they spend looking into each other's eyes. They return to the hotel, bid each other a reluctant good night, and unlock the doors that face each other.

Later she hears a knock at her door; she opens it to find him, long hair hanging loose around his shoulders, his shirt unbuttoned. Too jet-lagged to sleep, he says, could he come in just to talk for a while? And although she's wearing only her nightgown, she lets him in. He starts out sitting on the chair next to the desk, his bare feet propped up on the foot of the bed. A little later he moves onto the bed and stretches out beside her, occasionally reaching over to touch her hair, her face. He tells her she's beautiful, and they kiss, easily at first, then going deep. His lips nuzzle her neck as he slides the nightgown off her shoulders, then down around her hips. She in turn slips off his shirt, and he helps her remove his slacks, then his briefs. He eases his body down onto hers. I want you so much, he murmurs, burying his head between her breasts. She invites him to enter her. He responds with the full heft and motion of his sex, thrusting inside her again and again until–

Two fire engines from the third district station raced down 17th Street, all roar and screech. Her trance abruptly halted, Denise bounced up onto her elbows, her heart racing. What had she been thinking? As she pulled herself upright she sensed moisture and a pleasant tingling between her thighs.

She jumped out of bed and ran into the bathroom, grabbed a washcloth and frantically began to scrub between her legs. As she worked the soap into a lather, Denise could hear a chorus of accusations from a familiar choir. Afraid you might give him some? We don't admire white men, sweetheart. Afraid you might like a little cream in your coffee? She rubbed and rinsed until she was sure she'd removed every trace of her sweet, sticky essence. Scoured herself until she felt dry and raw.

Despite her efforts to purge herself, Denise was still consumed with guilt when she wearily climbed back into bed. Had she lost her mind, imagining herself and Ian making love? Ian Phillips was a white man, a white man she worked with. She shouldn't be attracted to him and she damn well shouldn't be having erotic fantasies about him, making herself crazy. No way, not if she had to go a thousand years without a man. She'd been unable to face her own reflection in the bathroom mirror just now, and she was sure she'd never be able to look Ian straight in the eyes again.

Chapter 10

"Hey!" Ian crashed into the office on Monday morning, carrying the bags he'd left with and tall coffee. He had arrived early, for him, and in good spirits.

Denise nearly jumped out of her skin at Ian's greeting. She had been standing by the window, studying the pale blue sky that graciously accompanied the first day of spring. She wasn't ready to deal with him after getting caught up in her little fantasy on Friday night. She almost believed he could read her mind sometimes, and she couldn't take the chance of showing anything that might betray her attraction to him. She walked back to her desk with a quick step, her eyes fixed on the floor.

"How was San Francisco?" She sat down and pretended to look for something in the lower left drawer.

"Not nearly as much fun as it would have been if you had come along," he answered readily. Ian fell into his chair as he tossed his bag and backpack on the floor.

"Oh?" She didn't dare look up.

"Hell no! Just suits and geeks. I didn't have anyone to talk to. I ended up eating alone most of the time; you know how much I hate that. And at places you would have liked, too. I didn't even have the heart to walk around, check out the clubs after. I just stayed in my room watching bad movies all night and was like the walking dead each day after. We could have hung out, had some decent meals, and taken the edge off the jet lag. I guess I'll just have to kidnap you if there's another show before we're done here."

"That's not funny," she cautioned darkly.

"My weekend wasn't a laugh riot, either. You should have come with me when I asked you," he added petulantly.

"Damn it, Ian!" She whirled around to face him, a sudden rush of anger overcoming her usual reserve. "What the hell makes you think I'm supposed to rearrange my life every time you want just because I'm stuck here on this stupid detail with you? There are a hundred other things I could be doing right now, including being on my own damn vacation. You're the one who screwed up, remember? That's why I'm here!"

Ian fell silent, knowing she was right. But old habits died hard.

"I thought you were my friend," he sniffed. Having claimed the last word, Ian sprang from his seat and walked out, slamming the door behind him.

Denise pounded her fist hard on her desk, tears of pain and frustration springing to her eyes. How did he always manage to push her buttons so easily? A day with Ian Phillips was like a trip through the fun house. She could ride through one setting and laugh herself silly. Then the next scene could scare the hell out her.

A noise at the door roused her from her thoughts. Ian was standing just inside the room, his hands jammed deep into his pockets.

"I apologize," he murmured softly. "You were right, Denise, absolutely. I'm worse than what I said about your family taking advantage. I have no right to make any demands on you." He didn't wait for her to respond, but simply walked over to his desk and took his seat. Denise could see his reflection in her monitor as he leaned forward on his elbows and rubbed his eyes. The shadow of her anger receded; she wanted to make a conciliatory gesture.

"That's okay," she said, rolling her chair around to face him. "I don't like traveling by myself, either."

He turned full around as well, a grateful smile playing across his features. He acknowledged her acceptance with a nod yet continued to look at her, much as he had that day at the Spanish restaurant. Denise tried to look away but something in his eyes held her, made her feel as if she were the one waiting for the answer this time. They stared at each other silently until Ian leaned forward, resting his elbows on his knees, the muscles of his jaw flexing as he chose his words.

"Denise, I believe there's more to this." He spoke hesitantly, and without his usual self-assurance. "While I was in San Francisco

I had some time to think about things and realized how much I... No, it's been longer than that. It goes back to the beginning of the year, when we first began working together. It's as if I've refused to deal with this because we're work mates, so things always come out so differently than what I mean. I think I have an idea why I tend to blow up around you for no apparent reason sometimes. It could be that I tend to become a little crazy whenever I'm feeling most–"

The harsh chime of the telephone on Denise's desk swallowed his words. She reflexively picked up the handset, her eyes still locked on Ian's.

"Denise Adams, how may I help you?" It was the receptionist from Frank's office, calling with the room number for their presentation. "Thirty-seventy-A? Two o'clock, right," she repeated, looking away for a moment to scribble a note on her blotter. When she looked up again, Ian had turned back to his work. Denise shrugged, deciding to focus her full attention on the phone call.

"Look, is there any way we can get in there the day before to set up? Uh-huh. Good. We'll need the usual: LED panel, a couple of body mikes. A headset? Oh, sure."

She hung up, shaking her head, then remembered Ian was in the middle of telling her why he tended to go off when he was feeling...what?

"Sorry about that. Now, you were saying..."

He didn't turn around.

"Nah," he mumbled to his monitor. "Forget it." His desire to discuss whatever was on his mind had obviously faded.

"You sure?"

"Quite."

Denise shifted her attention back to her work, but Ian's words floated just beneath the surface of her attention. Not nearly as much fun as it would have been if you had come along...refused to deal with this because we're work ... She was considering his words when something in her mind clicked. Her usual restraint vanished; she turned around and stared at the tawny tail of hair hanging over the back of his seat. No, that couldn't be what he was going to say. It was simply more drama from Denise's Wishful Thinking Studios, produced by an over-active imagination, directed by a starved libido, and starring an actor who never got a copy of the script. Damn it! All she needed was one good black man or maybe just a good shrink, as Lynn had suggested. But above all, she needed to get Ian Phillips out of her face. And that would happen in the natural course of events if she could keep herself from acting like a fool for the next two weeks.

Chapter 11

Their final presentation was scheduled for two o'clock on Thursday afternoon. Ian and Denise had worked feverishly up to the last minute to make sure the plan would be understood and accepted by the numerous division chiefs. Together they had chosen a theme that would tie in the paper, video and LED monitor components. Denise had insisted on setting up the conference room on Wednesday afternoon to make sure that no presentation materials or equipment would go missing at the last minute.

When Denise arrived Thursday morning, Ian was already in the office, leaning over a pile of papers. She nearly dropped her coat on the floor when he turned to speak to her. He was wearing a dark, European-cut suit, a silky abstract tie and polished loafers with tassels. His hair was neatly pulled back and the shadowy beard had vanished.

"You look great!" she exclaimed.

"You too," he responded, walking toward her. She was wearing a navy wool suit with a modified peplum waist. He reached out and yanked the blue velvet ribbon that held her braids like a mischievous schoolboy.

"Nice touch. You should have brought one for me so we could match." They stood and looked at each other for a few seconds until Denise felt her face flush warm with embarrassment.

They spent the morning rehearsing their "script," drinking too much coffee and pacing the tiny office in circles, one behind the other. At one-thirty they took deep breaths, bumped their fists together like athletes before a game and marched over to the conference room.

Ian commenced the presentation exactly as they'd rehearsed it. It was the first time she'd seen him not be totally sure of himself or totally in control. He was halfway through the first section when she heard him falter. She scanned the outline to make sure of the place, rose to her feet, and began to speak from where he had left off. She pushed back her chair, walked over to the LED board and stood slightly in front of him, maintaining a calm and measured tone. Grateful for a chance to regroup, Ian quickly shuffled through his notes until he was back on track. The rest of the presentation ran smoothly, even the question and answer period, with the two of them easily tossing their parts back and forth, even smiling at each other on occasion.

After nearly two hours had passed, Ian thanked the officials effusively for the opportunity to work with the government and acknowledged Frank for allowing Denise to assist him. He went on to recount in detail how critical her assistance had been for him, and how fortunate they were to have her as an employee. The room was silent for a moment, and then the office and division directors broke into applause. Frank came up, shook Ian's hand and patted him on the back, and kissed Denise on the cheek.

"I know that wasn't politically correct," he admitted, but I'm so proud of you!"

"You can talk to my lawyers tomorrow," she grinned. "You know I don't mind."

They lingered in the conference room for a while longer, answering a few questions and beginning to pack up their materials.

When they stepped back into their office, Ian lifted Denise off her feet and spun her around the tiny room several times. She shrieked from the surprise of finding her feet off the ground and the sensation of his hands around her waist.

"Thank you, thank you, thank you, Denise!" he cheered, setting her down on top of her desk.

"There's nothing to thank me for," she insisted, a little out of breath. "I was just doing my job."

"No false modesty allowed. I couldn't have done this without you."

"Suit yourself," she answered with a shrug and a smile.

"I intend to, by having you join me for drinks and dinner."

In the back of her mind Denise had wondered if, or maybe even hoped this might happen. It was probably an innocent offer, but she knew this invitation was different from the ones that preceded it. This wouldn't be like going to lunch and having to return within a reasonable time. This evening he would take her to a nice place, they'd have a couple of drinks and share a long, leisurely dinner. And then the night and all its possibilities would lie open before them. She knew Ian well enough to sense the danger. Hadn't he demanded enough from her? Come with me; talk to me; promise me. She was afraid of what he might ask of her tonight. Afraid she'd allow him to have it. She idly pulled the ribbon from her hair as she attempted to compose a graceful excuse.

"I'm sorry, but I sort of had my own little celebration planned: a hot bath and an early bedtime. But I appreciate-"

"Come on, you!" Ian scolded. It doesn't make sense for me to spend the evening at Neill's Inn alone and for you to go home and have your little glass of wine alone. This is the least I can do for you. Hell, we both deserve it! What do you say? Please?"

She knew Neill's Inn was a predominately white professionals' pub on Capitol Hill. Race and class divided the singles crowd in D.C. and the Hill was no exception. But what could it hurt? Have a drink, eat a little, and then go home. What could happen? They'd be out in a public place. You worked hard on this too, girl.

"You're right; I deserve it," she grinned.

"Yes!" He did another little victory dance around the office.

"Let's go, then. It's Thursday so there's probably a crowd." It was a mild evening; they decided to walk the seven blocks to the restaurant.

Neill's Inn on the Hill was a sea of oxford shirts and blue suits, the conservative uniform of congressional staffers, lawyers, and law students from Georgetown University. The march toward the NCAA Final Four was nearing its end, and this year Georgetown was a serious contender. The fans had gathered early to claim their places at the bar, already standing shoulder to shoulder and at least two deep. Denise scanned the room for non-white faces, a habit she'd never consciously learned but practiced as regularly as she drew breath. Her tally didn't take long; she counted only two African Americans in addition to herself, plus a couple of Asians. The red-haired hostess announced that no tables would be available for about fifteen minutes. Ian put his name on the waiting list and they proceeded to the bar to pass the time.

She felt the light pressure of Ian's hand against the small of her back, steering her through the crowd. It was then that Denise could have sworn she heard a voice, pitched low so only she could hear it. They'll always be ashamed of you; they won't take you around their friends. Where did that come from? Must be... Wrong lecture; this wasn't that kind of situation. They were just coworkers in for a drink and a bite after a hard day at work. At last they claimed a spot of standing room toward the end of the bar. The noise level was even higher in that spot, just below a large TV set aimed at the rest of the room.

"What would...?" Ian tried to ask without shouting over the blare of cable sports.

Denise turned to him, pantomiming that she couldn't hear.

He leaned closer and touched her on the shoulder.

"I said, what would you like?"

Denise leaned closer as well, her braids swinging forward to brush against his face. She smoothed them back, wishing that she had not been so quick to rip off the velvet ribbon that had held them in place during the presentation.

"Sorry about that," she apologized. "A glass of white wine, please."

"Nothing to be sorry about. I like it when you wear your hair loose like that." He looked at her a fraction of a second too long before he gestured toward the bartender to order a Molson ale and her wine.

Denise shifted uneasily on her stool. She hoped their drinks would come soon; she needed something to calm herself.

The order placed, he turned back in her direction. Their knees brushed under the bar. Denise jumped a little, surprised by the sensation of heat that seemed to spread from that point through her entire body.

"So," he began, smiling broadly, "how will you spend your time now that this crisis is over?"

"You're pretty familiar with our division by now. It's just more of the same." She sighed at the thought of returning to her predictable routine.

"I didn't mean that. I meant you'd have more free time away from work. What do you do with your spare time this time of year?"

"Oh, the usual. Church. Hang out at the boutique and help Jo. Baby sit."

"Those things smell like duty."

"But I enjoy doing them," she insisted.

"Nah. What do you do for fun? I'm talking about a little travel, a little adventure, doing things you've never done. Like going somewhere, maybe in D.C., or not, to take in some different scenery, see a play, try a new restaurant."

"I used to do that a few years ago with my girlfriends. But it's been a while," she admitted. "They've gotten married, have kids or are living with someone. I'm probably the only one left who's free to hang out or travel, but it's no fun doing those things by myself."

"I can think of a few ways to change that," he said, leaning in toward her. "I try to get out every weekend and do something; biking, hiking one of the trails, whatever. I know Wolf Trap Park has an outstanding jazz festival scheduled for later in the summer. We should check it out. Or if someone we like has a club date in town before that. I like spending time at the shore, too, especially old-fashioned places where you can walk around in swimsuits eating chips and ice cream and no one cares."

"Sounds like fun," she answered ruefully as she attempted to process his definition of "we." We should check out, someone we like... His "we" was probably tall, slender, and white; everything she wasn't. Here we go again, girl. Men use you to plan the itinerary, take someone else, and return to share the post mortem. Her shoulders sagged in disappointment, and her internal dialog nearly kept her from hearing Ian's next words.

"Then why don't you come with me sometime? I've been on my own for months now and I'm tired of it. And you haven't mentioned seeing anyone recently."

Ian used a finger to trace the outline of her left hand, which was resting on the bar. "Denise, I didn't want to ask this too soon, while we were still working together. I don't have a good grasp of what the rules are these days, but it wouldn't have been right, I think. And it was important that I get this right, because you deserve nothing less. But now that the contract's nearly done, I need to ask you something."

He leaned in close as if he were going to kiss her; Denise stiffened involuntarily, bracing herself for his touch. He did not kiss her, but the warmth of his breath against her ear was equally unsettling.

"I meant what I said just now, that you should come with me. Not that you have any obligation to, of course, but I've thought of you as a friend and I hope you've felt the same. Although we're quite capable of getting into it with each other, I think it says how much we respect each other as partners, and as friends. I tend to get a bit mental over people and things I care about. And the truth is, I've come to care about you, Denise. I've danced around the edges of this, teased you and behaved badly at times, for one reason only: from the first day I've been attracted to you. I've tried to deny it for the sake of our working relationship, to deny that I could care about anyone..." His voice trailed off, but resumed with new energy.

"I've come to like you a lot, and not only as a someone I happen to work with. So what I'm asking is, is there a chance you could think of me as more than a friend? Would you allow me to call you, see you?"

Denise's head was reeling; she thought she would tumble off the barstool. I was right, I wasn't just imagining it! He's asking me to go out with him. I've tried so hard to keep this white man out of my mind, out of my heart. I have to be loyal to our black men...but I'm so attracted to him...I want to go, I want to be with him so much... Lord, please don't leave me to make this choice. I should never have come here; I knew this was going to happen. Don't let him touch me again...

Their drinks arrived before Denise could answer. Ian slipped the bartender a couple of bills and handed Denise her glass.

"A toast," he began, "to partnership. Ours." He drank, not taking his eyes from hers. She took a sip of wine, hoping to slow her racing heart.

"Wait, wait," he directed, placing his hand over hers. "I'm not done. A toast to friendship. Ours, also." They repeated their salute. Ian gave her hand a gentle squeeze.

Denise was still pondering how she would answer the question he'd asked, wondering if he'd let go of her hand before the evening ended, when a strident female voice pierced the air between them.

"Ian!"

"Laura? I don't believe it! How are you?" He embraced the tall, willowy blonde who seemed to have appeared out of nowhere. Denise felt a flicker of annoyance. He spun the woman around to face her. "Denise, this is Laura Callahan, an old friend of mine. Laura, this is Denise Adams, a brilliant colleague and friend."

Laura had pale green eyes like a cat's, possessing a lazy, cunning, quality. Her clingy black dress defined her small breasts and concave stomach. His attention was totally riveted on her. Denise's heart sank; there was some history between Ian and Laura, history Laura clearly intended to repeat.

Denise extended her hand. Laura weakly shook her fingertips and quickly turned to shine her full attention on Ian. She immediately launched into a discussion of people and places Denise knew nothing about. Despite Ian's attempts to bring Denise into the conversation, Laura easily steered their talk back within the bounds of their previous relationship. Soon enough, Ian gave into Laura's manipulation, his eyes and attentions becoming fixed on her and, Denise was sure, anticipating Laura's slender form rising and falling beneath his own. Denise resigned herself to listening politely as their conversation lengthened and grew more intense.

When their table was ready, Ian invited Laura to join them. Then he ordered another ale for himself and a glass of pinôt noir for

Laura. Denise sat quietly, watching the mutual flirtation on the other side of the booth. After a few moments Ian rose and excused himself.

"As much as I hate to leave such lovely ladies I've got to go see a man about a horse." He reached over and affectionately squeezed Denise's arm before he set off for the men's room. She looked up only to see a feline pair of eyes checking her out thoroughly.

"So Diane," Laura began in a light, sing-song tone, as if she were a nursery school teacher and Denise were three-years-old.

"Denise," she corrected.

"Denise," she repeated with a dismissive wave, as if the difference were irrelevant. "How do you know Ian?"

"We work together," Denise replied evenly, struggling to keep her annoyance at bay.

"Are you his secretary?" Then she uttered a little shriek, causing Denise to flinch and spill some of her wine. "What am I thinking? No one has a secretary these days! Then you do data entry or something?"

"Or something. I'm attached to the office that's supervising his current contract. Ian and I were writing documentation for his network security program at the—"

Laura exhaled loudly, signifying acute boredom.

"Oh, please! I can barely find the 'on' switch. It's a pain to always keep Ian from veering off into whatever you techno-geeks are constantly babbling about. Especially," she purred, her eyes narrowing, "when he has much more interesting talents."

She gave Denise a sly, just-between-us-girls look, which she quickly cancelled with a toss of her thick, blonde mane. Something you'll never know, black girl, because you don't have what I've got. The platinum strands taunted Denise as they settled around Laura's bisque-pale features. Denise knew that she could not spend another minute in Laura's presence, with or without Ian.

"Look, I think I'm going to go." She slid across the vinyl bench and grabbed her purse. "Please tell Ian I'm more tired than I thought. Nice meeting you." Laura nodded, her thin lips then bending into a nasty smile, satisfied that Denise posed no threat to her plans for the evening. Seton Hall scored again as Denise plowed through the mob. It had become a bad night for the home team.

Outside of the restaurant, Denise tipped across the damp grass in the median in order to catch a cab headed uptown. Then she heard Ian calling her name.

"Denise, wait!"

She turned and saw him waiting for a thick stream of oncoming cars to pass. Then he darted across to her side.

"Please, Denise, don't go."

"Didn't Laura tell you? I'm really tired and my head's started hurting. Thanks for the drink, though."

"Can't you just–"

A Capitol Cab with its broad orange stripe pulled up at the curb. Knowing how Denise could be once she made her mind up to do something, Ian opened the door for her. After making sure she was settled inside, he motioned for the driver to roll down the window.

"Number 623, take this lady wherever she needs to go," he ordered as sternly as he could after a couple of beers. He pulled a twenty out of his wallet and thrust it at the driver through the lowered window. He knew taxis in D.C. often refused to take black customers to certain parts of town, especially after dark.

"She is to be let out directly in front of the door at..." He realized that he didn't know her address.

"Wherever she wants." He knocked on the back passenger window.

"See you tomorrow?"

Denise made no sign that she had heard. The cab pulled out into traffic and joined the sea of red lights headed uptown.

Chapter 12

The next morning Ian awoke with a roaring headache and a sense of failure. The previous evening had not turned out at all as he had planned.

Laura. Damn her.

He had taken her back to his place, a totally stupid move. He'd been unable to perform, a fitting punishment, particularly when he only had to think about Denise some nights and be hard for hours. Laura had jumped right in there, of course, with a reproach that reminded him of why they'd broken up in the first place. But worst of all, his longing to get close to Denise had come to nothing.

He had felt so good coming into Neill's Inn

with Denise. He had been looking forward to having a legitimate chance to ask her out and circumstances had finally come together to make that happen. He had liked the way her braids had brushed his face when she bent closer to hear him in the noisy bar, and had felt the jolt of electricity when they touched. Knowing Denise was still fragile from her breakup with Kenneth Hilton, he had been determined to draw her into his arms without hurting her more. And damn it, he had been getting there; he had been getting it right. He'd seen the expression on her face when he told her he wanted to see her; her big brown eyes had been as gentle and startled as a doe's. But then he'd let Laura ruin the best chance he was likely to have.

He was mulling this over when the telephone rang. The shrill, jangling noise rammed a steel rod through his throbbing head.

" 'lo."

"Ian?"

"Denise?" A good thing, a very good thing. At least she was still speaking to him. Hell, she was calling him at home! Whatever she wanted he'd give her. To hear her voice this morning was more than he deserved.

"Ian, you need to get here right now. Frank wants to meet with us at ten-thirty. I tried to hold him off but he's still caught up in the moment from yesterday. The man needs a life."

"Wha' time is it?"

"Nine-thirty."

He squeezed his eyes shut for a couple of seconds.

"Ian?"

"Coming," he mumbled.

"Okay."

"Denise." Those two syllables cost him the pain of a blow between the eyes.

"Yes?"

"Thanks."

"No problem." She hung up.

Ian stumbled in around ten-fifteen wearing dark glasses and balancing a venti cappuccino.

Denise looked at him with pity but was unable to suppress a giggle.

"Is this the official crash and burn uniform?"

"Cruel," was all he could murmur.

"I'm sorry," she laughed, leaning against her desk for support. "I'll earn the right to make fun of you, assuming I'll have to do most of the talking this morning."

Ian lifted one finger in agreement. A word or nod might have made the room spin.

Denise turned around on her way out to make sure Ian was behind her. He was following gingerly, but still wore shades.

"Wait a minute." She put down her armful of files and flipped off the switch that controlled the office lights. "Close your eyes."

"What?"

"Just close 'em, okay?"

She stood on tiptoe and gently pulled off each earpiece, one at a time. Then she lifted the keeper that held the glasses over his head. Even in his sorry state Ian could feel her warmth and detect the fragrance she wore.

"Try to open your eyes now. Slowly," she warned.

He squinted and cautiously opened his eyes to the shadowy office.

"Not bad," he mumbled.

"Okay. Just walk right behind me and do whatever I do. Short of sitting in my lap, of course," she added, heading for the door.

"Bless you, my child," he whispered.

"I really appreciate what you did this morning, easing me into that meeting and all." They had returned from their talk in good spirits; only a little fine-tuning remained to be done. Denise eased herself onto the tabletop and kicked off her shoes while Ian knocked back the remains of his coffee.

"For a good girl you sure seem to know the drill," he declared cheerfully.

"Good girl?" Denise suddenly jumped to her feet. "What is it with you? Every time I try to do you a favor, you end up insulting me!"

"Being a good girl is a bad thing now?"

Ian raised his hands, surprised by Denise's anger. "I didn't know."

"You didn't?" she snapped. "Good girls wait patiently and get nothing while the bad girls get it all! Therefore, good girls are losers! You want proof? I seem to remember a bad girl who was working it just fine, not even twenty–four hours ago. Based on your condition this morning, I assume she got everything she wanted." She was practically screaming at him.

Ian was genuinely rattled by Denise's fury. He moved quickly to apologize.

"Denise, I realize how rude Laura was last night and how wrong I was to let her get away with it. I know how she can be; I should never have left you alone with her. I should have sent her on her way, told her that our meeting was private. And I'm sorry, really and truly sorry about that."

She forced herself to sound more calm and composed than she felt. "There's nothing for you to be sorry about. You saw an old friend and decided to do some catching up. You didn't have to pay for the cab, either." She pulled open the desk's top drawer. "Here." She held out the twenty he'd given her the night before.

"I don't want that." He took her hand and closed it around the bill. Angered by his touch, Denise jerked her hand away, allowing the twenty to drift to the floor.

"Last night was supposed to be a special time for us to celebrate what we've accomplished here." Ian pressed on in the face of Denise's anger. "The way I acted I didn't deserve to have you call me and bail me out this morning. You're a good friend, Denise. If there's any way you can forgive me...I'm sorry."

The rage that had swelled to the point of explosion turned to ashes. It was hard for her to speak; her mouth was as dry as her heart was empty.

"No, I'm the one who's sorry. You haven't done anything that needs my forgiveness or anyone else's. Your personal life is none of my business. And vice versa, I suppose." She stopped to rub her temples. She had to get out of there.

"Look, I don't think there's anything Frank talked about that's worth beginning before Monday. I'm going to take off a little early. My head's starting to hurt again." She crossed the room quickly to get her coat.

"Hey, I've got the mother of all painkillers with me." He pulled the vial out of his jacket pocket to show her. "Please, let's go get some coffee or something. You'll feel better. I promise," he pleaded.

"No, no thanks. Really." She hurried out the door so he wouldn't see the tears of shame and disappointment in her eyes.

Denise found herself standing in front of

the receptionist's desk at the Niagara School around three-thirty. She hoped the young woman would recognize her and send her back to her sister's office quickly.

Tamara's glossy, lacquered hairstyle almost seemed to be a part of her headset. She finished taking a message and looked up at Denise.

"May I help– Oh! Dr. Adams-Vaughn's sister! How you doing?"

Denise nodded a little and mouthed 'fine.'

The young woman's welcoming smile faded.

"You don't look so hot." She quickly punched in Lynn's intercom number. "Dr. Adams-Vaughn, your sister's here. Can she come back right now?" She tapped her perfectly airbrushed fingernails against the telephone console as she waited for Lynn's reply.

"You go right back," she advised Denise. "You know where it is?" Denise was already on her way. She hurried down the womb-like corridor, hoping that none of her sister's coworkers would run into her and want to chat. The dam she had built to get herself across town was about to rupture.

She rounded the corner into Lynn's small but elegant office. Her sister had turned her chair toward the window to water one of her prized tropical plants when Denise burst through the door.

"Lynnie, please–" She collapsed into one of the leather armchairs in front of Lynn's desk. Her small shoulders trembled with violent, heaving sobs.

"My Lord, child! What's happened?" Lynn jumped to her feet and ran to her sister's side. "What's wrong, baby? Please tell me what's wrong!" Denise wept for several minutes before she could speak.

"I don't know. I don't know why..." She opened her hands in a gesture of helplessness. "I just don't understand..." Denise began to wail softly again. Lynn was a little anxious; it had been a long time since she had seen her sister in such a miserable state.

"Is this about a man?"

Denise nodded reluctantly.

"I didn't know you were seeing anybody. Are you pregnant, honey?"

"No."

Did he hurt you?

"No," she sniffed.

"Then what is it, baby girl?"

Denise was too exhausted from crying to try to speak. She could only shake her head mournfully and stare at Lynn, tears still flowing down her cheeks.

"Do you want to come home with me? Preston's got a neighborhood forum tonight."

"Uh-huh," she whimpered.

"Okay, then that's what we'll do. We'll even splurge and take a taxi. I have a bit of a headache myself," she admitted, rubbing her forehead. "Let me finish up a couple of things around here and then we'll go. How's that?"

"Okay." She tried to take a deep breath. "Lynnie, I'm sorry," she choked. And she started to cry again.

Preston and Lynn lived in a rambling Victorian close to the northeastern boundary of the city. Denise often dreamed of living in a similar house with high ceilings and wraparound porches. Lynn constantly complained about the outmoded appliances in the kitchen and the drafts that streamed through the large windows, but Denise loved it all the same.

Denise woke up around seven on Saturday morning, surprised to find herself on the couch in Lynn's living room. After a few sec-

onds her sore, reddened eyes reminded her of
the circumstances that had brought her there.
She wrapped herself up in the blanket Lynn
had given her and padded into the kitchen.
Tea, tea, English Breakfast, where are you?
she whispered.

"Morning." Preston's gruff tone startled
her. She whirled around.

"I didn't know anyone else was up. You
scared me."

"Sorry. His slippers made little scuffing
sounds as he walked into the kitchen. "Want
some coffee?"

"I was looking for tea, but now that you
mention it, coffee sounds good." She was a little curious; a whole minute had passed and
Preston hadn't teased her.

"Okay." He went to the pantry but
ignored the coffee tin, obviously searching for
something else. After rummaging further
Preston pulled out a bag of coffee beans from
a well known, upscale vendor. He reached up
in one of the cabinets and pulled out the bean
grinder.

"Looks pretty fancy," Denise remarked.

"Yeah. Wanted to do something different
for a change." The shrill whir of the grinder
briefly shattered the morning's peace. She

watched as he measured enough water for six cups and poured it into the coffee maker, inserted a filter, and poured in the fine dark grains. When the dark brew finally began to drip into the coffee pot, he walked over to the table and sat down next to her.

The two sat quietly until the old boards of the stairway creaked in protest, announcing Lynn's imminent arrival. Denise rose and got three large mugs from the cabinet.

"Good morning, Baby, Neecy." Lynn was bundled up in an old chenille robe, insulating her slim frame against the slightest chill. She stopped behind Preston and wrapped her arms around his shoulders.

"Lynnie, thanks for covering me up last night," said Denise. "I must have been out cold."

"I didn't do it," Lynn admitted. "Remember the pills I took while we ate? When I went upstairs I sat on the side of the bed for a minute, supposedly resting my eyes. I don't remember much after that. I had intended to come back downstairs so we could talk."

"Both of you were out, dead to the world when I came in. I just threw a blanket over you, Neecy.

"Preston!" Denise exclaimed in surprise. "Thank you. That was a nice thing to do."

"See, Denise. I told you Pres really cares about you." Lynn rubbed her husband's broad shoulders.

"I would have carried you upstairs to Marcus's room, but next thing I know, you'd say I was looking at you and Lord knows what else." Preston laughed, reaching around and pulling Lynn onto his lap. They pretended to tussle but ended up in an embrace that made Denise smile wistfully and look away. Malcolm's footsteps sounded in the hall but Lynn remained comfortably on Preston's lap, her arms encircling his shoulders.

"You better come in here and get some breakfast, young man," Lynn called out.

Malcolm rounded the corner into the kitchen, his face as sullen as only an adolescent's can be. He was dressed to go to Saturday morning practice, a basketball resting in the curve of his left arm.

"I can't eat all that stuff before I run," he protested.

"Nobody said you had to eat like a pig, but you've got to eat something. Cereal and fruit, something."

"It's too cold to eat cold cereal," he sniffed.

"How about a couple of eggs and some toast?" Denise suggested. "It's okay Lynn, I don't mind fixing it for him."

"Yeah." He dropped into one of the kitchen chairs, causing it to skid a little.

"Excuse me, your majesty?" Lynn's voice descended into its husky warning mode.

"Thank you, Aunt Neecy," he mumbled.

"Could you break a couple more eggs in there for his highness' chauffeur, please?" Preston asked, looking at his watch.

"No problem," Denise responded, rising to open the refrigerator. "Lynn?"

"No thanks, sis. Coffee's fine for now." Lynn tightened the belt of her robe and went out onto the back porch to smoke a cigarette.

Grabbing his coffee, Preston went upstairs to take a shower. Denise scrambled eggs and ran slices of bread under the broiler while Malcolm poured glasses of juice. When Preston re-appeared, father and son ate quickly and departed for the junior high gym. Denise fixed two slices of toast and poured more coffee before taking the seat opposite Lynn, who had returned and was skimming through the newspaper.

"I'm sorry. I shouldn't have come to your office like that," Denise apologized. "I just

didn't know where else to go. You would
think that I would get a little better at this. I
mean, the way he was acting ... I was just so
sure. And I've tried so hard..."

"Tried so hard to what?" Lynn laid the *3*
aside to look at her youngest sister.

"I don't know," she concluded with a sigh.
"I just really thought that something more
was going to happen between us. She warmed
her hands around the coffee mug. "So I'm
back where I started. Alone. I don't know
how much longer I can stand being on a constant emotional see-saw."

"What does that mean? You're young;
you've got quite a way to go yet."

"But you and Joanne were both married
and had children by the time you were my
age," Denise insisted.

"Well, if it's so important to you to be like
us, then go out and find yourself a paramedic!
We've pretty much exhausted the other divi-
sions of public safety."

Denise felt like laughing for the first time
in several hours.

"You've started with your dumb jokes so it
must be time to leave," she said, moving to
place her cup in the sink and pour more coffee
for her sister. "Thank you," she sighed, stop-

ping to give Lynn a quick kiss and hug. "You always give me a little hope."

"Want a ride to the Metro?"

"No thanks, it's a nice morning. I'll walk." Denise had walked into the living room to straighten up after herself and collect her belongings when she heard Lynn call her again.

"Neecy?"

Her heels made hollow sounds on the old floors as she hurried back to see what Lynn wanted.

"What's up?"

"The next time you get up and have to put on what you wore the day before, I hope it won't be in my house." She was smiling and lighting one of her ever-present cigarettes.

"Another reason for you to quit smoking," Denise laughed, pointing at her, "because I know I'll be an old lady when that happens. And I'm gonna need you to be here so I can tell you about it."

Denise reluctantly headed in the direction of the office on Monday morning. She had considered calling in sick but decided that it was probably better to finish the detail and get it and Ian behind her. And a small part of her needed to let Ian know that he did not have the power to upset her as much as he had seemed to, causing her to run out of the office.

As she approached the doorway, she could have sworn that she saw light coming from inside. Ian never surfaced before nine-thirty; what was going on? Denise held her breath and pushed it open.

Ian must have come in early. His backpack was sitting in the middle of the floor as usual but he was nowhere to be seen. She walked in slowly and uttered a little cry of surprise. The vase she kept on her desk had been stuffed to overflowing with pink and white tulips. As she bent over to inhale their fragrance, Ian hurried in, a little out of breath. He was carrying a large bakery bag.

"Morning," he said, looking at her cautiously. "How are you?"

He rarely engaged in polite small talk. She wondered what he was up to.

"I'm fine. You?" She busied herself with hanging up her coat.

"I was worried about you on Friday," he said quietly.

"Oh, it was just that headache I couldn't get rid of, and I was tired." She tried to sound more nonchalant than she felt.

"Are you sure there wasn't anything else?"

"Nope." She had returned to her desk and stood thumbing through her files, when she realized she had to say something about the flowers.

"The tulips–they're beautiful. Where did you find them?"

"At the place where I get fueled up every morning. You like them?"

"They're my favorites!" she exclaimed, immediately regretting her enthusiasm.

He grinned, clearly happy he had pleased her.

"I thought we could have a little something special for breakfast this morning." He turned to unpack the contents of the bag. "Fresh croissants–they're still warm, at least. And some fresh-squeezed fruit juice." He put two large plastic glasses filled with orange juice on the table.

"And finally, a café au lait for you and a double cappuccino for me." He looked at Denise expectantly as she continued to stand in front of her desk. "I didn't put all this out here so I could paint a still life, mademoiselle.

Please, come and help yourself." He extended his hand to her with a mock bow.

"But I don't understand. What's the occasion?"

"The occasion?" He rubbed his newly-shaved chin as he pondered her question. "It's Monday? The sun is shining? Frank didn't tell us we had to start over? Pick one. And pick a croissant, too. I think one of them has chocolate..."

"Speaking of Frank, we really need to get started on those changes–"

"We don't have that much left to do. I worked through most of it over the weekend. I need you to check behind me, as always, but it's almost done." When Denise didn't respond, he took a step toward her.

"Denise, I didn't want you to leave the way you did Thursday night, although I can't blame you. I should have sent Laura on her way, and not let her interfere in something I was trying to do with you. And nothing happened between me and Laura that night either." You took care of that, he reminded himself. "She doesn't mean anything to me anymore."

"I don't need to know that!" Denise cried, putting her hands over her ears.

"I think you do," Ian asserted. "The same way I think you know what I was trying to ask you before she showed up. And maybe this isn't the time or the place, but remember, I'm still waiting for your answer."

"I don't know what the hell you're talking about," she lied shamelessly. "And besides, we, I, need to look over those edits and I just don't have a whole lot of time. I took a look at my desk when we were over at my office last week and I really need to get back. So," she concluded, turning her back on his breakfast offering, "give me what you've done so I can make the corrections. I want to start moving my stuff back this afternoon."

Her eyes lit on the blaze of tulips again. He'd presented her with flowers and sweet things to say he was sorry, the kind of thing a man would do for a lover or a wife. Things she would never be to him. Denise turned to look at Ian once more and was surprised by his truly mournful expression. Something inside her yielded. She knew she had to say something; she didn't want whatever kind of relationship they had to end badly.

"Look, Ian. I'm sorry," she said quietly. "You've done something really nice here and I appreciate it, I do. So, thank you. For breakfast, the flowers, everything." She gave him the best smile she could muster.

At this he brightened, and beckoned her again to join him. This time she walked over and took her usual seat in front of the window, while he slid into his accustomed spot on top of the table. They took their time, sipping coffee, chatting about the project and predicting new uses for the Web. The most important business between them remained unspoken.

Chapter 13

Club Blue Nile was jammed between two car repair shops on a side street in the Adams Morgan district. Denise's heels resounded on the metal stairway as she hurried up to the quiet lounge to meet Karyn for a drink on a mild May evening. The two young women shrieked and hugged enthusiastically, then found a corner table and eagerly proceeded to share their news.

Denise was genuinely delighted for her friend, but also a little wistful.

"I'm so happy for you, but I miss doing stuff like this together. How is your Terence?"

"Oh, Neecy. He's just so-o-o good and fine.

There's nothing like a good black man. Know what I mean?"

"Wish I could say I did," Denise mourned, taking a sip of chablis. "It's been a long time."

"Have you heard from Kenny?" Karen asked.

"No. He's got a good sense of self-preservation. He knows even my mother still has him down for a major butt-whipping."

"She'll have to get in line behind me, then," Karyn muttered under her breath. "Whatever happened to that white contractor guy? Ian, right? Did you ever give him any play?"

"I think he liked me a little, but when all is said and done it just couldn't have happened for either one of us. Besides, the detail is over and he's been gone for weeks."

"I'll bet that boy was probably curious, or heard that black women were hot and decided to drop a few hints to see if you'd drop your drawers. You said he was fine, so he's probably used to getting what he wants. More power to you for holding the line, Neecy. If he wants a black experience let him work for it."

"I never said I thought he was fine," Denise insisted. "It's just that..." Karyn looked at her expectantly. "Do you think a white man can ever really love a black woman? Or is it something only for movie stars, not ordinary women like us?"

"That's not the point," Karyn chided Denise gently. "I don't know if I could love a white man day after day, knowing what we'd have to deal with. What if he were to come out with some foolishness like, 'You didn't get the promotion simply because someone else was more qualified,' or 'It was just your imagination; the salesclerk wasn't peeping up under the dressing room door at you because she thought you were trying to steal'?"

"You're probably right about that," Denise agreed reluctantly. "I can't understand why a man like that thought he wanted to be with me anyhow."

"Are you for real?" Karyn shot an incredulous look at Denise. "It's just like I tried to tell you back at Morris: there were guys who asked me about you all the time. You ran away from them, not the other way around! It wasn't so much about your weight; you were just so scared all the time. I can't believe you're still selling yourself short. Look at yourself, Denise. You're beautiful! Your skin is so clear and smooth, your hair looks great, and most women would kill to have a shape like yours! But the biggest problem with this isn't even about you."

"What do you mean?"

"It's always the kids who pay the price! And you want babies so bad that some nights I swear I can hear your clock ticking halfway across town. Neece, you only have to look in the mirror–you know what you are, everybody else can see what you are. In a society where everything turns on race, that's not always such a bad thing. This kind of living is hard," she said, pointing to her pale, freckled face with both hands.

Denise braced herself, anticipating Karyn's hurt and anger around the issue of color.

"Minimal acceptance from whites can be an advantage in the professional world, but how the hell can I ever feel good about it? On the other hand, I'm always fighting for acceptance from my own people who assume I think I'm better than they are. You know what I've been through, kids trying to kick my behind every other damn day because I'm light-"

"I remember only one or two of those fights," Denise interrupted, "mainly because somebody always had to pull you off those pitiful children before you beat them senseless."

"But I still had to do it, that's the point! I can't imagine some poor biracial child coming home after something like that, looking to their white mama or daddy, who can't even buy a clue! Ralph always knew what the deal was when I came home with my dresses torn and the ribbons yanked out of my hair. Vernelle assumed I was going around starting stuff, being a tomboy. But my daddy had been through it himself a hundred times, so he always understood." She paused to wipe the angry tear that was coursing down her cheek.

"Look," Karyn proposed, "suppose you and your boy decide to hook up? What if one kid looks like you, one looks like him, and another one ends up somewhere in the middle of the spectrum? What happens then?"

"I don't know." Denise's head was reeling from her strong drink and Karyn's stronger opinions. She was silent for a moment. "Yeah, I do," Denise rejoined, "The latest and best mama play: 'Mama, I Wanna Be White!' The one who looks like him disowns me until I die a premature, tragic death from a broken heart. Then he'll crawl through the doors of

Mount Zion at my funeral, crying, 'I always loved you, Mama,' while the choir wails a reggae jam of 'Soon Ah Will Be Done.' Troubles of the world, said troubles, mon," she pronounced in a rhythmic monotone, nodding to the beat.

"Screw you!" Karyn laughed and finished the dregs of her Long Island iced tea. Denise ignored her, flexing and spreading her slender fingers.

"I and I gonna meet mah Jesus!"

"Good Lord, child!" Karyn stared at her friend, unbelieving. "Are you drunk already?"

"I don't remember that verse," Denise grumbled.

"I bet you don't remember how to get home either, and that's only three blocks away. I guess I better take you downstairs and point you in the right direction. Mama Adams would have my head if you wound up downtown with some of those other professional females."

"I'm just playing with you, Karyn." Denise pulled herself to her feet. "This color stuff, though... You're right, it's pretty deep."

"Yep." Karyn also stood, then fell silent for a moment, thinking. "Neecy, if you really want to try some cream in your coffee, you should go on and do it. There's nobody stopping you; not the law, not me, not even your crazy sister. But remember," she cautioned, "somebody has to pay the price. It might not be you, and it probably won't be him, but somebody will pay."

Denise undressed and ran herself a bath as soon as she returned home from the Blue Nile. Seating herself beneath the froth of the jasmine-scented bubbles, she tried to unwind and think about the weeks ahead. No brain surgery there, she reflected. She was practically sleepwalking through work these days, compared to the period when she and Ian... She and Ian, indeed.

Many waking dreams of making love with Ian had followed the first; she no longer attempted to resist their power over her. She imagined his big hands around her waist as he swept her off her feet after their presentation; imagined the taste of his lips; tried to picture him lying beside her, or the weight of his lean body on top of her, and how he would feel inside her, wondering if he could please her.

It doesn't matter, she thought. He was on

his way to success and recognition and would not remember her name this time next year. He had likely forgotten the question he'd asked her that night at Neill's, not that she had an answer for it even now. It's all pointless anyway, she concluded, hugging her knees up against her bosom as the water cooled. I'll never see him again.

Chapter 14

On the second Tuesday in May Ian woke up early and went to the gym, working himself into a state of sweaty agitation. After a quick shower he returned home and cooked himself a large breakfast. Once he'd finished eating, he walked from room to room with a cup of coffee, opening windows to admit the warm, sun-washed breeze. He finished his task in the guest room, which he used for storage more than anything else. Taking a seat at the window that overlooked the tiny rear yard, he surveyed a patch of iris blooming in deep blues and yellows.

He had come to love this time of year in D.C. Exquisite formal gardens and smaller ones tended with loving determination by city residents all combined to give the city colors and smells he never experienced in New York. As usual he had begun his usual round of springtime activities: hiking nearby trails, cycling along the C&O canal, appreciating bare shoulders and legs that were revealed as the temperatures warmed. He even had gone out on a couple of dates. No bells, no magic, just evenings he didn't have to spend alone. For once he was not concerned to find himself between projects. His software sales were great, according to the accountant. He had even given some thought to setting up an office somewhere in the metropolitan area and going into development on a full-time basis.

But as much as he'd kept his mind and body active during this time, his heart was empty. He was simply going through the motions, and he knew it.Something–no–some-one was missing, and he had no doubt who she was. Denise Adams had firmly lodged herself in his consciousness from the first time he'd ever seen her, and even now she refused to leave gracefully.

But he'd been too damn scared to ask before that night at Neill's because every sensible indicator had predicted she would refuse. Sensible indicators...

It was odd how his life had changed after he'd started writing code full time. He'd actually started thinking in terms of cause and effect, actions and reactions, and consequences. He'd begun to see how his arrogance and combativeness made people throw up walls against him, much like the digital walls he fashioned to keep the crap out of computer networks. He was now starting to think before he opened his mouth. He was seeing the need to establish some goals and maintain a steady direction. He knew he needed to decide what mattered to him and go after it. He was thirty-two; he'd seen that number on the obits page. And most recently he'd seen it in a little wooden box, reduced to ash and specks of bone, the forlorn subject of eulogies and ancient sorrow songs.

He knew the Denise Adams issue had to be resolved before he could choose his path, before he could even take the next step. There was no question now: Denise mattered.

He'd clung to one hope for the past several weeks: she had never answered the question he posed to her that night. Didn't he deserve that, at least? He'd been tempted so many times to call and remind her of that fact. She would either say yes or no. He could either seize this last opportunity or always wonder. Either she would be a part of his life or she wouldn't. It was quite simple. Almost mathematical. Reducing his fears to an equation gave him confidence. He picked up the telephone and dialed the number he knew by heart.

"Good morning, this is Denise Adams. How may I help you?"

Ah, yes. Professional, to the point, just this side of curt. But like music to him.

"Hello? May I help you?"

"Denise, It's me."

Silence.

"Ian."

"Ian? Ian! How are you?"

"I'm good. You?"

"Fine."

"And how are the fruits of our labors?"

"Keeping out bad stuff and bad folks, just as you designed it."

"Glad to hear it. Anything to make old man Wagner happy."

Yeah, he's been real calm lately. That makes my job a lot easier. So..."

"So enough politics," he ventured. "How have you been, really?"

"All right, I guess. A little tired. Busy..."

Busy...With work? Socially? Tired? Was some good-looking brother squiring her around to the clubs and then to bed every night?

"Did you have a follow-up question about the contract?"

The question was tinged with a note of impatience, a warning shot. Here goes, I can't do this again.

"This isn't about the contract. This is about you and me." He paused, steeling himself to say the words.

"Denise, do you remember when we talked about finding someone for you a while back, that evening at Neill's? My motives were not entirely charitable. I kept pressing you because...because I was really talking about, well, me. I wanted to know if you could ever think of me as more than a work mate, more than a friend."

Denise felt her stomach drop as if she were in an elevator plunging toward the center of the earth. She nodded silently, as if he could see her reaction through the telephone.

"I guess that's part of the reason I was so mental when I came back from San Francisco. I spent every minute of those nights thinking about you, imagining what might have happened if you'd come with me, hoping we would have come back more than friends. I suppose that's why I wanted to be angry with you then, so I could stand to be near you for the next two weeks. That's what I nearly told you, that morning when the phone interrupted. Ever since then I've thought about you constantly, wondering if you've found a new guy, wondering if you're happy, wondering if I could ever have a chance to try to make you happy. And I want that chance more than anything else I can think of. So I'm asking again: would you be willing to see me, Denise?"

All her normal, orderly thought processes vanished. Disbelief and confusion rushed in to take their place.

"You can't be serious," she blurted.

"I've never been more sure of anything."

"But me?"

"Why not you?"

"You know D.C. is a conservative town. Not a lot of people, black or white, like to see interracial couples."

"And I didn't like seeing a Republican majority in Congress either, but I learned to live with it! Let the bigots look elsewhere; I like you, I care about you and I hope you can learn to care about me. If anyone stares, it will be for wondering what a beautiful, brainy woman like you sees in an overgrown moron like me."

She ignored his compliment. "Are you at all interested in what I think about this?"

"Haven't I always been interested in what you think? It's just that this time I definitely prefer that you not think and that you just go out with me."

"You don't get it, do you?" She bent forward over her desk and dropped her voice to a whisper. "This would be hard for me. I've never dated a white man."

"Me neither."

"Ian, I'm serious. My family...I don't know if I could..."

"Let's just go out together and have a good time, okay? We can worry about the remake of "Guess Who's Coming to Dinner" after our third date."

"Who said there would be a third date?"

"Remember how we used to tell each other

our dreams? This is one of my favorites."

"I don't know if this is a good idea."

"I don't either. Can we discuss it Saturday around eight?"

"Ian," she began, struggling to find the right words. "How can I trust you after what happened that evening? If that's how you treat someone you consider a friend, how can I even begin to think about..."

"I acted like a complete ass. I've kicked myself a thousand times." He knew there were no glib, easy answers to her question. "And I don't know that you should trust me. But if you'll give me this chance, I will do everything I can to give you a reason to try."

The sounds of the office outside her door faded. She was aware only of his voice and the beating of her heart. Denise thought back to the weeks they'd worked together in that tiny room, the nights she'd lain with him in her dreams. Did she dare take the step that could give those dreams flesh and weight? And consequences? Reluctant to breathe the word that could set those events in motion, she came back at him with another question.

"So, what if I agree to go out with you? What if another one of your old girlfriends walks up?"

"I'd hold her down so you could pound her with one of your little shoes."

"What if I want to beat you up instead?"

"If it means being with you, I'd take your worst and beg for more. Please, Denise?"

Interracial relationships were rare in her world. The few black people she knew who were involved in them tended to be artists, musicians or performers who traveled in an orbit well outside the daily grind of nine to five, commuting, neighborhood, church and family ties. And they were overwhelmingly male, as well. Denise thought about her mother, her sisters, and her friends. What would her mother say? Joanne? Denise was surprised to find herself without a clue.

Lynn was another story; she'd made clear her belief that there was a special, blistering corner of Hell reserved for those who crossed racial lines. Her views became only more vehement after Preston was denied promotions for years and ended up suing the city to get his due. Denise had unpleasant memories of that time; the stressful years of litigation had nearly destroyed Lynn and Preston's marriage. But at least Lynn had a husband and children, as did Joanne. She had only her books, her computer and a one-bedroom apartment. And her fantasies, in which Ian had starred for the last several weeks.

"Denise, are you still there?" he inquired anxiously.

His opening question had not surprised her six weeks ago and only the fact of its timing fazed her now. She closed her eyes to better hear her heart speak. The answer could not have been more clear.

"Yes, I'll go out with you."

"Great! Saturday around eight, then?"

"That's fine. Is this going to be casual, or what should I wear?"

"Anything that goes with a white tablecloth and matching knives and forks. I'm a high-class kinda guy. You'll see."

"You're a silly kinda guy." After she gave him her address and home telephone number, they talked a little more before she tactfully reminded him that she was working.

"Well, I think I hear Frank calling me."

"Are you telling me I have to hang up now?"

"Something like that."

"Okay, I can take a hint," he joked, but became serious again. "Denise, I'm really glad you said yes."

After she replaced the handset Denise

pushed away from her desk and walked over to the window. For the first time she noticed that trees lining the avenues below had already turned the fluorescent green of early summer. They seemed to shimmer in the waves of untimely heat that rose off the pavement.

What have I done, she thought, pressing her forehead against the windowpane. She tried to imagine herself dressed in various garments from her wardrobe. Nothing seemed to please her; she mentally discarded them all. She decided that she needed to make a call, and she'd have to swallow a lot of pride to do it. The number was on her speed-dial. She returned to her desk, pressed the combination and waited, too anxious to sit.

"Good morning, Mango Leaf."

"Joanne? It's Denise."

"Hey baby girl!"

"I need your help. Can you stay behind a few minutes this evening?"

"Possibly. What's up?"

"I need a dress. An outfit, really, for Saturday night."

"Uh oh. Sounds like you want to impress somebody, huh?"

"I haven't gotten myself anything really

nice for a while." Her brief surge of courage began to ebb away. "I'm sorry, I know it's your busiest time and I'll understand if you can't–"

"Of course I'll help you, darling! It's just so rare that you ever ask me for anything; you and Lynn have such a secret society. Come on over, I'll be here. In fact, I'll start poking around right now."

"Thanks, Jo. I'll leave here early so I should see you around six."

"No, thank you. This'll be my pleasure! Ciao, sweetie."

Having sealed her fate, Denise stumbled through the rest of the day's activities wrapped in a fog of anticipation and dread.

Chapter 15

A late-day shower dampened the sidewalk as Denise knocked on the Mango Leaf's locked door. She huddled under the awning, listening as her sister's high heels clattered down the steps from the storage area. Joanne waved and began to undo the series of locks Maurice had recommended many years before.

"Neecy! I can't tell you how glad I am that you called me," she bubbled as Denise stepped inside. "And I found just the thing. A few alterations, and he'll be ready to climb the stairway to heaven!" She was literally pushing Denise through the showroom and up the steps to the storeroom as she chattered. But

Denise stopped midway and turned around to face her.

"Joanne, I really appreciate what you're doing for me but you've got to promise me something." Her tone was solemn.

"What's that, sweetie?"

"You can't tell anyone about this. It's important that this just stay between you and me, at least for a while, all right?"

"Why, of course, if that's what you want."

"Please don't say anything to anybody, Jo. Not Lynn or Mama, either."

"If that's what you want, that's what you'll get, darling. Now, take a look at this!" She gently nudged Denise up the remaining steps.

Denise stopped and stared at the dressmaker's dummy standing in the middle of the storage area. It wore a sleeveless sheath in shades of azure, with each hue fading seamlessly into the next like an eastern sky at sunset. Its neckline scooped deeply in front and back. A shawl in the same fabric and a beaded evening purse lay on a chair nearby.

Denise tried to speak but could not utter a word. She simply walked around the mannequin several times with a big, foolish grin.

"Are you going to stare it down or try it

on? I'll need to get some measurements to start working on it tomorrow, so can ya move it?" Joanne demanded cheerfully. "Get those clothes off and, see that stool over there? Pull it out and hop up on it for me."

She then marked areas to be taken in or let out, and lowered the neckline even further. When Denise expressed her reservations about that step of the alterations, Joanne advised her, through a mouthful of pins, that if she had been sufficiently desperate to request her advice, she should also be sufficiently desperate to follow it.

"Okay. That will do it." Joanne stood back, finally satisfied with her adjustments after half an hour of work.

"Well, I'm glad there's a shawl," Denise complained as she stepped down from the stool. "Otherwise I'd be picked up for indecent exposure."

"You're just too prim and proper for your own good," Joanne observed as she slipped the garment off her sister's shoulders. "You've got a dynamite figure-you need to start showing yourself off more! That way maybe you'll be settled down with somebody by the time it all starts to drop." Denise began to laugh as Joanne sucked her teeth.

"You go on and laugh now, all right? Shoot, you better hold on to my word, as Pastor Shelton says. I could do aerobics twenty-four-seven and still not get back what I had before the girls came. I used to look like you, remember? Except I was smart enough to let it all hang out every once in a while. I'm collecting names of plastic surgeons right now 'cause I believe if it falls down, you should just stick it back up. I love Maurice with all my heart, but if he goes out like Daddy I'm gonna run out and find me a fine, healthy nineteen-year-old–"

"Are you getting this all down for your book, *The Ten Minute Widow*?" Denise asked, laughing heartily.

"Girl, don't you even spit onto this silk! Take it off right now!" Joanne screeched.

Denise executed a mock pirouette, then dipped into a graceful curtsy in front of Joanne.

"I really love the dress, Jo," she admitted. "And I really appreciate your taking the time to do this for me." She took her sister's hand and gave it a gentle squeeze.

Joanne looked genuinely surprised.

"You don't have to thank me, sweetie. I'm probably more excited about your big date than you are! Besides," she added, sliding the garment off Denise's shoulders, "I can't remember a time when you've ever asked me for anything, not so much as a piece of candy, even when we were younger. It was always you and Lynn, or maybe Mama."

"Really?" Denise carefully stepped out of the dress and handed it to Joanne. "But you and Lynn are closer by age. I always thought of you as a pair: my glamorous older sisters."

"But Lynn and I are six years apart," Joanne reminded her. "That's a lot when you're young. Plus being switched at birth and all..." She selected a quilted hanger from the freestanding clothes rack and carefully arranged the dress around its padding.

"Switched at birth!" Denise snickered as she eased her skirt over her hips. "What are you talking about? I crashed the party with my fat little self ten years after you did; if someone doesn't belong it's me."

"Oh you belonged, Little Miss Science Fair, more than I ever did." Joanne sighed heavily, collapsing into the overstuffed chair by the rack. She kicked off her Italian pumps and wiggled her toes. "I always felt I was Adams 'lite.' You remember how we had to discuss what we were learning about in school and

current events at dinnertime? Every night I
felt like Bozo the Clown at a congressional
investigation. There we sat: Dean Adams, the
great scientist and civil rights figure; Mama,
who could sing whole operas from memory in
at least four languages; Lynn, the teenage cultural nationalist intellectual; and yours truly,
lover of cartoons, fashion magazines, the
'Teen Dance Party Show' and McDonald's.
Everything that was loud and flashy and fun,
I was there! They actually suspended the
nightly interrogation when Lynn went to
Morris; she lived in the dorm so she was pretty much out of the picture. Lord knows I did-
n't have anything to say of interest to Mama
and Daddy. I thought I'd caught a major
break until you started talking in complete
sentences at two. It was like hallelujah time
for them: Salon Adams was back in effect!
You were doing long division in your pretty little head at seven. Hell, I was on my way to
college by then and I couldn't. Still can't."

"That's crazy," Denise declared. "You can
just look at somebody and cut a dress for them
that fits better than anything in a store ever
would. And while we're talking about stores!
You've stayed in business while twenty like
you have come and gone. Famous people call

you up and ask for stuff like it's a regular thing! You don't even run up and down the street screaming about it anymore. How many dresses have you done for Denzel's wife?"

Joanne shrugged.

"And Daddy couldn't have cared less. To him I wasn't much more than a seamstress, as if something was wrong with that. Try to find a decent one these days."

Joanne leaned forward, resting her elbows on her knees. Denise looked around for a place to sit, then settled herself on the modeling stool.

"I think Daddy was—no—he wasn't exactly ashamed of me. It was more like I was a bit too Booker T. Washington for his taste. You know, manual labor and all that. Like I was taking a step backward. He would have preferred to see me become a buyer for one of the big department stores rather than doing my own stitching or sweeping the floor in my own shop. From the time I was 13 I dreamed about having my own boutique one day.

"I know I'm blessed because I'm doing what I love, what I know, what I'm good at. The two of you are good at the academic thing, and that's great. I am so proud of you and Lynnie."

"I know you were the first one in line when Niagara opened."

"Uh-huh. And Joy will be going into Pre-K before you know it." Joanne broke into a wide smile just thinking about her plump, laughing toddler.

"And you, Neecy," Joanne continued, "you're incredible! Now, you know I don't believe in telling folks what to do with their lives but damn, girl! You could be one of those Internet millionaires or something. You hooked me up on the Web, you fix all our computers, you teach this stuff to people... You're back on your feet health-wise, aren't you? If you got yourself out there a little bit you could go all the way, I know it! Could probably snag some rich computer nerd for yourself, too, if this deal doesn't work out." She nodded toward the blue dress.

She and Jo had never talked so honestly before; she'd never known Jo felt she was an outsider in the midst of their talented family. Denise had always assumed that with Joanne, what you saw was what you got. At least, that's what Lynn always said. Jo was the one who couldn't keep a secret to save her soul, yet somehow she'd managed to hide something so fundamental about herself. Denise remembered how she'd observed her older sisters for years, how she'd taken her lessons on womanhood from watching their every move. But she'd never had a clue that Jo saw herself as a misfit. If anything, Joanne had been like a junior movie star in Denise's young mind. Pretty, confident, and always with a pack of friends in tow, especially boys. She'd seemed supremely happy. Denise was tempted to tell Joanne about Ian, to return secrets for secrets. But feeling unwanted by one's family was the fodder of every daily talk show, a far cry from this-white-boy-asked-me-out-and-I-think-I-like-him. Besides, she'd already given Joanne one confidence to handle. Time would tell if her chatty sister could keep her tongue still.

"Well," Denise began, picking up her purse and briefcase, "shouldn't you be getting to the babysitter's?"

"Oh, I called and told her I'd be late after I talked to you," Joanne responded, looking at her watch. "But there's no need to hang around, really. I'll start on this tomorrow." She reluctantly jammed her feet back into her shoes, pulled herself up from her chair and started down the steps, with Denise following.

Halfway down Joanne began to laugh softly.

"What's up?" Denise asked.

"What would they call our little secret on the spy shows–a black project?"

"A black project," Denise repeated, considering the irony there. "I think that's probably the best name for it."

"In that case I'll bring the black project over to Mama's Friday night. Maurice and I will run you home, so Lynn won't know a thing."

"Bless you, my sister. You're sneaky when you want to be."

Once they'd locked up and stepped outside, Denise waited while Joanne lowered the mesh security gate and locked it. They hugged each other warmly and set off in the directions of their separate homes.

Chapter 16

Denise purposely did not begin to get ready for her date until the last minute. She knew that if she gave in to her normal tendency in these situations, she would be bathed, dressed and waiting before five o'clock. Joanne had shooed her out of the boutique around three-thirty, passing her a twenty and telling her to go get her nails done.

She'd twitched like a distracted queen on the spa chair as the technicians filed, painted, and gossiped about boyfriends and coworkers. She could have kicked herself for gushing about her dress when they asked what shade of polish she wanted. Their selection, "Pearly

Mica," only gave her something new to worry about.

After leaving the salon, she'd slipped into an empty booth at a nearby bookstore café to linger over a cup of tea. She finally headed home and let herself into her apartment around six-thirty.

She took a leisurely bath, applied sparing makeup and approached the dress with butterflies in her stomach. She paused to look at it, wondering if it would send the wrong message, not that she had any idea what the right one should be. She zipped herself into it, finding that the alterations granted no mercy from any angle. Denise slipped a pair of pearl drop earrings through her earlobes and gathered a few braids up and to the side with a pearl-trimmed barrette. A pair of strappy, high-heeled sandals she'd borrowed from Joanne completed her costume. Then she walked into the bathroom, closed her eyes and pushed the door shut. When she opened her eyes, she felt as if she were looking at a stranger in the mirror instead of her usual plain self. A stylish, sexy stranger, down to her Pearly Mica toes. She turned and looked over her shoulder; the result was the same. Her new look would have alarmed her on any other occasion, but if she wanted Ian to see her as a desirable woman...Or perhaps she should run over to Kenny's house, ring the doorbell, and taunt him when he answered. She dismissed the foolish thought, knowing she had enough to worry about that evening.

She was pacing back and forth between the living room and the kitchen when she heard a knock at the door. She took a deep breath and went to answer, her shoulders squared as if she were marching to her execution.

Ian was carrying a large bouquet of pink roses and baby's breath. He was wearing a white, tab-collar shirt with a dark, silky suit. He'd tied his hair back neatly and his face was shaved clean. He stared at her helplessly, his jaw gone slack with astonishment.

"Denise, I,..." he fumbled. "Wow. You look great."

"Thanks. You look pretty good yourself. Shall I put those in water?" she asked, pointing to the flowers. "Come in, please." When she closed the door behind him she realized her hands were shaking. He presented the bouquet, his eyes still fixed on her.

"Make yourself comfortable–I'll just be a minute," she called as she dashed into the kitchen to look for a vase. She was vaguely aware of pricking her fingers on thorns, but was far too nervous to cry out or worry about bloodstains on Joanne's inventory. She rushed back into the living room and set the vase on the coffee table.

"They're gorgeous, Ian. Thank you."

He nodded wordlessly.

"I'm sorry to keep staring like this, but, wow! I thought you looked great every day we worked together, but..." He trailed off, shaking his head.

"Thank you." Denise lowered her eyes demurely, with genuine embarrassment. She heard him clear his throat.

"Well, our reservations are for eight-fifteen, so–"

"I'm ready," she said, picking up her shawl and clutch purse from the end of the couch.

As they walked down the stairs side by side, his hand light on her arm, Denise realized she had no idea what kind of car Ian owned. When he held the front door of the apartment building open and led her up to his boxy, battered Jeep, she briefly wished the sidewalk would open up and swallow her whole. But as Ian helped her up she overcame her initial dismay. The vehicle was scrupulously clean; she could detect the odor of polish even with its interior open to the sky.

"It was so warm I had the top down on the way over." His tone was apologetic as he closed the passenger door. "But if you want me to put it up–"

"Please don't," she appealed. "It's a beautiful evening."

He gunned the motor and they sped downtown into the night. The national monuments loomed before them, reflecting the glow of a thousand floodlights, then receded into the distance as they headed west toward the Georgetown district of the city.

Ian had chosen a restaurant located just off Washington Circle. The evening was unseasonably warm, so he asked that they be seated outside on the courtyard patio. Silver maples in full leaf and the surrounding buildings absorbed the harsh sounds of the streets, permitting them to enjoy the jazz quartet playing inside.

"I've been here only five minutes and I love it!" Denise whispered once they had been shown to their table.

"The food's not bad either," he noted. "And the company has never been better. Or more beautiful."

They shared a bottle of sauvignon blanc Ian ordered from the cellar. After salads and expertly prepared seafood entrees, they shared a single crème brulée.

Afterward they decided to walk a little and ended up at a small jazz club not far from the restaurant. The venue was crowded that evening, but the waitress pointed out a tiny table against the rear wall. A few of the patrons stared openly as they squeezed through the crowd. After they were settled with their coffee he took her hand, almost shyly, and they listened to the saxophone quartet until almost midnight

When they returned to her apartment, Ian took the key from her hand and opened the door himself. Not appearing to be in a hurry to leave, he helped her remove her wrap and then took off his jacket. Denise felt a little nervous, not knowing what to do next. She started walking in the direction of the kitchen.

"Would you like some coffee? Or decaf, I guess. It's late for more coffee."

"Whatever you've got is fine." He followed

her, unbuttoning his cuffs and rolling up his sleeves.

He leaned against the doorjamb and watched her fill the kettle.

"I'm going to have a little tea," she announced.

"Then tea it is."

"Is chamomile okay? I don't want you to doze off on your way home." Denise watched as Ian entered the room, his eyes fixed on hers again. It was that look, the penetrating gaze that had unnerved her in a public building in the daytime with people around and employee conduct regulations. Now it was one o'clock in the morning in her apartment; no one was around and there were no rules. Nothing between them but her tight little dress–damn Joanne anyhow! Perhaps if she kept moving...She pretended to search the cabinet for the box of tea although it sat on the shelf right in front of her.

"Is there something I can reach for you, babe?" Ian walked up behind her and placed one hand lightly against her waist. He bent his head close to hers, his voice soft and deep.

"Uh, no," she replied, undoing his hold on her as she reached up and grabbed the box. She stepped away from him quickly, filling the kettle and setting it on the stove. After she'd lit the burner, she stood back and crossed her arms over her chest, not daring to look at him again.

"Denise, is everything all right?" Ian asked, taking a step toward her. She took another step back, shaking her head.

"Do you remember what I said when you called me? The part about this being hard for me?"

Ian nodded.

"This might sound silly to you but I really need to know..." She paused, gathering the nerve to continue. "Have you ever been with a black woman before? Or is this, am I, some kind of experiment?"

He sighed and rubbed his forehead with both hands before he answered.

"That's fair. Yes, I've been with a black lady before, briefly. But my being with her had nothing to do with race, just as my being here with you now has nothing to do with it either. She wasn't anything like you except in the most superficial way. She simply wasn't you. I'm attracted to who you are, not what you are." His brow furrowed for a moment, then smoothed as he broke into a familiar, clever grin. "I guess I'm entitled to ask the same question, whether I'm an experiment for you."

Her lips curled into a smile at this.

"You know I wouldn't have said yes unless I..." She dropped all pretense of protecting her heart. "Unless I really liked you, which I do. And I've fought those feelings for a long time; they go against everything I was raised to believe in. But I couldn't stop thinking about you."

"And I couldn't stop thinking about you either. I've missed you so much." He stepped closer again; this time she didn't move away.

"Denise, there's more than a silly fantasy of jungle fever between us and you know it. We're two smart, difficult people, you and I, and we've seen things in each other nobody else can and we manage to bring out the best in each other, too. We both know this isn't really a first date; we're not starting from square one with each other. It's more like taking something we started to the next level."

They stood facing each other in silence as she pondered his words. Did she dare believe he was capable of loving her? She could not deny the strength of the mutual attraction that had brought them both to this point. Could she risk everything one more time, especially in a relationship that by its very nature carried a high and hurtful cost?

She closed her eyes to steady herself. The moment she had both dreaded and yearned for had arrived. There was only one question but two possible answers. She knew which one was right: to tell Ian to get out of her apartment and out of her life. That would be the thing to do, the act that would finally atone for all the crazy things she'd thought and said and done from the time she'd met him. To say no would free her from strangers' cruel remarks, release her from her father's accusations from the grave and Lynn's anger here in the flesh. She could live with the pride of knowing she'd honored history, held the line, stood her ground. No doubt that was what she should do. But then she looked back into Ian's hazel eyes, which had turned soft and sleepy with wanting her.

"I want to, I really want to, but how can I?" she whispered. "How can I trust you?"

Ian sighed deeply, bending forward so that his face was close to hers.

"All I have is what I know and how I feel. I know that I've been attracted to you since the first time I saw you. I like everything about the way you look and I like looking at you. I know that I like the way your mind works. I like your sweetness, your sense of humor, the way you put me in my place when I need it. What do I feel? What I feel is that I'm in love you, Denise. All I ask is that you–perhaps–like me a little. Is that possible? Can you?"

The warnings, the fears, the beliefs she once held without question were crumbling, turning to dust as she looked into his eyes. She held out her hand. He clasped it tenderly as he had earlier that evening, brought it to his lips, then pressed it to his cheek. Another door closed behind her; she could almost hear the tumblers turning in the lock. All that was honest and best in her was rising. Her inner voice spoke clearly and without reservation. She leaned forward to accept his kiss, claiming the warmth of his mouth on hers, the moist glide of his tongue between her lips. She felt as if she were in a dream, her feet lifting off the ground as Ian's lips sought the hollow of her neck and her arms crossed behind his head. They explored the new touch and taste of the other until the kettle mocked their passionate embrace with a hiss. Denise reluctantly extracted herself from Ian's embrace and went about arranging the teapot, cups, saucers, and a container filled with honey on a small tray.

"Please, have a seat." She nodded toward the small tiled table with two chairs in the window alcove.

"No, thanks." Ian casually leaned against the counter again. "As I said, I like watching you."

"Is that why you're always looking at me with those puppy dog eyes?"

He reached for her hand and brought it to his lips with a slow, swirling lick.

"Woof."

"You're hopeless."

"I'm not hopeless! I'm just like a good little puppy: housebroken, affectionate and willing to please."

She shook her head and laughed. "I worked with you for three months, remember? You've barely achieved the first and I completely disagree about the others."

"Yes, but you weren't really in a position to know about number two. And I didn't know enough about you to succeed at number three," he whispered as he nuzzled the back of her neck.

"Please don't do that," she murmured without conviction.

"You know I'm a quick study. Now that I know what gets you excited," he whispered, "it will stick forever." He ran his hands up and down her bare arms, his fingertips lightly brushing the sides of her breasts. Denise could feel the twitch and swell of his sex as he pressed his body against hers. She would have been happy to stand in that spot for the rest of the night but the kettle's incessant screech forced her to move.

"If you don't let go," she cautioned, wriggling away from him once more, "you're gonna have some scald scars forever."

She poured the steaming water into the teapot and pointed in the direction of the kitchen table again. This time he acquiesced, carrying the tray and then pouring tea for both of them after it had brewed. They sat in silence, sipping tea and holding hands.

"That's funny," she said after a while.

"What, babe?"

"We've always talked so much before. Now we don't have anything to say at all."

"Everything we've said and done before has been simply a prelude to tonight. I really believe that. Now we've finally said the most important things. And if you'll have me, I will give you more than words," he promised, looking directly into her eyes, "because you've already given me more than you'll ever know." Denise melted onto his lap and rested her head against his shoulder.

Ian rose to leave around three. They walked slowly, hand in hand, into the living room. When they reached the front door he suddenly turned to lean against it, pulling her into his arms, close to his heart.

"Are you really going to make me go now, like this?" he breathed into her ear. "I want to make love with you so much! Just hearing your voice the other day I got so excited, and then you show this side of yourself to me...I'm mad for you, Denise."

She sighed, resting her head against his chest.

"Ian, please be patient with me. I won't play games with you but tonight–"

"I know, I know," he lamented, nodding in agreement. "I just can't wait to see you again, that's all."

"Why don't you let me cook for you next weekend?" she suggested. "That is, if you don't have something else to do." She lowered her eyes. "Maybe I'm assuming too much."

He raised her chin with his fingertips.

"Where else would I be if you want me here?"

"Maybe you could bring a movie or something. I'm not a bad cook, if I say so myself."

"What time?"

"Is around six okay?"

"Around two?" he asked, his lips brushing her cheek.

"Around six."

"Friday?" She felt his mouth make its way down her chin, curving back toward her neck.

"Saturday," she insisted.

"Stay right now?" His tongue darted into her ear.

"Ian, I'll see you next Saturday at six."

He cautiously pulled her closer. She initially tensed, but then relaxed in his arms. He kissed her once more, savoring her warmth. Denise felt as if she were on fire, starting with her lips and blazing down into her center. She knew that she had to break his hold on her before she changed her mind. She took a tiny step backwards. He gently pulled her to him again, so close that she could feel the beating of his heart. He slipped his tongue inside her mouth, tentatively exploring and urging her to do the same. She responded eagerly, surprising them both with her bold and playful maneuvers. She became aware of the sweet flow of pleasure from her center; her knees nearly collapsed. She had no choice but to press herself against Ian and hold him even tighter. Ian leaned over to kiss her once more, quickly.

"Oh, Denise," he sighed heavily, his eyes on her soft and full of longing. He stroked the curve her cheek with his hand. "Goodnight, my little love," he whispered, then slipped out, closing the door behind himself.

Denise locked the door and turned out the lights, then went directly, if a little unsteadily, to her bedroom. She was going to take off her dress, but decided to go into the bathroom instead. Flipping on the light, she closed the door and stood in front of the mirror. She touched her fingers to her lips. They were still warm; the taste of him lingered. She slid her hands down her dress, tracing where his hands and body had been.

Remembering what she needed to do, she carefully peeled off the dress, then bent down to doff her panties. Her cheeks burned as she felt another gush of wetness issue from inside her, almost as much as had soaked that handful of flimsy lace and silk a few minutes earlier. Taking a seat on the side of the bathtub, she dropped her head into her hands. She could not remember the last time she had been so happy.

Chapter 17

Denise barely managed to slip into the ushers' office just before the door closed for instructions and prayer. She had just taken her shower when Joanne knocked on her door around nine-fifteen, and her blissful stupor had made it difficult to answer Joanne's questions, coordinate the required uniform, find her way to her Sunday School class, or pay attention once she got there.

Standing in the left rear aisle of the sanctuary in her dull navy suit, white gloves and usher's badge, Denise barely heard a word of the sermon. Repeated waves of joy, shame, and desire swept over her even as she tried hard not to think about Ian. A couple of times her knees actually started to buckle as she imagined what could happen during the upcoming weekend. Unfortunately, she had the remainder of the day and the whole week ahead to wait.

Once the service ended Denise left through the rear entrance. She didn't want the obligatory pleasantries at the front door with Pastor Shelton to dislodge the sensual thoughts that were occupying her mind. Hurrying over to the side street where Lynn and Preston usually parked, she spotted Lynn first, elegant in a turquoise silk buba and matching gélé. Malcolm was sitting on a retaining wall nearby, swinging his ever-lengthening legs.

"I love that dress," she exclaimed as she ran up beside their car. "Why do you have to be so tall?"

"Have you seen Preston? Probably somewhere running his mouth..." Lynn was clearly agitated, pacing as she complained. She longed to be away from the church property so she could smoke in peace.

Denise stood on tiptoe, peering back in the direction from which she had come.

"I think I see him. Grey pinstripes, red tie?"

"Uh huh." Lynn set her purse on the trunk of the town car. "And how was your date last night?"

"I don't believe it! Especially when I told her..." Denise groaned. "Tele-Jo, on the job as usual."

"And I want to see the dress."

"She just couldn't hold it in, could she?"

"Joanne will be telling people's business from beyond the grave, you know that. While all the other ghosts are rattling chains and telling folks to get out, she'll fluff their pillows, pour a couple of drinks and settle in for a chat about what their husbands are really doing when they say they're working late."

"I believe it. I brought her dress with me this morning. It's in her car."

"You still haven't answered my question."

"If I give you a cigarette will you stop? Besides...," she whispered, tilting her head in Malcolm's direction.

"That good, huh?" Lynn's eyes widened. "In that case we'll have a meeting in the basement. We won't even invite Mother!"

Preston came running up beside them, grinning and pulling out his keys.

"Sorry, ladies and gentleman." He seemed to be in a good mood as he popped the locks open from the key fob. Lynn rolled her eyes at her husband as he opened the front passenger door for her.

"Lord, what have I done now?"

"Just drive, brother," Denise advised, sliding onto the rear passenger seat next to Malcolm. "Or else Maurice will have to name the tobacco companies as accessories to your murder."

The ride to the Adams homestead was short, no more than ten minutes from the church. Preston arrived first, as usual, and had parked when Maurice and Jo pulled up with their girls and Julia. Lynn was already strolling up the walk, lighting a cigarette as she walked, while Preston and Denise admired Julia's early roses.

"Lynnie!" Joanne called from the passenger window. "Come back here! Don't you want to see the dress?

"The dress? You mean the wild dress!" Lynn directed Malcolm to follow his father into the house and hurried back down the steps and into the street.

Joanne popped the trunk as Lynn and

Denise gathered beside her. She unzipped the garment bag and carefully moved the gown out into the bright May sunshine.

"Ooh! That color!" Lynn swooned. "And that neckline!" She looked at her usually prim younger sister in disbelief. "Neecy, you wore that? I have only one question: did the paramedics come before or after dinner? You're right, girl. That's one fierce dress."

"Now being returned to captivity," Joanne pronounced, re-zipping the bag and placing it carefully in the trunk.

"Joanne, you better sell that one with a license and insurance," she advised, then turned to Denise. "Come on, you—give it up! Is the brother still alive or what?"

"And are you going to see him again?" Joanne chimed in. "Was my dress torn off in the heat of passion and crumpled up on that man's dusty floor?"

"Nope. I was all by myself when I took it off."

"Well, that's no good!" Joanne slammed the trunk shut.

"Are you going to see him again?" Lynn pressed.

Denise looked at her sisters, calculating. How much could she or should she tell them?

Lynn's prejudice and Joanne's loose tongue could easily prove substantial obstacles to her happiness if she and Ian became seriously involved. She decided to keep her plans to herself.

"Maybe."

"I hope you will," Lynn encouraged with an unexpected burst of warmth. "I saw your face this morning while you were on duty. You looked all lit up from the inside." She reared back to look at Joanne, cocking her hand on her hip. "And Neecy, I'd be careful about who you tell your business to from now on."

"Don't you trust me after all these years?" Joanne fluttered her lashes in a caricature of innocence.

"Hell, no!" Lynn and Denise shouted in unison. The three women linked arms, laughing, as they marched up the steps to their childhood home.

Chapter 18

Denise was struggling to keep her mind on the report she was editing when the office receptionist asked if she could come up front for a few minutes. Grateful for a legitimate reason to leave her desk, she slipped on her jacket and strolled through the maze of cubicles. The mood of the office was still subdued; at ten-thirty on a Monday morning large servings of caffeine were just beginning to kick some signs of life into her colleagues.

The small group of women who had gathered around Phyllis' desk laughed and joked quietly as Denise approached.

"What's up, ladies?" she asked as she stepped into the waiting area. Then the lush arrangement of lavender, blue, and white iris on the front counter caught her eye.

"That's what we want to know, girl!" Phyllis' plump, motherly arms rippled as she laughed. "They're for you, dear."

Denise felt a wave of surprise, then embarrassment, in front of the small audience. She stepped forward and checked the small envelope; it was clearly addressed to her. Risking a bemused smile for the benefit of the group, she carefully lifted the vase off the counter and returned to her office.

After setting the vase on the corner of her desk, she closed her door and simply stared at the arrangement. It had been a long time since she'd received flowers at the office. After a few minutes she pulled the envelope out of its holder and opened it. The note was scrawled in a familiar hand. She read its two lines over and over: "To my goddess in blue. Love, Ian."

By five o'clock on Saturday afternoon Denise had little left to do other than work herself up into a state of panic. She had cleaned, washed, or waxed everything in the apartment at least twice during the week. The two Cornish hens were roasting on a bed of wild rice, mustard greens simmered on the stove and the salad was wrapped and ready in the refrigerator. She had gone to Koehler's for a pound cake first thing that morning and found fresh, local strawberries to go with it.

She soaked in the bath for while, pondering how she had gotten herself into this situation. She was trying on a third outfit, a blue and white flowered sundress, when she heard a knock at the door. She slipped on her white sandals and hurried to answer.

Ian arrived promptly at six, bearing flowers, a bottle of wine and three videos. He was wearing a dark polo shirt and a neat pair of khakis. His hair hung down his back, long and loose. When he bent over to kiss her she noticed he had left all the shirt's buttons undone. The sight of his smooth, bare chest made her want to duck past him and run all the way to her mother's house.

Ian's presence in her home unnerved her; her hands shook as she stood at the sink and clipped the delphiniums' stems before placing them in water. He was leaning against the kitchen doorjamb when he noticed the buttons she'd left unfastened in her haste.

"Let's do this for now," he said, stepping behind her to finish the job. His fingers seemed to give off heat as they brushed the nape of her neck. Denise arranged the flowers in a vase as he worked, fighting a sudden urge to scream. When he finished, Ian gently ran his hand down the length of the track of buttons.

"I hope this is only a temporary measure." He took a deep breath and smiled. "Something smells great. Would you give me a hint? Is white okay?"

"Is white what?" she nearly shouted, her anxiety spilling out into the open.

"Will the white wine I brought go with our dinner? I can run down the street and get something else if it doesn't." He peered into her eyes. "What did you think I meant? Is something wrong?"

She covered her face with trembling hands and shook her head.

"I'm sorry. I'm just anxious about you, about everything."

"You shouldn't be. I grade on a curve, and I have an incredible bias in your favor." She relaxed a little, laughing.

"Good. Now, let's try this again. Is white wine okay?"

"It's perfect," she assured him. "Would you open it, please?" She remembered she had left the corkscrew on the counter so she could find it easily.

"Certainly, mademoiselle."

The dinner was a success. Ian had double portions of everything and insisted on helping her clean up. She would have actually preferred a few minutes to herself to calm her fears concerning what might or might not happen later on.

When they finished the dishes, Denise excused herself and went to her bedroom. She perched on the side of the bed, absently smoothing the sheet that had been turned back to display its flowered border. She couldn't decide what she feared more: ending up in this room with Ian or without him. You won't find out by hiding in here, she silently scolded. Taking a deep breath, she rose and walked back into the living room.

Ian was examining the framed photographs that decorated the far wall. She smiled when she noticed the shoes he'd kicked off and left by the couch. He obviously felt comfortable in her place. Time would tell whether that was a good thing.

"Make yourself at home," she announced with a cheerful note of sarcasm. "We don't stand on ceremony around here." She slid her feet out of her sandals and kneeled on the cushion at the end of the couch, close to where he stood.

Ian was examining the formal portrait that had been taken when she was twelve years old. Her parents were seated, Dean Adams in an elegant pinstriped suit, her mother wearing a gown with a portrait collar. Denise stood behind their father, her hands resting on his shoulders. Joanne mirrored her pose behind their mother, with Lynnette standing between them. Joanne had created similar dresses for the occasion; the sisters wore violet blue bubas, each featuring a different pattern of embroidery around the neckline.

"Wow." He let out a slow whistle. "No wonder you're pretty, such a good-looking family. Your dad must have been amazing, I can tell from the picture. And your mom's beautiful." He took a step back. "Now this," he said, indicating the right side of the portrait with an outstretched hand, "this must be

Joanne, right?"

"Right! How'd you know?"

Denise was curious.

Ian bent his head to the side.

"She has that slightly crazed, artistic look. No, really," he insisted over Denise's giggles. "Wendy gets it when she's inspired. Ed was always very orderly, had a schedule that allowed him to write early in the day, then teach or whatever else in the afternoons. But when the muses called Wendy Phillips, Andy and I had peanut butter or Chinese for many, many nights. And I wouldn't have a bath until the teachers began to complain. Andy was always easier to handle about those issues than I was." He turned back toward the wall, continuing his inspection.

"Who's the white babe?"

"White babe? No white babes on my wall, I'm sure."

"Here, in the pictures with you," he insisted, pointing to a couple of the photos.

"Humph. Don't ever say that around her! That, sir, is no white babe. She's Karyn, my heart, my sista-girlfriend for almost as long as we are old. I've told you about her, about us."

Ian nearly pressed his nose against the

glass of one of the picture frames.

"But she's almost blonde!"

"And your point is–?"

"She can't be your sister-girlfriend, as you say, if she looks as if she could be my sister! We could have been separated at birth!"

"No, we were the ones who were probably separated at birth. That's what her father used to say. If you saw one of us, the other couldn't be more than a step behind. You're a few years too old."

Ian shrugged, then moved to take a seat beside her on the couch.

"Quantum physics is easier than this race business. I don't think I'll ever understand it."

"Consider yourself lucky," she advised, gracefully moving from her knees to a seated position. "You don't have to."

"Yes, I do," he insisted. As long as anyone says we shouldn't be able to spend time together like this," he said, taking her hand in his, "I have to understand. As long as you have to live with it, it's my problem."

He leaned over and brushed his lips against hers once, then again. In no time his other arm was around her waist, gathering her to him. Their kisses slowed, becoming deep and leisurely. She forgot she was kissing a white man, even when her eyelids occasionally fluttered open. After a while she no longer cared. They broke their embrace reluctantly, chests heaving like mad, then laughed easily at each other.

"Weren't you supposed to bring a movie or something?" Denise asked, grateful for a chance to slow down.

"Take a look," he replied with a nod, indicating the three boxes he had placed on the coffee table.

"Hmm. *Sophia's Tapestry*; that's romantic," she murmured, picking up the first one. "*Flight from Zero Point*? I saw that once in the theatre and again on video with Malcolm. I have the feeling he'll have to see it at least ten more times before he'll get it out of his system. What else?" She picked up the last box. "*Spirit Dwellers*! Ooh, is this okay? I wanted to see this but was too busy when it was in the theaters. On a detail, as I recall," she added with a wry smile.

"I hope this isn't your commentary on the evening so far." Ian removed the videocassette from its box and got up to go to the VCR. "I come bearing wine, romance, and adventure, but you choose horror instead."

"How could it be any other way?" she teased.

The movie turned out to be perfectly awful. The screenplay and the acting were so poor that Denise and Ian ended up cheering for the monster instead of its inept victims.

They checked the TV listings as the video rewound itself.

"Nothing much, huh?" Ian turned to look at her as he replaced the booklet on the coffee table. His expression was the one he often wore when working his way through a problem or trying to reach a decision.

"Something wrong?" Denise sat up straight, sensing a change in his mood.

"Nothing. Absolutely not a thing." Ian reached out and ran a hand up and down her bare arm, not taking his eyes from her face. Denise looked back, realizing what he'd decided. Yes. Now.

"Would you mind if I turned on some music?" he asked.

"Help yourself." She nodded in the direction of her stereo.

He got up and switched off the TV.

Finding the tuner, he searched the FM band, pressing buttons until he found the strains of a familiar, jazz ballad. When he returned to the couch he sat down close, not leaving an inch of space between them. Denise could barely hear the melody for the pounding of her heart as Ian slipped his hands around her waist. He touched his lips to her forehead, her temples, her cheeks, making her skin tingle. The fingers of one hand rippled down her face, past her shoulders, coming to a halt on her left breast. He drew back for a moment, raising liquid, inquiring eyes toward hers. He wanted to know if he could, if she would permit this.

Until this moment, Denise had known that a small part of her was still unsure. But now her body and her heart were as one: firm, unquestioning, and ready. Her mind would just have to hold on tight and enjoy the ride. She took his hand in hers and molded it against the broad curve of her breast, then brushed the tips of his fingers against the swollen nipple. Ian drew in a ragged breath and closed his eyes. Denise took the other hand and repeated the gesture. He moaned softly and whispered her name.

Ian rose from the couch, effortlessly

pulling Denise up with him. She molded every curve into his embrace as they swayed to the subtle rhythms. Ian's hands moved up toward her shoulders again, undoing the first three buttons of her dress and unhooking the clasps of her bra. She trembled as his hands stroked her bare skin. Hungry for his touch, Denise slipped out of his arms just long enough to pull the bodice of the dress down around her waist and slide the undergarment off her shoulders. Ian looked at Denise intently, then tugged his own shirt over his head and tossed it aside. Denise drifted back into his arms, her breasts pressed against his chest, close to his heart. She could feel his sex, aroused and seeking, pressing against her. After a few moments Ian lifted Denise's arms from around his neck and placed her hands on his belt buckle. She slid the leather tab from its keeper and unbuttoned his khakis, unable to conceal a smile as they fell easily from his slim hips. He stepped out of the legs and kicked them aside. He gently pushed her dress down until it dropped like a blue cloud around her ankles. He stood back and looked her up and down again before bringing her back into his arms. They held onto each other tightly, barely moving. A rumble deep in Ian's chest erupted into a groan of insistence and surrender. His steps began to guide her away from the living room and down the short hallway.

On reaching her room, they stripped off their underclothes and fell into bed. He gently caught her arm as she reached out to extinguish the lamp on the bedside table.

"Don't you dare," he playfully admonished her. "I've waited so long to see you, to know every inch of you. A man would be either blind or insane to choose to make love to you in the dark. You can't imagine the things I've dreamed of doing with your beautiful body." He placed the tip of his index finger against her lips, then traced a line down her chin, between her breasts, across her belly, through the tight curls of pubic hair and into the folds of soft, moist flesh. He closed his eyes, stroking her until she released a muted sigh.

"So you like me a little, then?" He withdrew his hand, bringing it to his lips to taste her essence.

When he smiled, Denise saw the beginnings of feathery lines around his eyes. She didn't speak, but let him read the answer in her trusting eyes.

"My sweet lady," he whispered, "my sweet

Denise." He rolled over to straddle her, kissing her lips and retracing his path from before.

Liquid fire seared her womb, ran up her spine, and flickered behind her eyelids.

What was that crazy theory, that the flutter of a butterfly's wings ultimately causes a hurricane on the other side of the world? It had to be true; how else could she explain the pale, lanky man on top of her, or how his thick, heavy sex pulsed against her? It could all be quite reasonable and way beyond her control that this man should rub his body against hers, that he should draw an inky-dark nipple between his lips and release it with a soft, smacking sound, that he should return to tease its stony little peak with the tip of his tongue. She held his head between her breasts so she could feel his moans reverberate against her heart.

He cupped his hands beneath her bottom and drew her to the edge of the bed. Dropping to his knees in front of her, he swirled the beginnings of a slow, wet kiss between her thighs. At first she resisted, reluctant to lose control. But he held her so she could not pull away, so she could neither deny herself pleasure nor prevent him from giving it. And soon she surrendered, no longer caring about the reflexive arch of her back or her breathy cries.

Ian climbed back onto the bed and spread himself over her like a canopy, balancing his weight on his forearms. Denise briefly wondered if she would ever get used to the expanse of his pale skin, the way his straight hair fell around her face like a veil, or the rosy flush of his erection. But her concern faded as he came closer, rubbing his whole body against hers again, seeking access. She raised her legs, clasping them around his waist, drawing his hard thickness deep inside herself.

"Oh babe," he sighed into the curve of her neck. "You give it up so sweet, so sweet"

She watched Ian with open curiosity as he plunged inside her again and again. He watched her, too, occasionally offering a besotted grin or a breath-seizing kiss, and telling her how beautiful she was, how he loved all of her colors. But Ian's speech soon left him, leaving him to moan with every stroke as his pleasure mounted. He slipped his hands under her buttocks, gathering her to himself, and cried out as his body angled in repeated spasms of release. Once his passion was spent he collapsed on top of Denise, still trembling, then worked his hips to withdraw from her in one smooth motion. He rolled over onto his back and groaned loudly, dragging a hand through his damp hair. Denise rose onto an elbow and looked at him with concern.

"Are you all right?"

"Oh yes." He exhaled heavily and rubbed his forehead. "I've never..." He closed his eyes for a few seconds before he turned to look at her again. "You're incredible. So amazing..." He reached over to stroke her cheek. "And how are you?"

"I'm okay," she answered hesitantly.

"Only okay?" Ian repeated with concern.

"It's just that, well, my head tells me that it's impossible, it's crazy. And I need for it to be impossible because..." She faltered, avoiding his eyes.

"What is it, Denise?" He pressed her, lifting himself to look at her fully.

"Nothing," she answered, snuggling up against him. "Nothing I want to think about right now."

"Good." He lay back and collected her into his embrace. Breathing in shared rhythm, they dozed in each other's arms. And each time Ian reached for her that night, Denise was very pleased to be found.

Chapter 19

Joanne Thurman ran up the stairs to Denise's apartment a little after nine. Usually her sister would be downstairs in the vestibule waiting for her ride to church, as reliable as Sunday morning itself. She hoped that this wasn't further evidence of depression settling in. She had dealt with designers and other moody, artistic types over the years and she knew the signs, probably as well as Lynn did with all her degrees. If Denise's pattern held true, the Big Date last week had probably come to nothing and the poor thing was too sad to get out of bed. Pausing in front of the door, Joanne shook her key ring lightly to find Denise's, the one with the spot of blue tape on its cap.

Letting herself in, she was about to call out her sister's name when her sixth sense for other folks' business silenced her. Soft jazz flowed from the stereo speakers. Alert as a bird dog, she tipped into the living room, drawn by the scent of fresh flowers that had been set on the bookcase. As she moved in to get a better look at the bouquet, her breath caught audibly. Her curiosity demanded that she take a quick inventory of the pile of abandoned clothing: one sundress, one polo shirt, one pair of khaki pants, one pair of boating shoes, one pair of white sandals, and one bra. She bent over to pick up one of the big deck shoes, making a mental note: size 12. That's my girl, she thought, smiling.

She looked down the hall toward the bedroom. The door stood slightly ajar. Lead me not into temptation, but You know I'm nosy as hell. Unable to help herself, Joanne crept down the hall, praying that the old building's floors would not betray her presence.

When she reached the door she turned at a slight angle to peek in. Denise lay facing away from the door, curled tightly into herself, her breathing deep and even. Then Joanne's hand flew to her mouth just in time to stop the scream. A tall white male sprawled on his back beside her, one arm thrown back behind his head, long, light brown hair flowing onto the pillow. She could see the strong, symmetrical cut of his features, the lightly bronzed skin. Not bad, thought Joanne, allowing her eyes to roam the length of his naked form.

Joanne knew she needed to get out of Denise's place before one or both of them got an eye open, before the tang of their mingled sex reached her, forcing her to scurry downstairs, toss her children onto the sidewalk and jump Maurice in broad daylight. She crept back up the hall as quietly as she could, her mind struggling to wrap itself around what she'd seen, then quietly closed the door behind herself and made her way down to the second floor landing on tiptoe. She stood there, blinking for a moment, as if the image of Denise curled up next to a white man had been burned onto her retinas.

For heaven's sake—it's no wonder she didn't want anyone to know! The girl never came to me for anything in twenty–seven years until two weeks ago, when she wanted a nice dress. A nice dress to attract a white man! But he wasn't in that bed by himself; she was right there, curled up under his arm, both of them as knocked out as two children after a day at the beach. Probably were up half the night ... Oh Lord, Neecy and a white man! And the hell of it is, I've always had a feeling ... I don't know if I'm more shocked because she actually went and did it, or because I've always believed I wouldn't be surprised if she did. Didn't I even say it to Lynn and Mama one time?

Lynn and Mama. She could see the Adams homestead in her mind's eye, then a bright flash, followed by the inevitable mushroom cloud. Lynn's wrath, gone thermonuclear. Ground zero for the end of her world. There would be nothing left but piles of ash and the next generation of cockroaches.

And I'm all up in this mess. Encouraged it. Held a pep rally for interracial seduction. Accessory to the crime of miscegenation. Lynn will have my head on a stick; she'll tear my heart out and show it to my babies.

Her ankles wobbled a little; she reached out and grabbed the railing for support.

If the Lord continues to be as good to me as He has been, this will all blow over. Denise will get her little heart broken again but...

Damn! I know this mess ain't gonna blow nothing but hotter. I saw the look in her eyes last week, that boy with half a smile on his face even dead asleep. Fools, both of them! All the black men and white women in this city and neither of them could find anything better to do than start smelling each other...

Glancing out the stairwell window, Joanne saw her car and remembered the reason for her errand. She squared her shoulders and continued down the steps, into the bright morning.

I can't ever breathe a word of this to anyone, living or dead; family, friend, or foe. My lips are zipped, she murmured to herself, raising a hand to shield her eyes from the sudden glare. Trouble is, this mess is so crazy it'll probably bust right out of my chest just like that damn alien...

Maurice was tempted to shatter the Sunday morning stillness with a blast from the Saab's horn. What were those women doing up there other than running their mouths? Why couldn't they do that in the car? He was twitching behind his seatbelt more than Jocelyn, who was starting on her 14th chorus of "God Is So Good." Joy weighed in occasionally from her car seat with an unintelligible stanza of her own. He was just about to send Jocelyn upstairs when he saw Joanne marching down the walk, vibrant in her yellow silk suit.

"It's about time," he started. "Where's Denise?"

"Denise?" Joanne repeated, hoping to buy some time. She'd forgotten she'd have to explain her sister's absence. Her mind stubbornly refused to invent a plausible excuse as she fastened her seatbelt.

"Denise?" Think, girl. You can't say her name again. Maurice was looking over his glasses at her.

"Well?"

"She's uh...asleep! Yes, she's asleep, poor thing. So let's go!" she urged. Maurice looked at his wife again before he started the engine and pulled away from the curb. Joanne gave a sigh of relief but, true to her nature, couldn't leave well enough alone.

"I think she was doing some volunteer work or something yesterday. Wasn't it Christmas in April or something?"

Jocelyn broke off her performance.

"Christmas in April's in April, Mommy. It's been May for weeks now."

"Girl has a point, Jo."

"I said I didn't know, didn't I?"

"Is everything all right? Did something happen up there?" Maurice asked directly.

"Why?" Joanne tried to sound light and casual, but she knew Maurice was an expert at carving reluctant witnesses into blubbering fonts of truth.

"It doesn't take fifteen minutes to tell if somebody's asleep."

"Well, she'd obviously been in a rush, her place was a mess. I just picked up a little as long as I was there."

"You won't even use a public toilet when you're wearing that suit! And if you really feel the need to 'pick up a little,' then why have you been after me to clean up the storage area for the past two months?"

"I miss having you involved with the shop, darling." The outrageous lie caused the corners of her mouth to quiver.

"Too bad y'all Baptists don't have confession," grunted Maurice, a lapsed Catholic. "Cuz baby, you need to make one right now. In fact, why don't you just get out and walk the rest of the way so the children and I won't be struck by that lightning bolt that's got your name on it?"

Joanne erupted into a giggling fit, a blessed release from the combined pressure of her lie and what she'd seen in Denise's apartment.

"What's so funny, Mommy? And the radio didn't say it was going to storm today!" Jocelyn wondered what had gotten into both her parents.

"I don't think it will, sweetheart." Maurice made a left turn and pulled into the church parking lot. "We're sorry Mommy made you late for Sunday School. You've got your offering?" The child nodded, one hand on the door handle. "Go on, then. We'll see you at eleven." Jocelyn barreled out of the car and across the lot, her small features tight with concern over her tardiness. Maurice and Jo sat in the car for a few more minutes, allowing Jo to compose herself.

"Jos is so much like Denise," Maurice observed as the tail of the pink dress disappeared inside the Church School building. "Just as smart and sweet, and even resembles her a little. It's almost scary, you know?"

It was Joanne's turn to give him an odd look. What made him come out with that on this of all mornings?

"You don't know how scary," was all she could manage in reply.

Chapter 20

"'Morning, babe." Ian greeted Denise with a yawn. "How are you?"

"All right, I guess. I didn't get to sleep until late."

"I didn't know. You should have waked me. Or is it woken?"

"So you could be tired, too? That doesn't make a lot of sense."

"I only meant that I could have rubbed your back or something until you fell asleep."

"Oh. I think I'm a little sleep-deprived," she admitted, rubbing her eyes. "I'm not angry with you. Sorry."

"Sorry's the last thing I am this morning." He wrapped his arms around her and kissed her. "Do you want to sleep some more?"

"No, it's after ten. Might as well get up." She wriggled out of his embrace and stretched as if to underscore her words.

"What's the hurry? I thought maybe we could fool around a little bit, shower, grab some breakfast. There's a diner near the Circle that serves breakfast all day. We could just hide out in the back booth with the Sunday papers..."

"I was thinking about making breakfast."

"You cooked for me last night. I want to take you out somewhere."

She sat again on the edge of the bed, stretching.

"Sounds okay to me." She swallowed a yawn. "Guess I'll shower."

"What about the fooling around part?"

"You can fool around while I shower."

"I'd rather fool around with you while you shower."

Denise smiled at first, then looked up and screamed. Ian jumped out of bed, startled.

"What is it?"

"Oh no!" Denise sprang to her feet and began to pace back and forth beside the bed. "I can't believe I'm so stupid! What have I done?" She ran into the hallway, with Ian following.

"Denise! What the hell is it?"

"I forgot to tell Joanne not to pick me up this morning!"

"Well, she didn't, so why are you so upset?"

Denise shook her head violently.

"You don't understand. She has a key. She was here, I know she was." She surveyed the discarded clothing on the living room floor with mounting distress.

"So she saw our clothes on the floor. I'm not your first lover; she figured it out and took off."

"I hope that's all she saw." Denise collapsed onto the couch.

"What makes you think it wasn't?"

"I know Joanne. If the bedroom door was open..."

"Then I should be worried because she probably saw a lot more of me than she did of you. But I'm not and I really don't care." Ian sat down beside her.

"Maybe you should."

"And why is that?"

"I told you about my family. They have strong attitudes about things."

"Things like a white boy boffing their little

girl?"

"You got it." She picked up the bra and fastened its hooks, her brow still furrowed with worry. Then she laughed out loud.

"I guess we look pretty stupid sitting in the living room as naked as jay birds." She tossed her lingerie back on the floor. Crawling onto Ian's lap, she straddled him, her arms wrapped around his neck.

"I don't know why you would say that. This is my favorite outfit," he responded, his eyes eagerly taking in her form. "You're beautiful, desirable, and everything I need, right here, right now." His lips met hers tenderly, but with an undercurrent of insistence. She could feel him becoming hard against her thighs.

"What I need right now is a hot shower," Denise declared, rolling her hips for emphasis.

"Hot? Are you talking water or..."

"You'll have to come with me to find out."

He dutifully followed her down the hall and into the bathroom. Under the steamy torrent they soaped each other into a renewed state of passion, followed by a gentle, playful encounter.

They finally straggled out of her apartment a little past noon, both of them weak
from hunger and making love. He took her to
a restaurant on the wharf, where they cele-
brated their relationship with champagne and
seafood omelets made to order. Although she
felt light-headed from the alcohol and her
intense feelings for Ian, Denise was not blind
to the chilly stares of disapproval they attracted from many of the establishment's black
patrons. Only a child would not know, or at
least suspect, how they had spent their most
recent hours or how they would spend the
time yet to come. But hadn't she appeared in
public with Kenny, behaving the same way?
They'd pushed their chairs close together,
held hands, and laughed at everything and
nothing. What was different, other than Ian's
pale skin and straight hair?

She found her answer on the lips of a
church sister who was being shown to her
table. Resplendent in her white suit, her eyes
had locked on Denise's almost as soon as she'd
entered the dining room. Ian was pouring
more champagne into their glasses as she
passed; he didn't see the look or feel the current arc between the two women. But Denise

felt as if the stranger had taken a picture of her soul and handed it back to her, all in the hiss of a single word.

"Shame."

"Is there anything you need to do, anywhere you need to go before I take you home?"

Denise had begun to descend from the state of euphoria in which she'd spent the past twelve hours. It was time to think of her real life again: her family, the job, choir rehearsals and a thousand mundane details.

"If it's not too much trouble could we stop at a grocery store? I was so busy concentrating on last night's dinner I forgot to pick up a few things for myself."

"Sure, no problem." He veered off in the direction of the only large chain grocery remaining on the Hill, which happened to be located a few blocks from his home.

The store was teeming with a diverse mix of Sunday afternoon patrons, yet Denise noted the absence of interracial couples like themselves. Ian, as always, seemed oblivious to the fine points of his surroundings. He was content to push the shopping cart along, occasionally whistling as he followed her up and down the aisles.

Once she had found the items she needed, they found a checkout line that had just opened. Ian piled her choices on the conveyor belt while she watched the electronic monitor. When it showed the total Denise reached down in her purse for her wallet. To her chagrin Ian had already peeled off a couple of bills and was handing them to the cashier. Before she could protest he gathered up the bags and was on his way out of the store. She followed as swiftly as her high heels allowed, her anger rising with every step. Before she could catch up Ian had stowed the bags and opened the passenger door for her. She glared at him as she got in but he didn't seem to notice. He slid into the driver's seat, still whistling. Unable to hold in her anger any longer, she finally yanked the keys out of the ignition.

"Denise! What–"

"Now that I've got your attention, what the hell was that back there?"

"What was what? Would you calm down, please? What are you talking about?"

"You know what you did, damn it."

"No, I don't. Why are you so upset?"

"Who told you that you could–" She tried to shove the roll of small bills into his hand. "Oh here, just take the money."

"What is this for? I don't want this!"

"I was going to pay for my stuff myself."

"So you didn't have to. Go get yourself some shoes this week, or dye your braids red. Have something pierced, whatever." He thought for a second. "Hey! How about one of those nipple rings? We could each get one and–"

"The point is that I don't want you doing stuff like that!"

"Stuff like what? I don't know what you're talking about."

"I can't feel like...I can't feel like I owe you or something."

"You owe me? Where did that come from? What makes you think us being together is about owing?"

"We're together? Is there a 'we'?"

Ian sighed and placed his hand over hers. "I've never experienced anything like making love with you last night and this morning. And right now it's all I can do to keep from locking the doors and hijacking you and your little apples and oranges to my place because I want you in my bed so much... But this is your day with your family and I accept that because it's very important to you. But how can you say you don't know we're together?" He reached over to stroke her cheek.

"I can't see the future, my love; very few of us can. But I know I can try to shape it, and these last months have made one thing clear–I want, I need you to be with me so I can make a future for both of us. I want you to be part of my life and me to be part of yours. And as long as you'll let me be part of your life, I intend to take care of you in every way. Everything I have is yours. And that's how it is. You got that, babe?"

He slid over as far as the gearbox allowed, then kissed her slowly, honestly. Denise's concerns seemed to vanish with his touch.

"And now Ms. Adams, I'll take you back to your own apartment so you can read your own newspaper, go see your mommy, wrap yourself up in your own sheets tonight and maybe miss me a little."

When they returned to her apartment, Denise hurried to the kitchen to unpack the perishables while Ian gathered up the videos and checked to make sure he didn't leave anything behind.

"You've got a message!" he shouted from the bedroom. She suspected it was from Lynn, wanting to know when to pick her up to go their mother's.

"Thanks. I'm sure it's just about dinner today. Did you find everything you need?"

Ian had just walked around to the kitchen doorway.

"I think I've got it all, except you." He paused, regarding her with longing in his eyes. "You're sure I can't convince you to come with me, my love?"

Denise put down the paper bag she had been folding.

"After last night it scares me to think what you could convince me to do. You know I'd like to, but..." She walked toward him and slipped her arms around his waist. He wrapped his arms around her to pull her even closer.

"I know, I know. I think it's great you and your family are so tight. But do you think they could give you a bye for next Sunday? It's Memorial Day weekend and I'd really like you to spend it with me at my place. But I also have an idea for a short trip we could take

Sunday night."

"That sounds interesting."

"It's settled, then. I'll start working on the arrangements as soon as I get back." He leaned over and gave her a hug.

"Thank you, Denise."

"For what?"

"For saying yes, for being with me, for giving me the best evening of my life."

"You don't have to thank me," she began, but he silenced her with a hard, fast kiss.

When they parted, he wove his fingers between hers and continued to look down at her. He backed into the living room toward the door. "It won't be easy but I guess I should go now."

Carrying his belongings under one arm, he opened the door, pausing to look into her eyes once more. Then he pulled the door closed behind him. Denise wandered back into the kitchen, missing him immediately. She wondered if she had made a mistake.

The sound of a knock at the door made her heart jump. Yes! He had returned for her; she would go home with him after all. She ran to answer, her fingers trembling with anticipation as she undid the lock. She yanked the door open with a welcoming smile, only to see

Joanne's amused grin and Lynn's puzzled look.

"I didn't know there were any white people in this building," Lynn remarked. "Some tall white man held the door for us on the way up. You've probably seen him."

"He tried to speak, too," added Joanne, "said hello as if he knew us."

"Looks as if they're gonna take this building back, too. Are you ready to go, baby girl?" Lynn asked as she stepped into the living room, unaware of her sister's startled expression. Joanne studied Denise's face closely, almost as if she were intending to sketch her from memory.

Denise closed the door and followed them, hoping no traces of her company remained. Joanne veered off in the direction of the bathroom to look for aspirin, claiming a headache.

"I'm sorry, but what are you doing here?"

"You got my message, didn't you? I said we were coming down to Koehler's for a pound cake and that we'd pick you up on the way to Mother's. Neecy, I left it around nine o'clock last night. What were you–" Lynn stopped, noticing Denise's atypically bare sundress and high-heeled sandals for the first time. The furrows that had been deepening over her eyebrows suddenly went smooth and a smile played across her lips.

Denise's features remained blank, her mind more intent on what Jo was doing in the bathroom. The aspirin was in the medicine cabinet as always; didn't she know that? Or was she about to bounce down the hall and ask why there were two damp towels on top of the hamper?

"Oh." Lynn's mind had finally wrapped itself around the implications of Denise's pretty dress. "Oh! Guess you had other things on your mind last night, and this morning. Into this afternoon, too?"

Denise looked away, her face going warm with embarrassment. Lynn folded her arms and looked her up and down.

"Jo, you and your dress must have started something," Lynn called in the direction of the bathroom. "I've never seen Denise look like this before, not even with Kenny. And she's glowing! Indulge me one question, baby girl: same fella as before?"

Denise nodded, involuntarily breaking into a big grin. Joanne finally emerged from the bathroom, holding a wet washcloth to her head with one hand and carrying a paper cup in the other.

"Why don't you change before we go to Mother's?" Lynn eased herself onto the couch and began flipping through the magazines that fanned across the coffee table.

"Yes, girl, please do," Joanne chimed in. "Your poor old sisters need to hold onto their husbands at least until all the children have finished college. No telling what could happen if you come strutting into the house like that. Poor little Malcolm would probably end up on some shrink's couch twice a week for the next ten years."

"I'll just be a minute," Denise replied, grateful for the near miss, and to have been let off the hook about last night so easily.

"Hold up, Miss Thang," Joanne ordered, staring at the front of Denise's dress as she walked by. "What happened? Lose your bra?"

Denise gave her a wisp of a smile. "Well, even I don't have to wear one all the time, do I?"

"I suppose not," Joanne answered tartly. "Just toss it on the floor and go on about your business, I guess."

Denise set off down the hall but stopped abruptly. She turned to look at Joanne, who lifted her drink in an almost imperceptible motion.

"Nothing like a long, tall, pale glass of water after a dry spell," she said quietly. Lynn, immersed in an article, didn't appear to hear.

But Denise did.

Denise drifted in and out of the usual kitchen chatter among her mother and sisters. Careful to maintain a blank expression as she chopped tomatoes and tore curly romaine leaves for the big dinner salad, she could not suppress a smile when she remembered something Ian had said or recalled the mutual pleasure their bodies had summoned from one another. At one point she couldn't help laughing out loud. Three heads immediately swiveled in her direction.

"I'm sorry." She covered her mouth with both hands but couldn't conceal the delight in her eyes.

"You'll have to excuse Neecy," Lynn advised Julia. "It seems she's got a little fella."

"What makes you think he's a little fella?" Joanne challenged. "He could be tall, like a basketball player. Remember how you used to complain about how tall guys always seemed to be attracted to little women? Well, Neecy's little."

"Yeah, yeah. Whatever, as Malcolm would say." Lynn lifted a hand in a dismissive wave.

"Oh, excuse me for breathing, doc! I only had to share the burden of your fatal attractions from the time I was seven years old, usually when all I wanted was to draw my dresses in peace. 'Doesn't this one have the baddest 'fro?' Yes, Lynn. 'Doesn't that one have the cutest little smile?' Yes, Lynn. 'Don't tell Mama 'bout my birth control.' Yes, Lynn."

"I seem to remember that somebody dropped the ball on that last item," Lynn objected. "Told Mother you wished your vitamins came in a little pink case just like I had, didn't you?"

"That's nothing!" Joanne shot back. "There's no telling what damage you did, imposing your romantic exploits on my tender ears."

Julia ignored their bickering.

"Is he anyone we might know, baby girl?" she asked.

"No, Mama, I don't think so. I met him at work and he's from New York.

"Where did he go to school, then?"

"Harvard." Denise didn't bother to mention the roving curriculum that followed.

"Hmm." Julia grunted with preliminary approval. "What does he do at the agency?"

"He did programming. He's not there anymore; he was a contractor and the project's finished." Denise nearly broke into giggles again. Her answers were strictly true, weren't they? In a few brief phrases she'd sketched an educated gentleman and a responsible employee. Husband material, as far as her mother and sisters were concerned.

"Then why didn't you invite him over for dinner, baby girl?"

"It's way too soon, Mama."

"Yeah, we don't want to scare him away yet," Lynn and Joanne echoed in agreement.

"We some crazy black folk up in here," Joanne added. "No telling what we might do."

Denise looked hard at her older sister for a moment but soon returned to her task. Ian was probably right, she decided. *I need to lighten up. Jo let herself in, saw the clothes and let herself out. That's what all her lip is about. No way she knows anything more about Ian than his shoe size.* Besides, she reasoned, the most important fact about Ian was

so staggering, so potentially explosive, that
there was no way in hell Jo would ever be able
to keep it to herself if she knew.

Denise lay awake as darkness gave way to
a brightening in the eastern sky. Her delight
had given way to worry, but she had managed
to slip into a troubled sleep for a couple of
hours. She'd spent much of Sunday night bat-
ting her newfound passion for Ian off the
brick wall of her family and their expectations.

From as far back as she could remember
she had always accepted the family's unwritten code. That had had a lot to do with her
desire to be with Kenny. After she had time to
reflect on their breakup, Denise had been genuinely surprised to discover that she had
never been madly in love with him. That had
been her dirty little secret for some time now.
Sure, she had been proud of his intelligence
and his reputation. And their physical relationship had allowed her to launch into a
long-delayed exploration of her sexuality.
They had liked the same kinds of restaurants,
entertainment, and friends. Her family had

seemed so happy with the arrangement.

Theirs had been a "mature" relationship. Who needed all those messy emotions when she, with her dark skin, round hips, and tenacious intellect had been chosen by the ultimate African American alpha male? She would have been content to stand by his side at university functions, wearing a freshly pressed smile and expensive clothes. She would have presented him with two or three offspring and reared them in a manner befitting descendants of the late Dean Adams and future Morris graduates. She would have worn, taught, learned, done, or been whatever was necessary to become the perfect Afrocentric soccer mom. And everyone would have been happy. Everyone...

Ian would not suit them, no way, nohow. His impatience, his quick temper, his arrogance would rub them the wrong way even if he were black. She imagined him striding into their midst on a typical Sunday afternoon with no proper introduction, speaking his mind with no interest in the consequences. He had few credentials, no civil rights pedigree, no esteemed connections to power. How could someone who loved her, someone she'd begun to let into her heart, have the potential to disconnect her from the only life she'd ever known?

Having Ian in her life would be much like having a fireplace, she reflected. As long as the fire was contained it would bring her a sense of warmth and security. But let one spark pop beyond the safety of the hearth, and she could lose it all.

Chapter 21

On Sunday afternoon of the Memorial Day weekend they drove to a bed and breakfast deep in the West Virginia mountains. The air was heavy with the buzz of insects and fragrant flowers that surrounded the converted farmhouse. They enjoyed a sumptuous chateaubriand for dinner, followed by cappuccino and tiramisu for dessert. Later they sat on the front porch to watch the sun set over the valley below. After chatting with the other guests for a while in the common room, they returned to their room to wash away the day's heat, make love and watch a movie from the innkeeper's library of videos.

Later that night a storm broke over the

mountains. It seemed to sit directly over the old frame house, Denise thought, as the rafters shook with each peal of thunder. The lights flickered and soon went out, plunging them into darkness occasionally lit by brilliant flashes of lightning. They played the childhood game of counting the seconds between the flash and the answering roar for a while, but Ian suddenly went silent and pulled her even closer to him. She tried to shield herself from the tumult in his arms, but she sensed that something was troubling him. She lay quietly for a while, watching him focus on a point in the distance. When he raised up slightly to rest an arm beneath his head, she decided to speak.

"Ian, is something wrong?"

At first he made no sign he had heard but turned his head toward her a few moments later. Denise was surprised to feel the heat that rose from his face, and a blast of lightning revealed eyes that were moist and full of pain.

"I want to be able to protect you," he whispered.

Denise reached out and stroked his cheek.

"What do you mean? You've taken care of me so far."

He shook his head violently.

"No. I lost the best friend I ever had because I was careless. If only I hadn't..."

"Tell me," she said, shifting to wrap her arms around him. She felt his chest contract as he exhaled with a ragged sigh.

"I lost my best friend last September. His name was Josh Morgan. This belonged to him." He lifted his forearm to show her the watch. "I'd been in D.C. since July, trying to make sense of the mess your previous contractors had left behind and not doing a very good job of it. Josh was still out West, out of rehab for a few months. He had a job lined up to start in November. He was going back to school in January, too. He was determined to get a graduate degree in psychology. He'd talked about becoming a counselor or a therapist.

"It was a sweet time for him. He felt he'd gotten his life back, that he was free, really free... He wanted to take this last fling, like a bachelor party on the night before the rest of his life. So he kept calling me: come on, Ian, this trip will clear your head so you can go back to D.C. and take care of business. We have to do it one last time before the 'burbs and the babies kick in. He'd met someone at the job he'd taken on work release, Yvonne. She had this amazing background: Spanish, Asian, Irish... He was crazy in love with her, he was going to ask her to marry him when we came back. I didn't want to hear it. I'd been blowing up relationships left and right and the agency project was headed down the toilet. You can imagine me, arrogant and sarcastic as usual, then add a log of resentment on each shoulder."

She tightened her embrace.

"So even after we got to Cozumel I taunted him about his new addiction to commitment. That pissed him off, naturally. A person can't be more of an idiot than I was; Josh had hit bottom and still I envied him. I hated that he was finally putting it all together. I knew he and Yvonne had the real thing and that I was going to be left on my own. So I shoved it up his ass; we really tore into each other. He walked out, I didn't know where he went and didn't care. I shrugged it off and went out to find a few drinks.

"I came back to the room a little after dark. I just wanted to wash up, collect Josh and get some dinner, hang out a while. We never stayed angry at each other for long. I didn't get past the front desk. The clerks recognized me and one of them pushed me out the door and into the hotel van. They drove me to the police station. I don't remember. I can't..." His words trailed off.

Denise waited quietly, sensing he needed to finish his story, no matter what emotions were brought to the surface.

"We used to have a ritual. I'd check his oxygen tanks and he'd check mine. The equipment for rent isn't always in the best shape. That last time Josh must have been too angry to be careful because of all that I'd said. The tank was faulty and he went too deep. The next time I saw him they were pulling back the sheet...

"Josh's parents flew in the next afternoon. We all went back home the day after that: Josh, his parents and me. I was drinking from the moment they rolled the service cart down the aisle until they locked it away for landing; I don't know how they got me to Ed and Wendy's place without a stretcher. Wendy tells me that I sat Shiva with his parents but I don't remember... It's what Jewish people do when someone dies; it's almost like a wake. I don't remember putting on a suit or going to their flat. But I must have been there," he insisted, his voice rising. "No matter how bad

I was I couldn't have been anywhere else. Josh used to say we were spiritual brothers. I was far closer to him than I've ever been to Andy. And once he was gone I felt so alone.

"But now that I've found you," he murmured, tracing the outline of her face, "my grand passion, my blue moon lady, I'm so afraid I'll lose you, and through my own fault."

"Blue moon?" she repeated, tilting her head back to look into his eyes. "Is that another one of your British expressions?"

Ian chuckled softly.

"It's the one thing I've always remembered, I don't know why, from Ed's first man-to-man chat with me. He told me that one day I'd meet one amazing woman, and that she'd literally knock the wind out of me. He promised that my heart would literally beat inside her own, and, if she'd have me, we'd have mind-altering, once-in-a-blue-moon sex. I knew it was all rubbish, of course. Until the first moment I looked at you. Every word I ever knew went out of my head, and my chest began to ache as if it were on fire. It still does sometimes, I want to be with you so much. I've never felt this way before. You must be the one." He pressed his lips to her forehead.

"I love you, Denise. I don't want to lose you."

"You're not going to lose me," she whispered. "I love you, Ian." She had not planned to speak those words to him, not this soon and perhaps not ever. But the words had come straight from her heart.

"I love you more."

"You always say something like that," she laughed softly.

"I'm serious," he replied, touching a finger to her lips. "It means you get it all: my body, my mind, my heart... Everything, babe. Always. And how do you love me?"

She looked into his eyes, finding no trace of their previous sorrow.

"With all that, and more."

Chapter 22

Most evenings Ian would come for Denise after work. They took turns preparing meals at his home on Capitol Hill. He favored steaks and vegetables done on the grill in the small backyard; she cooked fish or chicken with corn on the cob with freshly made slaw or a tossed salad. He shared his successes and frustrations with his ongoing development projects; she voiced her weariness with her daily routine and agency politics. Some evenings they worked side by side on his computers; other nights they'd watch videos or simply sit on the front steps, hoping to catch a rare breeze. They made love in his big bed and fell asleep with their bodies still entwined.

By mid-June Denise had become accustomed to bringing a small suitcase to work on Fridays. On the first occasions Phyllis and a few of the other women in her office had looked at the luggage, then looked at her, their expressions arch and questioning. Denise would allow her eyes to meet theirs for a second, then dart away nervously, deliberately shy. Even if she called the name of her traveling companion, she decided, no one who had the most passing acquaintance with either of them would have believed her.

They spent most weekends at the shore, usually in one of the small towns on the coast of Delaware. Ian would drive to the agency a little after five o'clock, restlessly circling the block until Denise emerged from the building. On returning to his home they would share a light supper, make love, and nap until midnight. Then they would fill a thermos with coffee, load the Jeep, and head out east, taking advantage of the waning of the city's weekend exodus. Once they crossed the Chesapeake Bay, Ian would turn off the main road and take them across the coastal plain, passing through a patchwork of small towns and farms. Denise found that she could doze and estimate their progress simply by smell: the choking exhaust of the highway was followed by sweet scents of produce ripening in the fields, then punctuated by the sharp stench of industrial chicken houses. And finally, the briny scent of the ocean, borne inland on the feathery early morning breezes.

Sometimes they rode in silence while Ian mentally rearranged equations and code, his eyes fixed between the bright beams the Jeep cast ahead of them. More often he would fish out a cassette from the pocket, or ask Denise to make a blind pick. They had their favorites: John Coltrane with Johnny Hartman, Cassandra Wilson, Chet Baker, Dianne Reeves. They sang along in their odd counterpoint–his beat-perfect, yet tuneless baritone nestled against her smoky alto.

On one of these night journeys Denise remembered the dream she'd had early on the day they first met. She could scarcely believe that she was giving form and flesh to those images, living out that fantasy, after a fashion. Her azure sky had been replaced by stars twinkling in endless matte-darkness, or sometimes a glowing red shade ripped by flashes of lightning. Her driver's arms were pale bronze but still strong at the wheel. And he had a face, one that often turned toward her with affectionate concern as they rolled toward their destination. A face she'd never have associated with caring for her in the most general way, and certainly not as one particular, special individual.

But for all the joy and closeness, Denise had discovered a wedge of loneliness in Ian's attention. She missed being able to share her happiness with anyone. Karyn's somber warnings quenched any desire in her to talk about her feelings for Ian, even to mention the places they'd visited. And to disclose any of this to Lynn was out of the question. So she simply remained silent in their presence, clutching his love tightly to herself, reminding herself that she really wasn't alone.

Maurice Thurman hailed the bartender and ordered another bourbon with a splash. He was out with a few colleagues from the U.S. Attorney's Office, celebrating his fifth straight win as a rookie in the Narcotics Division. He understood that these little jaunts were just another part of paying dues, as important as his hard work in the library and the courtroom. Sure, he would rather be home in his recliner, snoozing in front of the TV or playing grab-my-nose with Joy, but this was simply another diversion on the path he hoped would lead to a seat on the Court of Appeals. Besides, he wasn't being tortured here, he reasoned, so why not relax and enjoy a sweet moment of victory? He took another sip from his drink, turning away from his co-workers slightly as he loosened his tie.

He could see the bar and part of the adjoining restaurant from this new angle. Plenty of Capitol Hill types, fresh faces full of hope and privilege. But he and his colleague Iris Moore were the only dark faces in the room. In a city full of black folks, there was no excuse for a scene like this, he thought, with a flash of bitterness. Forgetting his co-workers for the moment, Maurice slipped back into an old habit from his days on the street, making quick profiles of the people around him. His eyes flickered restlessly over the crowd until he focussed on the tall man standing near the entrance. Was he alone? No way, he was repeatedly looking down and to the left. Maurice recognized the look of supreme confidence, the look of a man who knew he was going to get some that night. Look at him;

he's not the least bit concerned about it. First dinner, then dessert. He was wearing those little oval glasses, but he wasn't a nerdy type. No, this one was too easy in his skin, too tanned and fit. He wouldn't be out of place on the cover of one of those adventure magazines, trekking across Nepal or sailing down the Amazon.

Maurice wished he could see the woman the guy was with but a panel of decorative smoked glass blocked his view. Wait a minute; wait a damn minute now! A small hand reached up to touch the guy's cheek. A small, dark hand. No, it couldn't be. The light in here isn't that great. After all it's a bar, Thurman, not an operating room. Anyhow, she's probably a Latina, Filipina, whatever. Oh good, their table's ready. Maybe now I can...

Maurice leaned forward a little for a better view. I'll be damned, he whispered to himself. My man's got a case of jungle fever! Sure enough she was a sister, and a pretty one at that. Had he ever seen a white man with a plain black woman? This one faintly reminded him of Jo: petite, nice figure, but a shade darker, with braids instead of dreadlocks.

The next thing Maurice knew he was

standing behind the room divider, watching the couple slide into a corner booth. It was Denise, he knew it. Denise and a white man. This wasn't their first date either. There was an easy intimacy between them, without a trace of awkwardness or formality. He jumped when he felt a hand on his shoulder.

"Hey Maurice, what's up?" Something wrong?" It was only Bruce Carter; they'd been sworn in together as assistants nearly two years ago.

"Nothing, man. Just thought I saw someone I knew." He took one more look back at Denise and her date, then reluctantly followed Bruce back into the bar. I saw someone I thought I knew, he whispered to himself.

He listened to more shoptalk for a while, then decided to finish his drink and head home.

"Look, I've got to go meet a young lady, folks. Sorry to take leave of this fine gathering."

"A young lady?" Iris teased, already knowing the answer. "Anyone we know?"

"Oh, some of you have met her a couple of times already," he answered with a wry grin. "You know, the little dominatrix with the diaper fetish. I'd do anything for her." Maurice departed under a shower of back pats and well wishes, but his mind was racing ahead to dinner tomorrow night and what, if anything, he would say to Denise.

Joanne Thurman climbed into bed shortly after she tucked Jocelyn in that Thursday evening. She wasn't really sleepy, so she browsed through the European fashion trades that had begun to pile up under her side of the bed. She paid no attention to the shots that rang out from the television; it was simply another cop show. When Maurice was still on the street she couldn't bear to watch those things–the sound of fake gunplay would make her jump ten feet out of her skin. Now she barely noticed the programs and was at a loss to tell one from another.

She felt a tingle of anticipation when she saw Maurice standing in the doorway.

"Hey, Jo." Maurice usually brought law books or files from the office upstairs, dozing over them until Joanne would set them aside and tuck him in as if he were one of the children. Tonight his hands were blessedly empty. He pulled the bedroom door closed behind himself.

"Hey baby." Joanne looked up with a smile.

Her husband stretched out beside her on the bed.

"You talked to Neecy lately?"

Joanne's eyebrows arched, but she was careful not to betray her concern. Why would he be asking about Denise? The burden of her secret had already begun to weigh on her.

"No." She pretended to examine a spread of Helmut Newton stills, slowly and deliberately creasing the pages. "Any reason?"

Maurice rubbed his eyes, then his forehead before answering.

"Naw," he said slowly, as if he weren't quite sure. "Just asking."

Joanne closed the magazine and stretched out beside her husband.

"No really, what's up? Fresh from confirmation you're the best thing since Thurgood Marshall and the only thing on your mind is my baby sister?"

"I'm just concerned. She's been seeing a lot of somebody lately, huh?"

"How would you know?"

"Been a while since we've been able to have one of our weekends, know what I mean?" He reached out to stroke the outline of her hip. She grabbed his hand and pressed it between her thighs.

"You're telling me! I was hoping that's why you came up early."

"Damn! I knew there was a reason I should have passed on those drinks!" He rolled toward her, drawing her into his arms. "Don't eight-year-old girls have pajama parties or something? Too bad they aren't posted on the Internet. I'd book Jos for one every week." Maurice kissed Joanne slowly and deeply. But their embrace also reminded him of the question he needed to ask. He lay back, propping one arm under his head, Joanne snuggled close in the curve of the other.

"I saw Denise in the place where we were this evening. I think I saw the man she's been spending so much time with. He's white, Jo." He paused to let the news sink in. "She didn't see me. Hell, I don't think they saw anything except each other. I don't know why they even bothered to eat. Or eat first, I should say. No question what's on their agenda for tonight."

"Hmm." Joanne decided to say as little as possible, hoping the inquiry would pass quickly.

"You don't seem surprised."

"But I am!" she exclaimed, remembering to play her part. "I'm surprised, in a way. But not really."

"Objection; the witness is contradicting herself, as usual."

"Well! It's just that...I've just always had a suspicion that Neecy might jump the fence. Call it intuition or something, I don't know. Even as tight as she was with Kenny. I decided I was wrong only after they'd been together for a couple of years. But now..."

"Even with Lynn always up in her face with that 'get whitey' stuff all the time?"

Joanne could feel Maurice's muscles grow tense under his skin.

"Honey, between Daddy and Lynn I just kind of got used to it. When we were younger Lynn used to be all up in my face about my work not being 'sufficiently immersed in the black aesthetic.' "

"Whatever the hell that is."

"Just academic jargon for look to the 'hood for your artistic inspiration. She was pissed with me all the time I was in school because I was seriously into my French studio mode. It passed, as most obsessions do," she shrugged. "Besides, I do my part. I really like being able to help our young designers get started in the business. It's pure pleasure for me, not politics or duty."

"Jo, are you sure you don't know anything about this?

What do you mean, am I sure? I said so, didn't I?"

"You didn't ask what he looked like."

"You just now told me about this! I'm trying to get used to the idea." She paused. "What did he look like?"

"Oh, no," Maurice warned, "you're not getting off that easily! Tell me more about this intuition of yours. How did you know?"

"It's not that I ever thought she would go chasing after one of them. I just had a feeling that sooner or later, some white boy was going to find her and get his nose open big time. It doesn't take intuition to figure that out. She's into all that white boy techie stuff. Sooner or later some little nerd on her job was going to push his glasses up on his nose, take a good look, and fall madly in love. And why not! She's always had a pretty face, and now she's got the body to go with it. Plus, she's damn near brilliant; I can't understand why she won't leave that awful little job of hers. It was okay when she was just getting back on her feet after the surgery, but now? She could be her own boss and make some serious money. Anyway, if she liked the guy a little, and if she were lonely enough, why would she prevent it from happening? If he loved her, if he treated her well, why should she? According to what you saw, he found her, she liked him a little and the rest is history."

"She likes him more than a little, Jo. That part's obvious. I don't know about him, though. If you dressed this one up in an Armani suit–"

"Prada, sweetie," Joanne interrupted. "Armani's played. Or Dolce y Gabbana..."

"Whatever he wouldn't look out of place on the cover of *GQ*. He's the kind who could be real slick if he wanted to. We're not talking about some young kid with bad skin who wears a pocket protector to bed."

Joanne fought the impulse to tell her husband exactly what the man wore in bed.

"You're not intending to play the daddy now, are you?" she teased. "Like, what are your intentions toward my sister-in-law? Or is this your dress rehearsal before the first car pulls up for Jocelyn?"

"Somebody should do something! She hasn't had a lot of experience with men, period.

And this interracial stuff is dangerous even when you're used to messing around. And a white man and a black woman? That's almost always bad news, even when they've got money. No offense baby, but Lynn and your mother really overprotected the girl"

"Yeah, you're right. But aren't you simply doing the same thing, not trusting her ability to make her own decisions?"

"I hate it when you make sense, you know that?" He playfully squeezed her inner thigh.

Pleased with her modest victory, Joanne became reckless.

"Besides," she continued amiably, "I have a feeling she's got that big old boy's nose open wide enough to fly the Concorde through! The President probably could have run through the bar butt naked and Romeo wouldn't have looked up. Even if his family threatened to cut him off, he'd probably say thank you, Jesus! Now I can enjoy my little brown sugar in peace!"

Maurice was nodding in agreement when he realized he hadn't mentioned the man's size. He hadn't mentioned the man's rapt attention either, fixed on every word coming out of his sister-in-law's pretty face. Unable to resist courtroom tactics, he decided to give

Jo a little push to see if she'd roll all the way over the cliff.

"But the hair's got to go, you've gotta admit that," he offered with an innocent grin.

"Did he have it tied back? That's not so bad," she insisted cheerfully. "Both white men and brothers look really stupid when they pull it back and there's just this much worth of hair," she said, illustrating with a thumb and forefinger. "If you've gotta have a ponytail you might as well have some hair to put in it, whether it's yours or not. No, Romeo reminds me of that hairstylist—you remember the one—'shake you' head, dahling!'" Joanne lifted her dreads through her fingers and tossed them, thoroughly enjoying her performance until she realized she was laughing by herself. Maurice looked at her sternly over his glasses.

"Uh-oh." The last giggle died in her throat. "I messed up, didn't I?"

"Joanne, Joanne," he murmured, shaking his head. "Joanne Adams Thurman. Wife of my youth, mother of my children. What kind of example—"

"I was trying to be an example," she huffed with as much dignity as she could muster, having merrily danced into Maurice's trap. "I promised, kind of."

Maurice rolled into a sitting position beside his wife.

"Kind of promised? Is that like being a little bit pregnant?"

"Well, I promised Denise one thing but I promised myself something else. That's why it's 'kind of,' Mr. U.S. Attorney. Kind of like U.S. can stand for 'universal smart ass.'"

Maurice ignored her weak attempt to save face.

"Which part did you promise yourself?"

"That I wouldn't tell anyone that he's white."

"How'd you find out?"

"The morning she wasn't ready when we came to take her to church. I went up and let myself in. Things had obviously gotten hot and heavy—they left their clothes all over the living room floor. And you know me: the bedroom door was open and I couldn't resist taking a peek. And so I went, expecting the usual, but the deck shoes should have tipped me. I spied around that corner and nearly hollered and peed my pants at the same time. There he was, with that hair spread out all over the pillow. I probably would've thought he was a woman except for..." she trailed off.

"Didn't take but a second to clear that up. And then I left."

"So how are we going to handle this?" Maurice sounded brisk and businesslike, as if one of them should be taking notes.

"We?" Joanne repeated shrilly. "Handle what? We're going to do what we've always done and stay out of her business."

"But it's a white man this time, Jo," he insisted.

"So? Either he loves her or he doesn't. Either she loves him or she doesn't. Based on what we've both seen, neither is an issue right now. Why don't you just let nature take its course?"

"That's the problem," he muttered. "A little too much nature going on. What if she gets pregnant?"

Joanne feigned a horrified look, then bent her lips close to her husband's ear.

"If the baby is chocolate brown with blue eyes, I'm keeping it. I'm gonna kidnap it and run away to Europe where it'll be a supermodel. And baby and auntie will be rich, rich, rich! I might even let you and the girls come and visit us up at our villa in Tuscany sometime."

"Negro, please," he laughed, gently pushing her away. "But seriously, about your mother, and—Lord help us—Mother Afrika!"

"Ooh, ooh! I'll come stand behind you when they're introduced."

"That means you're gonna be standing behind the civil disturbance squad and the National Guard. In fact, let's just take the girls and go away for a while when that action goes down!"

"I guess Mama'll have to live with us after it's over. There won't be two bricks left together of the house." Joanne thought for a second. "We'll have to figure a way to sneak out the china she promised me. Otherwise it's all just gonna get broken upside that poor boy's head!"

They shared a good laugh, imagining Lynn's ire.

"That settles our agenda, baby. Not a word to either one of them. Seriously," he added.

"You don't have to tell me twice!"

"And I don't mean your 'kind of' promise, either."

"Look, the only agenda I have is for Denise to be happy. Denise is the only one who can decide whether Mr. Size 12 rocks her world tonight or for the next fifty years. If he treats her well, it's okay with me. I think it's good, in a way. Somebody might as well try to get beyond all this race madness."

Maurice relaxed for a moment but his mind was still worrying the issue.

"You know we've always agreed Jocelyn would go to Assumption Prep when she finishes Niagara. What if," he trailed off, lines creasing his mahogany brow, "what if she does the same thing, brings home a white boy?"

"I don't know what I'll do," Jo began, "but if his mama or daddy happens to be Secretary of State or a Supreme Court Justice, you'll be calling in an engagement announcement to the *Herald*."

"You've got an answer for everything tonight. Do you still promise we're not going to say anything?" Maurice asked again.

"What do you want me to do, seal it in blood?"

"I was thinking about some other bodily fluids, to tell you the truth," he murmured, rubbing her belly.

"I've been a bad girl, Mr. U.S. Attorney," she whispered, her eyes half-closed. "And I'm ready to make a deal."

Chapter 23

Denise could smell fried fish and corn bread before she started up the familiar brick walk. She'd nearly forgotten that this was the Independence Day holiday weekend. Her mother would be in one of her nostalgic moods, slipping Leontyne Price's recording of "La Forza del Destino" into the CD player and cooking as if she were preparing everyone's last meal.

Denise had wished Ian well when he left for New York that morning, staying behind because her absences from regular family gatherings were beginning to make her uneasy. But events were neatly falling into place; she could make an appearance without having to present, explain or exclude the white man who was sharing her life and her bed.

Preston was on her as soon as she walked through the door.

"Would somebody please tell the stranger that this gathering is for family only?" He was steadying a ladder in the hallway as Marcus replaced a bulb in the light fixture.

"In that case, don't let the door hit you on your way out," she shot back.

"Hey!" Marcus shouted, nearly dropping the pin that held the fixture in place. "Is that Denise?"

"Denise?" she repeated, stopping next to the stairway. "Oh, so you're a sophisticated college man now, no more 'Aunt Neecy.' Are you too cool to give me a hug?"

"I'll be right down," he called, giving the pin a final twist. He scrambled down quickly and squeezed past his father to nearly lift Denise off her feet.

"Good Lord, what did they feed you down there?" she teased when Marcus finally set her down again. "Just as tall and good-looking as your grandfather," she observed, rolling her eyes in Preston's direction. "Did any of your little girlfriends try to follow you up here?"

"No, but they keep the phone tied up every night!" Lynn walked in from the dining room, holding a glass of white wine. "I made his daddy talk to him, give him the speech again. I'm too young to be a grandmother."

"No, you're not," Denise contended. "And it ain't an issue for aunts."

"Ain't an issue for aunts," Malcolm echoed from the living room.

"Isn't," Denise corrected in a loud voice, "for everybody under twenty–one. Aren't you supposed to be in computer camp?"

"His session doesn't start for another couple of weeks. That commute's going be a pain in my ass," Lynn mourned, dreading the daily trek to the outer suburbs and back. "And this one," she said, nodding in Marcus' direction, "lined up a little gig with the Recreation Department. He's working at one of the centers over near you so he gets to practice his Spanish."

"Are you all going anywhere else, like a real vacation?" Denise asked.

"You remember Annette Gary, the novelist, my roommate for my first two years at Morris? She read about Niagara over the wire services and got back in touch after all these years. She's doing a reading from her latest book here in August. Anyway, she's invited us to her folks' place up on Martha's Vineyard."

"That sounds nice."

"The beach is supposed to be quiet. I could work on the notes for my book. She's got a son Malcolm's age, too."

"So why not go, Lynnie?"

Lynn sighed.

"Ann's parents, girl... They're a couple of prehistoric, bourgeois throwbacks, always reminded me of that quotation, 'I seek the integration of Negroes with black people.' Who said it anyhow?"

Denise shrugged, giving her a blank look. "You should just go and enjoy it. I can't believe everything always has to be about politics."

"We'll see. But you're in a good mood," Lynn observed, studying her sister for a moment. "And you look great."

"Yeah, you're looking really good, Aunt Neecy," Marcus agreed.

"Don't you have a ladder to put away, young man?" Lynn asked sternly.

"Still look good," Marcus muttered to himself as he folded the ladder's legs together and hoisted it away on one shoulder.

Lynn shook her head and sipped from her glass. "That boy's nothing but a walking hormone these days! But with you, there's something different. You seem more confident somehow. Definitely happy. Maybe a little in love, huh?" she suggested, nudging Denise with an elbow. "Same fella as Jo's wild dress?"

"Girl, please," Denise responded with a laugh. "Where's Mama?"

"I'll give you three guesses," Lynn sighed, nodding toward the kitchen.

"So where's Leontyne?"

"Oh, I cranked her down soon as we got here. I bet they could hear the "Ritorna Vinctor" aria up on the tennis courts. Mama's almost as bad as Marcus."

At that moment the kitchen door swung open and Joanne emerged carrying a platter stacked with steaming fried fish.

"Well ah declare!" she called out in an exaggerated drawl. "If ah had known we was havin' a fish fry, ah'd a worn mah Daisy Dukes!" She set the large plate down in the middle of the table, moving a few glasses to accommodate its breadth.

"I've seen those shorts," Lynn sneered, "and it wouldn't take but one bite of cornbread to make you bust out every seam!"

Joanne tossed her head and swung her hips wide as she returned to the kitchen.

"Don't hate, Doc, don't hate. You might have gotten the brains, but Neecy and I got the boom-boom-BOOM!"

"It's that last 'boom' I'm talking about!" Lynn insisted, laughing hard. "Little bits of denim plastered onto the walls from the force of the explosion."

Joanne stopped, turning to glance back at Denise.

"Neecy has obviously learned to work that thing, too! I'm glad you're getting out more, sweetie, 'stead of sitting up under a bunch of old married folk all the time. Don't pay doc or the fire boy any mind. Been anyplace good?"

Denise thought for a moment, deciding how much she could safely tell.

"The beach mostly," she said, the memories spreading a smile across her face. "I got a bikini. It felt kind of strange at first but I think I like it."

"And turning heads, I bet." Joanne smiled as she spoke.

"One in particular," Maurice added. The three women turned as he walked down the last couple of steps and into the dining room,

Joy riding high on his shoulders. He stopped next to Denise.

"Anything you want to tell us about?" His words sounded light and playful but Denise noticed that his eyes were serious. He couldn't know, she told herself. She had deliberately steered Ian away from clubs and restaurants that were popular among African Americans. She had tried to be careful in every way she could think of, tried to keep word from getting back before she was ready. If she would ever have a reason to be ready…No, it was just her guilt on duty, making her see things that didn't exist.

"Not much to tell at this point," she answered breezily. Maurice kept his steady, sober eyes on her. Denise reached up and stroked Joy's cheek, provoking a bubbly giggle.

"Now if you all don't mind, I think I'll go in and say hello to Mama," she began, pulling away from the group. "She probably needs some help since everyone is hanging out here looking at me, as usual." She quickly walked away, leaving the kitchen door swinging in her wake.

Andrew Phillips, M.D., leaned against the doorway of Ian's boyhood room. His younger brother was slouching by the window, but his eyes were clearly turned inward.

"Okay, I give up," Andy called out. "What's up with you?"

"Nothing, man. Nothing."

"I don't think so. You've been trying to act as if you were somewhere else ever since you got here."

"Well...Maybe. Yes. I wish I were somewhere else."

Andy drifted into the room and stretched out across the bed next to the wall.

"So?"

Ian fingered the change in his pockets, looking at Andy, calculating. What the hell. He walked over to the other bed, extracted the short stack of four by six photos from his duffel bag and tossed them at his brother.

Andy's sudden intake of breath made a whistling sound. He wordlessly shuffled through the pictures that had a single subject: a pretty, dark-skinned young woman. In some of the photos she wore a white sundress and a shy smile; in others she had donned shorts, a T-shirt and an attitude of amused contempt toward the photographer. In one of the photographs Ian stood behind her, his arms about her waist.

"Operating outside your normal parameters, aren't you?" Andy thumbed through the photographs once more to make sure he hadn't missed anything. "Not only is she black, but a blind man could tell she's a decent girl from a mile off. Sure you're not hiding one of your pale, anorexic glue-sniffers in the deck?"

Ian returned to his post by the window, his arms folded across his chest.

"You know what you can do with your parameters," he said calmly, looking out at buildings tinted shades of red and orange by the setting sun. "I won't be needing them anymore."

"Whoa, gentlemen! Return your seats to the upright position! When did this happen?"

"The first of the year. I was expecting a typical geek to come in for a limited detail on a contract I was seriously running into the ground. And I was a little worried, too, because there was a chance that I wouldn't be able to get more government programming work if I didn't get the contract finished.

"Anyway, I'm just getting in and there's a knock at the door. And this soft voice says,

'Mr. Phillips?' And I turn around and there she is, all big brown eyes and braids and a posh little figure. I'm assuming that she's probably one of Frank's luscious assistants, there to request that I come to his office to be executed or something. And then she says, 'I'm here for the detail.' And there I am, just staring at her like a dunce."

"Nothing new about that," Andy observed.

"So here I was with this hot-looking woman an arm's length away every day. And here's the thing man." He gestured toward the photographs. "If all that weren't enough, Denise is smart as all hell. She pulled my rump out of the wringer so many times on this thing, I can't begin to tell you."

"While your eyes were coming out of your head."

"Spent a lot of time holding a book in front of me those first few weeks, believe it.

"So D.C. is having this incredible winter. There's a load of snow every other day, and you know how they panic down there if six flakes fall. People were crazed, spent the days looking out the windows, waiting to go home. Not much work got done.

"Anyway, while everybody else is running up and down panicking, we start this habit of kicking back and having these deep, I mean deep, talks. Stuff I never even told you or Josh. As if it were the most natural thing in the world to be sitting on a tabletop, toe to toe with this beautiful woman talking about all kinds of wild stuff."

"I presume you did all the talking?"

"No. She told me things, too. Things I couldn't believe—how like this engineer ass she was dating for three years dumped her for someone else out of the blue. And that except for him, she'd never really had a serious boyfriend."

"And you volunteered."

"Not at all. I guess I couldn't believe it on some level. I don't know. I thought maybe she was just trying to keep me out of her business. Anyhow, we got close." He launched into a detailed account of the hits and misses in their courtship.

When he finished, Andy asked, "So have you had any problems? Being with a black woman and all?"

"Did you cut that day in med school? The parts are all the same."

"You know bloody well that's not what I meant."

"She says black guys mouth off to her

sometimes. I've never heard anything but the next bloke who tries will be collecting his teeth from the sidewalk."

Andy shook his head in wonder.

"I thought I'd never live to see it: the Iceman, whipped at last!"

"Iceman?" Ian questioned. "Me?"

"Yes, you boob," Andy replied evenly. "I can remember when Mum and Dad used to worry about you, especially in view of Josh's, ah, issues. I always assured them that Gibraltar would crumble indeed before you would consider giving yourself over for a line of powder or a pair of pretty legs. I reminded them of your passion for control, and told them that you might sell but you'd never use."

"How reassuring," Ian murmured sarcastically. "You must have one hell of a bedside manner."

"When we were small," Andy continued, ignoring Ian's comment, "you always hated bedtime, fighting sleep even as your eyes were closing and your skinny legs were sliding out from under you. Always afraid you might miss something. Always afraid to let anyone else handle the reins for even a moment." He glanced down at the pile of photographs again. "You've finally proved me wrong. So what's the arrangement ? Are you living together?"

"Not really. I'm at her place as much as she lets me. She comes to my place every now and then."

"So, what do you want?"

"What do I want?" Ian echoed.

"What are you going to do about it?"

"Every time I look at her the second thing I think about is a house in the suburbs and a minivan filled with little brown rocket scientists.

"Okay. You've found this incredibly beautiful, smart, sexy woman who has inspired you to mend your ways, conquer your chronic instability and assorted personality disorders. Why isn't she here?"

"I thought it was a little soon to bring her up."

"I don't believe you!" Andy sat up, blinking at Ian.

"What?"

"Are you insane? This is your life calling, man. And not many of us get a call like this." He brandished the sheaf of pictures in Ian's direction. "No way, man. There is no way in hell I would leave this woman alone. Call her, damn it! Pick up the phone, ask her, nicely, to bring her beautiful self up here; put down the phone; pick it up again and leave a ticket for her at the airport. Then go pick her up. Lead her to think you're a stable, dependable human being–even if the rest of us know the truth."

Preston Vaughn was crossing his mother-in-law's living room with his second piece of iced lemon cake when the telephone rang. He balanced the plate on the sofa's armrest and picked up the receiver.

"Speak to whom? Just a minute."

"Nee-cy!" Preston bellowed her name into the far corners of the house.

"I'm right here!" Denise snapped, appearing in the hallway. "What on earth are you hollering about?"

"Girl, it's not my job to know where you are every minute. Sounds like some old white lady on the phone for you."

"I don't know any old white ladies."

"Sounds like one knows you." He handed her the phone.

"Hello?"

"Hello, is this Denise Adams?" The voice sounded faint, but somehow familiar.

"This is Denise. Who is this?"

Ian reverted to his normal timbre.

"Somebody who wants your sweet, round ass on the next shuttle, babe."

"Ian? What the–? Why are you calling my mother's house and disguising your voice? Have you lost your mind? And watch your mouth; anybody can pick up the extension. Besides, I just gave you this number for an emergency!"

"It is an emergency. I need you. I'm here smack in the valley of the shadow on the Upper East Side and I need you to comfort me. And my brother thinks that having you here will give me extra points with the old folks and with you."

"Your brother must be as crazy as you are. I can't come to New York."

"Sure you can."

"At seven-thirty on a Friday night?"

"The shuttle goes out until eleven-thirty. I'll arrange a ticket for you and drive out to meet you up here. Don't worry about the money, it's not an issue. Just grab a couple of things and get here. Please, babe?"

"Oh-h-h..." She glanced around at the

undulating pile of arms and legs in front of the TV that was her nieces and nephew.

"I don't know if I can get away."

"Just leave."

"You don't know this crew. Saying see ya, then taking a late shuttle to New York won't get it. They'd like to sit me down and shine a light in my eyes until I confess!"

"Leave fast, then. Don't explain. Please, don't make me beg, babe."

"Don't call me babe, either."

"Why not?"

She turned away from the hubbub of the living room.

"I've seen your eyes when you say it. It's like when your beard tickles my neck."

"O-h-h babe…"

"Why do I keep letting you do this to me? All right, damn you."

"Yes!"

"Which airline?" She turned to the scrimmage behind her. "Malcolm, sweetie, go get me a piece of paper and a pencil please."

"Is it all right if it's a pen, Aunt Neecy?"

"That will be just fine, sweetheart."

"Can't wait to get into your panties, Aunt Neecy," Ian murmured sweetly.

"What did I tell you about your nasty

talk?"

"Remind me when you get here."

She dutifully recorded the information and hung up. Dreading the next step, she took a deep breath.

"Look, you guys, something's come up and I gotta go."

"Something like what?"

"Girl, I know nobody on your job is calling you at this time on a holiday weekend," Preston protested. "What you got to do that's so important?"

Denise raised one hand in Preston's direction and grabbed her purse with the other.

I can probably get out of here quicker by giving up just a little information, she thought.

"A friend of mine has invited me up to New York for the weekend. I've got to get the shuttle out tonight, though."

Preston, as could be foreseen, jumped on her offering.

"Well, Missy, if this is a male friend, I'll take you to the airport. I'll drive you up the turnpike myself because I need to see this man. You're going up there to see his people? How come you haven't brought him around here? We're not good enough or something?"

"I haven't known him that long. Well, I guess I have...I don't know!"

She turned, pleading, toward her older sister.

"Lynnie, can you please just run me home?"

Lynn studied her for a moment and nodded. Denise knew that she could always count on her older sister, but she also recognized the ride would come with a price.

It took them only ten minutes to get back to Denise's apartment. Denise was out of the car and halfway up the steps before Lynn could shut off the ignition.

"Damn it, Denise! Can you at least wait for your old chauffeur?" Lynn hollered after her.

"Sorry," Denise yelled back from the front door. She bounced from foot to foot waiting for her sister to join her. Lynn was puffing a little as she entered the building.

"You just go on up and leave the door open for me. I haven't been young and in love for twenty years so there's no way I can keep up with you." She rested against the stairway rail, waiting for her breath to return.

Denise paused for a second. "Who said anything about love? I clearly said 'a friend.' I didn't even say it was a man."

"Girl, I've been looking in your face for the last few weeks. If it isn't a man, it must be some new kind of drug. And if that's what it is, I want you to get me some, too. I need it. Bad."

Lynn resumed her arduous climb moments after Denise. By the time she reached the third floor, Denise was already in the apartment.

"Don't bother to look for clues; there aren't any," Denise announced.

"Moi? Looking for clues about your man?" Lynn pretended to take offense as she walked in and collapsed on the couch.

"Toi, girl," Denise tossed over her shoulder as she hurried down the hall to the bedroom. "You may be more quiet about it than Joanne, but you're looking just as hard, I know."

"Shoot. There's always a clue or two."

"And don't try anything while I'm gone either. If one piece of paper has been moved I'll know it."

"I won't have to mess up your place to find

out what I want to know." Lynn struggled up from the sofa cushions and followed Denise. "A friend of Preston's is a U.S. Marshal. We'll just run your man's name through their computer and give you a complete profile on him when you come back. Or else we'll just come up to New York and kill him, if we have to."

Lynn perched on the edge of Denise's bed, reflexively exploring her purse for a cigarette. She stopped when she remembered her sister's rule against smoking in the apartment.

"It's okay," Denise told her. "For what you're doing for me tonight I'll buy you a carton sometime. Nah, I won't! I love you and I want you around." She stopped scurrying about for a few seconds to plant a kiss on her sister's forehead.

"I know!" Denise exclaimed. "Preston and I will tie you up, drive you out to California and leave you at Betty Ford's. Detox with the stars."

"With my luck I'd probably end up sitting between Rick James and Robert Downey, Jr., during group therapy."

"So? You wouldn't be bored. You might get a little banged up, though."

Lynn laughed heartily, leaning back to watch Denise toss articles of clothing into her suitcase and snatch them out again.

"For heaven's sake, Denise, try to focus!" Lynn ordered.

"You're right," she muttered, stopping to count on her fingers. "Okay: one nice dress, something casual, something to travel in…"

"Why do you need a nice dress? It's the Fourth of July, not Thanksgiving! People have picnics, not formal dinners."

"You're right again. Why don't you go instead? This is stressing me out."

Lynn glanced down at her watch.

"The clock is moving, Neecy. Do you want to get with your man tonight or what?"

The thought of missing the chance to be with Ian in a few hours unnerved her more than she expected. Denise packed her weekend bag without another word; she and Lynn rejoined the evening traffic crawl fifteen minutes later.

"Girl, I owe you one, but you don't have to take me all the way to the airport."

"Don't worry, I'm not. I'm just going to take you to the Hilton so you can catch one of those shuttle buses. It's probably faster that way."

Denise reached out and squeezed her sister's thin arm.

"Lynnie, thanks. I really appreciate this."

Lynn blew a jet of smoke from her nostrils.

"You nearly had me fooled back at Mother's that evening. No big deal, we've been to the beach, blah, blah. And now he's flying you in for the weekend! Who knew?"

Denise stared straight ahead into the southbound traffic.

"Well?" Lynn pressed. "What does he look like?"

"He's tall. He's got a nice build, he works out."

"And?"

"And he's got nice eyes. He has been doing some programming on his own but he's thinking of expanding. You know, hiring some people. Maybe doing some teaching."

Lynn showed a rare smile.

"Sounds like a brother on the way up."

Denise frowned and unzipped her purse. "I hope I didn't forget…" Anything to get her off that track.

"Seriously, Denise, I'm real happy because I've been praying for something good for you for such a long time. It isn't easy for an intellectual woman like you to find the kind of man she can respect and be respected in return. I've been so afraid you would end up alone. Or with a white man."

Denise tried to keep emotion from creeping into her voice.

"Well, neither one of those is the end of the world, you know."

"They're not the end of the world, you're right. But they're not what I'd want for you either. Maybe I'm prejudiced but I think any decent man would be lucky to get with you. You'd be such a good wife and you're great with kids. It's just hard for men to see you because you're so conservative and quiet. But a white man? Ugh," she shivered.

"Why 'ugh'?"

"It's just that they're so much trouble–their families and all. And then you have to deal with the kids; how do you teach them to cope with racism and their identity and all that? And what would he think they are: black or white? Something in-between? And before kids there has to be...I can't even imagine one putting his hands on me."

Denise knew that she was both too tired and too excited to pursue this turn in the conversation. She sighed and leaned back against the headrest.

"Could I at least get a name?"

Denise felt a cold hand in the pit of her

stomach. What were the chances that Lynn would remember her talking about him earlier in the year? Would she suspect something or treat it as a simple coincidence?

"Ian," she whispered, holding her breath.

"Ian." Lynn repeated the name with a tone of approval. "I knew an Ian from Trinidad. Is he from the islands?"

"No."

"You know anything about his family?"

"He has an older brother who's a surgeon and has two kids. Both his parents are still living."

"And he's good to you, right?"

"Are you talking about money?"

Lynn laughed.

"I'm talking about everything!"

"Well, he's just...nice."

"Nice enough to have you almost nodding off into your plate these Sunday evenings? Girl, I am so relieved. I was worried; I almost thought you were getting sick again or something. Now I know what it is you're getting!" Lynn reached over to give her a playful shove. "I don't know why you were doing so much fussing over what clothes to take. Hell, you're probably not gonna need 'em! Look, tell the brother that it's okay to get a little sleep in between; you both have plenty of time to be together."

Denise frowned again and looked away. Lynn laughed at what she presumed to be her sister's shyness.

"So are you just hanging out and having fun or is this going anywhere? Not that there's anything wrong with hanging out," Lynn added, careful not to disturb Denise's good spirits any more than she had to.

"I don't know," Denise answered, fearing another unsettling turn in the conversation.

"No clues at all?"

"He likes to talk about being married and having kids."

"Is he talking about being married in general or married to you?"

"About being married to me," she admitted in a small voice.

Lynn abruptly pulled the car into the first vacant space she saw. Unbuckling the seat belt, she turned to face her youngest sister.

"Denise! Girl, what is your problem? How long has it been since we had this conversation? You say you can't read men's signals? You aren't kidding, are you?"

Denise shrugged and peeked at her watch.

"So why haven't you said anything?" Lynn

insisted. "Why haven't you brought him around?"

Denise shifted as much as the seatbelt allowed to look directly at Lynn.

"It's not that simple. It's complicated. I can't, well, I don't want to explain it right now, okay?"

"What's complicated? He's crazy about you, obviously, and you're crazy about him. And I bet you're going to meet his family while you're up there. I might not under-stand physics, like you and Daddy, but I know chemistry, the human kind. Honestly, I hope you don't let this one slip through your fin-gers."

"You sound like Preston now."

"And I don't mean to, Neecy. But you're always asking me about how romance and love and marriage all work; this is it!" She reached over and gently touched her sister's cheek. "I truly want you to be happy, baby sis. And the look in your eyes makes me think you've got it right this time. Don't over-ana-lyze everything; be happy."

Denise relaxed enough to smile.

"Now you sound like Ian."

"My brother-in-law, Ian," Lynn corrected her, rebuckling and checking both rear mir-

rors before merging into the surging holiday
traffic.

When they reached the Hilton Lynn pulled
into the drop-off zone.

"Now go to New York and have a wonderful time, you hear!"

Denise leaned over and hugged Lynn as if
she were going off to war, not a weekend visit.
As Denise pulled away and gathered up her
purse and small suitcase, Lynn felt a damp-
ness on her cheek.

"Neecy girl, what's wrong?" she called out.

Denise was out of the car, on the sidewalk.
She waved and tried to speak as she backed
away. Then she turned and walked into the
Hilton.

Chapter 24

Ian easily spotted Denise in front of the airline gate. He nearly leaped out of the vehicle before Andy came to a complete stop. He grabbed her satchel and led her to the van.

"Denise, this is my brother Andy." He slid the back door open, helped her up, and climbed in beside her.

"Hi, I'm Denise." She leaned forward a little and extended her hand between the seats.

"Yes, I know," Andy replied, grinning, as he reached back to take her hand. "It's a real pleasure to meet you. You're even prettier than your pictures."

She slid back onto the seat and gave Ian a worried look.

"You showed him? Did you show them to everybody?"

"No, just Andy. The chauffeur has to know."

"This isn't a good idea," she fretted, suddenly overcome with nameless fears. "Maybe I should just go back right now."

"But you haven't even said hello," Ian said, leaning over to kiss her as Andy pulled out into the main traffic lane.

They pulled up in front of the distinguished old apartment building around eleven o'clock. Andy loosened his seat belt to lean around toward his passengers.

"It's been a pleasure, Denise. Say Ian, why don't we get together for brunch Sunday morning with Ed and Wendy and you two? It'll give Lily and me a chance to get acquainted. I'm sure the kids have had it for tonight."

"Your second good idea in four hours! You're on a roll, bro. I'll make it happen."

"And send my family down here, while you're at it."

Ian grabbed her bag and jumped down onto the sidewalk while Andy motioned for

Denise to stay.

"Nice meeting you, Andy," she offered with a shy smile. "I hope I'll see you again on Sunday."

"Looking forward to it." He leaned forward, lowering his voice. "Ian is happier than we've seen in a long time. You must be as special as he says you are."

"I didn't do anything," she demurred.

Andy squeezed her hand. "Believe me," he said with a serious look, "thank you."

Ian poked his head back into the car.

"It wasn't enough for you to suck all the brains out of the gene pool, big brother? Are you trying to steal my girlfriend, too?"

Andy waved them both away with another reminder about Sunday. After passing through the elegantly appointed lobby, the elevator whisked them up to the twelfth floor. Ian led her down the hall to number 1202 and opened the door into a small, tiled foyer. The sounds of jazz and muted conversation floated down the hallway.

"Ready?" he asked.

"I think so." She tried to sound more confident than she really was. Ian gave her a quick kiss and, taking her hand, led her into the book-lined living room. A middle-aged couple sat in a pair of armchairs talking quietly.

"Ed, Wendy," Ian announced, "this is Denise Adams."

"Hello." Denise struggled to keep her voice bright and even, despite her natural reserve and the late hour. "It's nice to meet you all, I mean, all of you."

"And it's so nice to finally meet you, dear." Wendy was already crossing the living room, her arms open. Ian felt a rare surge of appreciation for his mother's natural warmth. She hugged Denise with a big smile.

"You are beautiful, exactly as promised."

"Thank you," Denise whispered, a little embarrassed.

Denise immediately found the source of Ian's good looks: his father was tall, with a head full of light brown hair that was beginning to go gray. He also had the same self-confident swagger when he stepped forward to take her hand, despite his cut-offs and bare feet.

"It's a pleasure to meet you, Mr. Phil–"

"Ed. That's what Ian has always called me from the time he was in the nursery. No reason for you not to do the same."

"Ed," Denise repeated with some discomfort. "My mother loves your books."

"Then by all means take some back with you. At least then I won't be able to say I can't give them away. Oh, here's Lily."

Lily emerged from the hallway carrying Jacob. Emma followed, dragging a large tote bag. Lily introduced herself and the children but was obviously in a hurry to take her sleepy brood home. Remembering Andy's idea, Ian suggested that they all meet for brunch on Sunday. The issue was easily settled, and Lily said she looked forward to seeing Denise again.

After Lily and the children departed, Ian set down Denise's bag and led her to a seat on the couch.

"Are you sure there's nothing we can get for you, Denise?" asked Wendy.

"Well," she sighed, hating to be a burden at the late hour. "Only if it's no trouble, a cup of tea would be nice."

"Herbal? We've got loads, just follow me." She turned with a knowing smile. "Tired, but too wired to fall asleep?"

"Exactly," Denise agreed.

"You're in luck, then. I picked up some chamomile while I was out this morning."

Ian made a choking noise.

"What is it with you women and that crap? Denise tried to force me to have some on our first date. I fixed her, though."

"I'm sure I don't want to know," Wendy called out as she ushered Denise into the kitchen.

Ian hung back for a minute, turning to look at his father who was shuffling through a loose pile of CD jewel boxes. Ed Phillips glanced up into the eyes of his youngest son. He smiled and nodded. Ian grinned back at him, pleased by his father's affirmation, and followed the women into the kitchen.

Wendy and Denise returned to the sitting room carrying steaming mugs of tea, and Ian followed with a plate of shortbread cookies. They sat and talked for more than an hour, Wendy and Denise huddled together on the love seat while Ian sat on the floor, resting against Denise's legs. Edward Phillips presided over the impromptu gathering from the depths of his armchair. Ian was relaxed and happy, telling the story of how their meeting and friendship had blossomed. Aware of her tendency to be shy, he was careful to draw Denise into the conversation, pressing her for details about her education and her family. Both Ed and Wendy responded with approval, just as he'd anticipated.

A little past midnight he noticed that Denise's eyelids had begun to flutter every few minutes. He gently shook her hand. Denise, startled from her doze, blinked at her unfamiliar surroundings.

"Where can we put her, Wen?"

"I thought your old room." Wendy reached over to give Denise's hand a gentle squeeze. "We're so pleased to meet you, at last."

"Thank you—I mean—thank you," she replied, sufficiently awake to be flustered in the presence of her potential in-laws. Ian took her arm, grabbed her satchel, and led her down the hall to the room that once was his own.

"This was your room?" Denise looked around her at the dark, heavy furniture, bookshelves nearly sagging from the weight of their contents and the faded posters of mountains and skiers.

"Yep. It just took a little drywall and paint after the exorcism and everything was as good as new."

"You are so bad! And your parents are so nice," she remarked in a sleepy voice.

"They have to be. They couldn't live up to their billing as major liberals if they mistreated you, especially in front of me. I'm the family scoundrel, remember? They've got to do better. They really like you, though."

"What makes you think so?"

"Wendy told me after you left the kitchen. She said she hoped I wouldn't botch this up, 'this' being you and me. And Ed definitely gives you two thumbs up."

"But they don't know much about me."

"They only had to see you to know you're different from any other woman I've ever brought home. And that has absolutely nothing to do with your color. They see exactly what I see, a woman who's brilliant and beautiful and sweet."

Denise sat on the side of the bed for a few seconds, then decided to stretch out. Ian lay down next to her and stroked her cheek.

"As much as I hate to admit it I am a little tired," she yawned.

"Well, get ready for bed then, and I'll see you later."

"What does that mean?"

"Be sure to leave the door unlocked."

"But Ian, this is your parents' home."

"It's every boy's fantasy, babe."

"So Ed! So Wen!" Ian rhapsodized, dropping onto the love seat beside his mother. "How would you feel about a house full of grandchildren?"

"This is serious, then?" asked Wendy Phillips, leaning forward a little. "Good for you! She's a lovely young woman. Does she feel the same?"

"God, I hope so."

"You have doubts?"

"Well, I believe she loves me. She says she does. But her family is something else again. She's going to be torn, I know it."

"Have you met them?"

"No, and that's part of the problem. She was low-key about it in front of you, but her father was a major figure in African American academe. I checked up on it. Her mother sits on the board of the foundation that was set up after he died. Denise tells me her oldest sister tries to pattern herself after him and is really into Black Nationalist cant. I keep telling her I can take care of myself but she really believes someone might take a bite out of me should she ever take me home."

"That's quite something to overcome. Is she close to them?"

"Absolutely. Before we got together she spent most of her free time with her sisters and their kids or her mother. The middle sister I don't know much about. She's run a chic Afrocentric boutique in D.C. for years and years. Denise is closer to her older sister, Lynnette. In some ways they're more like mother and daughter."

"Yet she's in love with you."

"It wasn't easy to get through to her either. From the first day she wouldn't take any nonsense from me."

"That's worth several points in her favor."

"Absolutely," Edward Phillips agreed. "I was expecting your usual type: tall, blonde, tiny waist, long legs, I.Q. of a gnat..."

"Aahhhnnn!" Ian mimicked the blare of a game show buzzer. "Sorry, Ed! You only get points for the tiny waist this time, but thanks for playing. You will receive our home version of 'Name Ian's Lover.'" He leaned forward, shaking his head. "I still can't believe how it's turned out, you know? I was determined never to get close to anyone again and one morning there she was, standing right in front of me like a gift. We spent a lot of time talking about our families, how we grew up, things like that at first. Later I started to press my case a little, trying to be sneaky about it. She, of course, would always see through me and try to change the subject. And once we weren't together every day I missed her so much.

"I just wanted you to know how great you were with Denise tonight," he added, turning toward Wendy. "She can be terribly shy but you were your usual warm, gracious self. That helped her relax a lot faster. You were always so good to all the hoodlums I've paraded through here over the years, and if I've never said—"

"I know. If I hadn't, I would have seen far less of you." She reached out and squeezed his hand.

"I'm just crazy about her," Ian sighed.

"You must be," Ed agreed. "We gave up trying to get you to use 'please' and 'thank you' after sixteen years of trying. Now you seem to have mastered them in what, under six months?"

"Let's face it, her incentives are a hell of a lot better than anything you had to offer!"

They all laughed at this, but Ian soon became serious again.

"Now, I have to ask you both something hard. Are you really okay with the racial aspect? I know how you've lived and what you taught Andy and me, but..."

"Would your feelings for Denise change if we weren't?" Edward Phillips asked tentatively.

"Hell no." The set of his mouth was firm, his hazel eyes blazing.

"And that's all that really matters, isn't it?" Wendy responded. "As a parent I fear for you to some degree because of all the hatred and bigotry in the world. No one wants to see her child hurt, physically or emotionally. Have you thought about what your own children would face? You and Denise will love them and your father and I will spoil them silly, but if what you say is true, what of her family? And of the rest of the world that wants so badly to put them in a box and will be happy to knock them about if they don't quite fit?

"To answer your question, Denise's race doesn't matter to us." Ed spoke slowly and thoughtfully. "Frankly, she's just the kind of woman we've always hoped would come into your life. She's decent, stable and educated. And lovely, of course. And being with her has changed you immensely. You seem to have a sense of focus, a sense of direction I've never seen in you. Frankly, I'd become concerned over the years that you would continue to run from everything that required a commitment and end up a bitter, lonely old man. I always hoped that you would eventually find a place you could call home. And now you seem to have found that, with her."

"Yes. One day, quite soon after we'd met, I looked into her eyes and realized I'd found the place you spoke of, my home."

A warm ray of morning sun stole through a gap in the heavy drapes and woke Denise the next morning. It took her a few seconds to remember where she was as she looked at the boyhood memorabilia around her. You're with Ian, your lover, she told herself silently, in his parents' home in New York City. This would have been so hard for her to believe only a few months ago. When she sat up Ian grunted and rolled over, snatching most of the sheet with him. She was wearing one of her more modest nightgowns, but he slept unclothed, as always. She observed him for a while, until she became aware of the sound of a radio playing nearby. Before long she recognized the familiar theme music for a public radio weekend program. But wasn't it early for that now? She reached for her watch on the nightstand and was shocked to discover that it was a little after ten.

"Ian? Ian!" She was shaking him, her whisper harsh with panic. "We've gotta get up! Your parents are up and they know we slept together!"

He struggled onto his elbows, his eyes barely open.

"What?"

"I said your parents are awake! They know you spent the night in here!"

"That?" He dropped heavily back onto the pillow. "Of course they know."

"Won't they be upset?"

"They assume we sleep together and wouldn't expect us to pretend we don't," he replied with a yawn. "That's how they are. They'd probably cart us off to the nearest emergency room if they thought for a moment we weren't doing it. Aging hippies are good for stuff like that. And they know a lot more

now about how things are between us. We
talked for a while after you crashed. Talked
about you, mostly."

Denise cringed. "What did they say?"

"Why do you assume it's bad, babe?" He
rolled over on his side and reached for her.
"To make a long story short, you've won the
Ed and Wendy Phillips Peace Prize: the right
to sleep with me under their roof and still be
thought of as the premiere potential daugh-
ter-in-law on the planet."

She wriggled out of his grasp and off the
bed.

"Let's keep things status quo, then," she
said, padding across the worn carpet. "I don't
want to press my luck." She reached into the
closet for the peignoir that matched her nightgown. Ian flipped sideways across the bed,
watching her.

"Hey, Neecy!" he called as he crawled out
of bed. "Are you busy today?"

"I don't know; I'll have to ask my
boyfriend. Why?"

"Dump that horse's ass! Tell him I want
to marry you."

They spent the day indulging in the urban

delights they loved best. Ian led Denise in and out of tiny bookstores on the Lower East Side. She coaxed him into a few department stores and boutiques on the premise of checking the styles for Joanne, but ended up making a few purchases for herself.

That evening the Phillipses and Denise took a taxi to a Fourth of July party at the home of friends. The elevator opened on a scene Denise recognized from her early life as Dean Adams' daughter: blazing chandeliers, table decked with expensive foods and liquor, and the hum of cocktail chatter occasionally broken by shrieks of laughter. But she observed that most of the people at this gathering were white, with a sprinkling of Asians, Latinos and African Americans in addition to herself. The younger people were dressed casually in shorts and t-shirts, but quite a few of the older women, including Ian's mother, wore chic linen dresses and jewelry. She would have to tell Lynn she wouldn't have been out of place with a good dress, she thought. On the other hand, she wouldn't mention it all, she decided, remembering who had brought her there.

Ian introduced Denise to everyone he knew. A few looked at her with curiosity, but most were gracious, inviting the two of them to stop by while they were in the city.

When the fireworks began, Ian steered Denise out to the balcony to watch the show with the younger crowd. As she leaned against him, his arms around her waist, Denise finally chased all doubts and fears from her mind. She and Ian loved each other. And that was all that mattered, for now.

Chapter 25

Denise was nearly overwhelmed by the urge to sleep as she dabbed pats of butter on top of the raw dinner rolls. On that Sunday afternoon in mid-July she tried to follow the three-way conversation that rebounded among her mother and her sisters, but the heat and her sluggishness convinced her to do only one thing at a time. When she finished, she stood up and yawned, pulling her braids back behind her head. Never one to miss a detail, Joanne uttered a little shriek.

"Diamonds! Those are diamonds, right? Girl, let me see, let me see," she chanted as she flew to Denise's side and lifted her hair. "I knew it! These are real; nothing else in the world sparkles like that! Nice Euro-wire setting, too. And they're huge. Huge!" Her mother and Lynn rushed over to inspect the goods. Denise showed them off with a mixture of pride and reluctance.

"Are these from our future brother and son-in-law?" Lynn asked.

"What!" Joanne and her mother responded with one voice.

"That's what Lynn wants to believe," answered Denise, rolling her eyes in Lynn's direction.

"Don't even try it," Lynn warned playfully. "You were sitting in my car on Friday, July third, at approximately eight-fifteen. You said it yourself, or at least you didn't object when I said it. By the way, I never found out what happened in New York, so give it up. Give it all up!" she ordered, making herself comfortable at the kitchen table. Joanne pulled up a chair as well but their mother went back to turn the chicken that had begun to pop and sizzle in the frying pan.

Joanne peeked over at their mother, then turned back to the table.

"Girl, what are you into these days?" she whispered. "You must be throwing down in bed to rate these! You young women got some new technique or something? I need to know because there are too many young female lawyers running around that damn courthouse and I need to protect my investment!"

"Still waters run deep," Lynn murmured. "Why do you think she's always so sleepy these Sunday afternoons?"

"You know what they say about whispering," Julia admonished from the stove.

"I'm gonna get the R-rated version later," Joanne mouthed silently, pointing at Denise.

"Shoot, probably more like double 'X.' One for each carat," Lynn advised.

"Are you through?" Denise yawned.

"Yes, baby girl." Lynn tried to pull herself together. "Let's get New York on the record before the men come in here and start meddling."

"Okay." Denise sat up as straight as she could manage. "New York: I flew up Friday night; Ian and his brother met me at Newark. We went back to his parents' apartment in Manhattan. That's where we stayed; they're very nice. He took me sightseeing the next day and we watched the fireworks from a friend's balcony at night. We all went to brunch the next day and I flew back home later that afternoon. End of story."

"You stayed in his parents' home?" Julia walked over to the table, wiping her hands on a dishtowel. "This was a couple of weeks ago, wasn't it?"

"Yes, Mama," Denise answered.

"How come we haven't met the young man then?"

"It's complicated, Mama." She couldn't meet her mother's eyes.

"I've got a dozen pieces of chicken left to cook. Your father once explained Einstein's theory of relativity to me in less time than they'll take. I think you can manage to do the same."

"Uh, let's go see what the fellas are up to," Lynn suggested, slowly rising from her seat. She recognized her mother's tone; after forty-four years it still retained the power to make her uncomfortable. She rose without another word and walked through the door that opened into the dining room. Joanne reluctantly followed.

Julia Adams took the chair Joanne had vacated.

"Denise? Is everything all right?"

"Everything's fine." Denise picked at a thread that was hanging from the seam of her skirt.

"If everything's so fine, why do the young man's parents know you but we don't know him?" Julia Adams let a few seconds pass before she asked her next question.

"Neecy, is he white?"

Astounded, Denise stared at her mother until she found her voice.

"How did you know?"

"I've been looking into your face for the past month or two, just like everybody else around here. You're almost a different person, you've been so happy. Even Marcus mentioned it when he came home. If your young man were one of us you'd have brought him around by now. So by process of elimination that left me with a married man and a white man. I know it's not in you to break up another woman's home; I raised you better than that.

"How did I know?" Julia Adams repeated, shaking her head. "You girls never fail to amaze me." She sighed as she stood to return to the stove. "You all just can't believe I had a life before you and your father. That I was young and pretty, had a career, dreams of my own..." She trailed off, her attention back on her cooking.

Denise, now fully awake, jumped to her

feet and followed her.

"Mama! You?"

Julia let Denise wait while she expertly removed the crispy chicken to drain and added several flour-coated pieces to the pan.

"Why don't you pour us a little iced tea?" Julia suggested. Denise quickly retrieved two large glasses from the cabinet and filled them with tea from the pitcher in the refrigerator. She set the glasses on the table and waited impatiently for her mother to sit down again.

"I was graduated from Morris' School of Music in the early 1960s. I knew that I wouldn't have the same opportunities as white classical singers my age, so I made up my mind to go to Europe and try my luck there. Back then I loved music so much that I was willing to sacrifice being with my parents and brothers and sisters and starting my own family. My favorite instructor at Morris arranged some introductions for me, and I won a few small roles in some of the opera houses.

"But music was not the only thing in my life during those years. The Europeans, the French and the Italians in particular, found black women very attractive. The fact that I was with the opera was just icing on the cake

"There was one white man in particular,

from Stockholm. He was in Milan on business. He heard me sing Despina one night in *Cosi Fan Tutti*. Karl was waiting for me at the artists' exit after the performance and asked if he could take me to dinner; being young, adventurous and away from home, I went. In spite of the fact that he was ten years older, we shared similar ideals and interests beyond music. We were friends and lovers for nearly three years."

At this revelation Denise nearly tumbled off her chair. Her mother had never spoken so frankly in her presence.

"My room was always filled with flowers. We took wonderful trips together. If I happened to admire a gown in a shop window, I would find it in my room the next day. And beautiful jewelry, like yours."

"But what happened?" Denise asked, impatient again. "Why didn't you stay with him? Your life would have been so much easier!"

"Who's to say, Neecy? I don't know if it would have. Anyway, I began to think about the future. I couldn't turn my back on the civil rights movement in this country; there was so much to be done! And I had to think about having a family. It's still difficult raising interracial children, so you can imagine what I had to think about back then. And, when I put all my thoughts together, I decided to end the relationship and return home."

"And is that what you're telling me, that I should stop seeing Ian?"

"No, that's not what I'm telling you. I know you've already spent too much time up on the shelf. And I was the first one who put you there," she said ruefully. "I've always felt guilty about not spending more time with you. You've had to make your way in the world by yourself more than you ever should have. When I've seen you alone and struggling so much over the last few years I've felt that I was at fault, that I didn't teach you the things you needed to know."

"How can that be? You never left me, Mama."

"Yes, I did. In all the ways that matter, I did, baby girl. When your father was at his lowest point, you were still a little girl and you needed me. But I couldn't tend to your father and also meet your needs. I couldn't answer your questions about the world and what was happening to your body and why boys act the way they do. It was all I could do to thank God every day that Lynn was here to do so much of that for me. But sometimes I've felt that we've never reconnected since then. Never really been close, the way we should be. Does it seem that way to you?"

"You were always here for me. Maybe not when Daddy couldn't do much for himself, but since then I've depended on you a lot, and you've always been here. How many Friday and Saturday nights have we sat on that couch watching TV, or movies after we gave you a VCR? Or the times you took me shopping or out to dinner when I was so depressed about being by myself? Lynn and Joanne always meant well but they always made me feel like I had failed basic womanhood; you never made me feel worse. You shouldn't blame yourself because I'm awkward. Lynn tried and tried to socialize me and Joanne tried to dress me up, but if it's not an equation or a formula, I just don't get it!"

"You don't seem to be doing so badly now. Can you tell me a little about him, this Ian?"

Denise broke into a wide grin, but immediately lowered her eyes in an attempt to hide it.

"I figured that much out for myself!"

"I didn't say anything," Denise protested.

"You didn't have to–that devilish smile

said it all! What I meant was, does he have a last name, where is he from, who are his parents."

"Okay, Mama, okay. I think I told you before that Ian's from New York. His father is Edward Phillips—"

"Not Edward Phillips the novelist."

"One and the same."

"And you came back into this house without asking him to sign a copy of *The Glass Forest* for me?" She could tell her mother was only half-joking.

"Relax, Mama. I think I can get you as many as you'd like. He was pleased to hear you're a fan. Ian's mother, Wendy, is an artist. His older brother Andrew is a surgeon. He's married and has a little girl and a baby boy. They were all really nice, not just polite, but relaxed and treating me as if I were already their relative."

"Speaking of in-laws, Lynn seems to be taking all of this in stride."

"She knows only what I've told her."

"What are you saying, Denise?"

"She doesn't know the one thing that would bother her the most."

"I can understand why you're reluctant to let on, but the longer you wait," she warned.

"How did you stand it all those years, when Daddy and Lynn got into their anti-white rants? Didn't you feel guilty or something? Did you ever tell anyone?"

"I never told your father. He wouldn't have married me when we were younger and he would never have understood when we were older. I believed it was something best left unsaid. To tell you the truth, I don't know whether Karl is dead or alive but at least there's little chance of him showing up on this side of the Atlantic. But your young man is something else again. Doesn't he have any interest in meeting us?"

"That's an understatement."

"Then aren't you afraid he just might turn up at this door one Sunday afternoon?"

"It's crossed my mind."

"And what would you say to Lynn and Preston? They're two peas in a pod when it comes to whites. Jo and Maurice probably wouldn't be as bad but you never know until you have to face the situation in your own family."

"I know you're right, Mama, but I just can't deal with it yet. I was raised hearing and believing that white people can't be trusted; that it's better for us to stay separate from them and their world. And it almost made me reject someone who's made me happier than I've been in a long time."

"I can see you're happy, and that he treats you well. You need to keep thinking about that future, though. Think about whether he's willing to make a commitment to you and all that will mean. Think about whether you'll have children and how you'll raise them to see and define themselves and honor all their roots. But if you're as important to him as all his attention seems to say," she remarked, gently pushing Denise's hair back to reveal the sparkling earrings, "and as the look in your eyes says, then there's no reason for you not to be together."

"Knowing you feel this way might make things a little easier. If Ian had his way we'd have been married weeks ago. And his family seemed to be impressed with me, believe it or not. I'm the one who's trying to make up my mind."

"And there's nothing wrong with that," Julia assured her. "You need to take your time. And why shouldn't they be impressed with you? Maybe I wasn't here for you as much as I should have been, but among the four of us we raised a lovely, intelligent young woman."

"Mama, I just can't get over it, that you knew right away."

Julia laughed again in high, crystal notes.

"To tell you the truth, I'd always thought I was saving this talk for Joanne. She was always my free spirit, especially after she lived in Paris for a couple of years after graduation. But if Jo was involved with any Europeans she must have kept it to herself."

Denise sighed audibly. "Let's just see how things go for a while, Mama. No sense in getting excited over something that might never happen."

"I've got news for you, baby girl." Julia carefully rose from her chair and headed back to her cooking. "You two might not have had the benefit of clergy, as my mother used to say, but it has already happened. The rest is in your four hands and two hearts."

Chapter 26

Lynnette Adams-Vaughn readjusted the straw tote bag on her left shoulder, then wearily resumed her trudge up 17th Street. She'd felt quite faint earlier during Ann Gary's noon reading, but she'd recovered sufficiently to stay for the entire program and bid her former roommate good luck as she set out on her book tour.

The relentless sun and high humidity felt lethal on this August afternoon. Neither did much to ease Lynn's blinding headache, one of many she'd suffered lately. And what was more odd, considering the oppressive heat, she wasn't even perspiring.

She considered lighting a cigarette as she

stood in a stick's worth of shade, waiting for the traffic signal to change; it was too hot even for that. At least now she could see the lower end of U Street where New Hampshire crossed 17th...Neecy! The apartment building where her younger sister lived gave off shimmering waves of heat about three blocks ahead.

"Thank you, Jesus," she whispered as she stepped off the curb. The prospect of air-conditioning, something to take the edge off the pain, and a cool drink quickened her steps a little. And perhaps when her agony subsided, she could tease out the latest details of her youngest sister's love life.

About ten minutes later Lynn climbed the stairs and used the phone hanging by the entrance door to be buzzed in. She almost felt better as she reached the third floor landing. She knocked on Neecy's door instead of using her key. That was the respectful thing to do, now that Denise had a man. But Lynn's knees nearly gave way when a thirtyish white male with long, taffy-brown hair opened the door.

"Hello, may I help you?" His tone was pleasant, curious.

Lynn shook her head in disbelief. Had her confusion led her into the wrong apartment building?

"I'm sorry...embarrassing... my sister's apartment...my head... This heat must be doing a job on me..." She seemed to have lost the ability to speak in complete sentences.

"You must be looking for Denise; she should be back in a few minutes. You're one of her sisters?" Not waiting for her answer, he opened the door wide and took her hand, gently steering her inside.

"Please come in and sit down, have something to drink. It's brutal out there today."

Lynn was so undone that she allowed him to take her by the arm and guide her to the couch. A laptop computer was propped open on the coffee table in front of her, its screen filled with figures she couldn't decipher. She shut her eyes, attempting to regain her bearings, and get some sense of what this white man was doing in Denise's apartment.

"We made fresh lemonade this morning; you must have some." Lynn noted the clipped consonants and the unfamiliar lilt of his speech. Was it English? Australian? Her brain was too fuzzy to identify the accent. She stared at the long tail of hair, gaping tank top, and the tiniest athletic shorts she'd ever seen as he marched purposefully into the kitchen. So little of his body was covered that he might as well have been naked.

The man returned with a tall glass of lemonade and a plate of sugar cookies. He set both on the coffee table in front of Lynn and perched on the sofa beside her, his hazel eyes round with concern.

"Are you sure you're all right? Sorry; I'm Ian Phillips, by the way." He extended a large, tanned hand toward her.

Lynn stared at him, her mind struggling in waves of pain and disbelief. Let him assume that her lack of enthusiasm was caused by heat prostration.

"Lynnette Adams-Vaughn."

"Lynnette! Of course you are," he exclaimed. "It's an honor and a pleasure to meet you. You're the principal of one of the charter schools, right? And you're the first relative of Neecy's I've met. But you've probably heard about me."

"You know Denise," Lynn replied with a trace of sarcasm. "She's so quiet you have to pry everything out of her."

"Yes, that's Neecy, all right," he agreed with a knowing chuckle. Lynn flinched; she didn't even like the way her sister's pet name sat on his lips. But as long as she was here, she figured she might as well get some basic information.

"And, ah, how do you known Denise?"

"We met at the agency at the beginning of the year. I was a contractor at the time. Neecy's boss had detailed her to my office to keep me out of trouble—now there's an impossible task! Both of us can be quite stubborn, so it was rough going at first. She decided early on not to have much to do with me. But because her beauty only exceeds her brilliance, I had to ask her out after the detail ended. It took some work on my part to convince her but..." He trailed off for a second, then looked at Lynn as if he could see clear through to her soul.

"Your sister is very special; I've come to care for her an awful lot," he admitted softly. "She's quite an amazing lady, but you already know that."

"She's something else, that's for sure." Lynn hid her displeasure behind a long sip of lemonade. Her last hope, that Ian Phillips was an overly familiar super, had evaporated.

Of course he walks around here like that. This is the man who's been taking up all Denise's time. This man is your sister's lover. This white man. His chiseled features and tall, lean physique probably made him a real head-turner in some circles, she thought. Yet the idea of him touching, kissing, lying down next to her sister and... Lynn took another long sip from her drink to keep from screaming, either from the pictures forming in her mind or the throbbing pain on the right side of her head.

Ian hunched forward to punch a few keys on the laptop, then turned back toward her again.

"Denise has a programming course on Saturdays, you know."

Lynn turned a baleful glance in his direction.

"No, I can't say that I did. Otherwise I sure wouldn't have come here."

"Sorry, I didn't mean to imply..." He seemed concerned that he might have insulted her. "It's just that she should be back any minute now."

Lynn bristled. He was staring at her again. Nice eyes, Denise had said.

"That's a beautiful dress you're wearing,

Lynn. Does the pattern have special significance?"

"Uh-uh." She closed her eyes and leaned back, resting her head against the upright sofa cushion. Yeah, I'm ignoring you, you nasty son of a bitch, she thought. All those years in the church wasted because I must be both dead and in Hell with this dumb white boy who's screwing Denise—Jesus! How the hell did this one get past me? Can't even have a damn cigarette. A bullet to the head's starting to look good, compared to this. Couldn't hurt much more, at least...

Denise could not help smiling to herself as she turned the corner onto 17th Street. She was sailing through her class with Ian helping her over the rough spots. Perhaps she could think of a way to thank him. She could show her appreciation as soon as she walked through the door and perhaps for the rest of the afternoon.

The city's heat burned through the soles of her flat sandals. This morning they had talked about driving down to Bethany on the south Delaware Coast after midnight. In this heat the beach was definitely looking better all the time. But first she needed to go upstairs and take care of her man.

She could hear footsteps hurrying to the door as soon as she inserted the key. Ian pulled the door open, grinning broadly. Dropping her purse and tote bag, she jumped into his arms. Her kiss trapped his tongue in her mouth, teasing him until she heard him sigh. But as she slipped her hands inside the elastic band of his shorts he froze and gently pushed her away. Puzzled by his resistance, she looked into his eyes. He grinned sheepishly.

"Uh, we've got company, babe." He stepped aside, allowing her a clear view of Lynn's grim expression. Denise's eyes grew as round as Lynn's were narrow.

"Lynn!" she shrieked. "You never said–" She was still clinging to Ian, fearful she would collapse without his support.

Lynn glared back silently, arms crossed, tapping her right foot against a leg of the coffee table. Let Denise twist in the wind for a while, she decided, just like I did when the big white boy opened the door.

"Excuse me, ladies, I just need to..." He strolled over to the coffee table and turned the laptop so it faced Denise. "Babe, I think this might help with what you asked me about last night. And that trip we were talking about this morning? I'm still well up for it if you are; I'll fill up the Jeep while I'm out."

"Do you really have to go right now?" Denise was pleading with her eyes and her voice. As long as Ian stayed in the apartment she knew Lynn couldn't harm her. If he left, all bets were off.

"You remember the guy I met at the last trade show? I promised I'd look at the cabling in his new office and," he lifted her wrist to look at her watch, "I'll be late in about ten minutes. One of the many bad habits your sister is slowly purging from my life," he added, looking at Lynn.

"How nice of her," Lynn mumbled, cutting her eyes at Denise.

"Lynn, it's been a pleasure." Ian extended his hand to her again, but Lynn simply stared at him, keeping her arms folded across her thin chest. He seemed oblivious to both her rudeness and the chill that hung between the two women.

"I hope I can see you and meet everyone else soon. And you," he said, pulling Denise close to him, "I'll see around six." Ian gave her a leisurely kiss that seemed to resound off the walls when they parted. "Love you, babe." Grabbing his keys, he hurried out with a wave and a smile.

Both sisters watched the door shut. When the slap of Ian's sandals could no longer be heard on the stairs, Lynn struggled off the couch.

"I have always respected your place," Lynn began, "but right now I have got to have a cigarette. In fact, you really want me to have this cigarette. It will give me something to do while you figure out when you were going to say something, babe." The endearment dripped acid, coming from Lynn. Her hands trembled as she tried to light the cigarette she had drawn from her purse. She leaned against the kitchen doorjamb for support.

"Was it going to be right before the wedding, in the church bridal room? Oh yeah: 'Mama, Lynn, Joanne, did ya know?' And we'd all say, 'Hmm, we were wondering what all those white people were doing on the groom's side; must be one unusual brother!' Or was it going to be in the hospital, so we'd be wondering what the white boy was doing in your room holding your dingy little baby? Is he the doctor? Lord no–that's the daddy! What were you thinking!" She did not give Denise an opportunity to answer.

"But," Lynn continued, arms waving, her cigarette tracing curls of smoke, "but I should have known something was up. Our little Denise being flown up to New York for the weekend? I knew something about that didn't sound right but I was so happy for you I wanted to believe... Yeah, nice build, nice eyes, nice everything! And for what? Just so he can use you like a whore every Saturday night until you're too tired to hold your head up on Sunday?"

"Stop it!" Denise shouted.

"I'm not the one who needs to stop! You need to stop because you're the one who's gonna get hurt, not him, not me."

"What are you talking about? We love each other; we're just doing what people in love do. Or can't you remember?"

"Just tell me; what are you getting out of this?"

"That's a stupid question. What do you get out of Preston?"

"This is not about Preston! Preston's people never enslaved my people! Preston's people never degraded me or my sisters!" Lynn lowered her voice. Her tone became quiet, almost pleading. "Is there something you need? Is it money? If you need money you have a family, you can come to us. You don't have to humiliate yourself this way…"

Denise suddenly banged her fist against the wall beside her, shocking Lynn into silence.

"Damn it, Lynn! I know what your problem is. You just can't believe that a man like Ian could possibly care about me, plain and simple. Poor little Denise can barely get a man and can't keep one when she does. That's the way it's been and that's the way it should always be. So here comes Ian, and he's smart and funny and rich and he's white, so what could he possibly see in our poor little Neecy?"

"That fool's only interested in using you as his 'black experience,'" Lynn shot back. "How long had he known you when he decided he couldn't keep it in his pants any more? Three weeks? Three dates? Three cups of coffee?"

"Try five months, sis. And did it ever occur to you that we both decided when we'd sleep together? If I went only by your standards I could say that I haven't opened a door or my purse since May. But that isn't what matters to me. If I don't know anything else, I know Ian loves me."

"Of course he says he loves you! Girl, you might be smart in books but you're a few bricks shy of a load when it comes to real life! Do you think for a minute that boy really loves you? Sure, he'll be in your bed tonight and maybe a few nights after that, but the day will come when you'll be looking for him and he won't show up and you'll call him and he won't pick up the phone. The next thing you know, he'll be smiling back at you from the wedding announcements in the *Herald*, next to some little blonde bitch wearing a dress I'd have to take out a second mortgage for! You'll just be a memory he uses to make himself come inside his little white wife."

"When you thought Ian was an 'up and coming young brother,' you thought it was great. 'Tell him it's okay to rest in between,' wink-wink-nudge. But now that you've seen him, I'm a whore!"

"That's all you are to him! It's history, girl, history! You know what white men have always done to black women in this country. And damn near everywhere else, for that matter."

"I know about all that, Lynn. You and Daddy beat that stuff into my head every day for as long as I can remember. But Ian is just one person. He's not all white men."

"That's what you think." Lynn's eyes narrowed for a moment. "Wait, wait a minute. He's the one you came crying into my office about a couple of months back, isn't he? He did that to you? I hadn't seen you fall apart like that since Daddy died; I thought you were having a nervous breakdown! And you're letting him use you this way? Girl, are you crazy?"

Denise looked away while Lynn took another draw on her cigarette. Calmed by the infusion of nicotine, Lynn decided to take another approach.

"Look, Denise. I'm just trying to keep things real here. I know we act as if we don't respect you sometimes, calling you 'baby girl' and things like that when you're nearly thirty years old. You're a grown woman," she said, lowering her voice. "And with Kenny you became accustomed to having a partner who was constantly available to fulfill your physical needs. I understand that. In fact, Kenny mentioned to Preston one time—"

"Mentioned what?" Denise asked warily.

"Oh, he just said that he hadn't expected you to–well–he hadn't thought you would be as eager or adventurous sexually, that he was pleasantly surprised by that."

"That's just great!" Denise began to pace back and forth. "Kenny had to tell Preston about what was totally personal between us and Preston had to tell you. Did you tell Jo? Obviously not, unless I missed the headline: 'Civil Servant Is Real Freak!' Thank you for that small favor."

"All I'm saying is, you can't always wait until true love comes along. There's nothing wrong with that, either. Preston knows so many nice young fellas and he'd love to hook you up–"

"That sounds horrible," Denise protested, "like letting a cat out at night to mate with whatever's in the neighborhood."

"Isn't that just about what you're doing now? And I know it can't be that good! I can understand why he gives you jewelry and takes you places, but what about your needs? He can't be doing all that much for you in bed."

Denise collapsed onto the sofa, shaking her head.

"I can't believe you're saying this. If you

must know, he's pretty amazing."

"I find that hard to believe! Listen to you, the dateless wonder! You couldn't even get a boy to walk you around the block when you were in high school! When did you lose your virginity? It hasn't even been five years, has it? I'd had an abortion and more scares than I could count at an age when you were still juggling test tubes at some damn science fair! But hey, you're the expert! Move over Dr. Kinsey, Dr. Ruth, and Sherry Hite," Lynn shouted, "because the real sex authority is in the house this afternoon!" Lynn's desperation had driven her to outright cruelty, but she was willing to use any means to deliver her sister from the evil that was Ian Phillips. As she expected, these last darts hit home; Denise began to cry. But she kept fighting back.

"I know he's totally focussed on me whenever we're together that way," she whimpered through her tears. "He's not thinking about work, or some other woman he wants to talk to, or sports, or anything else, just me. It's just the two of us, totally into the moment. I don't have any complaints and I know he doesn't."

Lynn knew she was running out of arguments and patience. She aimed full throttle for guilt.

"How could you do this to us, Denise? How could you!"

"I haven't done anything to anybody! I'm just trying to be with someone who loves me. You have that; why can't I?"

"Don't try to play stupid with me, little girl! I can't believe I've been looking in your face for the last three months hoping maybe, just maybe, you finally got it right this time. And all the time you could not have been more wrong, playing the whore for this white bastard who's probably laughing at you every time you spread your legs! I hate to say it, but I'm ashamed. Ashamed for you since obviously don't have enough sense to be ashamed for yourself!

"I'm almost glad Daddy's gone because this certainly would have killed him! When I think about what he stood for, what being a member of our family means...And Daddy adored you, Denise! Not only were you his precious late baby, the walking, talking proof of his masculinity, but you loved math and science, where Jo and I were hopeless failures! You were the one he put that little desk in his study for; not me, not Jo! I can still remember being too ashamed to ask him for help when I couldn't make heads or tails out of basic statistics at Morris, while he had you drawing root diagrams when you were in fifth grade!

"And when he was dying all he could think about was you. He was so torn at the end, barely able to scratch out a 'D' on his scratch pad, but always refusing if Mother or I asked if we should get you. He didn't want you to see what he'd become; he wanted us to protect you from that. He had such high hopes for you; if he had lived long enough to see you degrading yourself this way I know it would have destroyed him!

"You need to stop it! Stop it right–" Lynn halted in mid-sentence, her eyelids fluttering. Denise froze, still angry, but with a sense that something had gone terribly wrong. As she watched, the cigarette flipped end over end out of Lynn's fingers and her sister's tall, slim frame gradually slid to the floor like an abandoned marionette. Denise rushed to her side, screaming.

"Lynn! Lynnie!" She knelt to check her sister's pulse; it was weak and her breathing was labored. A thin line of drool leaked from the side of Lynn's mouth. Denise felt a sensation of wetness; she looked down and realized she was kneeling in a puddle of urine. She jumped to her feet and ran for the telephone, nearly tripping over the coffee table in her haste. She dialed 911 with one eye on Lynn while she rubbed the reddening bruise on her leg.

"Nine-one-one? Please, I need an ambulance; my sister's unconscious! A minute ago. Her pulse is weak and she's barely breathing. Address?" Her panic had risen so quickly she could barely remember her own name. Denise's hands were shaking when she hung up the phone. She returned to where Lynn lay by the kitchen doorway and kneeled beside her again.

"It's okay, Lynnie, it's okay," she whispered. "The ambulance should be here soon—it's just a few blocks." The wail of a siren in the near distance seemed to confirm her words. She prayed it was on its way to them. But the front door, she remembered, needed to be unlocked. Otherwise the paramedics wouldn't be able to reach them. She didn't want to leave Lynn but they had to get up to the third floor somehow.

Denise stood up and grabbed one end of the coffee table. She dragged it across the floor, ignoring the sharp pain in her lower back. Propping the front door open, she crawled across the tabletop and out into the hallway. She limped over to 3B and knocked as hard as she could. She stepped back slightly while she waited for someone to answer, trying to see if Lynn stirred or spoke. There was no movement inside her neighbor's apartment, but she could hear a series of loud knocks from the bottom of the stairwell.

Denise ran down the steps, her dress damp with perspiration. She flung open the heavy front door, nearly striking the paramedic who carried the front end of the stretcher. Barely pausing to apologize, she directed them to follow her to the third floor. The sturdy young man and young woman easily pushed the table aside and began working on Lynn.

After what seemed an eternity to Denise the paramedics lifted Lynn onto the stretcher and fastened the securing belts over the orange blanket. They were taking Lynn to Metro Hospital, they advised as their hands flew. She would probably need emergency surgery. Denise would have to take a cab and bring insurance information. The man and woman cued each other and stood, lifting the stretcher with military precision.

Denise was still standing in the hall holding the door as the siren keened and the ambulance pulled away into traffic. She stared into her apartment as if she were waiting to be invited in. Then her eyes focussed on Ian's laptop. She'd tossed it onto the couch when she moved the coffee table. He'd wonder why when he came back home. Home...

She roused herself and walked back into the apartment. The cigarette butt still lay on the carpet. She noticed the burnt spot where she'd stubbed it out. She picked it up and walked into the kitchen to throw it away. Then she tore off a paper towel and soaked up the mess where Lynn had fallen. When she was done, she went to use the bathroom and wash her hands. She didn't bother to turn on the light. She did not need to see the red toothbrush, cheap razor and can of shaving cream.

Denise took a last look around before she left and saw the computer. She went over to the couch and sat down, placing the laptop on her knees. She exited the program, powered down, and closed the lid. Setting the unit back on the table, she thought about leaving a note. That would have been the decent thing to do.

Denise rose to her feet, grabbing Lynn's

purse and her own by the straps. The room's quiet roared in her ears as if she were under water. She walked to the door and closed it behind her without making a sound.

Chapter 27

Denise was filled with a surreal sense of indifference for the rest of the afternoon, as if she had become an observer in her own life. As if another pair of legs had stuck to the seat of the airless taxi on the way to the hospital. As if a stranger had calmly negotiated the insurance paperwork at the emergency desk. As if she were merely an empathetic concierge calling Preston, her mother, Joanne, telling them where Lynn was and what had happened.

Preston arrived first. Even from the depths of her apathy Denise could tell that Commander Vaughn was well-known and respected among hospital personnel. He'd been ushered immediately to the interior emergency area while she had been told to remain in the public waiting room. He emerged about ten minutes later, looking for her. He sat down next to her on the battered sofa and talked about MRIs and neurologists, clot-busters and surgeries. She took it all in without comment. Too worried to notice Denise's inattention, he rushed back to Lynn's side.

Julia and Joanne eventually appeared, quiet as shadows. Her mother hugged her desperately, squeezing Denise as if she could make her daughter part of her own flesh. Denise wanted to scream and keep screaming until she roused all the sick and the dying from their beds.

Marcus and Malcolm soon followed. Marcus was trying very hard to behave as he thought a young man ought to, but Denise could see the tears floating just below the surface. Malcolm just sat quietly, staring at the backs of his hands. They sat together on a couple of worn couches, barely conscious of the TV grinding out its tired Saturday afternoon schedule.

Preston reappeared half an hour later, reporting that Lynn was about to undergo surgery to remove blood clots from the brain cavity. He could barely form the words, and her mother and Joanne cried openly. Denise simply stared into the distance.

Ian pulled up in front of the apartment building a few minutes after six. Hopping out quickly, he walked around the Jeep, pulling down its tarp cover, making sure it was fastened securely at all points. The bank of greenish-black clouds overhead emitted dull growls of thunder. A streetlight flickered on, illuminating the eerie, early darkness.

They were in for a serious blow, he knew it. He paused on the steps, his eyes scanning the western sky. It was the kind of storm that could sit on top of the city for hours, or dog them all the way to the coast if they chose to make the trip. Perhaps they'd take a pass and just order in. Eating Chinese in bed naked on a stormy summer night, he thought, could be better than the beach. Fat drops splattered onto his head and around his feet. Lightning popped close, as bright as a photographer's flash. Ian pictured himself licking a dab of plum sauce from the deep curve of Denise's back, just before it curved steeply into her magnificent rear. He unlocked the front door and headed upstairs.

"Neece?" he called out as he entered the apartment. The rooms were dark but for intermittent flashes of lightning. He moved forward carefully, feeling his way until he could switch on the overhead light in the kitchen. Nothing and no one there. He charged down the hall toward the bedroom, then poked his head into the bathroom. He returned to the living area, looking for a note or at least a clue to where she'd gone. This wasn't like Denise; she usually called or scribbled a message. He went back to the bedroom to check the answering machine only to be greeted with a big, red zero. A bolt of lightning struck close to the building and the thunderous reply shook the floor under his feet. Rain began to fall in thick, gray sheets. He didn't like this, not knowing where Denise was, especially under these conditions. But he was her lover, not her father, and she was more grown-up in a lot of ways than he'd ever be. He decided to lie down for a few minutes; she'd either show or call soon.

Fifteen minutes later Ian was turning the pages of Denise's personal telephone book.

Each entry was exactly alike: names in blue ink, addresses and telephone numbers in pencil, all in Denise's precise hand.

"Begin at the beginning," he muttered, "'Adams, Julia.'" He dialed the number and listened to it ring for a few seconds, then switched the phone off. He exhaled heavily, then erupted into a coughing fit, realizing he'd been holding his breath. Breathe, old man, breathe, Josh would urge whenever he saw Ian heading over the edge. Ian forced himself to concentrate, breathing deeply and slowly, holding both hands out until they stopped shaking. Then he dialed the number again and listened to it ring.

"Plan B," he grunted. "'Adams-Vaughn, Lynn. Vaughn, Preston.'" She'd be home by now. But she'd had that awful headache, remember? Perhaps Denise went with her, to make sure she got there safely. The number rang, then clicked into a deep bass greeting: "Vaughn residence, please leave a message at the tone."

He kicked off his sandals and stretched out on the bed, leaning back against the pillows on Denise's side. The number of names he could recognize had been reduced by half. He turned the page. "Mitchell, Karyn Baker."

And beneath her, "Mitchell, Terence." Answering machines picked up at both numbers.

Ian hesitated, shaking out his hair and pulling it through the elastic band again before he thumbed his way to the end of the book.

"Last chance," he mumbled as he entered the number. "'Thurman, Joanne Adams. Thurman, Maurice.'" More ringing again, until a male voice uttered "Thurman residence." Ian hesitated, unprepared for this final success. He sat up straight, as if the person on the other end could see him.

"Joanne or Maurice Thurman, please." He used the British pronunciation, Morris.

"This is Mau-reece Thurman," Maurice corrected.

"Maurice, I'm Ian Phillips, a friend of your sister-in-law, Denise Adams. I'm calling because," he faltered, suddenly feeling ridiculous, "we were supposed to meet at her place. She's not here, she hasn't called, and she didn't leave a note, none of which is like her, and with this storm..." He gestured toward the window as if Maurice could see it. He hoped his concern didn't sound silly as he put it into words.

There was silence on the other end, then a roaring noise followed by a high-pitched squeal: "Dad-dee!"

"Hello?" Ian ventured, not sure whether the connection still held.

"Yes, I'm here. Sorry, the girls are a little excited with the storm; it's bad over here, too. Can you hold on for a second?"

Ian could hear an attempt to cover the mouthpiece, and Maurice's muffled voice saying there was nothing to be afraid of. Then he came back on the line.

"You're Denise's friend." It was a statement, not a question. When Ian didn't respond, Maurice continued. "About six-two, slim build, long hair, glasses. Hopkins Grill, one night back, say, June?"

"Could have been," Ian admitted uneasily. What was this guy, a cop? Yes, exactly what he'd been. Denise had told him that.

"Hmm. Look, uh, Ian?" Maurice hesitated.

"Yes?" Ian's hand tightened around the handset.

"There's been an emergency. It's not Denise," he added quickly, "but she had to get Lynn to the hospital this afternoon. I'm sure she's still there with my wife and their mother. I haven't talked to Jo for about an hour but Lynn might have had a stroke."

"Jesus! Which hospital?" asked Ian, scrambling to his feet.

Maurice hesitated again.

"Ian, man, can you hear me out for a minute?"

"Excuse me?" What the hell did Maurice have to tell him that was more important than getting to Denise right away?

"Look, man, I'm not trying to get in your business, but if you really care about Denise you won't go running over there right now."

"And why not?" Ian snapped, feeling a rush of anger.

"Look, I don't know you, I don't know anything about you, except that you're white. I saw you out with Denise that evening. Joanne knows, too, and we're the only ones in the family who do. Now, don't get me wrong, I understand how it is. You're a man, you want to run over there, show the flag, take care of your woman. You want to do the decent, honorable thing; no problem, usually. But this isn't a 'no problem' situation. There are at least two reasons why Denise didn't feel she could introduce you to the family: Lynn and Preston Vaughn. I can't speak for Mrs.

Adams, but Lynn and Preston, there's no telling how they'd react. And Lynn's condition being pretty much touch and go as it is... I'm not asking you to do this for me, I'm asking for Denise. I'm just suggesting you do it on her terms, let her make the rules here. Now that you know where she is and that she's all right, please don't make things any more complicated than they need to be right now. Do you understand what I'm saying?"

Ian slumped forward, relieved to know Denise was all right, yet shaken by the news she'd never mentioned him to her family. After so much time, after he'd introduced her to his folks, after she'd sworn she loved him? He was familiar with her shyness, her tendency to keep her feelings well hidden, but this was entirely different. Here he was, on the verge of making an old-fashioned, down-on-his-knees proposal, but only three members of her closely-knit family even knew he existed. And their knowledge had only come by chance.

"You still there, man?" Maurice asked.

"Yes. Okay. I'll try to wait for a little while," he conceded.

"Good, good. I know Denise will appreciate it." Maurice cleared his throat, then fell silent.

"Thanks, Maurice." Ian knew he needed to end the call. "And good to meet you, sort of."

"Same here, man."

Ian heard Denise's key turn in the door around nine-forty-five. He jumped up from the couch to meet her. Denise's clothes were completely soaked from the storm. Her face was drawn and tired from the hours of waiting.

"Why didn't you call me?" he nearly shouted. She froze in the doorway, almost seeming to look through him.

"I'm sorry," she answered, her voice flat and expressionless. "It's Lynnie. They're pretty sure she had a stroke when she was here this afternoon. It happened after you left. May I come in now?"

He tried to take her hand but she brushed by him, heading straight for the bedroom. Ian shut the front door, then followed her down the short hallway.

"God, Neecy! Why didn't you call me?" he demanded, following her into the bedroom. "I had no idea; I would have come to be with you. How is she?"

"She's been through surgery, she's stable, but we still don't know how much damage..." She sat heavily on the side of the bed and slipped off her waterlogged sandals. He went to the closet, pulled out the silk robe he had given her and laid it across her pillow.

"The doctor told us to go home."

Ian sat down next to her and closed his beefy hands around hers.

"I'm sorry. I'm so sorry, babe. Is there anything I can do?" He lifted her fingers to his lips.

"No," she replied wearily, pulling her hands from his, allowing them to drop into her lap.

"How are you holding up? You look exhausted." He reached over to put his arm around her but she arched away from him.

"I'm–I'm okay. I just really need some time to myself."

"Are you sure? I could run a bath for you, or rub your back. Or both, if you want me to."

"I said no!" Her voice was suddenly sharp, but then she drew a long sigh. "I'm sorry. I guess I'm just tired. I can take care of myself. I just really, really need to be alone right now."

He stood reluctantly, not ready to leave her side.

"Sure I can't fix you anything to eat?"

A flash of lightning illuminated her blank stare.

"Okay, okay." He walked out slowly. The door closed behind him as he stepped into the hallway.

He perched on the edge of the couch and tried to distinguish the sounds of water running into the bathtub from rain lashing the kitchen windows. There had been an undercurrent of resentment toward him during his exchange with Denise that he couldn't understand. It made him uneasy. He'd wanted to tell her that he'd spoken to Maurice, but was glad he'd held back, sensing she wouldn't have handled that piece of news well, either.

The minutes ticked by, punctuated by the sounds of wind-driven rain and occasional rolls of thunder. Ian flopped back on the couch, trying to talk himself out of his apprehension. He tried replacing Lynnette with an image of Andy to imagine how Denise might feel. She's tired and she's scared, he rationalized. I'd probably be on edge myself. That must be all it is. Sure, her sister isn't out of the woods yet, but Neecy will get a better handle on it after a little food and sleep. He began to relax a bit, stretching his legs out along the length of the couch and closing his eyes.

Denise emerged about an hour later, dressed in a frayed old tee shirt. Ian sat up, wondering why she wasn't wearing her silk as she usually did. She ignored his questioning look and padded into the kitchen. He pulled himself up off the couch to follow her.

She was standing in the dark room, staring at the refrigerator as if she couldn't figure out how to open the door. Ian decided it was better to act than ask more questions. He walked in and flipped on the ceiling light.

"I'm hungry," he announced as he brushed by her. Opening the refrigerator, he reached in and stacked a carton of eggs, cheese, and sliced ham under his chin. "So what else is new?" he answered himself as he balanced the ingredients on the way over to the stove. Reaching into one of the lower cabinets, he pulled out a shallow frying pan.

"It's not bangers and mash, but this munch should fix us up jolly good now, what!" he blustered, turning to observe her reaction. His affected brogue usually provoked a laugh but Denise gave him a weary look instead, making her way over to the small table and dropping heavily onto one of the chairs. Making no further mention of sausage and potatoes, Ian quickly set about preparing a light supper. He broke four eggs into the pan; when the omelet was ready he cut it into two sections and added slices of buttered toast to both portions.

Denise didn't respond immediately when he set the plate before her. She stared at it over the mug of chamomile tea, thinking of the shunt on the back of Lynn's hand. After a few minutes passed she reluctantly picked up her fork, cut off a few pieces of omelet and nibbled at them. She flinched when Ian pulled out the adjacent chair and sat down. He smiled and reached over to squeeze her hand reassuringly, then tucked into his eggs.

She put her fork down and watched him as he ate, eyeing him critically as she hadn't done in a long time. She noted the straight brown hair, now with lighter streaks from the sun; the pale skin under its summery cast; thin lips that flexed slightly as he chewed; one bare foot resting atop an equally bare knee.

Who was the sum of these parts? she wondered. The one man she'd ever loved? A white man who loved her, not perfectly, but more than anyone she'd ever known? She was more sure of his feelings for her than she was of her own. What did she really know about love anyway? How could she talk about love or sex when she barely knew her own heart?

Denise looked up to meet his eyes. Ian had finished eating and was watching her, his square chin resting on one hand. His expression was questioning, yet gentle, much as it had been the very first time he'd touched her.

"I know it's hard to work up much of an appetite under the circumstances, so I won't nag you to eat." He looked down at her plate, which was still half full. "At least I'll try not to. Is that all you can manage right now?"

"Yes." She looked away, shamed by his compassion despite her abrupt manner.

"All right, babe," he sighed. He stood and carried both plates over to the sink. "I'll wash up. Why don't you go on ahead and lie down?"

She nodded and tried to muster a weak smile for his benefit before she left the kitchen. Ian could be very sweet when he wanted to. And he usually wanted to, where she was concerned. About ten minutes later he came into the bedroom and began to undress.

"Everything's done: we're all washed up, I

checked the door and put out the lights. Is there anything else you need me to do, babe?"

"Uh-uh," she mumbled, burrowing deeper into her pillow. Her eyes flickered open for a moment, catching a glimpse of him as he stood next to her side of the bed. He walked around to the other side and climbed in, sliding under the sheet until his body lay flush against hers. She could feel his erection, thick and heavy, pressing against her thigh. She winced and tried to squirm away.

"Please forgive my friend there," he begged. "I know you're probably not in the mood to make love. I understand, but I'm afraid empathy isn't his strong suit. Just ignore him and eventually he'll go away. But Denise," he whispered, "may I hold you?"

He had called her by name, not Neecy, not babe. She didn't dare turn to look at him, not then. She knew his eyes on her would be soft and sleepy, still holding a glimmer of desire should she change her mind.

"I'd like that," she replied quietly. He obliged her with a shift of his weight and the favor of warmth that seemed to flow into her bones.

"I am so sorry about your sister, about Lynn," he murmured, his lips brushing her ear. "I know you love her and I know you're scared. But it's times like this I want you to come to me, Denise. Please don't shut me out because..." He trailed off, his fingers carefully combing through her braids. "Because that scares me more than anything else I know."

She reached back and touched Ian's hand; he gratefully pressed it to his lips. Relieved that he had not lost her, Ian arranged his body around hers, his hands clasped just below her breasts. Denise lay motionless, listening to the rhythm of his heart. And once Ian's breath became deep and steady, Denise's heart and mind went to war.

Whore. A simple word, one syllable. An expression that drew blood and burned down to the bone. A word never to be exchanged between sisters. Unless it fit...Lynnie, Lynnie, please...

What could he have said to Lynn? He didn't have to say anything; it was enough that he was there, walking around as if he owned the place, owned me. Lynnie's going to die and the last thing she ever said to me was that I'm a whore and that she was so ashamed. I want her to live and I want one more chance with her. A chance for her to look in my face and call me something besides...I should never have had him in my place, never should have let him into my life. I always knew it was wrong, so wrong.

Lord, just give me the chance to make this right. I won't ask for anything else, ever. Please, just bring my Lynnie back. I've lived my whole life without Ian but I can't begin to imagine life without Lynnie. I can learn to be strong. Please, please...

Chapter 28

Denise had been awake for at least an hour when she felt Ian raise his head from the pillow beside her. She could visualize him even with her back turned, propped up on his elbows, trying to determine whether she was awake. Lord help her if he nuzzled the back of her neck or ran his hand down her thigh, or worse, did both at the same time.

"Neece?" His baritone whisper was sleepy and tinged with hope. For what? Her forgiveness? Her body?

She frowned, pulling the damp sheet up around her. Last night's rain had turned to steam; their bodies were moist with a light sheen of perspiration. Denise felt his hand strong on her thigh, fingers creeping toward the cleft between her legs. She dragged herself away from his tentative exploration, off the side of the bed and to her feet. She took a stumbling step in the direction of the hallway, her head reeling from the sudden movement.

"Babe?" Ian swept across the bed in one motion and rushed to her side. He lifted her arms with his own, inviting her to rest her weight against him. Denise stiffened against his touch, shaking her head from side to side until she could speak.

"No!" She pried his fingers loose and set off down the hall, pulling her old T-shirt down over her hips as she went. Ian followed as quickly as he was able, pausing only to step into a pair of shorts. Denise slammed the front door shut as he entered the living room, then slung the Sunday paper she'd retrieved onto the couch. She marched deliberately toward the bedroom, her heels banging hard against the old hardwood floors. Ian stepped in her path, blocking her exit. She exhaled angrily and stomped back in the direction of the kitchen. When he attempted to follow her there she quickly reversed direction and headed back down the hall. She barreled into the bedroom headfirst, slamming the door shut behind her.

Ian slumped onto the end of the couch, running both hands through his hair. Soon he could hear sound of rushing water from the bathroom. A few minutes passed before he stood again and went to try the bedroom door. Locked. He rattled the knob in exasperation, finally smacking it with the flat of his hand. No response.

Ian gave up, cursing and slouching back toward the kitchen. He popped a cookie into his mouth and set about making coffee.

Twenty minutes had passed when he heard the high-pitched squeak of spinning faucets. The gush of the shower was soon replaced by the yank and slam of drawers and closets. Ian winced as he thumbed through the *Herald*. He suspected this would be one of those days when anything he said would be wrong. Saying nothing would likely be wrong as well.

This was the first Sunday morning in months they had not enjoyed a slow, natural awakening, gratefully embracing each other and making love, sometimes not putting their feet on the floor until well past noon. He watched the last drops of coffee slide into the glass pot, absently wondering when the current siege of odd, ill temper would end.

"Bring back my sweet, sweet Denise," Ian half-sang to himself as he rose to get a mug from the cabinet. He stood at the counter and filled the cup. He was about to take the first sip when he sensed someone watching him. He looked up to see Denise standing in the doorway.

She was wearing a mustard-brown dress he'd never seen. The shapeless garment billowed around her small frame and hung nearly to her ankles. She had pulled her braids back from her face, not leaving a tendril or two loose to soften the effect. The absence of jewelry and makeup made her appear very young. Ian quickly renounced his plan to maintain a respectful silence.

"Coffee, babe?" he offered, extending the cup toward her. She lifted a hand in refusal.

"No, no thank you," she said softly.

Ian breathed out a sigh of relief. The rampage had ended; his sweet, sad Denise had returned.

"My poor little love," he murmured, setting the cup down, approaching her with arms outstretched. Denise gave him a wary look, then took a step back. Ian was surprised by her reaction but glanced down to see he was wearing only his briefs. He looked up at her with as innocent a grin as he could manage.

"Sorry, I've not been able to reach the closet for a bit. I can hop in the shower right now, then we can get breakfast and go to hospital–" He paused, seeing her shake her head slowly, negatively.

"Ian, I'm sorry," Denise began, "but there's something I have to tell you. I–"

"You needn't say a word," he interrupted, his smile warming with reassurance. "Only a fool wouldn't understand why you were so angry before. I know, remember, I know what it's like to see someone you care for..." He trailed off, trusting Denise would understand he meant Josh. But she shook her head once more and folded her arms across her chest.

"No, it's not about that, although I'm sorry for carrying on like I did with no explanation. It was more about what I need to tell you."

"Then what is it, babe?" Ian tried to keep an even tone despite a growing sense he wasn't going to like her answer.

"Ian,   after   what   happened yesterday...Well, you don't really know about that, do you?"

"Tell me," he urged.

"Lynn and I were fighting," she admitted, her features falling with the hard memory. "Fighting about you. I always knew, I told you Lynn would react exactly the way she did. She said terrible things. She said you–" Denise hesitated; she didn't want to hurt him any more than she had to. "I called her on all of it. Everything she said I shoved right back in her face. And right after she started on what Daddy would have thought, that's when she..." Tears started to her eyes when she realized she was standing where Lynn had fallen. She took a deep breath, struggling to go on, to finish what she had to do.

"That's when Lynn fell. And I called an ambulance and, you know. And so I was with her all afternoon, and sitting there so long... Well, Ian, I realized she was right. About some, a lot of what she'd said." Denise looked up to gauge Ian's reaction. He hadn't moved an inch. He stood across from her, nearly mirroring her posture, arms folded across his chest. She could see the left corner of his mouth twitch, imperceptibly at first, then settling into an odd, steady pulse. She pushed on.

"You need to understand, Ian, it's not personal. It's not really about you. It would be the same if you were the President or a movie star. As long as you were a white man. She was only trying to look out for me because she knows I'm not... To be honest, I don't think we should see each other any more." She clasped her hands together in front of herself like a little girl.

Ian was quiet, his eyes fixed on her, the lines across his forehead deepening.

"You're joking," he said at last. It was a statement, not a question.

"You know I would never joke about something this serious," she responded.

"Do I?" he snapped. "Because I desperately hope you are. I hope you're joking, or out of your mind with grief, or scared out of your mind because your sister nearly died before your eyes. Because if you're not..." His chest was expanding like a bellows with each breath.

"Because if I'm not, what?" Her tone darkened in answer to the perceived threat.

"No," he protested, raising his arms and taking a step forward. "Let's not do this. Things are bad enough with your sister so ill. I've stood in your shoes, Denise, for months I did. You lose someone, or you nearly lose someone and you just want to tear up everything else in your life.

"Babe," he continued, softening, "your sister's still here. If it had been otherwise your mom would have called. I really think she'll recover and be as contentious as ever. So there's no reason to throw us away simply because you're going through a rough patch with your family."

"This isn't about Lynn being sick," Denise insisted. "The fact is, there is no 'us,' if there ever was."

"Denise, how can you say–" Ian's voice surged with emotion. "I thought we settled this a long time ago, that we loved each other and that we wanted to be together."

"And I thought I did! I'd really started to believe the things we talked about were possible. But now I realize I'm not the kind of black woman who can be in an interracial relationship. Ian, I can't fight the world any more. Things are how they are. Look at you: you're a brilliant, healthy, white male in America. Anything is possible for you! Anything, that is, that you don't screw up by antagonizing everyone in your path. And you know what? Sometimes I think that I'm just another symbol of that.

"Look at me, you say, I did everything my

way! I got rich; I've got multi-million dollar corporations and the government depending on me to protect their networks! I didn't have to kiss ass in grad school or work my way up in some cutthroat, back-stabbing corporation for a hundred years only to be tossed out on my ass the day I turned thirty–five ! And you know what one of my best rewards is? I get to sleep with this hot little black chick every night and who among you who needs my product is going to tell me that I can't?"

"Oh, so it's all right for you to speak for what's inside my head?" Ian finally interrupted.

"I don't have to be inside your head," Denise shot back. "I know you! But I'm not like you, Ian. I just can't abandon everything I know and tell everyone to go to hell the way you do! I have things that are important to me, too! Family, history, traditions! Ian, you need to face it. Our time together has always seemed unreal to me. I don't know why. But it's as if I haven't even been myself. When I think that I allowed you to sleep with me in your parents' home..." She shook her head. "That's not me. I don't do things like that, or at least I didn't before I met you."

"You didn't seem to have a problem with

us yesterday morning."

"You're right. But yesterday afternoon, sitting there in that emergency room all those hours, I had a lot of time to think. Time I haven't had lately because you always seemed to fill it with your talk and your dreams and jokes and presents and sex.

"I've had a lot of fun the last couple of months, I can't deny that. I've enjoyed your company and sometimes even tried to imagine a future with you. But yesterday real life was up in my face for the first time in months. I know that it's time for me to wake up, grow up, and walk away from my part in your adolescent fantasy. But don't worry, you'll find another big-legged colored girl who'll be willing to stand behind you and sing doo-wop. I promise," she added dryly.

Ian's lean frame crumpled as if she'd landed a blow to his gut. "How can you say these things? I love you, Denise! I don't want anyone else, not now, not ever! Everything I've done, or said or dreamed about for the last seven months has been about you! About us! You want proof? Let me show you something." He went into the living room and quickly returned with several presentation folders marked with the symbol of a national investment house.

"Do you see this? Do you see what I was trying to read before I nearly went ballistic with worry about you last night? You're right, I'm starting to make a nice pile of money. For the longest time I didn't know what I had or where it was or how much of it I had blown. Do you know what this is for? It's for our kids, Denise! Yours and mine! If anyone had told me this time last year that I would get off my ass and start making plans for a real life, thinking of setting up a real firm, saving and making serious investments, I would have said he was out of his flaming mind! I even went to my parents for advice, and you know what that took! I wasn't going to make any final decisions without you, of course, but I just wanted to get things started so when I asked you to marry me—"

"Ian, you've asked me to marry you almost every day for the past two months."

"What's wrong with that? We love each other, don't we? Yes, I joke about it but I was planning to do it right; I was going to surprise you next month. I've already made the reservations at our favorite B&B in West Virginia; a jeweler friend of my parents is making your ring. I wanted everything to be special and have meaning, just for us. And then I was going to tell you about the plans for the firm, show you the blueprints for our home, all of that. Neecy, I'm only trying to say that everything I've tried to accomplish lately has been about us, you and me."

Denise stubbornly folded her arms, staring through and past him. "We shouldn't see each other any more. You'll have plenty of time to get your stuff together; I'll be at the hospital all day." She tried to walk away but Ian caught her hand, forcing her to turn and look at him.

"Denise, you are my future! Please don't tell me to go away! There isn't anywhere for me to go without you," he pleaded. You're my best friend, you've been like a business partner to me. You're my lover; I want you to be my wife, I want us to make a family together. Being with you has helped me find what I want my life to mean, as an individual, a husband, what kind of father I want to be. Being with you has changed me, changed both of us. Together we can do, be so much more than either of us ever could alone." She tried to pull away but he held her fast.

"I don't understand what this is, why this is all of a sudden! Help me understand. Did I do something wrong with your sister yesterday? Did I say something to make both of you angry? If I have, I'm sorry; just give me a chance to fix... Denise, I love you," he whispered. "Why are you doing this to me?"

"I'm not mad at you, Ian, and you have every right to hate me." Her tone was brisk. "I'm just making the choice I should have made months ago when you first asked me. You were right that night during the storm. You can't protect me. We never should have"

"We never should have what? Were you wrong about loving me, too? It was the first time you told me you loved me, that night." His hands trembled as he took hold of her shoulders. "How do you think I could ever hate you? How could I ever look into your eyes and even remember the meaning of the word?"

She tried to turn away, but he gathered her into his arms insistently. "Look at me, Denise! Look at me and tell me you don't love me anymore!"

She looked away, her resolve withering in the light of his honesty.

"Tell me, Denise, please tell me!" he begged. "We never should have what?"

"Don't—" she whispered, her eyes welling

with tears.

Ian took her face between his hands, raising her eyes to meet his own. She could see that he was on the brink of weeping himself as his lips touched hers. She could taste his warmth as it traveled directly to her heart. She could not savor these last moments and finish what she'd begun. She struggled to escape his embrace and backed slowly into the front room.

"You should try to get everything out by eight; that's when visiting hours end. I left the things that belong to you on the dresser." Denise could taste the tears coursing down her face. She turned and left the apartment, slamming the door behind her.

Karyn Mitchell hurtled off the elevator, only to come to an abrupt halt in front of the nurses' station for the intensive care unit. As usual, heads turned, the women's with envy of her expensive attire, the men desirous of the tightly packed curves on her slender frame.

Karyn hated hospitals, hated passing one more door opening on a sick or dying soul than she absolutely had to. Then she saw a small figure emerge from behind the door marked "Lavatory." Denise at that moment appeared frail as she had when she lay in this same hospital years before, struggling to maintain a hold on life. Karyn marched down the corridor to surround her with a fond embrace and a haze of Joy perfume.

"Oh, Neecy. My sweet girl. I'm so sorry."

"Me too." She took a step back to look at her best friend. "I'm so glad you're here."

"I didn't hear until church this morning, otherwise–"

"You couldn't have known. It was too late to call when I got home last night and–"

"Girl, I know I was the last thing on your mind. No problem." Karyn slipped an arm around Denise's shoulder as they headed down the hall.

"Pastor Shelton's on his way over, I know, as soon as he can get away." Karyn stopped suddenly, placing herself in front of Denise.

"Neecy, is Lynn really going to be okay? That's what Shelton said this morning but..."

Why was everyone demanding truth from her today?

"I think so," she responded slowly. "We still don't know whether the surgery was really helpful. And still it's going to take time because she lost–" Denise hesitated, feeling her throat tighten. Perhaps a more detached, clinical approach would keep her emotions at bay.

"And the protocol is so different now from when Daddy–"

Daddy. That one word, carrying the sum of all her losses, forced her to her knees in the middle of the corridor despite the harsh lights and hum of activity around her. Her father. Kenny. Her sister–mama, almost. And now, Ian. Denise felt as if she'd stepped away from her own body, was barely aware of Karyn's wiry arms bearing her back up.

"I'm not gonna let you fall, Neecy. Come on now, girl. Come on," she murmured. "It's all right, girl. It's all right." Karyn was right there, holding her close. Denise summoned the strength to stand once more, struggling to lift herself up toward the woman who exuded the fragrance of a thousand white flowers and years of honest affection. Her dear friend's presence lifted her flagging spirit more than she would have ever expected.

"Well," Denise sighed, slipping her arm through Karyn's as they resumed their walk down the corridor. "I know you didn't just come here to see me. Mama'll be glad you're here." She stopped in front of the ICU's small waiting area. Karyn pushed the door open and stepped aside to let Denise enter first. She followed, stopping to greet Julia and Preston with her fragrant embrace and words of reassurance. Once she'd spoken with Joanne, Karyn sat down next to Denise on the worn, vinyl couch and placed an arm around her shoulders. The two women waited silently, heads bent forward, as when they were young girls waiting for a summer storm to end so they could go out and play in the sunshine again. Pastor Shelton and his wife arrived a few minutes later.

"Shall we all join hands for a word of prayer on behalf of Sister Adams-Vaughn?" Pastor Shelton's words were strained, spoken in whispers instead of his broad, cadenced baritone. The petitions for comfort and healing streamed through Denise's consciousness without finding a resting place. Surrounded as she was by her families by blood and by Spirit, she'd never felt so alone.

The air had begun to moderate late on

Sunday evening, working itself into a light, dry breeze that stirred the sheer curtains in the Adams dining room. The family sat around the table, listlessly picking at takeout chicken, not one of them displaying the exuberant celebration usually associated with the product. Even little Joy had absorbed the somber mood, fussing and refusing to be held by anyone but Joanne.

The surgery had been successful and the doctors cautiously ensured Lynn's recovery. Once permission to hope had been granted, exhaustion set in. Plates half-filled with food were abandoned without so much as an "excuse me" as people drifted out to the living room to sit and stare at the TV without comprehension.

Denise hoped they would all leave. She wanted to clear the table in peace, have a little time alone in the kitchen to practice not thinking about Ian. Practice going home and not finding his long legs dangling off the end of the sofa, followed by his puppy eyes begging for "just a little taste" to sweeten his Monday morning coffee. Visualize herself returning the empty vase to the office storage closet. Get used to a voice mailbox without "I love you/can't wait to see you tonight/let's get out of town." Forget greeting the dawn with their personal, sweet rocksteady. She was just thanking the Lord to have her Lynnie back, not to mention her mind and her pride.

Maurice stubbornly remained, standing when she rose and helping her scrape and stack the plates. She shot darts of irritation at his back as he passed through the kitchen door, then gathered up a few grease-slicked glasses and followed him.

Maurice was standing at the sink, rinsing and arranging plates in the dishwasher.

"I can do that," she said edgily, walking up behind him.

"Not much left to do." He transferred two handfuls of utensils from the sink to their basket. "Why don't you go back out front and relax? It's been a hard couple of days. I just wanted to do something to help since we're gonna have to pack up the girls and go soon."

She ignored him and went to open the back door. She stood there for a few minutes, staring out into the darkness, barely noticing the moths that banged lazily against the screen.

"Did you ever get your boy to chill last night?" Maurice asked casually.

"Huh?" She'd allowed her mind to wander. Then his words slowly registered.

"What did you say?" Denise turned away from the door.

"Your boy. You know, Ian. He was about to lose it," Maurice recounted as he placed glasses on the top rack. "Almost went off on me, and I was only trying to help him out."

"What the hell were you doing, talking to him?" she shrieked, not really caring whether anyone else could hear.

"Isn't that what you do when someone calls you on the phone," he responded sarcastically, 'talk'?"

"He called you?"

"I guess he was calling around trying to find out where you were. The man was worried–who wouldn't have been? I know you had other things on your mind, but that was one hell of a storm last night. You could have taken two minutes to let him know, Neecy. You almost had another problem; I had to beg him not to go running over to the hospital."

"You know what?" Denise stabbed an index finger at Maurice as she headed for the dining room. "Don't talk about Joanne's meddling, you hear me! Where do you get off, all up in my business?"

"I was trying to help you out," Maurice

responded with an edge of anger.

"Well, don't!" she shouted. "Don't help me out! Next time you hear about anything that has to do with me, stay the hell out of it!" She rushed through the swinging door, nearly crashing into her mother.

"Denise! What on earth–"

"I'm tired, Mama. Please..." She quickly stepped around Julia and grabbed her purse from the sideboard table in the hallway. "I'm going home. I'll just take the bus or a taxi, whatever comes first. I've just got to get out of here."

"But it's too late for you to be walking around by yourself. If you can just wait a minute..."

Denise shook her head, knowing she might start to cry at any minute. She hurried out the door, down the steps, and walked as fast as she could toward the main street.

Wendy Phillips ended her shopping trip early on Tuesday afternoon. The city was unbearably hot and not an item on her list seemed worth the effort.

She let herself into the flat, shuffling

through the day's mail as she walked. As she headed down the rear hall she noticed a shaft of light emerging from Ian's old room. Nothing else in the apartment seemed to be out of place. Her heartbeat quickened as she placed her bag and the bundle of letters on the sideboard and slowed her steps, nearly inching along the interior wall. Wendy stopped just short of the doorway and peered around the corner.

Her younger son was lying on what had been his bed, one leg stretched out in front of him, the other dangling to the floor. His face was listless and blank, his shoulders hunched in despair.

"Ian! What-"

"She left me, Mum. She's gone."

He had not called her "Mum" since he was thirteen, not even when Josh died.

"Oh, Ian." She went in and sat on the side of the bed, as close to him as she could. "I can't tell you how sorry I am," she murmured, reaching up to stroke his cheek, "what happened?"

"I don't know. She just decided that she couldn't handle it any more. Maybe her family put pressure on her to end it. I'm just guessing; I don't know..." He shrugged his shoulders in a helpless gesture. "For once, though, I don't think it was me, you know? Not that it matters."

"Ian, I'm so sorry. I had such great hopes for both of you; she is a lovely young woman. You must be devastated."

He acknowledged her words with a nod.

"Why don't you change?" Wendy suggested. "It's so hot in here. You'll feel better."

"I didn't bring anything."

"I'm sure your father has something. Let me look." She touched both hands to his face, shielding the thin creases that had emerged to frame his lips. This most recent blow to the heart was aging him before her eyes. She stood wordlessly and went to her bedroom, feeling herself older as well.

Alone again, Ian slid his other leg over the side of the bed and stood up. She'd been in this room, slept beside him in this bed, and they'd walked the streets below together, hand in hand. His knees sagged; he dropped down on the floor beside the bed. Ian had never known pain like this before; he ached from the inside out and back again. No morning after, no bodily injury he'd ever sustained was like this. And that sound...Blinded by the tears that hung in his eyes, he tried to turn his head toward its source.

Then he knew–the howl was coming from inside him, from the same place that had glowed like the heart of a stoked fire the first time he'd looked into her eyes. Everything was gone now, nothing left behind except this howling grief, threatening to tear him apart.

Wendy re-entered the room quietly. She knelt beside Ian, stroking his hair, then pressing her cheek to his as if she could draw out his pain by taking it into herself.

Chapter 29

A week after her stroke Lynn was moved to the National Rehabilitation Institute. Located across the street from Metro Hospital, the Institute was a state-of-the-art structure, its soaring lines enhanced by bold colors and full-spectrum lighting. Lynn found the place more disturbing than the hospital's intensive care unit, despite its anti-clinical design. The sight of people wan and ill, huddled in their beds or taking slow, cautious walks down the corridors of Metro Hospital, didn't faze her. But patients at the Institute seemed to be in constant motion, whether they rolled by in motorized wheelchairs or lumbered across the reception area with jerky, halting steps. Many of them wore medical appliances that starkly resembled medieval torture devices. Heads were held rigid with steel halos; missing limbs had been replaced with varying combinations of metal and plastic. The children affected her the most. They were oblivious to the magnitude of their injuries, performing their daily rounds of study and play as did boys and girls everywhere.

Lynn shuffled back to her room from the Sunday afternoon physical therapy session to find her husband, mother, and sisters clustered outside her room, waiting for her to return. She was surprised by the prick of annoyance she felt on seeing them there. Never one for exercise even when her health was good, this new, exhausting activity had wrung the last ounces of strength from her weakened body. She would have been happy to collapse headfirst onto the hospital bed and remain that way for the rest of the afternoon. She braced herself for the fuss she knew her haggard appearance would cause.

"Lynnette! What on earth?" Julia approached first, dropping her guise of a smile.

"Are you all right, baby?" Preston took Lynn by the arm and directed her through the door Denise held open.

"I'll live," she assured them with a wan smile. "But Amnesty International needs to know about those folks in physical therapy." Her hesitant steps took on a final burst of determination as the lovely hospital bed with its smooth white sheets was nearly within her reach. Joanne was standing beside it, encouraging her like a mother beckoning a child's first steps. Lynn found the image profoundly disturbing.

"Make yourself useful, girl," she barked at Jo as she eased herself into bed. "Go get me a popsicle, a lemon one! That's what I liked best when we were growing up."

"Fool," was all Joanne could manage in reply as she swung the heavy door open and disappeared down the hall.

"Takes one," Lynn murmured, drawing her legs up under the covers.

The room went quiet, allowing Lynn to close her eyes and rest for a while. Preston had just taken the chair closest to the bed when he suddenly jumped to his feet.

"I don't know what I hate more," he complained, yanking the pager from his belt, "the damn beep or the damn vibrate! Somebody needs to invent one that does magic fingers.

For a whole minute, if it's bad news." He pulled his cell phone from his pocket, heading out of the room. Then he stopped, squinting down at the pager again. "Hey Neece," he called out, "whatever happened to that computer fella you used to work with? If he can put something together I'll be willing to go fifty–fifty on the profits!" He chuckled to himself as he strolled out of the room.

Denise, who was standing in the bathroom doorway, cringed and glanced over at Lynn. Lynn looked back at her intently. Their mother was preoccupied, updating her list of those who had sent cards, flowers, or gifts. Denise looked around for the bottle of spring water, still cold from Julia's refrigerator. Finding it in her mother's tote bag, she pulled it out and approached Lynn's bed.

"Why don't you go ahead and have a sip," she urged, breaking the seal on the cap. "Jo must've gone to Rome for authentic Italian ice instead." Lynn nodded, reaching for the bottle. Denise passed it to her, closing both hands over Lynn's.

"It's over," she mouthed, her face expressionless.

"Good," Lynn pronounced with a grim smile.

Lynn was taking a few sips of water when Joanne returned, peeling the wrapper from the popsicle as she walked.

"Neecy, there's someone outside who wants to see you."

Denise stopped suddenly, the bottle nearly slipping from her hands.

"Hey!" Lynn shouted as cold water splashed across the front of her gown. "If I need a bath just say so!"

"I'm sorry! Sorry!" Denise grabbed a handful of tissues from the bedside table and dabbed at the wet fabric. "Do you know who it is?" she asked Joanne, trying to sound as calm as she could.

"Yes I do! And forgive me, Lord, but I'd love to put that man in traction, personally." She broke the frozen treat in half with a sharp grunt as if to emphasize her point, then stepped to the other side of Lynn's bed. "Go on, I can handle this phase of Lynn's return to childhood."

Denise wiped her hands on the sides of her skirt, walked slowly toward the heavy fire door and pulled it open. There in the hallway stood Kenny, talking to Preston. Her heart sank; Kenny was the other last person she wanted to see.

Preston saw her over Kenny's shoulder. He stopped talking and pointed in her direction. Kenny turned and looked at her, his face a study in mourning.

"Hello, Denise." He approached her tentatively. "I was so sorry to hear about Lynn. She's so young; it's quite a shock. I know this must be very hard for you, being so close to her. How are you?"

She studied him for a few seconds before she responded.

"I'm fine and she's recovering. Thanks for coming by." She turned to go but he caught her by the hand.

"Look, Denise, I need to talk to you about something. It's important. I know you've got other family here," he nodded in Preston's direction, so please..."

She looked over at Preston, still standing a few feet down the hall. He gave her a slight nod, as if to say it was okay.

"Fine." Denise frowned and set out for the fifth floor visitors' atrium with Kenny following. She glared at Preston as she passed, hoping he understood the look to mean "come get me if this takes more than five minutes."

The visitors' atrium was an attractive space, topped with a skylight and furnished with comfortable seating. A few patients and visitors were present, talking quietly. Denise led Kenny to a corner with two armchairs. She perched on the edge of one and leaned forward on her elbows.

"Your meeting," she murmured, eyes on the floor.

Kenny laughed softly and sat down in the adjacent seat.

"You still have that same sense of humor, I see. That's good, that's good, under the circumstances."

"What circumstances?" Denise responded angrily. "Ever since you got here you've been talking as if Lynn were dead! She's going to be fine; it's just going to take some time."

"And that's exactly what Preston was telling me. It must be a relief for you." He reached out to touch her hand but Denise avoided him, sliding back into the chair.

"Kenny, what do you want?" she asked in a flat tone, "At least in the immediate sense. I don't think you've ever known what the hell you really want in the long term."

"What makes you think I want something?" He shifted a little in the soft chair and grinned uneasily.

"I haven't heard from you since you drop-kicked me out of your life almost a year ago. I thought you got rid of me to pursue your happily-ever-after with Valerie."

"I didn't 'get rid of you,' as you put it. I just needed a little space, you know how it is."

"No, I don't. Was there enough space in Antigua for you? I hear those honeymoon cottages are kinda cozy."

"All right," he admitted, putting up his hands, "you're right, I was wrong. Last year I messed up, did something I shouldn't have done. And if I hurt you–"

"If!"

"Okay, once more, you're right. I did a terrible thing, leaving you the way I did. And I want to apologize to you for that. And even more," he said, sitting forward," I wanted to ask if you could possibly consider us getting back together again."

Denise crossed her arms over her chest and regarded Kenny's strong jaw line, as sweet and handsome as if it had been chiseled out of milk chocolate. She remembered how grateful she had been for his time, for his kisses, for his delicacy as he sought his pleasure with her. Her relatives had been grateful because he was safe; the fact that he was an EE professor practically made him part of the family. He loved her mother; he revered her father; he talked sports with Preston and laughed at Maurice's jokes. Her sisters had always smiled when they called his name: "Is Kenny coming? Kenny's on the phone. Denise, it's Kenny." And yet...

Ian would not let her go. He was out of her life but still making trouble, just as their relationship had caused trouble from the very beginning. Ian and his plans, his dreams, his love for her that had the power to consume everything in its path like a fire burning out of control. Those flames had nearly killed Lynn, had nearly separated Denise from the person most dear to her on earth. That same fire had made her call out his name in the dark, crying, sometimes, when she climaxed, because she felt so known for the first time in her life. How do you want me? she would say. In every way, he would reply. Mind. Body. Heart. Soul. Our babies. Everything.

"Denise?" Kenny interrupted her reverie. "I know you weren't prepared for this, with everything else you've got to think about. Look, would it be all right if I call you sometime? I'd really like to see you again." His dark eyes were eager and sincere. And safe.

She looked at him, wishing she could read

him over and over until she finally understood him completely, like a theorem in a textbook. At least she already knew the factors in this equation.

"Why don't you do that." She stood decisively, ready to return to Lynn's room.

He flashed one of his killer smiles as he looked her up and down.

"Denise, baby. Uh, uh, uh! You're still as fine as you ever were, you know that? I'm going to make things very special for you. For both of us." He took her right hand and kissed it. He smiled again as he moved in the direction of the elevators.

She heaved a sigh of resignation and turned back in the direction of Lynn's room. Two sisters, she thought, both out of danger.

Chapter 30

Kenny brought Denise home a little before eleven o'clock. She had put him off for several weeks, but now she had to admit she'd enjoyed cruising the familiar jazz clubs along Georgia Avenue, seeing Kenny's musician friends and their ladies. She even saw some members of her father's circle, older and moving more slowly, but still making great sounds. It was only when they pulled up in front of her building that she had a sense of dread.

She was sure Kenny believed she was being coy when she'd asked him to take her home earlier than usual. She was tired, but she was also curious to know whether she could lie down beside him and have her life return to its size and shape before Ian. Damn! Why couldn't she get him out of her mind and heart as easily as she'd pushed him out of her life?

Kenny opened her door and helped her out of the late model Jaguar. They had started up the steps when he needed to go back to the car. She stopped for a second but decided to continue on; she could unlock the entrance door, at least.

She hesitated again when she saw the shadow of a man sitting on the front steps. The neighborhood derelicts usually weren't quite so bold. She stopped and looked around for Kenny. He was stepping back onto the sidewalk, locking the car by the remote as he walked. She decided to keep going; Kenny would be by her side soon. Keeping her eyes on the ground, she approached the steps. It was then she noticed the man's shoes. Winos usually didn't wear fine Italian sandals. Her eyes involuntary traveled up to his hands, which were holding a bouquet of roses.

She knew those hands, knew them in the dark as well as she did in the light of day. Those hands had smoothed her hair, massaged her weary shoulders, and cooked her a meal or two. There was a time when they had made her ache with desire and soothed her once that hunger had been satisfied.

Ian stood and stared at her. His forlorn expression barely masked the anger beneath its surface. She hadn't recognized him because he'd cut his hair. The long, tawny veil that had fallen around her face when they made love was now as short and spiky as the bristles on a brush. He nodded in Kenny's direction and asked his question without saying a word. Her eyes searched his, as on their first day so long ago, now needing his forgiveness. The tears she'd refused to shed for weeks were coming fast.

"Leave the lady alone! Don't make me kick your ass down these steps," Kenny commanded, barreling up between them. "Give me the key, baby." When she didn't respond he reached down and grabbed the key ring from her hand. Once he had unlocked the door and led her inside, he pushed it shut with a loud bang, as if to punctuate his warning.

Kenny draped his arm protectively around Denise's shoulders as they climbed to the third floor. He was probably grateful for the encounter at the door, she thought. The perfect opportunity to prove his devotion, defending me from the man who loves me more than anyone on this earth, she thought, struggling to blink back her tears.

Denise regarded Kenny sorrowfully as he unlocked the door to her apartment and stood aside for her to enter. Every piece of furniture, even the very walls, had a tale to tell about her recent past: the coffee table she had used to prop open the door when Lynn collapsed; the couch where she and Ian had made love; the spot where she and Ian had joined in that first explosive kiss, the one in which she'd discovered she could love him.

"What's wrong, Denise?" Kenny asked.

"Nothing." As she walked toward the kitchen she felt him take her hand and gently pull her in the direction of the couch.

"You know I don't drink coffee, so don't waste time making any. Please." He motioned for her to sit, then seated himself uncomfortably close to her.

"Let's take advantage of every minute we've got to get reacquainted. You're a good church girl and I intend to see that we get you there on time tomorrow." Kenny took her face between his hands and kissed her, his tongue darting into her mouth too quickly, his hands prematurely sliding down to squeeze her breasts. Denise tried to pull away; he had been apart from her too long to permit a rush into intimacy. She forced herself to give him a good, hard shove back against the pillows. Kenny looked at her in disbelief.

"What the hell—? Look, I asked before if anything was wrong and you said no. Why are you being this way? I slept with you for three years—don't try to act as if you don't know me! I've seen parts of you you've never seen yourself!"

Denise was tempted to laugh at this in spite of herself. Vintage Kenny, she thought. But she sat up as straight as she could and folded her arms across her chest.

"I think you put your finger right on it. I don't know you and you don't know me. Otherwise you never would have left the way you did."

"Why do you keep throwing that up in my face? I came to you, I confessed, I let you have your little fuss, and now I'm trying to continue the nice time we were having.

"But we haven't really spoken to each other for almost a year. I don't know what's up with you, what your goals are, what might have changed in your life. I enjoyed hanging out with you tonight, going back to our old haunts and all, but we were with other people most of the time. If we're going to get back together, I need to know more about where you are, who you are now."

Kenny looked into her eyes, shaking his head.

"I wish the Dean could have lived to see you now, the beautiful woman you've become. You were always smart, no doubt about that. I used to laugh to myself about your little desk whenever we went into his study. If I'd had any idea that plump little girl would turn out the way you have, I would have made him promise you to me a long time ago."

She frowned, remembering Ian's words: so he was a child molester, too.

"That's nonsense and you know it," she responded sharply.

"You don't need to be so serious all the time, baby girl," he purred, leaning back and slipping his arm around her once more. He removed his glasses and set them on the table in front of them.

"You don't need to call me that, either. It's bad enough that my mother still does it."

"You're right about that, too. You're one hundred percent right and you're one hundred percent woman. And now that I've got you back again, I'm never going to let you go."

He began to kiss her again, one hand combing through her braids and the other sliding up between her thighs. Denise summoned her strength once more to free herself from his embrace.

"Kenny, please! When I said I was tired I wasn't kidding. There's just been so much going on lately with Lynn. And other things," she said, thinking of the man on the front steps. "We need to talk but I'm really not up to it tonight."

"That's all right. I was thinking of something else we might do to help you relax."

"Sorry. That's not going to work either. I'm really not in the mood."

"You might fool yourself, Neecy, but you can't fool me. You can't tell me after almost a year that you don't want to, don't need to–"

"Are you saying– No! Do you really think that I've been sitting here waiting for you all this time? You think there hasn't been anyone else since you?"

"I know you, girl!" Kenny replied with a little laugh. "You're not the type of woman who goes out to clubs looking for men. Especially after your little girlfriend got hooked up with the city desk. What's his name? I know you've been sitting either right here or with your mama."

"Kenny, did you ever think that somebody might come looking for me? That's right, that somebody might want me, your dependable, boring, church girl, Denise." She jumped to her feet and began to pace back and forth in front of the couch.

"Baby, I never said you were boring. To the contrary, you're quite unpredictable. Especially in bed, when you want to be. Come on back and sit down," he urged, patting the sofa cushion next to him. "You're making me dizzy. And if you want to work off that excess energy you seem to have found..."

"I'm standing up because I don't feel so hot." She stopped, holding a hand to her middle. "I don't know what was up with that fish batter." She eyed him with a new sense of hope.

"I hate to ask you this, but maybe you might want to duck out a little early. I'm on the verge of doing something that's not very attractive." She grimaced and pressed her stomach again."

Kenny's smile faded into a look of concern.

"Are you sure you don't need me to stay, then? If you're so sick all of a sudden it could be food poisoning. I can run you over to

Morris emergency right now..." He stood and patted his pockets for his keys.

"Oh no, Ken. It's nothing that bad. I just think I'll be better off on my own, for now." She patted her foot impatiently.

"Are you sure, baby?" He walked over to where she stood and touched a hand to her forehead. "You do feel a little warm. Can I make you some tea or something? I hate to just leave you like this."

"I'll be fine," she insisted, steering him toward the door.

"I'll call you as soon as I get home," he promised, kissing her lightly.

"Well, if I don't answer, you can guess where I'll be." She tried to sound cheerful despite her distress, like a good little soldier. There should be an award for the best performances in real life, Denise thought as she closed the door behind Kenny. She stood quietly for a few moments, waiting until she heard the entrance door slam shut. When she was sure enough time had passed, she stole down the steps quietly and walked outside. Ian had left the flowers where he'd been sitting, their fragrance still delicate and pure. Denise wanted to reach out, pick them up and inhale their perfume. And remember...

She turned sharply on her heel instead and headed back upstairs. The door locked behind her, safe and secure.

Kenny came to church the next morning, and had the nerve to sit down right next to her mother. Denise had sunk down into her seat in the choir loft, grateful to be at a remove from both Kenny's enthusiasm and her mother's displeasure. Julia Adams aimed a distinctly evil look up in her direction when she came down front for the altar call.

Kenny invited himself to dinner that afternoon as well. Preston and Maurice were happy to welcome their prospective brother back into the fold. It was as if little had changed from this time last year. The men sprawled, jackets removed and ties undone, in their favorite spots in Julia Adams' living room, watching the first pro football games of the season.

Denise looked miserable as she mashed potatoes by hand at the kitchen table, every so often passing a furtive glance in her mother's direction. She couldn't discern the exact meaning of the look Julia sent her· in response, but she suspected her mother was equally disturbed by Kenny's presence.

Lynn was pleased by Kenny's unexpected appearance, and smiled as she snapped the green beans. Joanne had apparently forgotten her anger toward Kenny as well; she and Lynn were recalling amusing stories about their weddings and wondered aloud what tales Denise would soon add to their collection.

Julia cut a few extra carrots and turnips into the bottom of the Dutch oven before she covered the roast and slid it into the oven. She removed her apron and wiped her hands, watching as Denise repeatedly slammed the potatoes with the full weight of her unhappiness. Julia couldn't ask Kenny to leave, as much as she wanted to. But her daughter was hurting and she had to do something.

"Joanne, could you finish the potatoes, please? I need Denise to help me with something upstairs."

"Sure, Mama," Joanne answered, oblivious to her mother's mood.

Denise was all too glad to put as much distance as possible between herself and Kenny. She followed her mother out of the kitchen, down the hall and up the stairs, avoiding eye contact with anyone in the living room.

"What is he doing here?" Julia asked pointedly, closing the door to her bedroom.

"I don't know. I didn't invite him here. Or to church either."

"But where is your young man?"

"I broke it off with Ian."

"For heavens sakes, why? You were so happy just a few weeks ago!"

"Mama, you're the one who told me to think about things, think about the future. Well, sitting in that emergency room I had plenty of time to do just that. I decided that a future with Ian wasn't realistic, so...Anyway, Kenny came to the hospital to see Lynn and we talked. We decided to get back together; we went out last night for the first time since last year. But I didn't invite him here today. Frankly, I wish he'd leave."

"What made you decide to go out with someone who obviously is making you very unhappy? Ian might not have been what any of us would have expected, but that glow you had when he was around went right out the door with him! Tell me this: how are you going to be with someone when you don't even want him around? I know if Ian were here, I wouldn't be able to get you within ten feet of that kitchen unless he came with you. Why on earth did you decide to start seeing Kenny again?"

"Because it's easy, Mama! Is that so bad? This way I can get married, have kids, have a nice home, and have some respect for myself! So I can walk down the street with my man and not have to hear every lunatic's opinion about my choice. I'll tell you just what I told Ian: I'm tired of fighting the world. I just want what everyone around me seems to have."

"Has Kenny actually said something to you about marriage?"

"No, but–"

"There is no 'but' when it comes to this, Denise. Either Kenny loves you and he's ready to settle down with you or you need to move on. I don't need to remind you about his track record. Didn't you tell me that Ian wanted to marry you months ago? Then why on earth aren't you with him? You didn't use him as a chip to bargain with God, by any chance?"

"What do you mean?"

"Oh, I think you know. Was it something like this: 'Lord, if you spare my sister I'll give up the one man on earth who makes me happy'? And now you think it's time to hold up your end of the bargain."

"Aren't you listening to me at all, Mama? I said that I couldn't imagine a future with Ian."

"And I never imagined that I would marry a man like your father and have so many beautiful, accomplished children and grandchildren. And my life is so much better for having all of you in it! Denise, I would be the last one to tell you that interracial marriage is an easy thing. But there's no honor in marrying a man you don't love and, as far as I can tell, one who might not truly care about you."

Her voice dropped to a whisper.

"The relationship I had with Karl was deep and satisfying for both of us. But when I met your father I fell in love with him in a way I can't describe. And there was never a day I doubted he felt the same way. We came to each other with everything we had, and I'm not talking about material things. I mean–"

"Everything," Denise chanted, "body, soul, mind, spirit. Everything."

"So you know," she said, stroking Denise's hair, "because that's what you had with Ian. I saw it in your eyes, baby girl. If Ian were one of us, you would have brought him home and there would never have been an issue.

"What I am going to do, Mama?"

"You're the only one who can answer that, Denise."

Denise sat on the edge of her bed and unzipped her dress. Maurice and Jo had dropped her off after dinner; she'd claimed a headache and urged Kenny to go home.

Scenes from the afternoon's gathering were still playing in her head. Kenny's voice had grated on her nerves like a fingernail on a blackboard. He'd been trying hard, too hard, to regain his old seat on the couch, to win back his place at her mother's table. But nothing had really changed in a year, had it? He was definitely the same old Kenny, and there was nothing wrong with that. With the exception of the Valerie skirmish, he was the same man she'd admired since she was a child. He hadn't changed. She'd changed.

Her meditation was disturbed by the telephone's ring. It was probably Kenny, still on the job, trying to get back into her good graces and her bed.

"Hello," she began, hoping her voice would

not betray the sense of resignation she felt.

"Denise."

It was Ian. She felt as if the ground had shifted beneath her.

"Ian," she repeated, the name she'd dared not breathe for weeks now.

"I'm sorry about Saturday night. It was awkward but I just felt I had to try–"

"I know."

"That was Kenny, wasn't it?"

"Yes." She was afraid to say more, afraid the emotions she'd held at bay would come crashing through.

"Please don't hang up, Denise. I need to ask you one question. Then you'll never have to see or hear from me again, I promise."

"What is it, Ian?" She waited, holding her breath.

"Denise, are you happy? Is this what you want?"

She clutched the handset tightly, her eyes filling with tears. She had searched her heart for the answer to a similar question of his months ago. It did not lie to her then and it would not lie to her now.

"Denise?"

"You know it's not," she whimpered.

"What do you want then?"

She nearly choked on the few words she needed to say.

"I want you."

"And how do you want me?" he asked quietly, daring to hope.

She took a deep breath.

"In every way. Your mind, your body," her voice caught as she began to cry, "your heart, your soul, your children. Everything."

"And you know I'm asking you to be my friend and my partner and my wife and the mother of as many babies as you're willing to give me?"

"Oh, yes. Yes!"

"No matter what people think or say?"

"No matter what. Oh Ian, I love you!" The tears were coming too fast for her to continue.

"And I love you, Denise, more than you could ever know. Just try to hold on for a few minutes; I'm on my way."

Denise was waiting on the front steps when Ian arrived, no longer caring what her neighbors thought or said. When he saw her he jumped out of the car, leaving it running in the middle of the street. They fell into each other's arms with such force they nearly tumbled to the ground.

"I am so, so, sorry," she cried.

"Just promise you'll never leave me again. Please, please..." He held her as close as he could manage.

"I promise. I promise you everything. I love you, Ian."

"And I love you, Denise. You are my life. I promise you everything."

After they made love they lay on their sides, looking into each other's eyes.

"I can't believe you did this," she said as she ran her hand over the spiky remains of his once-trailing hair. "But I like it."

"I was in mourning for you, my love. You remember when Bishop Tutu shaved his head when his friend Bishop Walker died?"

Denise nodded, her eyes misting.

"When we became friends, I felt as if I'd found a part of myself and then lost it again when you went away. I wanted to do something, make some visible, physical sign of that pain." He paused, running his hand across his head.

"I never had much use for religion and such, but I'm beginning to come around, you know? At least to the point of understanding why rituals are important, why signs and symbols mean so much.

"Speaking of which, a package came for you about a week ago." He climbed off the bed and padded over to the spot where his jeans had landed when they'd shucked off their clothing. He removed a small envelope from a back pocket and returned to bed, stretching out beside her. "Open it, please."

Denise took it from him, wondering what would come in such a tiny package. She peeled back the flap and shook it over the space between them. The gold band, weighted by a diamond and a sapphire, made a soft thunk as it settled.

"Oh Ian," she whispered, beginning to cry again. He took the ring and slid it onto her finger.

"If this is how becoming my fiancée makes you feel," he began, "you're not going to commit hara-kiri in front of the reverend, are you?" He reached over and tenderly brushed away her tears.

"We're going to do this by the book," he continued, "because I want to make it as difficult as possible for you to slip away from me again. I intend to know what you'll be like when you're a senior babe with long gray braids and I'm be stooped over from looking into your eyes for fifty years. Just don't ask me to live through anything like the past month, ever again."

"You won't have to, Ian. I promise."

"Good! And while you're talking to the Big Guy next Sunday, tell him that of the two of us, I go first, okay?"

"I talk to Him more often than just one day of the week! But if you're interested, why don't you tell Him yourself? I'd like you to come to church with me next Sunday. It'll be practice for the gauntlet waiting for you in the afternoon."

"What's that, babe?"

"Haven't you heard of the famous Adams equal-opportunity gauntlet for prospective in-laws? Don't worry, we're unplugged now."

"Unplugged?"

"Yeah. There used to be cattle prods, but having a brother-in-law who's a U.S. Attorney kinda took the fun out of that. He kept babbling something about civil rights..."

"You know how I feel, babe. If that's where you want me, that's where I'll be. Wearing my bullet-proof jock, of course."

"Good idea. That's the spot Lynn's liable

to aim at first when she hears about us."

"In that case," he whispered as he eased his body onto hers, "maybe we should try to make at least one little brown rocket scientist before then."

"At least one," she agreed. Soon all their words abandoned them, leaving only waves of motion and sighs.

Chapter 31

"May I drop you at work?" Ian was standing by the sink, rinsing out their coffee mugs.

"Thanks but no, there's an errand I have to run first." Denise was standing in the doorway, dressed for work in a beige wool suit. She didn't want wear anything that would outshine her engagement ring or her bright smile. "If you could just run me over to Dupont Circle…"

"No problem, mademoiselle." He followed her into the living room and grabbed her briefcase from its place by the door.

"Mademoiselle," he repeated, holding the

door open for her, "only for two more months." They ran down the stairs together, hand in hand, and into the crisp autumn morning.

"So what will you do for the rest of the day?" Denise asked as Ian turned onto R Street.

"I'll see if I can reach my folks. They'll be relieved; I'm your problem now!" He thought for a second. "I might even try Andy, although he's probably been playing with some poor sod's spleen since dawn. Where should I drop you?"

"Just as far as the Circle is fine."

"You mean in front of a certain elegant ladies' establishment?"

"All this and psychic, too," she teased, placing her hand on his khaki-clad thigh.

"I'd watch that if I were you," he growled cheerfully, "or else we'll simply go back to your place and not be seen again until spring." He pulled the Jeep over in front of the bright orange and green awning. They shared a slow good-bye kiss before she alighted and watched him join the stream of downtown traffic.

The air inside The Mango Leaf was redolent with potpourri when Denise walked in.

Joanne looked up sharply, surprised to see her sister so early on a weekday morning. She quickly marched out from behind the counter.

"Neecy, what's up? Is everything okay?"

Denise beamed back at her.

"Things can't get any better! But you're gonna need to sit down," she cautioned, pointing to the brocade-covered chair in front of the dressing room.

"What, what, what? Girl, don't do this to me; you know I can't stand it!" Joanne was nearly jumping up and down.

"Okay." She paused dramatically to torture Joanne for a few more seconds, but was forced to give in to her own delight. "Ian and I are getting married!"

Joanne screeched like a mockingbird and embraced Denise, rocking them both from side to side. "Oh baby girl, baby girl!" Joanne had begun to cry as well.

Denise backed away a little, holding her at arm's length. "Does this mean you're happy for me? No regrets, no problem with Ian?"

"Hell no! I know that big old boy loves you. I could tell by the way he looked that morning. I could've sworn he was smiling, even in his sleep!"

Denise frowned and backed away a few

steps.

"You were in the apartment that Sunday morning!"

"Uh huh. Tell him he's got one hell of a nosy sister-in-law coming, so he better be good to you. He better not be caught wrong because you never know when I'll turn up!"

"But Jo, you never told..." Denise trailed off, thinking for a moment. "You never told anyone, did you? You just kind of hinted to me that you knew. How did you manage that?"

"I guess even I knew this was important. I only knew you were happy, happier than you'd ever been with Kenny, happier than I'd seen since you were a little girl. I wanted to give you a chance to hold onto that. It damn near killed me, but I just had a feeling that this guy was going to be The One, no matter what color he is. I don't give a damn about you jumping the fence, I just want you to be happy! You deserve that more than anyone I know."

They shared another happy, teary embrace before it was Joanne's turn to step back.

"Are you pregnant? I need to know because of your dress and all..."

"No. Well, could be," she teased. "I'm not,

although I almost wish I were. Is that crazy?"

"Just more proof you're in love, sweetie. And I was asking because we had talked about something a little on the old-fashioned side. It seems so long ago now. Almost like another lifetime."

"It was another lifetime, one that's over and done with," Denise asserted. "So I want something different, I don't know what, but it's gonna say something about me and who I am now." She paused and looked around the showroom.

"Is it all right if I use your phone for a moment?"

"Sure is; I left it on the counter," Joanne replied with a wave.

"Don't go away Jo–I'm calling Mama. I want you right here."

Joanne looked surprised. "Me, not Lynn?"

"I know you've lost your mind! I'm gonna have to take annual leave to deal with her." She put the handset to her ear, listening to the lines connect. "Mama, it's Denise," she began. Jo pressed in closer to hear. "Guess what?"

Denise was late for work on Monday, quite

late, as a matter of fact. But everyone understood once they saw the ring flashing fire from
her left hand. She finally walked around to
Frank's office a little after five o'clock.

"That's the last time I send you on a
detail," he grinned, indicating one of the
leather armchairs. "I thought you could hold
your own with Ian, but as always you exceed-
ed my expectations. You went and trans-
formed the beast into a puppy dog! You have
my best wishes, Denise. And tell Ian I'll be
calling with my congratulations."

"Thank you, Frank," she accepted, smiling
as she had all day, but suddenly becoming
serious. "You're right, though, it probably
was the last time. I'll be leaving sometime in
the spring. Ian is starting a software firm out
in Chantilly and we're going to manage it
together."

Frank's face clouded over, but he quickly
recovered.

"So now Ian's a puppy dog and a thief!
Forgive me, but I'm just feeling a little selfish
right now. I couldn't be happier for both of
you, but I'm disappointed for me. I'll never be
able to replace you, you know that."

"Frank, you don't need to worry. Do the
same thing you did six years ago: take your

recruitment team to Morris and look for another short girl with thick glasses who's carrying a load of programming manuals. Just be sure to keep her away from your contractors, though!"

Denise returned home that evening to find Ian sitting on the couch, waiting for her. He swept her into his arms as the door closed behind her.

"What's up?" She could barely get the words out between kisses.

"Oh, Denise," he sighed, touching her face, sliding his hands down to her shoulders, then around her waist. "I had to come, just to be sure we're back."

"Want me to pinch you?" Denise grinned as she jammed her hands into the back pockets of his jeans.

"Among other things. Put your little arms around my neck, please." When Denise complied, he scooped his hands under her bottom and carried her to the bedroom.

It was nearly nine o'clock when Ian returned from the bathroom and slipped back into bed beside Denise. Denise rolled over and propped herself up on her elbows.

"A quick question, Ian. How many diapers have you changed?"

"During what span of time?"

"Your whole life, roughly."

"Um." He paused for a moment, thinking. "None."

She made a sucking sound between her teeth.

"I thought so."

"I'm not worried. You'll be a wonderful mother to little Zeke.

"Are you out of your mind? I have no intention of going through pregnancy and childbirth to end up with a big-head boy named Zeke!"

"What's wrong with Zeke?" He slipped an arm behind his head. "It's a honorable, Biblical name. Wouldn't your family like that? Anyway, Zeke'll be a good big brother to the twins, Hannibal and Harriet. And his sister Fanny, and his other brother Zack."

Denise pulled herself up into a sitting position.

"And you accused Kenny of child abuse? Those names! Poor, poor babies." She shook her head. "And my poor, poor body."

"I'm not worried. These will be even bigger, right?" He reached over and fondled her breast with his free hand. "My babe!"

Denise pushed his hand away with a smile. Thoughts of having children with Ian, at this moment, seemed entirely possible. Even likely. But her smile faded as the question that had roiled just below the surface of her hopes asserted itself. She rose from the bed and went to the closet. Finding her pink robe, she slipped it on and firmly tied its sash around her waist.

"I don't know about you, but I need to eat. There's a little roast beef from Mama's left. I can defrost something and stretch it a bit. Is that okay?"

Ian stifled a yawn as he climbed out of bed once more.

"I'd rather have canned peas with you than a four-star dinner with anyone else," he responded, pulling on his jeans. "What can I do to help?"

"You can answer another question for me," she said, leaning against the doorjamb to wait for him.

"And what would that be?" He pulled up the zipper and fastened the button as he followed her into the kitchen. "Sounds serious."

"It is." Denise pulled the foil package of roast beef from the refrigerator, along with a head of red-leaf lettuce and a couple of potatoes. She took her time, arranging the slices of meat on a plate and preparing the potatoes for the microwave.

"Ian?" She set down the knife she'd been using and turned to look up at him. "What will our children be to you?"

Ian looked down at her, his brow furrowed in thought. He opened his mouth as if to speak, then closed it again.

"What will they—what will they be besides yours and mine?" He paused again. "Are you talking about race?"

"Yes," she answered in a small voice.

Ian gently framed her face between his hands.

"Denise, I don't care whether our children are chocolate or vanilla or butter pecan; whether their eyes are brown or blue; whether they're tall and skinny like me or short with sweet little legs like yours. They can call themselves whatever they want, they can be whoever they want to be, acrobats to zoologists. The thing that matters—the only thing—is that they're ours, and they know we love them. If society says they're black, then we prepare them for that. You know better than I about these things; I'll follow your lead. We belong to each other now, Denise. That must count for something under these crazy rules, right?

"If there's anything on earth worth more than the two of us sharing our lives, I haven't seen it and wouldn't waste one second looking for it. This is all to say that what I will see when I look at our children," he said quietly, "is you. And that will make them precious and beautiful to me. Does that answer your question, my love?"

Denise struggled to speak around the lump that had formed in her throat.

"I didn't think there was a right answer, but somehow you found it," she whispered.

"It's the only one I have." He pressed his lips to her forehead.

They stood in that spot for a long time, holding onto each other, supper all but forgotten.

Chapter 32

"Karyn?"

"Hey girl! What's up with you? Is everything okay?

Denise hesitated.

"If you're not sitting down, well, maybe you better."

Karyn Mitchell nearly dropped the handset.

"Neecy, are you all right?" she quickly demanded. "Is it something with Lynn? Your mother?"

"Oh no, nothing like that," Denise assured her. "It's a good thing, or at least I think it is."

"Are you going to stop being a fool and tell it, then?"

Denise took a deep breath.

"Ian asked me to marry him. I said yes." There wasn't a sound from the other end of the line. "We're going to do it right before New Year's." The silence was abruptly shattered by a high-pitched squeal.

"Neece! How the hell–? When–?" More shrieks. "Why didn't you tell me? How long?"

"Yes ma'am, I'll take your questions in order. How the hell: damned if I know. When: two nights ago, Sunday. Why I didn't tell you: the last time we talked about this you were the self-appointed grim reaper of romance. You sounded just like the old gypsy lady in *The Werewolf*. 'Cream in your coffee,'" she intoned solemnly. "'Someone will pay!' But I digress. How long: how long it is ain't none of your damn business. There, did I get them all? But if you really must know the answer to the last question you should go to the source," she said, handing the telephone to Ian.

"Hello, this is Ian. Is this Karyn?" Ian mumbled from the depths of a pillow.

"You know your girl is off the hook, don't you? I didn't ask her any such thing! Are you two over there drinking? She can't hold her liquor anymore. But seriously, I'm glad to meet you, talk to you, whatever! Excuse me, but you have to understand this is–I mean I'm happy for her, for both of you, but it's like, whew..."

"That's quite all right," he said, propping himself up on an elbow. "I imagine it is a bit of a shock. But I've seen your pictures, you and Denise together. You've proved one of my earliest theories, that beautiful women all hang out together."

Denise playfully snatched the telephone from Ian's grasp. "I don't know what he thinks this is. Marry one black woman, get one free?" Ian settled back, grinning broadly.

"Terence mentioned having a fantasy like that about the two of us," Karyn admitted. "Don't let the glasses fool you; my baby can get his freak on when he wants to."

"That means the four of us will have to get together soon, drive them both crazy. But the two of us have to talk first; so much has happened! I thought I'd go insane, holding it all inside. It's so weird, though, I have to keep saying it–married! Maybe I'll start to believe it myself."

"Want me to come over there and pinch you? No, that's Ian's job exclusively now. Speaking of pinching, are you out of the will now? Has Lynn held a memorial service for your wicked, fence-jumping soul?"

"Not yet. Lynn and I are going to have our little prayer meeting tomorrow. And everybody else meets Ian on Sunday."

Lynn held the door for Denise, who was carrying the tray with the teapot and cups onto the front porch. It was a mild day in early October, with a hint of frost in the air. Denise set their snack down on the spindly table that had been squeezed between two rockers.

"I can get that, thanks," said Lynn before Denise could pour her tea. Lynn picked up the ceramic kettle carefully, and was able to direct the liquid into both cups without a spill.

Denise smiled and nodded with gratitude. "You're doing great, Lynnie."

Lynn eased back in her chair, occasionally sipping from the cup she balanced on her lap. "You know, I haven't sat out on this porch since the summer I carried Malcolm."

"That's what I keep telling you. This is a beautiful house; you should take advantage of it. I'm sorry this had to happen for you to find that out." They rocked in silence for a while, enjoying the afternoon sun.

"So what's up baby girl? Are you and Kenny going to tie this thing up once and for all?"

"Lynn, that's what I came here to talk about. We did go out, a couple of times."

"And?"

"And nothing. It's all over, Lynn."

"Oh, Neecy," Lynn mourned, her features crumpling with honest sorrow, "I'm so sorry. Good Lord, girl, you've had a hard time."

"That's true. And I'm sure there'll be some hard times coming. But the point is," she asserted, turning to face her sister, "I won't be alone when they do. Lynn, Ian and I are getting married." She paused to allow the words to sink in.

"What!" Lynn's head snapped around as if she had been struck.

"We are, Lynn, in a couple of months." She reached into the pocket of her jeans, pulled out her engagement ring and slipped it on her finger. "Mama, Joanne and Karyn already know. I didn't come in wearing this because I wanted to talk to you first. There are some things you should try to understand."

"No! No! I'll never understand this. After everything that's happened? You can't be serious!" Lynn's bony fingers balled into fists, pounding the arms of the rocker.

"Lynnie, please calm down and listen to me. I don't want you to get upset about this."

"Calm down? You must hate me to come into my house and tell me this mess!"

"If you don't know by now that I love you, well, I don't know how else to prove it to you. I've been by your side almost every minute since you got sick and you know that."

"But you told me, Neecy, or did I imagine it? You told me that you weren't seeing him any more."

"No, you didn't imagine it. And we had stopped seeing each other. But we both realized that we never stopped loving each other. I thought at one point that maybe God had struck you down to punish me for falling in love with Ian. And I prayed, I really prayed, that if God made you well I'd never see him again. I blamed Ian, too. And then," she paused to give Lynn a significant look, "I realized all of that was pretty crazy For instance, you've smoked like a chimney forever, at least since I was born! I'll never understand why you continued to do that after seeing what happened to Daddy. The fact that this is how I feel really doesn't change anything between you and me, or our family or anyone else. I'm still going to be the same person; I'm still going to be proud of who I am and the people I come from. And I am determined to instill that pride in our children; Ian understands this and he will support me.

"You can't believe that," Lynn countered.

"I just came to this point, Lynnie," Denise insisted, sliding to the edge of her seat, "when I realized that I didn't want to be alone, especially once I knew what it meant to really love someone and be truly loved in return. 'Poor Neecy, good, brave, strong Neecy.' It's not enough to live on, Lynn, it's not enough! You, Mama and Joanne all had or have men that love you and beautiful kids. Why shouldn't I? I didn't plan on the package Ian came in, but I always dared to hope I would feel this way when I found the man I'd love enough to marry. It's probably the only one of those damn signals I ever learned to read! So please, I know it's hard for you, but try to be happy for me?"

"But what would Daddy–"

"Lynn, I'm not going to let you use Daddy to get to me, all right? Neither one of us knows for sure what he would have thought about interracial marriages if he'd lived this long. And maybe he would even like Ian. But I don't know that, and neither do you."

"You still have to deal with Mama."

Denise laughed out loud.

"You and Jo should be ashamed. Mama had the whole thing figured out while the two of you were tinkering with your fantasy brother-in-law!"

"How the hell could she have known that?"

"Remember that Sunday afternoon in the kitchen when Jo was screaming about my diamond earrings and Mama chased you all out to talk to me? She just sat down and it was like, boom, is he a white man! I nearly fell on the floor!"

"I'll bet you did! But still, how did she know?" Lynn had begun to relax a little.

"Our mother," Denise began, searching for the right words, "is an extraordinary lady. I'm beginning to think that we don't know her as well as we think we do, or as well as we should. She always hid her own light so Daddy could shine brightest. She didn't have to do that; and she's always been so good to us. Maybe we can't give her the opera career she deserved, but she should have whatever she wants to be happy and comfortable for the rest of her life."

"That's for sure," Lynn agreed, shaking her head. "And I've always thought you're a lot like her; extraordinary in every way." They sat quietly for a few more minutes.

"So..." Denise began. "Can you answer my question now?"

Lynn rubbed her arms and stared out across the park.

"Can I be happy for you? You know this is not what I would have wanted for you, for a variety of reasons. And as far as I'm concerned, he's still on probation for whatever happened back in the spring when you came crying into my office as if you were on the verge of a breakdown. My office," she repeated wistfully. "Sounds funny now, doesn't it?"

"You'll get it back, girl. It's just going to take time." Denise reached out and took Lynn's hand.

"But about you—and Ian. Aren't you just jumping into this? Have you made any plans?"

Still clutching Lynn's hand, Denise described their partnership, the software firm, the blueprints for the house in the country and their desire to start a family as soon as possible. Lynn listened, really listened, and Denise saw the beginnings of a smile when she talked about babies.

"I'm going to miss you, baby girl." Denise saw her sister's eyes brimming with tears. "In some ways I've always felt as if you were my little girl, even though I've only carried boys."

"And you know that you've always been like a mother to me," she answered, on the brink of crying herself. "But you're not getting rid of me that easily, no way!" she insisted. "At least until the babies come, we'll be in for dinner every Sunday. And we'll have to alternate holidays with his folks in New York, but Lynnie, you're not going to lose me. Not now, not ever." She gave Lynn's hand a gentle squeeze.

"Oh, and there's one more thing." Denise let go of Lynn's hand and slid back into her chair. "We're starting a foundation to do connectivity projects with rural and inner-city schools. We'd provide all the equipment, do networking, and maintenance." She hesitated. "We wanted to ask if Niagara could serve as the location for the pilot project."

Lynn slid to the edge of her seat, reached

out and took Denise's hand again.

"Girl, you know," she began, practically trembling with excitement, "you know how long I've been looking for, praying for something like this! Spent every spare minute looking for grants, writing letters, before I got sick. And to have it come from my own sister makes it... Thank you, Denise. Thank you."

"There's a hook, as Mama would say, before you get too happy," Denise cautioned. "Ian wants me to write a study of the project I can use as a thesis, so I can work toward getting my doctorate." She shrugged. "He says one of us should have real credentials, but since he'd be likely to murder half the tech faculty before completing the preliminary exams, I guess it's up to me."

"Whenever I used to ask you about getting your final you'd roll your eyes and change the subject." Lynn withdrew her hand from Denise's and sat back quietly, thinking for a moment.

"You know this is going to be hard for me. This isn't something I'd ever want for you, and I'll never understand why you would choose to spend your life with a white man. You've been a witness to my marriage; Preston and I have had some hard times despite the values and vision we share. If you're expecting me to condone this relationship, give you my blessing—"

"I don't expect any of that," Denise countered. "All I want to know is whether you're still my sister."

Lynn stared out into the distance, her eyes narrowed against the slanting rays of autumn sunlight. Shunning the rocker's comfort, she drew her shoulders high until her back was as straight as a ramrod. A slight tremor shot through her limbs. She exhaled heavily, then allowed herself to relax against the padding once more. She pressed her feet against floorboards and commenced a gentle, rocking motion. Lynn extended her right hand. Denise clasped it gratefully.

Denise stared out at the familiar, elegant homes that lined 16th Street as Ian waited to make the left turn. This morning they'd attended church together. She couldn't decide what seemed stranger: sitting in the middle of the congregation with Ian, or anticipating their wedding ceremony, which would take place within those familiar walls in a few short weeks.

"There, the one on the left with the brick walk." She pointed to their destination. Ian swung into a space directly in front of the house on the opposite side of the street.

"Are you ready, babe?" he asked, squeezing her hand.

"As ready as I'll ever be. You?"

"Let's do it." He leaned back to grab the large bouquet that lay on the floor behind their two seats.

When they reached the house Denise pushed the front door open, knowing it wouldn't be locked this soon after church on a Sunday afternoon. Just before she could step inside, Ian kissed her and took her hand once more. She led him through the foyer and into the middle of the living room, where Preston, Maurice, and Joanne were boisterously debating whether any member of the men's chorus could sing worth a damn.

"Hey! Could you all be quiet for a moment!" she shouted. The noise level diminished rapidly as heads turned to inspect the visitor.

"I'd like to introduce someone in case you missed seeing him at church. Everybody, this is Ian Phillips, my..." She paused, looking up

at him. "My fiancé. Ian, this is everybody."
Her family checked him out from head to toe,
their eyes switching back to her as if a silent
signal had been given.

"Now we all know the drill. You have to be
nice to him until the last Saturday in
December. It's only a couple of months; you
can do it. After that," she said, raising their
twined fingers to show off her ring, "he's
going to be family. Then we can all go back to
being our usual evil selves. And don't try to
play him either," she added. "He's mean
enough to hold his own."

Breaking away from her mother's grip, Joy
ran up and grabbed Ian by the legs.

"Mean!" she shrieked with delight. Ian
reached down, dropping the flowers, and
whisked the toddler into his arms.

"Mean old Uncle Ian," he chanted, giving
her a little bounce with each word. "But I'm
not so bad once you get to know me."

"Neither am I," said Denise's mother, gently nudging her way through the group. "I'm
Julia Adams and I'm so glad to meet you, at
last." Extending her hand to Ian, she gave
Denise a significant look. "I don't know where
this girl, excuse me, this woman has been hiding you, but welcome, young man. I've heard

some very good things about you."

Ian shifted the baby over to Denise, then embraced his future mother-in-law and presented her with the lavish bouquet. Lynn's greeting was reserved but graceful; Joanne ogled him shamelessly, later advising Denise to give him jewelry. Jocelyn soon wandered over and stood in front of her aunt.

"Did you want to ask me something, sweetie?" Denise asked, bending down while supporting Joy's sleepy head.

"Does this mean I won't be your flower girl, since you're not marrying Uncle Kenny?" the child asked with a worried look.

"Not only are you going to be my flower girl," Denise assured her, "you're going to be my flower-girl-in-charge! Ian has a niece who's a little younger than you; I'm depending on you to show her the ropes, make sure the job gets done right." Jocelyn responded with a grin as bright as the mums in her grandmother's spray.

Maurice pulled Ian off into a corner to introduce himself and Preston.

"Welcome to the brotherhood, otherwise known as the Adams Outlaws. Our motto is, 'We do what we're told.' "

"And we like it," Preston added. "Say

goodbye to your backbone."

"Too late. Mine disappeared back in January." Ian gratefully shook their hands and looked up to wink at Denise. She answered with a nod, still cradling Joy in her arms.

"Then we won't even have to teach you the secret handshake. You're in! It's a funny thing about these ladies," Maurice began in a conspiratorial whisper. "They can break you down, no doubt about it. But they'll move heaven and earth to build you back up. And when they do, man, you can do things you never thought you could."

"I'll second that," Ian agreed with an affirmative nod. Maurice slapped him on the back, turning to Preston.

"Hey Pres, you think we can apply for some government funding now that we're an equal opportunity organization? We could get that pool table for the basement..."

"Who would have thought?" Preston mused aloud, rubbing his chin. "And you're the computer guy, right?"

"Guilty as charged."

"Wait a minute. You know about fixing crashes, about error messages, bombs and things?" Maurice's voice rose in anticipation.

"And network administration," Preston added. "Well damn! What took that Neecy girl so long anyway? Welcome to the family, brother!"

Preston led Ian to the spot on the couch that had long been reserved for the youngest sister's man. Maurice sprawled out nearby, Malcolm wedged himself between them, and Preston dropped into Dean Adams' favorite armchair. Julia gathered up her flowers and disappeared into the kitchen with Lynn, Joanne, and Jocelyn in tow.

Denise had taken a couple of steps back to watch as Ian settled in and the family fell back into its usual Sunday afternoon patterns. As she moved, Joy's drowsy head fell against her shoulder. With luck, she thought, you'll have a little cousin this time next year.

"Uncle Ian and I will start working on that real soon, sweetheart," she whispered.

Ian, her man. Soon to be her husband and part of her family. All hers at last.

INDIGO

Winter & Spring 2002

❧ May

Magnolia Sunset	Giselle Carmichael	$8.95
Once in a Blue Moon	Dorianne Cole	$9.95

❧ June

Still Waters Run Deep	Leslie Esdaile	$9.95
Everything but Love	Natalie Dunbar	$8.95
Indigo After Dark Vol. V Brown Sugar Diaries Part II	Dolores Bundy	$14.95

Love Spectrum Romance

Romance across the culture lines

Forbidden Quest	Dar Tomlinson	$10.95
Designer Passion	Dar Tomlinson	$8.95
Fate	Pamela Leigh Starr	$8.95
Against the Wind	Gwynne Forster	$8.95
From The Ashes	Kathleen Suzanne Jeanne Summerix	$8.95
Heartbeat	Stephanie Bedwell-Grime	$8.95
My Buffalo Soldier	Barbara B. K. Reeves	$8.95
Meant to Be	Jeanne Sumerix	$8.95
A Risk of Rain	Dar Tomlinson	$8.95

OTHER INDIGO TITLES

A Dangerous Deception	J.M. Jeffries	$8.95
A Dangerous Love	J.M. Jeffries	$8.95
After The Vows (Summer Anthology)	Leslie Esdaile	$10.95
	T.T. Henderson	
	Jacquelin Thomas	
Again My Love	Kayla Perrin	$10.95
A Lighter Shade of Brown	Vicki Andrews	$8.95
All I Ask	Barbara Keaton	$8.95
A Love to Cherish	Beverly Clark	$8.95
Ambrosia	T.T. Henderson	$8.95
And Then Came You	Dorothy Love	$8.95
Best of Friends	Natalie Dunbar	$8.95
Bound by Love	Beverly Clark	$8.95
Breeze	Robin Hampton	$10.95
Cajun Heat	Charlene Berry	$8.95
Careless Whispers	Rochelle Alers	$8.95
Caught in a Trap	Andree Michele	$8.95
Chances	Pamela Leigh Starr	$8.95
Dark Embrace	Crystal Wilson Harris	$8.95
Dark Storm Rising	Chinelu Moore	$10.95
Eve's Prescription	Edwinna Martin Arnold	$8.95
Everlastin' Love	Gay G. Gunn	$8.95
Gentle Yearning	Rochelle Alers	$10.95
Glory of Love	Sinclair LeBeau	$10.95
Illusions	Pamela Leigh Starr	$8.95
Indiscretions	Donna Hill	$8.95
Interlude	Donna Hill	$8.95
Intimate Intentions	Angie Daniels	$8.95
Kiss or Keep	Debra Phillips	$8.95
Love Always	Mildred E. Riley	$10.95
Love Unveiled	Gloria Green	$10.95
Love's Deception	Charlene Berry	$10.95
Mae's Promise	Melody Walcott	$8.95
Midnight Clear (Anthology)	Leslie Esdaile	$10.95
	Gwynne Forster	

You may order on-line at www.genesis-press.com, by phone at 1-888-463-4461, or mail the order-form in the back of this book.

ORDER FORM

Mail to: Genesis Press, Inc.
315 3rd Avenue North
Columbus, MS 39701

Name _____

Address _____

City/State _____ Zip _____

Telephone _____

Ship to (if different from above)

Name _____

Address _____

City/State _____ Zip _____

Telephone _____

Qty	Author	Title	Price	Total

Use this order form, or
call
1-888-INDIGO-1

Total for books _____

Shipping and handling:
$3 first book, $1 each
additional book

Total S & H _____

Total amount enclosed _____

MS residents add 7% sales tax